Daemon Handler

Crispin propped the gigantic, warped wooden hood of Lily 6 on its rods. The whole vehicle shuddered gently. "Hold up," he shouted to the roustabouts. "Stand clear."

He ducked into the hot, reeking interior. As a handler, he could feel the stink of the daemon, a powerful, localized source of tension. It stung his nostrils and eyes. He bent to gather hammer and pliers out of his toolbox. A daemon handler had two skills: the purely mechanical, which was just knowing the ins and outs of the transformation engines and the daemonological. Not dangerous, per se, for a celled daemon was a defanged daemon. And yet . . .

Crispin slid back the hatch in the top of the cell anchored in the middle of the engine. The entire body of the truck jounced upward, and then sank on its wheels. Crispin held on. His bones shook.

Two thousand pounds' worth of fury glared up at him. The face pressed against the silver mesh under the hatch was just like a human child's, except that it was bright green. A silver collar gleamed, pinched cruelly tight around the daemon's neck, trapping most of her mane of black hair. She sat in the three-by-three-foot oak housing with her knees drawn up to her nose, her arms by her sides. The cage was too small to allow her to change position. Her lips moved as if she wanted to speak.

She seemed properly angry. Supposedly, you could eke a powerful daemon out for fifty years with the right care and feeding, but Crispin had never heard of one that had lasted that long. If you were cooped up in a cell too small to stand up or lie down in, and the touch of the walls irritated you beyond pain, driving you mad with the urge to escape, so that you pushed and pushed and pushed—just as you had been trained to do. . . .

Whispering obscenities, Crispin tapped the sides of the cell. Probably a loose join. Daemons could not stand oak, so that was what must be used for the cells, and every crack must be sealed with silver. The catch, of course, was that silver is infuriatingly weak. He had just located the loose place, and was fishing in a pocket for silver nails.

Concentration shattered. Black bubbles danced in front of his eyes. Swearing, he dived into the engine cavity to retrieve his hammer, and the daemon shot a tentacle of power out through the loose join and sent fierce shivers up and down his spine as his fingers closed around the handle. The lip of the engine cavity caught him in the stomach. He heard a faint shout and knew that Lily 6 was standing on her port wheels, her center of gravity tipping dangerously high.

Every last kink in his hair straightened on end as he banged the vital nail in.

A squelching thud shook the earth as the big truck dropped back onto all eighteen wheels. The daemon shuddered with misery.

EVER:
The
WAR
In The
WASTE

FELICITY SAVAGE

HarperPrism

A Division of HarperCollinsPublishers

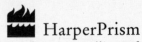 HarperPrism
A Division of HarperCollins*Publishers*
10 East 53rd Street, New York, N.Y. 10022-5299

HarperCollins®, ▥ ®, and HarperPrism®
are trademarks of HarperCollins*Publishers* Inc.

HarperPrism books may be purchased for educational, business, or sales promotional use. For information, please write: Special Markets Department, HarperCollins*Publishers,*
10 East 53rd Street, New York, N.Y. 10022-5299.

Printed in the United States of America

Cover illustration copyright © 1997 by Romas

First printing: September 1997

Designed by Lisa Pifher

Library of Congress Cataloging-in-Publication Data

Savage, Felicity.
     The war in the waste / Felicity Savage.
         p.   cm. -- (Ever ; pt. 1)
     ISBN 0-06-105678-2 (pbk.)
     I. Title. II. Series: Savage, Felicity. Ever ; pt. 1.
PS3569.A8237W37   1997
813'.54--dc21   96-22951
                                                          CIP

Visit HarperPrism on the World Wide Web at
http://www.harpercollins.com

97 98 99 00 ❖ 10 9 8 7 6 5 4 3 2 1

The War in the Waste
is dedicated to my mother, Helen, with love
and thanks for everything.

"A mother is the strongest educator, either for or against crime.
Her thoughts form the embryo of yet another
mortal mind, and unconsciously mould it, either after
a model odious to herself or through divine
influence, 'according to the pattern showed
to thee in the mount.'"

—Mary Baker Eddy

Table of Contents

Book One

The Immediary of Inevitable Sorrows

A Filthy Thing

1876 A.D. Ferupe: Greenslope Domain

The circus convoy rumbled along at thirty miles an hour: the daemons were really kicking in tonight. Inside Daisy 3, one of the big trucks whose body had been honeycombed with partitions to make living quarters, Anuei sat ungracefully on her sembhui mat. It was the only genuine relic of Lamaroon she had managed to preserve for this long. Her birdcages swung from the ceiling, linnets and nightingales silent under their cloths. She was knitting a sweater for Crispin and keeping an eye on him at the same time. He scrambled on a pile of the boxed props she didn't allow him ever to look at, trying to press his eye to the crack through which he'd be able to see the back of Roddy Colbey's head and the road between the dark, rolling fields ahead. During the day, Roddy was Fred the Fearless, a tiger trainer; at night, he was a reasonably expert truck driver. Crispin banged his head on the board ceiling as the truck jounced, let out one cry, and wiped his nose on the back of his hand.

He wore nothing except a shirt filthy with snot and what else Anuei didn't like to think. It didn't matter that his little penis bobbled in full view; he was only three, and the night air was warm. But before the end of the year, Smithrebel's Fabulous Aerial and Animal Show would enter the northern domains, where winter was one long swirl of whiteness and spring was a hillside or two covered with eyebright. By then Anuei wanted her son to have a wardrobe that wouldn't shame a squire's child. The circus's itinerary was so long, six full years between shows at the capital, that all Crispin had known in his short life were the plains of the east and these fertile, balmy hills of the heartlands. Saul Smithrebel said that this time, he'd timed the itinerary so that they'd make their swing through the northern domains during what passed for summer there. But it was already spring and they were not yet north of the capital. Anuei had twenty-five years of experience with Saul's timing. *Miserable man!* she thought. *He frets to get to our next stop, and then all he wants is to get the show over with and move out! I'd wager my last penny that every day when he sees the sun rise, the first thing he thinks is, "My hat and coattails, we're late, save the Queen!"*

Earlier in the day they had shown a farming town called Amisbottom. (*What a name for a town, no lilt, not like Eirhazii or Faiina or Redeuiina. Oh, Redeuiina, where it's always summer, and I was young and thin and wore hibiscus in my hair!* A pang of loss, the taste of sea-salt, memories of an ocean so blue that even the drops she splashed at her friends were turquoise. . . .)

As the circus rolled in along the main street of Amisbottom, sweeping carts and wagons aside, patchwork-coated clowns tumbling ahead of the parade, the band screaming its siren song, the lions in their open-sided truck and the elephants plodding behind, Anuei had known it was going to be a good show. Of course the respectable citizens were muttering behind their lace curtains. But out of sight was out of mind. And the lower classes, by contrast, were unashamedly visible. Scruffy street urchins trotting along behind the trucks. Farmers in town for the day showing their rotted teeth in laughter as the clowns plucked live birds out of the children's ears.

A good show.

In the east and west, circuses were seen so rarely that they carried no stigma. Here in the more populous domains of the heartlands, where the map was freckled with towns, everyone knew a circus was scarcely better than a music hall. The audiences were composed solely of the lower classes. But the lower classes of Amisbottom seemed far happier than they had any right to be. And happy people generally had coin in their pockets. Clink! Clink!

Anuei found the idea of saving her earnings—as her friend Gift "Mills the Magificent" did—ridiculous. She spent them on things that made Crispin laugh. Cypean lanterns, lollipops, paper dolls. She would have been happy to stay for two days, maybe more, in Amisbottom. Even Saul had known it would be a good show: he'd grinned as he sat in his paper-flower-covered throne on top of the first truck in the parade. Anuei believed that these were the best moments of his life, the rare triumphs of a ragtag general.

But the grin hadn't lasted long. Almost before Anuei finished with her last patron, the show was over and the roustabouts were dismantling her black top over her head.

Twenty-five years of this. Never slowing down.

She was forty-one, and she would spend the rest of her life with Smithrebel's. Sometimes she wondered how long that life would be; sometimes she didn't care.

If it weren't for Crispin . . . ! She didn't know why she'd waited so long to have a baby. What had she been afraid of? Should've gotten pregnant twenty years ago. Spawned a whole gang of little halfbreeds. Blown up to the size of a baby elephant.

She cocked her ear at a knock on the planking partition. Not Millsy, *he'd* come right in; and only one other visitor ever came to her quarters—unless one of her Amisbottom patrons had somehow managed to conceal himself in the convoy, and was now emerging to confess his undying love! She expelled a long sigh as she got to her feet. "Must shed just a little, just a little of this weight," she whispered as she unhooked the door curtain. Saul came in, sliding his feet and jerking his head about—like a crow, she always thought. A scavenger. He did not even look at her, but took up his stance in the middle of the tiny room, eyeing Crispin as if he thought the child might be good to eat. Beads tinkled as the curtain slid closed.

Anuei yanked up her skirts—she wore ordinary Ferupian clothing when she wasn't "on"—and slapped the mountainous, dimpled expanse of flesh as black as five-thousand-year-old oak. "Hey up, Saul, I'm going to lose some weight!" she said, silently cursing the soft-accented timidity of her voice.

"What, the Balloon Lady relinquish her rotundity? I forbid it!" Saul said pompously. "Skinny women are not female. They are Kirekunis." He chuckled at his own joke and squinted at Crispin, who balanced precariously on the rail from which swung the vast "Lamaroon" gowns Anuei wore for her patrons, picking wood lice out of the juddering partition. "Always climbing!" Saul said. "I tell you he is going to be an aerialist!"

"And *I* tell *you*," Anuei said, "the men of our race grow to be giants! He'll be six-foot-five by the time he's fifteen! More'n three heads taller than the tallest aerialist I ever saw. Millsy says he's not meant for the circus at all." Millsy was a truck driver, and also a daemon trickster who filled in between the elephants and the aerial ballet. In the scheme of Smithrebel's, he was so far down the pecking order that he was practically ignored, but he was one of the few people in the circus who took a real, human interest in Anuei and her son.

"Gift Mills spouts more hot steam than a kettle!" Saul said. "Don't believe a word he tells you, my angel."

Anuei looked at her son. His pudgy little hands were intent on their task. Anuei felt a pang of desperate sorrow: he didn't yet know he was a half-breed.

Annoyed at her inattentiveness, Saul tapped one foot in its meticulously shined shoe. "I expected to find you abed," he remarked.

"You don't remember Lamaroon, do you," she said sadly.

She had been fifteen when she met Saul. He had been eighteen. He was making a sight-seeing tour of the islands of the Pacific Ocean—his father, the then-owner of Smithrebel's Fabulous Aerial and Animal Show, heir to five centuries of circus life, had sent him to learn something of the rest of the world. For the young Saul, Ferupe, with its vast territories spreading from the frozen north to the equatorial savannah which bordered Izte Kchebuk'ara, had been enough world and more; he had refused to sail to the Americas, and he had stubbornly refused to have his mind changed by anything he saw in the islands. His itching, jumping eagerness to get back to the circus infected Anuei. She could not believe it when he offered to take her with him.

At fifteen everyone is prone to thinking they have fallen in love. But Anuei wondered, later, why she had never seen what her friends and family told her: that the short, maggot-pale tourist in his absurd black top hat could not hold a candle to the men of Redeuiina who flirted with her every day. Island men wore nothing but char-dyed pantaloons, so it looked as if they were balancing naked on the decks of the fishing boats. Dusty black gods with grins like double rows of cowries. But back then, Anuei knew only that she had heard stories of husbands drinking too much and bashing their wives' faces in. She had not yet learned the lesson of the circus: appearances are everything. So young, she placed no value on sheer physical beauty, on the positive impact of having that beauty come home to you every day. But of course, back then she had been beautiful herself.

She had been a valued addition to Smithrebel's Fabulous Show. But Crispin was even more valuable. A circus baby, he could be taught skills that no hiree could ever learn to the satisfaction of the born-and-bred performers. And a freak to boot! Saul prided himself on having one of everything. Among the roustabouts numbered a Green Eye from the Mim, a Red Nomad from Izte Kchebuk'ara, and a tiny, sallow, truck driver named Kiquat who supposedly came from deep within the snowlands. There was a man who called himself The Cultie, who did an epileptic trance dance to fill in between the lions and the high-wire acts, though Anuei very much doubted any apocalyptic cult would recognize him as a member. Saul even employed a couple of Kirekunis, though Queen only knew what they had done at home to have to live as exiles in a nation that was locked in war with theirs. They were tall men with glossy hair tied back from their faces, dead white skin, and long tails. They wore the brightest-colored clothes they could find and spoke Ferupian liquidly, adding vowels to the ends of words.

Then there was her. And Crispin.

She drew the line at including him in her act, as Saul wanted. But she couldn't stop people from staring as he toddled around the circus lot. When he learned to talk properly, she would teach him a comeback to spout when people asked him what he *was*: a precocious, improbable little speech ("I'm the child that the wind and the earth had when they danced with each other") that would make them laugh and forget. And she'd have to devise a last name for him. She hadn't given that thought yet. All she knew was, he wasn't going to go through life with a Lamaroon surname, let alone one as unpronounceable as Eixeiizeli.

"My beauty. Even when you are silent, I revel in your proximity." With the half-apologetic grin that meant he was now going to flirt, Saul bent, clamped his hands on her thighs, and hefted her into the air. He bounced her slowly up and down, smiling with pleasure, letting her long hair waft across his face. His arms shook visibly, but that was only because he wasn't very strong. Like all Lamaroons, Anuei weighed no more than a Ferupian child. Her patrons never seemed to get over the fact that although she was too voluptuous for them to put their arms around, and her face bore evidence of her age, her stomach didn't droop, and her bosom was as pert as a young Ferupian girl's. Crispin was lighter than a Ferupian child his age—but nothing like her.

*At least my baby will have half his heritage. Heir to five centuries of the circus—even if he is illegitimate. But if you, Saul, tell him before I'm ready for him to know—*she stared impassively down at her lover—*I will break your scrawny pigeon legs, little man. Smithrebel or no Smithrebel. Crunch.*

> *Although*
> *There's not a man can report*
> *Evil of this place,*
> *The man and the woman bring*
> *Hither, to our disgrace,*
> *A noisy, filthy thing.*
>
> *—* W. B. Yeats, "The Dolls"

Keep Your heart from Foolish Fears

1876 A.D. / 1192nd Year of the Lizard. Kirekune, Okimachi

Saia Achino wiped sweaty hair off her forehead and squinted at her sister. Saonna's black eyes were flat, distant. She held her baby against her shoulder, stroking its little back hard, as if she were trying to rub off a stain. Yet Saia knew the child was less present in its mother's mind at that moment than the amulet of the Glorious Dynasty around Saonna's neck. She caressed it constantly.

Saonna might as well be in Ferupe already. It had been pointless for Saia to come all the way out here just to say good-bye. She had had to hold Yoshitaro between her knees while the cart jounced interminably through the smothering dust of the Sayonoshima Road. She had been squashed between her sister and brother-in-law, breathing Saonna's soapy scent one minute and Vashisune's perspiration the next, trying unsuccessfully to avoid his elbows as he manipulated the traces. He slouched now on the front seat of the canvas-covered cart drawn up at the side of the road, floating his whip over the backs of the big, stupid draybeasts. He did not look at Saonna and Saia. She always felt a *vacuum* between the couple, a void of love—even though they had made so much of their passion for each other that everyone else had got tired of it. Maybe that vacuity was common to all culties—it certainly hadn't been in Saonna from the beginning—a symptom of their pretentious commitment to the Ferupian Queen.

Vashi was an initiate preacher in the Cult of the Glorious Dynasty, and proud as a tomcat. Saia despised him.

And the road was as busy as one would expect in late autumn. Everyone was rushing to get in or out of Okimachi before the weather changed. Carts, chariots, and rickeys drawn variously by draybeasts, mules, horses, pakamels, and bicycles vied with the new, noisy motor-chariots and an occasional black-painted Disciple tank for space on the paved "trunk strip" that ran down the center of the broad, packed-earth road. Out here, beyond the old city walls, beyond the new city walls, the misnamed "City of the Dead" spread nobody knew how many leagues into the plain. One supposed that at some point in history the City of the Dead had not been there; but Saia could not imagine when. It was so festered. Here, the road had no real borders, only a direction. Paupers' shacks, clustering together like soap bubbles, encroached on it only gingerly. Whenever the Disciples rumbled out of Okimachi, the tanks came twenty abreast, spikes whickering around on their treads, and anything that was in their way suffered.

The *soi-disant* "leisured" Dead shunned the Sayonoshima Road. Their tall, ill-proportioned houses clustered along the river far away, red and white and yellow columns dimly visible through the haze. They had been upstarts for longer than anyone remembered; Saia could not imagine that they would ever not be upstarts. When they came into the new city with their baskets on their arms, noses twitching under the brims of their too-fashionable hats, she could tell what they were without even looking. Even the girls laughed at Dead men. They took their money, though: *never sneeze at gold* was the first lesson Saia had taught each of her girls. Keep it warm and cozy, and it'll multiply, like baby rats.

"Sao," boomed Vashi over the hullaballoo of drivers' voices and the clatter of wheels. "Sao, let's go."

For the first time, Saonna looked straight at Saia. Her gaze was like a blast of cold air. Saia gripped Yoshi's hand so tightly that he squeaked. Docile little darling. He was sucking the tip of his tail.

"Tell June I promise we'll send word," Saonna said vaguely. "All right? Give him me and Vashi and Rae's love."

"I don't know how you expect to reach Ferupe in that thing," Saia said. "It's not a fit conveyance. It looks like something a Dead peddler would cart his wares to the new city gates in." Since Saonna's conversion to the ascetic Dynasty, Saia had found it increasingly embarrassing to be seen in public with her. Strangers thought Saonna was her servant, and it was impossible for Saia to explain. A lady never explains anything: that was another of the lessons she taught her girls. And this explanation would have been professional suicide. The Dynasty and its imitator cults, like the flamboyant Easterners, were self-declared enemies of the Lizard Significant: the only reason they weren't hounded out of existence was because the Disciples didn't take them seriously.

The most rabid ones always took themselves off into Ferupe, anyway.

As Saonna was doing.

That made-over brown dress wasn't fit garb for her! She said that the pauperish dress code of the Dynasty enforced absolute equality among its members. She loudly condemned her own family for their "vulgar show of affluence." Saia would have none of it. In Okimachi, showing who you were was a necessity not just for personal pleasure, but physical safety. She didn't know what roots the Dynasty's ascetism really sprang from, and she didn't want to. Only she couldn't help thinking it was strange that their dogma was near-identical to that of the Easterners, who dressed like harlequins and made nuisances of themselves in the streets until they had to scatter for fear of the Disciples.

On the other hand, she'd *seen* Saonna's leader, her Prince, or whatever they called him—and *he* wasn't wearing dull brown.

She could not refrain from speaking her mind. And in the corner of her eye quivered a drop of hope. Maybe—maybe—

"If that thing doesn't fall to pieces under you, you'll be luckier than I ever was," she said. "And, Sao, I wish you'd tell me how much money you have with you! What if you have to buy a new conveyance? What if one of you is sick, and you have to stay at an inn? What if—"

"It's not as if we're the first to have gone to Ferupe, Sayi!" Saonna's eyes crinkled as she turned to smile at Vashi. Saia felt cheated. Switching her tail, she stared at the cart.

Barely room under the canvas for two to stand up.

"Significant! What if you reach the pass in the middle of winter?"

"We'll be crossing the *plains* all winter," Saonna said patiently. "We'll reach the snows next spring, just at the end of the blizzard season. And the pass isn't *dangerous*, anyway. Thousands of people go by the northern route—even before there was a war, it was the only way to bypass the Raw Marches and the Daemon Waste. So of course it's well traveled."

Vashi says, Vashi says, Saia thought. The unspoken tag on each of Saonna's sentences.

If it wasn't for Vashi. He had drawn Saonna into the Cult of the Dynasty of the Glorious Decamillennium, he had planted in her this desire to journey to Ferupe, where their cult originated, where a goddess ruled the land. Neither of them seemed to care that Kirekune and Ferupe were at *war*! Saonna would not even *acknowledge* the dangers that she must be exposed to as a Kirekuni woman traveling in the hostile East! She seemed to think that all Ferupe belonged to the Dynasty, and that it would receive her with open arms. She had been full of plans for her "pilgrimage" so long Saia could hardly remember what the old Saonna had been like.

Ever since Saonna's conversion, Saia and their brother June had been running the Achino family business on their own. When Saia first confronted Saonna with not pulling her weight, Sao insisted she had never had a head for business, anyway. Saia could not deny that. But Sao had once had a real knack for dealing with the girls when they nourished grievances.

Love blinds the eye. (Better to believe Saonna really was in love.) And if blindness ran in the family, Saonna was probably about as perspicacious as a blind dung-pig! *Hari* . . . Saia thought, as she always did.

Yoshi whined, as if he could feel his mother's sudden distress. Saia scooped him into her arms, and desperately played her trump card. "What about *Rae*? Don't you care what happens to her? She's barely a year old! *Much* too young for a journey like this!"

Saonna had been shifting her feet, curling her tail around her ankles, as if she felt she had to wait for Saia's permission to make the final break. But when she focused on Saia, her eyes registered irritation. "Nothing is going to happen to her! Why should it? Vashi and I know the journey will be hard, but we're both committed to looking after her. It's not as if she's *replaceable*."

She curved her fingers around the sleek, scaly little tail that projected from under the baby's summer dress. Rae had got her strange, meaningless name because Sao and Vashi thought it sounded Ferupian.

"She's a child of the Dynasty."

"Yes, poor midget," Saia said.

"Oh, by the Lizard!" Saonna's brows knitted. "You're just jealous because I'm happy. But I tell you, it was the Dynasty that brought Vashi and me together. It's the only way. If you would just seek it out, you'd discover your true identity and stop pining after Harame! I promise you!"

Saia blinked, stunned. Not just because Saonna could speak of Hari and the Dynasty in the same breath, but because she spoke of him without rancor, using his full name, as if he had been somebody she knew only vaguely, in passing.

Didn't she *remember*? During that terrible time, the thing that saved Saia's sanity—beside Yoshi and his sisters, of course—had been sitting up at night with Saonna, crying in the candlelit kitchen, vilifying Hari and his fancy slut and his ancestors back to the nth generation. Flushed with indignation, Saonna had alternated between bursting into sympathetic tears and offering sisterly advice on tracking him down and ruining him.

Saia stared blearily at her dry-eyed sister. "I don't suppose you've thought about what your joyous union will be like after you've lived in a three ells by three space with him for a year."

Yoshi snuggled in her arms like a baby, sucking her earlobe. He was too big for that. She lashed him gently with the tip of her tail.

"But we're not just married," Saonna said. "We're joined in Waiting. That's the beauty of it. Everything else—even love—loses importance when you contemplate the end of the Dynasty! It harmonizes all disparities! You don't believe me, Sayi, but if you'd just—"

"We've been over this," Saia said evenly.

"*Now*, Sao," Vashi called.

Saonna spun around on her toes, lips parted. Saia hugged Yoshi tightly, sinking her chin into the top of his head, as her sister hurried to the cart, her chastely long skirt sweeping the dust, tail held high—pulling everything Saia cherished after her on a string. The end of the string was anchored in Saia's heart. What would happen to her when that doubtful cart bore the little family into the frozen north, and then, unimaginably, into Ferupe? Would she break in pieces?

She knew perfectly well what would happen. Slowly, stealthily, Saonna's absence would camouflage itself. It had happened with her mother and her father. It had happened with her older brother Kitsune who died at eighteen, a Disciple in the service of the Lizard Significant. It had even happened with Hari. You eat and you sleep and you pee and shit and you deal with business. And the sun shines, and the Disciples parade the streets on historic days.

"Is Aunt Sao leaving, Mama?" Yoshi said softly. "When is she coming back?" His wet little lips felt like the kiss of a lover.

"Never, dear."

The cart diminished into the distance, one brown-clad hump among hundreds wrangling slowly north. A convoy of Disciple troop carriers rolled past. The weight of them on the road shook Saia's bones.

"Don't want to walk," Yoshi said when she started to put him down.

"Oh, you lazy thing. I'll carry you then." He giggled with glee. Quickly, she added: "Only for a little."

Monkeylike, he wriggled around onto her back. "Giddy-up, Mama!"

"Mind your manners, Yoshi!" Then, when he squeaked an apology: "My little black-haired dove."

She began to trudge back the way they had come, walking beside the road.

Better suffer the dust than risk getting in among the paupers' shacks. The cart drivers and rickeymen looked at her strangely—a woman alone with a child—but that was because she was dressed so much better than the kind of woman who did walk alone beside the Sayonoshima Road. Her neatly coiffed hair, the tattoos on her tail, her red dress with the yellow satin flounces. Even in her frozen grief, she could take pleasure in the rich swish of the cloth, could derive comfort from the weight of her money pocket bumping her leg inside her skirt. These things as good as guaranteed her safety inside the walls, where the name of her business was her password into a web of friends the size of the new city. Flaunting her affluence (even during the year after Kit's death, when they were barely scraping by) had extracted her, in the past, from a number of unpleasant situations. Even the most unscrupulous in the new city tended to take the practical view, the long view, when it came to the question of whether to rape, rob, abduct, or not. If you were hated badly enough, you would be killed. So you just had to try not to make enemies. Money could extract you from all other situations.

The old city was another kettle of fish. In the old city, it didn't matter how rich you were. An old maxim: where you are determines who you are. Unwary night wanderers faced long odds against getting out alive. During the day, the steep streets thronged with sightseers from the provinces, and the hordes of Okimachites who came to prey on them; but when night fell the place emptied out faster than an overturned chamber pot. Even provincials knew that getting in the way of the Disciples—or worse, their Significant masters—was a one-way ticket to nowhere.

And the City of the Dead danced to another tune yet, one that no one in the city proper really understood. Certainly not Saia. She wouldn't toss a coin in the air for her chances here once night fell.

In a blurred way, walking was easing her pain. She never wanted to stop. But she could not get all the way home on foot. She had cut it too fine. Already the sun swam redly among the spikes and spires prickling the back of the huge slain beast ahead of her.

Okimachi was not built on a hill. Okimachi *was* the hill. At its highest point, the Significant Palace at the top of the old city, the Orange River ran in a tunnel buried under a thousand feet of solid architecture.

The limbs of the beast stretched out toward Saia, curling imperceptibly around her. Its rusty red scales sparkled with a thousand points of light.

She could smell something fetid cooking nearby. Yoshi was drifting off to sleep, a patch of child-drool soaking wet into her shoulder. There was a pain in her chest, as sharp and tender as that time she'd shattered a rib.

Can't have this, she told herself. *Home. It'll be all right once I get home. That young miss June hired couldn't get supper on her own if you threatened her with beheading.*

She stepped into the road and lifted her arm to hail a rickey. A man with the elegant logo of the Comashi Concern stenciled on his vehicle pedaled, careening, across traffic, nearly destroying himself under the wheels of a horse-drawn gas tanker, and screeched to a breathless halt five paces away. She walked toward him.

> *Mother, keep your eyes from tears*
> *Keep your heart from foolish fears*
> *Keep your lips from dull complaining*
> *Lest the baby thinks it's raining.*
>
> — M.C. Bartlett, *Baby's Skies*

A Caricature
of Infinity

1879 A.D. Ferupe: Kingsburg

Gift "Mills the Magnificent" bent to peer into the tiny mirror hooked on the wall of the men's quarters in the truck named Hollyhock 7. His fingers trembled as he wrapped a lace cravat around his neck. It had been years since he had done this. Ten years, to be precise. He was uncomfortably aware that ten years on the road with Smithrebel's had aged him immensely: at least in terms of appearance, he had reached the age at which style becomes a mere tautology. He looked as ridiculous as Sam Kithriss had; but at least Sam had had power to make up for it. Ten years ago, Millsy had cast aside his chance to inherit Sam's rings.

For ten years he had not written to any of them—until a week ago, to say he was coming. They must have thought him dead. He had been unforgivably rude.

And yet he couldn't *not* go back. Just to see. In the few hours since they had entered the suburbs of Kingsburg, the familiar restiveness had crept over him. Last time he'd been able to resist; but not now. Indeed, he was getting old.

"Goin' out?" a blurry voice said. Bru Wilcox lay in one of the lowest bunks of the men's quarters, caterpillar-wrapped in a blanket despite the heat of the Kingsburg summer. "Swear, Millsy, you're the most obscure fellow around. Show's in two hours."

"I have already told Mr. Saul I will not be taking part tonight," Millsy said, tugging at his lace. "Or tomorrow night, or next week."

Bru let out a low whistle. "What'd he say? This's *Kingsburg*, man."

"Precisely." Millsy had a horror of letting slip any crumb of information about his past, but punctiliousness compelled him to face Bru and explain, gesturing as extravagantly as if he were in ring center. "When I signed my contract, Smithrebel and I reached an understanding regarding Kingsburg. For six years of touring I would be his; when we reached the capital I could, if I wanted, take two weeks off. Of course it would be no good if everybody did it, but Mr. Smithrebel is an understanding and generous employer, and he realizes that I have certain needs." Bru's lip curled. Millsy hastily changed the subject. "Is your leg still bothering you?"

"Should be out with the rest of them. Whoopin' it up. Bloody pain in the ass." Bru slapped his blanket-shrouded limb, then winced. A war cripple, invalided home from the Teilsche Parallel, his only visible handicap was a rolling walk. According to him, he had blown his pension the first week after he got home, so that he now had to work to keep mind and body together.

Millsy, who had seen the Teilsche Parallel firsthand, wondered whether Bru had ever gotten his discharge—or whether he had taken his survival into his own hands. Many, if not most, so-called "invalids" were in fact deserters. *Real* invalids sat in their parents' houses, drooling. Men like Bru were regularly found guilty and incarcerated for unpatriotic behavior; but Millsy did not think that fair of the policemen, many of whom, after all, had joined the white-coats to avoid being recruited by the army. No one should be compelled to endure the ground front for a term of ten years. He had known men, and women, who had fallen in love with the war, and opted to stay on, and on, and on, until they were sent home in pieces. Perhaps they were even the majority. But whether you hated it or loved it, the conflict was still an atrocity.

In fact, it was a worse atrocity than most people knew, Millsy thought. After a hundred years, the population accepted war as a permanent evil, and resented the inconveniences of levies and forced recruitment no more than they resented the vagaries of wind and storm. But Millsy knew that in the last ten or so years the situation had become critical. Somehow—either through a religio-mystical connection such as culties rambled about, or through the understandable stress of impending defeat—the war was killing the Queen.

And Lithrea the Second was the last, the very last daughter of a dynasty which had held Ferupe stable for almost nineteen hundred years.

Like all who had spent time in the court, Millsy knew that although Ferupe was the most powerful empire east of China, it rested upside down, on its peak, and the Queen was that peak. And she was crumbling. Some of those who saw the awful truth of her decline with their own eyes lost their faith in life. Some redoubled their patriotic zeal. And a few, starting quite early in the war, had transposed the threat of the end of the dynasty into a strange doctrine of apocalypse and nothingness. All his life Millsy had watched—bemused and increasingly worried—as these slandermongers gained followers and imitators all across Ferupe. Cults were even in Cype and Kirekune. He'd seen them for himself. And since he knew their rants were based on *some* truth—the impending end of the Dynasty—he could not despise them, as most did.

It would have been suicidal for the court to confirm the royal illness in public. Officially, the cults had to be beneath the Queen's notice. So the disgust of the righteous citizen for the culties' excesses was encouraged, subtly, wherever possible. If Millsy had still been at court, he would have been intriguing against them himself. But he was a coward.

You are unworthy even to speak her name, he thought disgustedly, looking into the mirror. *Lithrea Mathrelia Lithrelia, Queen of men!*

As a young man he had worshiped her more devoutly than any other courtier. Each day, awaking, he had spoken her name aloud.

But he had not been a courtier for a decade, and what good could he do her now? Wasn't he returning only to solace his own heart with—pray—a sight of her? He was just a truck driver now. A midway magician. His sleight of hand wouldn't cure her illness. A daemon handler, member of the most royal of professions, and yes, a trickster (and that was his vocation if you liked, as diplomacy had never been). He had no daemon big enough to make an honorable gift.

"You old fool," he muttered to the mirror.

"What's that?" Bru Wilcox said loudly.

Millsy flung out his hands, nearly knocking over a precarious pile of razors. "What do you think?" He was attired in knee boots, baggy silk trousers, and a long tunic which was the smartest he had, though it had gone out of style ten years ago. All of his fingers sparkled with rings that signified the status he had once had at court. He had had difficulties remembering which ring went on which finger. He hoped he had them right.

"Not bad," Bru said. "Wouldn't fancy loaning me them boots tomorrow, would you?"

"Mmm." Millsy stretched out his hands toward the windows in the side of the truck, watching them shake. He was only thirty-six, yet the face in the mirror, with its hollow cheeks and ragged gray hair, could pass for sixty. He had once been tall and lean; now he was stooped and skeletal. That was what tricking daemons did to you. The combination of wrinkled skin and expensive regalia made him look like one of the scholars of Kingsburg University, at whom he and his friends had used to snigger when they tottered past with their spectacles falling off. Youth, the most cherished possession of a courtier, had been the price he paid for his freedom from the court. And he knew he had been lucky to get free at all. If not for Boone—there was a man he must see, if he got a chance—

"A fresh face is the stamp of a life unlived," he said aloud, and swirled his old cloak onto his shoulders.

"What?" Bru said again.

Irritation welled up in Millsy. Despite the heat he fastened his cloak all the way down. "Anon, my friend!" Before the young man could ask where he was going, he pushed through the curtains that partitioned off the quarters, strode between head-height piles of canvas, and leapt over the lowered tailgate into sewage-colored mud. Head down to avoid meeting anyone's eye, he crossed the vacant lot around which Smithrebel's trucks were parked. The carousel stood on a flatbed trailer near the gap in the fence which passed for a gate. The gaily painted side panels of the trucks glowed as brightly as the Ferupian flag that would fly from the peak of the big top when it was erected. Saul Smithrebel always had the trucks repainted in the last town before Kingsburg: the circus had to work to hold its own in a city where more than five traveling shows would be playing at any given time.

Millsy strode between the low mud-brick houses of the suburb. Guarze, it was called. Smithrebel's set up here every time it came to Kingsburg. Laundry filled the tiny front yards, flapping like flocks of birds descending onto scattered crumbs—but if there had been any crumbs, the scavenging cats, dogs, dragonets, and flightless crows would have gotten them already. Guarze. Spoken in the guttural drawl of Kingsburg, the word alone conjured long, dreary days at factory benches, bracketed by scant hours of sleep in rooms which no one had the time or inclination to beautify.

Much of the industrial north was like this, and none of the working people—whose fathers, or grandfathers had sweated their lives away, too, only in cornfields instead of factories—ever questioned their lot. Yet it was unthinkable that they should be content with such penury. One could almost despise them for it. And their country cousins, too, who knew no world beyond the perimeter of the squire's estate, whose ears were deaf to the call of filthy lucre even though they didn't know, as the slum-dwellers did, that the city's promises were all false. But these same men, women, and children were the ones who filled any circus's audience. One could not despise one's patrons. And in the years since Millsy had come to work for Saul Smithrebel, he had gradually realized that every single hayseed and slumrat desired liberation somewhere in his or her tarnished little soul. He knew he was crazy, knew that the pounding of life had driven him honest to heavens crazy, when he found his eyes filling with tears at the thought that they would never be truly liberated, because that was not the way the world was made. The circus was the closest approximation of joy they would ever see.

True freedom couldn't be bought. You had to reach out and grab it with both hands. That was what Millsy had done. He had been brought up on a tenant farm in the heartlands, barefoot and starving, but he had put that behind him. None of his cronies in the court had known he was born a peasant—just as none of his friends in Smithrebel's knew he had been the Queen's ambassador to Kirekune.

He'd only kept one of the vows he made as a child, and that was the vow never to have children himself. He never wanted to subject another human being to the misery in which he'd been born. The peace he had finally achieved as a ringside magician and truck driver in a small-time traveling circus was simply not worth it.

But now there was Crispin.

He sighed loudly, wrenching at his cravat as he walked.

Crispin, born in the back of a truck four years after Millsy arrived at the performers' entrance of the big top with his daemons, materialized, following him like dogs, to stage an impromptu tricking daemonstration for Saul Smithrebel that led to his being offered a position at a skinflint's salary of six shillings a week. (It had since risen to ten.) Millsy hated children. Hated them! But Crispin had wormed his way under his skin. He was six years old now, and looked ten or eleven. Being half Lamaroon, he was as easy to pick up as a baby: a specimen the physicians of Kingsburg would surely have loved to get their hands on. *What mysteries Nature conceals, the experts knoweth not,* Millsy thought. All the aerial acts would have had Crispin for a novelty turn, except that his mother, Anuei, wouldn't allow it. Elise and Herve Valenta, two-fourths of the Flying Valentas, even wanted him for apprentice when he came of age. Anuei violently opposed the Valentas. But Saul Smithrebel supported their claim. He might even have put the idea in their heads for all Millsy knew. And Millsy knew Anuei would never stand up to Saul. The conflict was still years off—a child could not start proper training until he was at least nine or ten—but Millsy could see it coming, like a black splotch on Saul's big map of Ferupe.

That meant it was up to Millsy.

The Valentas did not understand that once Crispin got a little older he would not take orders from anyone. But Millsy understood that perfectly. He would not make a single demand on Crispin. And because of that, Crispin would come to him willingly.

Millsy had already seen the small child watching the truck drivers coax their daemons into consciousness on cold winter nights. He'd seen him, entranced, sniffing the exhaust which filled the air as the engines warmed up. And after long nights on the road, he'd seen him sidle up to the handlers again, when they talked the daemons into quiescence, their heads and shoulders deep inside the engine cavities of the giant tractors. Crispin would listen, mouthing the words. *You ugly bastard . . . smelly snakely grass-eater . . .* Handlers used a limited repertory of persuasion on their daemons. The controlled violence of the relationship between men and daemons was what drew many to handling who would otherwise have been soldiers or policemen or criminals. Some said daemons understood every word out of your mouth; some said they were no more intelligent than fish. Millsy was a trickster, like the women who lived in the forests and captured wild daemons, and so he knew that the former was closer to the truth, but he would have had to be crazier than he was to give away trade secrets.

You're not going nowhere! So calm the hell down 'fore I flay the skin off your ugly skelliton!

There was less than no chance that Crispin, too, would be a trickster. But Millsy would not have wished it on him in any case. All he wanted was to be able to share the joy of handling with the child.

That animated little face, the color of clove honey . . .

Admit it, old man, he thought with a flash of disgust, *you're half in love with the child!*

Even in his days in court he had never been a pederast. He shook his head violently and tramped on, muttering.

In Guarze only the very small children stayed home from the factories. They looked up from their games, open-mouthed, dirty-eyed, as Millsy passed. The hem of his cloak swept the garbage-strewn dirt road. The weight of their neediness struck at him. How lucky the circus children were! Fate had not dealt Crispin and the others a particularly enviable hand—but all the same, they didn't know what it was like not to have enough to eat. He sank his chin into his collar, not acknowledging the children's whining pleas, and passed on beneath the ancient (and strikingly beautiful) stone arch marking the entrance to Guarze, into another mordant suburb named Hastych, and thence across the Eine into another world: one of the prosperous towns that snuggled against the walls of Kingsburg, Rotterys. Here all the houses had slate roofs like black paper hats, and their secret price tags were commensurate with the snotty manner of the maids hurrying through the streets. Everyone in Rotterys wished to be able to say that he lived in the Burg, and paid through the nose for the privilege of only having to stretch the truth a little.

The black worm of the Eine, oozing between the cobbled "river walk" on the Rotterys side and the sink-mud on the Hastych bank, fostered a sense of separation from the slums. But rich and poor alike breathed the same air. Thick with summer heat, evil-smelling, and vibrating with the far-off roar of the demogorgons in the factories. The noise was a contamination. It was everywhere. Even in the depths of the palace, if by a miracle everybody stopped speaking for a second, one heard it: *thud. Thud. Rrrrrrrr-thud. Thud.*

By the time he'd found his way through the twisting streets to the gates of the city proper, his body was dripping with sweat under the layers of regalia. He bought a fruit drink from a farmer-stallkeeper. As he counted out the coppers, he longed to be young again. Oh, instead of a mumbling, crazy old man in fancy dress, to be the boy with iron in his eyes and steel at his hip and gold in his pockets whom nobody in the court dared to cross. He had been a favorite. Once she had even spoken to him! He had crossed the northern pass into Kirekune and knelt as her ambassador before the Lizard Significant, full of high hopes, and failed to gain even the slightest concession from that august creature. And on his return she had said—

The failure of Millsy's mission had begun the pattern of defeats which was to drain Ferupe and her Queen. Soon Gift Mills was no longer the darling of the court, but a tool that had turned in its mistress's hand. He had left the capital because he could not bear the thought of living out the rest of his life in the shadow of his one-time celebrity. He knew also that if he stayed, that life was likely to be short.

The cold fruit juice cleared his head. His face heated with shame as he realized that for several minutes he had been lost in nostalgia. Nostalgia!

Standing out of the way of the bustle, he gulped the juice down.

Why should a ten-year-old failure matter in the least? Traveling with Smithrebel's, he was happy. *Happy!*

He lifted his eyes to the Salubrious Gates. Ajar, they looked as if they were about to fall and crush the market. Hundred-foot-tall marvels of black-painted wrought iron, they were the only entrance for miles into the stone wall that beetled like gray doom above Rotterys. He would not want to live even for a day with that hanging over him. Maybe that was why everyone here stared at the ground as they walked.

Moles! Blind, petty moles!

The haze of longing for the past which had clouded his mind since the circus came within a hundred miles of Kingsburg cleared. His thoughts were as lucid as crystal. Never like this anymore. Except with his daemons . . .

He threw his pottery juice bulb down to hear it shatter, and shouldered between shrill-voiced, foul-mouthed marketgoers toward the gates. Soon he would see his old friends. Then he would remember exactly why he had left the court.

The palace was unspectacular compared to the rest of the Heart of Kingsburg. It was the oldest building in the capital, built as a fortress before there ever was a capital by King Thraziaow, who had come out of the west to lead Ferupe under the flag of the Twenty-One United Domains. It was blocky and ill-proportioned. The buildings that crowded close around it, leaving mere cracks for streets, soared gracefully over the palace: the Hall of Justice; KPD HQ; Astrologers' Hall; the Crown Prince's Mansion (inhabited now only by servants); the Stock Exchange; the ancient church of God, now the Royal Opera House; and dozens of others. In the Heart of Kingsburg, there were no residential buildings, though in reality, the top floors of many of the public halls were in use as apartments.

The newer palaces dripped with balconies. They were airy with arches, and their spires strained toward the sky. If you stood in the maze of fountains on the plaza in front of the old palace, the spires hemmed in the sky like broken ice. It had been said that standing among the fountains was like drowning, looking up through the icy water to the surface.

The old fortress lay low like an old dog among children. Each block of pink granite was polished to brightness. The arrow-slit windows sparkled, and the heavy porticoes were freshly ornamented each day with flowers. Millsy entered in a river of people that got thinner at each police checkpoint. Every time, he flashed his rings and was shown through.

He had, in fact got the sequence of rings wrong. But none of the guards knew the difference until he penetrated the labyrinth to a depth where daemon-scented air whooshed out of grilles in corners, and the walls were no longer stone but carpet. Barkings, whoopings, and chee-cheeing sounds exploded close at hand. Millsy knew they could be traced to expensive pets (mostly animals that were never meant to be pets; he still had the scar where a bird of paradise had pecked him ten years ago). Niches displayed artwork from far countries and from every domain in Ferupe, with no glass to protect any of it. Visitors who got this far were expected to be above pocketing the knickknacks.

"You a *prince*?" the policeman said with disbelief, dropping Millsy's hands. "Whatcha wearing anyway?" He eyed Millsy's scruffy cloak.

Millsy felt shame climbing up his neck. "No, I—"

"You're a foreign prince. With connections to Kirekune. That's what this says."

The policeman sat on a camp stool in the middle of a small lobby. He had an antique gray-marble side table for a desk. The checkpoint was more for show than security.

"A foreign prince. Show you, mate." He began to flip through a ringbook printed specially for the illiterate, full of drawings of bejeweled hands. "Ain't no foreigners authorized—"

"I apologize. It has been years since I wore my rings," Millsy whispered.

The policeman looked up, eyes narrowing, sharp words springing to his lips. One hand went to his truncheon.

Millsy undid his cloak and swept it back from his shoulders.

An entering pair of courtiers who could have been twins, so ruggedly handsome were they, so springy their dark curls, laughed at the scene.

By the time Millsy found his way to the suite of Lady Gregisson, one of his oldest friends and a lady-in-waiting to Royal Cousin Dorthrea, he had lost all his desire for social interaction. Only loyalty drove him on. Through Christina Gregisson, and if not through her then through Sam Kithriss (if the old fellow was still alive!) or Boy Charthreron, he would wangle a glimpse of the Queen.

People were looking at him strangely. He realized he had been muttering to himself again.

Under the gaze of the lackeys at the door of Lady Gregisson's suite, he gathered himself and presented his rearranged rings.

The lackeys conferred. Then one of them vanished inside. The others resumed staring at him. They were all tall, red, and muscular. The skimpy tunics worn by Izte Kchebuk'aran men showcased their powerful arms and chests to perfection. Millsy wondered whether they resented having to dress like barbarians, now that they were employed in the most civilized place in the world. Such a question would never have occurred to him in the old days, but now it seemed of paramount importance. What were the Kchebuk'arans *thinking*? He was on the verge of asking them when the fourth one came back.

"Lady Gregisson is not in her suite," he said flatly. "However, her steward says that she is hosting Royal Cousin Dorthrea, Royal Second Cousin Sathranna, Royal Second Cousin Athrina, and Royal Aunt Melithra, as well as others, at tea on Sammesday. You are on the standing list of individuals who are welcome to join the Lady's parties at any time. Thank you."

"But she must be at home," Millsy said. "I sent her a note from Severidge saying I would be coming." He forced a laugh. "That was ten days ago."

"Thank you," another Kchebuk'aran said.

"Sammesday is the last day of my stay in Kingsburg. I am not sure whether I can—"

"Thank you."

And over the course of the next few hours he came to appreciate Christina's generosity, yes, the generosity she had displayed on leaving him on her standing list when everyone else had either crossed him off or presumed him dead. He wandered from door to door to door, jumping at servants, shaking his rings at them like a dancer jangling castanets for their entertainment, and with each rebuff he descended lower in the underground palace until he was in such rarefied territory that he had absolutely no hope at all of getting past any of the footmen who lined the walls like mannequins modeling different versions of the royal livery. None of his erstwhile friends had been Royals. Royals did not have friends. (Though he had spoken to her once, yes, spoken to her, and she had said . . .)

He should have expected this. But somehow he had assumed—the former ambassador to Kirekune, they couldn't pretend he didn't exist—

Then again, maybe he did not, or only in ghostly form. The footmen watched him without turning their heads, dozens of pairs of eyes swiveling as one. He flapped his hands at them as if he were shooing pigeons. His voice cracked. "Minions! Minions, do you hear me? The world is above your heads, and it is a bright sky which you will *never see*, cocooned down here!"

The underground palace was shaped like an inverted pyramid buried in the ground, with each level designed on the same basic floor plan, but as you descended, the plan got simpler and simpler, the area enclosed by the halls which you could reach without an entrée smaller and smaller. The lowest floor of all was a simple square of hallway with only three doors beside the one to the stairwell. Two doors had one dejected-looking royal footman each. The other had none. There was a smell of must. The carpet on the floors and walls looked water-stained.

Millsy walked around the square twice. The second time, both footmen thought about challenging him, and decided to do so if he walked around again (he saw every step of the thought process in each pair of eyes).

From their posts they could not see each other. Somewhat wildly, he wondered if they ambled to the corner to chat when no one was around. Would that be considered scandalous, a breach of loyalty to the Queen and to themselves? He did not know. He had lost his feel for the court code.

Lost his feel—

It had been slightly less than a decade. A blink, in the scope of the Dynasty. But things moved fast at court, even while they did not move at all. Not Sam, he wouldn't have started it. Probably Boy Charthreron: he'd been a back-stabber even at twenty. Millsy could just see him spring-cleaning his list of friends, standing perhaps in the middle of a whirl of servants who were industriously feather-dusting his rooms (Boy's life was one long, painstaking practical joke) declaring with a flip of the fingers that old Gift was probably dead, and if he wasn't, he'd always been a bore, anyhow. "If he resurrects himself from the provinces again, Moose, you know the line. Who's next?"

Thus is the past erased. Despair welled up in Millsy's heart like black syrup.

He turned the knob of the third door. It opened and let him into a pitch-black passage.

Warm, sewage-scented wind gusted into his face. He could hear water rushing fast and far down.

After a stunned instant, he chuckled. The sound echoed, bouncing off walls into infinity.

How could he have forgotten?

Tapping gingerly outward with his right boot, he encountered the crumbling stone edge of the walkway. Gravel bounced down and down and down.

His left hand encountered a clutch of wet pipes running horizontal to the ledge. The pipes were at the right height for handholds, but they were thick with slime; not many more people used this little shortcut, then, than they had ten years ago.

He hadn't felt ready for Boone earlier this afternoon. But now he did. How could he have forgotten Boone? *Boone* would not have forgotten *him*—in fact, within the bounds of propriety, he *could* not, since it was *he* who had incited Millsy to leave the court!

Millsy chuckled again and began to edge along the walkway.

Millsy was in the Kingsburg Waterworks. The light of the daemon glares nailed to the rock behind his and Boone's chairs cast a streaky brightness on the water of the reservoir, which stretched out from the cliff much farther than the light carried. Boone never permitted anyone except his subordinates to accompany him on his "routine" boat trips into the blackness, but Millsy had heard that it took several hours to reach the other side. It was difficult to imagine the years and manpower which had been necessary to hollow out such a vast space under the city.

Pipes at least three feet in diameter plunged down from the roof of the reservoir, into the water, like the proboscises of monstrous flies. Toward the edge of the light, the copper trunks grew as thick as a forest. Among them, stone support columns, inside which six of the pipes could have fitted comfortably, reached up to the invisible roof. The rumble of the pump daemons at work in nearby caves could be felt as a vibration. Boone's predilection for entertaining visitors on this sparsely furnished ledge mere inches above the reservoir, rather than in his sumptuous office, was, Millsy had deduced as much as fifteen years earlier, symptomatic of certain impulses, dangerously akin to sadism, which had grown from his boredom with his post.

Boone Skinner, Comptroller of the Kingsburg Waterworks, was king of his underground realm. He did as he liked. Valued by the Queen for his handling and administrative skills, and celebrated for his eccentricity, he was a treasure of the Burg, a rotund blond man who ought to have been jolly. In reality he had a gloomy manner far more pronounced now than the last time Millsy had seen him. His detractors said that he was not as pessimistic as he pretended: that, in fact, he thought better of himself than of any other man in Kingsburg. He lived in one of Kingsburg's rougher neighborhoods with his wife, Betsy, who was so common that she dropped the ends of her words. After absconding from the court, Millsy had stayed in their home while Boone taught him all he knew of the handler's art.

The comptroller's pale blue eyes stared meditatively at Millsy. His thumbs coaxed a thin ringing from the rim of his wineglass.

"It is that I regret my youth sometimes, nothing more," Millsy said, sipping the deliciously chilled ale Boone had served him. "And the indignity of the snub, perhaps. But that will pass. The last strings have been cut." He paused. "Now I know I could not live in court again."

"You are made of stronger stuff than the rest of them," Boone said. "I thought so from the beginning. Now I see I was right."

Millsy remembered the Teilsche Parallel. It was never far from his mind; but in light of what Boone had just said, the memory was especially painful. If Boone had seen him then, would he say that Millsy was made of strong stuff? Millsy had only been seventeen when he was in the army, but surely the stuff that a man is made of does not change. Once a coward, always a coward. All the machinations he'd put into getting his ambassadorship had been part of an elaborate, ongoing attempt to convince himself otherwise. Only when he discovered that he had the blood of a trickster had he finally accepted the truth.

"Perhaps the only difference between me and the rest of them is that I have weathered so many failures," he said. "Are you aware that when I was seventeen, I deserted? I was recruited into the Teilsche 198th Infantry. I only lasted three months."

"I was not aware of that," Boone said.

"I shan't bind you to secrecy. It's not as though it makes any difference now. The circus is effectively outside the law. At least half the roustabouts are deserters."

"Are you finding it satisfying?" Boone asked. "Commoners' entertainment. It's not much of a job for a handler. Especially one with trickster blood. You could be so much greater."

"But have no desire to be. Do I seem discontented?"

"I haven't heard from you in ten years, Gift. How should I know whether you are content? I did not even know whether you were alive."

The rebuke hung in the air. Millsy forced himself to look Boone in the eye. "I am not discontented any longer. I had to come here to know that, but now I am certain of it."

"Good," Boone said. "And good that you left when you did. They came to my house. I was in hot water for a while. It was lucky that Royal Sister Jacilithra spoke up for me." Pride rang in his voice as he mentioned the Royal.

Millsy sighed. "Boone, you are a better friend than I deserve. Tell me—they don't still hold that grudge, do they?"

"Gift, they were going to kill you."

"I had hoped it would be old news after so long. After all, I'm not coming back to reclaim my rings."

"Although you are wearing them."

"Only for a visit."

Boone nodded thoughtfully. "I don't expect there is any danger. But frankly, I was surprised to see you here. I thought that even if you were alive, you would not dare to come back. You have changed. In those days I thought you rather an amusing fellow, when you were allowed to be, but not very well attuned to reality."

"I don't believe it's possible to be in or out of tune with reality. After all, we live in it," Millsy said. But Boone did not respond, nor did his gaze leave Millsy's face. It was discomfiting. Millsy shifted in his chair in a vain attempt to get out from under the stare. *An amusing fellow . . . not very well attuned to reality . . .*

Was that really what he had been back then? Had he been vastly unsuited for the Kirekuni mission? Had his failure been—oh, blasphemous thought—not due to his own mistakes, but the *Royals'*?

There was no way of knowing. But it did not matter now.

He met Boone's gaze and laughed aloud. "Do you know what, Comptroller? I think you simply say whatever comes into your head." He took a drink of sweet ale.

Boone laughed: a prolonged rumble that carried out over the water. "I am still your friend, Gift. That is why I am telling you that you should not go to tea with Christina Gregisson."

"Who have you been entertaining while I lost my way in your damned tunnels?"

"Christina," Boone rumbled, glinting with joy.

"Is she planning to feed me poisoned pastries?" Millsy laughed.

Boone did not answer. He got up from his chair and stretched his massive shoulders. With the unhurried, rolling grace of the obese, he walked to the corner of the ledge, unhooked the front of his britches, and urinated into the reservoir. Millsy experienced a vague disgust as he watched the ripples spread into the drinking water of the masses of Kingsburg. "Even the Queen's morning tea is made with water from my reservoir," Boone observed as he returned to the assorted tables and chairs, on one of which Millsy sat. "A good joke, isn't it?"

"The Queen!"

Sparkles of hilarity danced in the blue eyes. "Oh, come on, Gift! I thought you were past that."

"No one calls me Gift any more," Millsy said stiffly.

"Shall I tell you what's happened to you?" Boone steepled his fingers. "I've figured it out. You've lost your cynicism. And if you'll pardon my saying so, that was the most amusing thing about you."

A torrent of words sprang into Millsy's throat. *Do you know how hard I struggled to lose my cynicism? It took me ten years and Queen knows how many setbacks to regain a measure of the innocence which I lost, not when I failed in Kirekune, but when I understood that because of that failure I must resign everything else in my life. Because it was all connected.*

"Perhaps you're right." He bowed his head to hide his face. He had to chew his lower lip until the blood came, just to hold back his laughter. Or was it tears? He cried very easily these days. It came from being a trickster. The men of Smithrebel's saw it as evidence of his craziness, but the women understood him a little better. "It's true that I've lost my feel for Kingsburg. The code of the court might as well be Kirekuni to me. I knew that tongue once, too. Have pity on me."

"Never fear," Boone said, and hoisted himself to his feet. Millsy followed suit. "No, no, bring your glass. You are not drunk yet. I owe you that, at least, for old times' sake! I think we've talked enough about the prize parrots in the palace. Come and see my daemons. I have two which I think you haven't met. One was seventeen thousand, the other was twenty; you will enjoy trying your hand on them." He shook his head. "Ahhh, where I'd be if I had trickster blood!"

Millsy paced himself to match Boone's slow strides as they entered a glare-lit archway in the cliff. "But I have no chance to practice with demogorgons. The beasts I use in my act are only small heartland ninnies. I have one southern daemon true-named Galianis that is twelve feet tall—I got him cheaply in Naftha. But all I can do with them is make them jump through hoops and tie themselves in knots."

Boone shrugged. "You work in a circus, not a house of trickery." Millsy knew the slur was unintentional. Everyone he had ever met— even those with democratic pretensions, like Boone—held the circus in low esteem. That was partly why Millsy himself had first been attracted to it.

"True, true." He laughed. "Do you know what? My act is like that stunt with macaws Sim used to do. Except that he had them on strings, poor creatures. Remember?"

"Just wait until you see, Gift," said Boone. "I have had a cave fitted especially for them."

They entered a big, brightly lit cavern where pale-faced young men were seated at desks. There was a smell of old books. All of the clerks scrambled to their feet and mumbled "Comptroller" as Boone and Millsy passed through. Millsy's palms were wet with anticipation. He glanced sideways: a half smile slackened Boone's normally expressive mouth. After all, they still shared one passion. It was a glimpse of this zest which had first interested Millsy in the comptroller. During his period of social decline, Millsy had tried his hand at every conceivable occupation. It had been through Boone, finally, that he discovered the quirk in his blood and his aptitude for trickery, a trade normally exclusive to women. And with Boone's help, he began to see a way out of his dilemmas at court. Very quickly they had come to share that all-devouring enthusiasm for the "business"; for a brief while, in Boone's house in Xeremaches, they had been as close as lovers, and Millsy had mistakenly believed they shared other things as well.

Now they had even less in common than they had ten years ago.

But there were still daemons.

There always had been daemons.

The vibration became a real noise. Thump. Thump. And simultaneously: Clatter-rattle-ratter-clattle . . .

There would always be daemons.

They rounded a bend, hurrying now, and came out onto the floor of a wide shaft whose roof was visible high up in the light of brilliant glares that did not leave a pocket of shadow anywhere.

"Sumenitas," the comptroller of the waterworks said in an odd voice. "Dorennin."

Against opposed walls of the shaft, thirty-foot silver treadmills housed in wooden scaffolding were turning so fast that they blurred. A huge axle hung horizontally fifteen feet off the floor, connecting the treadmills at the hubs. An assortment of wooden gears—a transformation engine many times magnified—rose from the axle's center into the roof, clanking and gnashing. And underneath that noise Millsy heard the booming of the pumps the engine drove, which sucked the water up from the reservoir into the pipes that ran beneath the streets of Kingsburg.

"Hallo!" Boone shouted at the top of his lungs, advancing into the cavern.

The handlers who stood guard, two to a treadmill, whipped around. For a minute Millsy thought they were going to crumple—as if the shattering of the tableau had shattered them, also. Then they dived for their levers, and the scent of burning rubber filled the air as massive brake pads contacted the sides of the treadmills. As the rpms decreased, the second handler of each pair ran up to his treadmill, carrying what looked like a seven-foot lance tipped with a silver spike. These they jammed into the mesh, into the flesh of the daemons inside. Millsy winced.

The daemons were silent. Collared daemons could roar and groan, but not speak. Another attraction of Millsy's little act ("The Only Exhibition of Wild Daemons to Tour the Domains in a Hundred Years!") was the eerie jabbering of the daemons as they obeyed his commands. Sumenitas and Dorennin obeyed the cue of the lance and crouched on the bottoms of their treadmills without making a sound. Tears poured down their faces. Millsy noted the way they constantly picked up their hands and feet to avoid contact with the silver slats.

One—Sumenitas, he guessed from the look of her—would have been about fifty feet tall standing upright. Her bones were coated with sweat-sheened mauve. Her breasts hung down like flaps. Even in the slave crop, her hair was bushy and black. Dorennin was shorter and stockier. His skin was pale, though his hands, feet, and joints, like Sumenitas's, were wealed and infected. Silver slave collars two inches thick encircled necks covered with sores. They would never see a bath: their natural smell was so overpowering that most handlers *preferred* it masked by the smell of dirt and feces. They turned their heads languidly to see who had come in, eyes the size of brimming teacups.

Oh, they were tricksy beasts! Demogorgons this big could only come from the Waste.

"How do you know their true names?" he asked Boone softly.

"I went myself into the northern Wraithwaste to buy them." Boone, too, spoke in a near whisper. Now that the last of the gears had stopped moving, his voice echoed up into the heights of the shaft. "The trickster woman told me their names, for a fee."

Most trickster women would sooner die than reveal a single bit of their lore to one of alien biology. That was why Millsy himself had never ventured into the forests of the Wraithwaste, never tried to seek out a house of trickery and get the training that would enable him to exploit the abilities his blood conferred on him. He had known it would be a wasted effort. Boone's bribe must have been handsome indeed.

"Sumenitas."

"And Dorennin."

There were many twenty- and thirty-foot daemons currently in use in the waterworks. But these were prize specimens. If Millsy had been trained as a trickster, he would have been able to step in perfect safety up to the sides of the treadmills and caress them through the bars. (The handlers hung back a good ten paces, aware just how far the daemons' auras of power extended, aware of the danger they were in. Boone would be rotating his men, putting different handlers on these daemons every day so that no man was numbed by the constant exertion of willpower that was necessary to keep the daemons calm enough that they didn't lash out. About seventy years ago a daemon had broken loose from its cage. That had not been in the waterworks, but in the gasworks, which lay about ten miles outside the city. The deaths had numbered in the hundreds.)

"Daemons are much like people," Boone said. He was fingering a small silver-threaded whip that he had taken from a pocket of his half-cape. "One learns a good deal from handling them. What one learns is that they are stupid."

"They're not." Millsy shook his head absently. He did not have to argue; he knew. "They are as intelligent as we are. That should be obvious even to you. I don't understand why handlers persist in believing them mindless."

"They are nothing like us."

"They do not *think* as we do. But they understand everything."

For the first time since they entered the cavern Boone looked at him. "Does it matter?" He laughed his deep, unhurried laugh. "They are ours. In *my* book, my friend, that which a man can best is not his equal." He strode to Dorennin's treadmill and flicked the whip through the metal. Millsy heard the faint hiss of silver contacting daemon flesh. A split second later he *felt* the power with which Dorennin lashed back at Boone. The comptroller leapt backwards, surprisingly fast for a man of his bulk, laughing as he deflected the invisible blow. Dorennin's handlers rushed up to the treadmill as the furious giant threw himself at the mesh. The whole scaffolding shook. The axle turned a half-rotation. On the other side of the cave, Sumenitas pitched forward in her wheel. Gears clanked like falling rocks in the roof.

The handlers pressed themselves against the mesh. Not for a second did they stop crooning to the daemon. *Ugly motherfucking beast . . . dickless ogre that you, that you are . . .* One of them, either bold or stupid, ripped one silver-woven glove off and stretched his hand into the cage. After an endless moment, the quivering giant let his head drop so that the handler could touch his neck, stroking around the cruel collar.

Boone walked back toward Millsy, grinning broadly, wiping sweat from his face. "All right! Start 'em up again!"

Dorennin's handlers withdrew. The daemons responded to the prodding lances. As the noise built, Boone shouted, "See what I mean? Eh?"

Millsy nodded. "Just so long," he shouted, grinning, "as you don't let them get free!"

"It's not even possible!" Boone tipped his head back to survey the workings of the machinery. "The mills are welded shut. We feed them through traps in the mesh."

Millsy felt exhilarated, as if he had shared in Boone's triumph. And as a handler, he *had* shared in it. It was the triumph of mankind over beast: pure, intellectual, and visceral at the same time. Inevitably his thoughts went to Crispin. This was the joy to which he wanted so badly to introduce the boy when he got old enough. He *felt* that Crispin had an aptitude for it. Just as, long ago, Boone must have felt that Millsy had an aptitude.

Boone was explaining some difficulty they had had in the construction of the shaft. Millsy could not make himself pay attention. Exhibitions like this were not routine to him, as they were to the comptroller. The episode with the whip had left his heart beating fast. A voice whispered in him: *This is all that there is in life. The rest is words on the wind; what does it matter if they are sweet or bitter? This is the essence.*

(Crispin, my child . . .)

And love, after all, the fast-fading cynic within him whispered superciliously, is just another form of control.

It was insupportably cold in Christina Gregisson's parlor. The Royals themselves seemed to emanate the chill—as if they were frozen stiff in their layers of draperies. They did not react to the conversation around them, except to flicker an eyelid when the company laughed. They were not dressed in the fashions of the court; instead, they had swathed themselves in what looked to Millsy's unaccustomed eye like landscape paintings torn out of their frames. The courtiers who fluttered around them, proffering cakes, finger-goblets of wine, conversational sallies, seemed small and thin as sprites—men and women both, for the fashions for women this year were body-hugging sheaths that would have caused a scandal in the streets of any city in Ferupe.

Only the boldest courtiers actually dared to address themselves to

Melithra, Athrina, Sathranna, or Dorthrea. The rest stood in the corners gossiping, slewing their eyes every five seconds toward the center of the room where the painted hillocks brooded.

Millsy's dulled aesthetic sense could not help equating the exquisite fragility of the parlor with beauty. He had been speechless ever since he came in. Common sense told him that none of them even knew who he was. Yet fear pounded maddeningly inside his skull, and every time someone offered him a cake he hesitated. He hated himself for it, but he hesitated.

He had been a fool to come!

But he had been so hungry for a glimpse of the Royals. And here they were. The women cousins. He had forgotten how unsatisfying they were, these women cousins. He remembered the Queen as far grander than any of them. *Her* skin was almost as dark as Crispin's. Strange, Millsy had often thought, how although the non-Royal ladies powdered their skin to make it whiter, among Royals darker skin meant purer blood. The court ladies' rejection of their rulers' standards of beauty had something not quite dignified about it. He could not help thinking of the women of Smithrebel's. Not Anuei Kateralbin, but the animal trainers like Mrs. Lee Philpotts, who feared and loved her smelly tigers so much.

There was a reek of daemons in the room. They roiled unseen about the Royals, worming their way in and out of the stiff folds of their drapes. Millsy knew that nobody besides himself and the Royal women could sense them. The tiny porcelain cup between his fingers glowed with warmth, but cold hung like a miasma over the room, whitening the air. Of course they were hundreds of feet underground; but that alone did not account for the chill.

Daemon braziers burned at the feet of each Royal. Green tea steamed as it issued from the spout of the samovar over which Christina presided, her wit brittle, her voice strained. Yet when Millsy glanced at the little gatherings of courtiers, the women were surreptitiously rubbing their bare arms, the men cracking their knuckles. It was almost impossible to remember that outside, overhead, up in the world of dirt and vulgarity and death, summer was in full force. Could the chill, Millsy wondered, be psychosomatic? It certainly wasn't produced by the daemons. He knew of no medical condition which would cause such symptoms. Therefore, it must be all in his head: a function of the extreme, unreasonable case of nerves which had overcome him the minute he entered the palace this second time.

And yet it wasn't just him.

He must try to join in the conversation. It would take his mind off the cold, and his fear. Yet he knew that if he tried to make repartee, he would betray his own redundancy. Anyhow, he was terrified of the courtiers. The kisses Christina had given him on his arrival, and the questions she had asked, had been so sincere that despite himself he got quite flustered. In the world of Smithrebel's, because of the close quarters in which everyone lived, reticence was valued almost as highly as patriotism, and Millsy did not have to throw up any false fronts. No self-explanations were required, and so he gave none—whereas in the half hour he had been at the tea party, he had already had to offer prettified accounts of himself to the Royals and to half a dozen other people whose eyes flickered away from him while he spoke.

"More tea, Martha? More tea, Frederic? No? Gift, surely you—"

"No, no." Millsy's voice came out husky. He cleared his throat. "Christina, did I forget to compliment you on that rosette? It is quite exquisite."

Her hand flew to her throat. She giggled. "You have an eye for fine craftsmanship!" Like most court ladies, she never tired of compliments, bland or clever, sincere or otherwise. The thing at her throat looked like a full-blown, perfect yellow rose, one petal edged with brown, but from the way it weighed down her neck ribbon, Millsy knew it was metal.

"I was given it by Melithra on my twenty-fifth birthday—last year!" The courtiers on either side of her chuckled indulgently. It was hard to remember that Christina was in fact forty unless you looked at the tiny lines in the masklike white around her mouth and eyes. "Of course I always wear it. Melithra!" She raised her voice. "Gift admires the rosette you gave me . . ." She whipped back to Millsy, a forced smile on her mouth. "If you won't have any more tea, then surely a pastry!" She picked several from the platters on the low table before her, arranged them on a saucer, and thrust them at Millsy.

"Really, no," he began, but she had already turned away from him. "Frederic!" she commanded. "Come over here and tell us again about your expedition to the south! Do they all look like my Kchebuk'arans, or are some of them moderately civilized? I am speaking of the people of the countryside, of course . . . Naftha is a perfect paradise, but then it is in Ferupe. Has anyone else been to Giorgio's in Naftha . . . ?"

Millsy's gorge rose as he stared at the assortment of microscopic pastries on his napkin. In order to keep their figures and simultaneously stick to a schedule which included four to seven meals a day, lady courtiers ate nothing that was not miniaturized. Baby chickens and quail eggs, fillets of minnow; wild strawberries, infant vegetables; doll-size scoops of sherbet, chocolates like bits of gravel. It was not a fad but a serious etiquette. If the food at a "mixed" party did not come in two sizes, the host was severely censured. What could be concealed in these dabs of flour and sugar? Should he choose cowardice or possible death?

He shook his head angrily and looked up.

The subject of the south had been a failure. Christina was frantically trying to entertain the Royals.

"And has your little Poche recovered from his canker, Dorthrea? We were all so concerned for the poor creature!"

Dorthrea turned her head, slowly. Millsy was surprised that the raised collars of her drapes did not crackle.

Silence fell over the guests: the Royal was actually going to speak!

"The dog is quite well."

Her voice was the grind of rocks falling. Her skin was sallow and lusterless, like that of her sister and her cousins. Her hair was a garden of china flowers. Beneath that hallucinatory mass, her eyes looked like rain puddles.

The Royals were not beautiful.

Once the Queen had spoken to him. And she had said—

"My bowels are about to move," Royal Aunt Melithra said suddenly. "Perhaps I will go home."

Far off, through the ground, Millsy heard the subsonic roar of the factories. The birds in the cages hanging from the ceiling were silent, their feathers puffed up in the presence of the daemons. Christina's voice rose high and gay over the silence.

"Well, of course, Melithra, if you are not feeling well, the last thing I should—"

The only light in the room came from the gas fixtures around the walls. It was yellowish, unhealthy. The tea in Millsy's cup had gone cold. He had not drunk a drop. He, too, would have to leave soon, or he would be sick; however, he probably wouldn't have to excuse himself. The Royal's announcement of her discontent meant the party would be over as soon as decency permitted. Knotting his fingers in his beard, Millsy stared at the curlicues of pastry on his knee, his heart pounding.

That night the trucks of Smithrebel's rolled out of the Guarze vacant lot. Millsy sat in a costume closet in the back of Daisy 3. He had left his pet daemons in the props truck so as not to frighten Crispin. If he had been a trickster woman, or a Royal, he could have forced them to stay invisible. But he was imperfectly trained.

He sat hunched in the dark as the trucks chugged through the streets of Guarze and Jaxeze. Little by little, they pulled free of the capital. Millsy could picture the half-mile-long convoy passing the gasworks, the Kingsburg Granaries, and nameless twenty-four-hour factories from which poured the noise of daemons in torment. At last the flattening of all outside sound told him they were on the northbound road. During the hours of daylight, ox-carts, dog-carts, private daemon limousines, police cars, foot travelers, men on horseback, and army trucks all vied for space, sometimes spilling across the hedges into the fields that bordered the road, reducing crops to mud. Now the road belonged to big game. Dump trucks, short-haul lorries, eighteen-wheelers bound cross-country for Naftha, Grizelle, Gilye, or Kotansburg, semiarticulated tankers full of natural gas; Smithrebel's trucks were merely the jesters of this powerful crew. The noise of the daemon-powered engines blended in Millsy's ears into a spine-tingling hum, as if a choir five hundred strong were voicing one endless note.

The winter clothes hanging in the closet swayed against his face. He inhaled a moth, and coughed. The vibration of the transformation engine went through his bones.

Long before he had ever thought of becoming a truck driver, as a twenty-year-old courtier, he had stood at the edge of the northern road and watched the stream of behemoths pour by. His fine silk hose had been sopped with dew. His suede boots had been ruined. (In those days he had tried so hard to be fashionable, despite his long stork's body that could not wear tight clothes without looking skeletal.) He had lost his hat. He had—if he remembered correctly—been wild with grief over some boy.

And yet—and yet—

The daemon of Daisy 3 was lulling him into a trance, all the way from the other end of the truck. He was in danger of falling asleep if he didn't rouse himself. Feeling like an old man, he extracted himself from the costume closet and passed along a dark gangway until he reached the nook behind the tractor where Anuei and Crispin made their home. Seven square feet to contain the debris of two lives. A chilling thought.

"Hallo!" he called, falsetto, and in a blurry voice, as if she had been sleeping, Anuei said:

"Come in."

But she was not sleeping, but mending clothes, while Crispin, as was his wont, clambered quietly around the room. Anuei's kind heart and clever fingers meant she got saddled with a lot of other people's sewing. In his present state of mind, Millsy did not dare to speak to Crispin. He pretended that he had come to visit Anuei. If she was not fooled, so much the worse for her, but this afternoon had left him with a desperate zeal to maintain the proprieties.

Despite his good intentions, it did not take him long to work around to the subject which, he now realized ruefully, was his only subject.

Daemons.

"Should you like to be able to command daemons some day?" he called to Crispin.

The little boy was hanging upside down from the clothes rail, half-naked, his thumb in his mouth, like some overgrown wingless fruit bat. His toes were on a level with the cages of Anuei's exotic birds, now covered with cloth, which swayed from hooks in the underside of the horizontal partition in the truck.

"Make them come to you, I mean? Should you like that? You could play with them, have them fetch things for you . . ."

"You are terrible with children," Anuei said. "Never offer them anything they don't need."

"I'd *like* that," Crispin said. His eyes shone like wet black stones. "D'you have some daemons with you right now, Millsy?"

"Don't build cloud castles for him!" Anuei said.

Millsy knew what she meant. *I'm warning you, Millsy!* But because she did not say it explicitly, he could ignore it—just as everybody else ignored what she meant. That difference between Ferupians and Lamaroons was the cause of Anuei's failure to influence Smithrebel's as the ringmaster's mistress should have.

Millsy took a deep breath and concentrated on ignoring the tragedy in her eyes. "Crispin, come down from there, and we'll have a game of cards—you, your mother and I. I'll show you a new shuffle."

"Don't wanna." Crispin flipped around on the pole so that he was hanging with his face to the wall. His cutoff shirt slipped down around his shoulders.

Millsy hitched himself closer to Anuei and murmured, "He has an aptitude. Look at the way he listens to the engine."

"He's always done that." Anuei bit off thread.

"Exactly! Don't you see—don't you see? If I started training him now, he would become so outstanding a handler that not even his father would think of making him into an aerialist!"

"Not so loud!" Anuei almost shrieked.

Millsy held up both hands to calm her. "He doesn't understand."

"The neighbors!"

"They can't hear, Anuei." Only a few people in Smithrebel's—Green Sam the chief cook, the elephant-training Philpotts brothers, and Millsy himself—knew the truth of Crispin's parentage. A secret shared, even among half a dozen, is barely a secret at all—but with Millsy, at least, it was safe.

"No child's got an aptitude for slave-driving," Anuei said in a flat voice, so that for a moment Millsy did not quite understand what she was saying. "Not no Lamaroon child."

Millsy rocked on his heels. "What most people mistakenly call aptitude is usually only a matter of early encouragement! And I feel it would be best to encourage Crispin to pursue the grandest of all professions, rather than making him into a mere entertainer!"

"I'm a 'mere entertainer'! And I know what you want from my baby," Anuei said, and for a paralyzed moment Millsy thought she was going to say something which should not be said by anyone. Then he remembered she was not like that. She sat hugely on the pillow of her thighs, on her cushions. "And I can't protect him all the time—not from you, because you are supposed to be our friend. Or are

you? This damn incestuous cesspit!" she spat suddenly. "Traveling monkey show! All I can ask you is not to put him in danger. And because you are my *friend*"— she stressed the word sarcastically—"I hope that you will respect my wishes."

The room smelled of cheap tallow, and those Lamaroon fumes Anuei carried about with her, whose virtues Millsy had heard graphically extolled in the men's quarters.

"I cannot," he said softly. Her eyes were on her mending, through which she jerked the needle viciously. "Anuei" —he knew she could not hear him— "this afternoon I tasted the poison. Henceforth I must push the cup away whenever it is offered to me—even when it is offered by a friend. I cannot."

It had taken him the greater part of his life to get the proportions right, but now he had it. From now on he was one hundred percent daemon handler. No more courtier. No more ambassador. No more failure.

No more misplaced scruples.

He had tasted poison, and he would have no more of it. The exhilaration of unrequited love, that obsession which frees the soul from gravity, buoyed him up. He felt as Anuei, the Balloon Lady, must feel when one of the roughnecks tossed her laughing into the air. His soul swelled with his desire for, and his complete belief in his own, altruism.

Twin tears sat on the shelves of fat below Anuei's eyes.

"Millsy! I'm begging you!"

He smiled in his beard and held a skinny, shaking finger to his lips.

The truck rumbled on through the night. Cows slept in the fields and tenant farmers slept in their one-room huts, dreaming of circuses.

The mask fell off the city, and she saw it for what it really is —a caricature of infinity. The familiar barriers, the streets along which she moved, the houses between which she had made her little journeys for so many years, became negligible suddenly.

—E.M. Forster, *Howards End*

A Fragile
Heaven

1884 A.D. Ferupe: Plum Valley Domain

Rae was nine. She had long, long, long black hair. Tangles didn't bother her, in fact she nourished her favorite ones with careful additions of burrs and thornbush prickles, and she always wore her hair hanging around her face, even like now, when she was playing down the stream and it kept getting in her way.

Black water gurgled along the bottom of the weedy gully. Elders and willows threw the summer sun down in shifting patterns. She crouched halfway up the bank, whispering to herself, pushing sticks into oblongs of wet clay. These would be her actors. Nearby lay a pile of scraps of material she'd cut out of curtains and tablecloths and things for their clothes. Dressing them up was her favorite part of the game—she enjoyed it even more than the plays themselves, since Daphne didn't want to help with the voices anymore. After their initial craze for theaters, Daph had lost interest.

Rae hadn't. She was like that.

She'd made the Prince. Now his consorts. "Sister Moira," she whispered. She giggled at her own daring, doubling over her knees, shaking silently. Sister Moira was the mother of Rae's enemy Colm, a towheaded twelve-year-old who lorded it over all the other children because their parents were lower in the pecking order than his. His father was the Prince's first courtier, and what with his mother being the first consort, you really would think he was the bee's knees! Rae's mother, Sister Saonna, was no less than the third consort. If it hadn't been for that, she suspected Colm would have given her a much harder time than he did. Even so, he pulled her tail every day in prayer. Morning, noon, and night. Her place was right in front of his. There was no escape.

Carefully, she scratched a scowling mouth onto Sister Moira's head. In the skit she was planning, Sister would get smooshed. Lovely.

Without thinking, she curled her tail around to hold Sister steady. Bad! Growling, she snapped it back over her shoulder. The tip hit a nettle; tears came to her eyes. She scrubbed them away with a handful of hair (so much glossier and stronger than any of the other girls').

She had a tail because she was Kirekuni. So did her mother—but her mother's tail was dark-patterned with tattoos, beautiful curly designs. None of the other children were Kirekuni, except for the Shard boys, who were much older, and a couple of the babies. But she'd never thought much about it until Daphne, her best friend, had told her they couldn't hang out anymore because Kirekunis and Ferupians were at war, they were enemies.

In the end it had proved to be just another of Daphne's things, like not wanting to play dress-up, or painting suns and moons on the knees of her breeches. But the idea had kept on bothering Rae, at meals and at prayer, and whenever someone slighted her, she couldn't help wondering if that was why.

Rae hardly ever spoke to her mother—though she watched her constantly. But at last, yesterday, she had sought her out in the kitchen. Over the clattering of cooking and washing up, she tried to ask her about being Kirekuni. Later she realized this was a bad mistake. Saonna hated kitchen duty. She didn't want to be distracted from the giant pan of scrambled eggs she was stirring. Sweating and biting her lip, she told Rae to go away.

So Rae went. She cried.

She didn't want to remember. Pinching her lips together, she pressed a piece of white curtain damask onto Sister Moira's torso for a dress. But she wasn't careful enough. The clay ball split, and half of it rolled into the grass. Rae gasped, threw Sister Moira down, and scrambled down the bank to dig more earth out of the muddy overhang.

Last night, feeling slightly desperate, she had gone to the third consort's bedroom to wait for Saonna. The bedroom was on the third floor of the mansion, right below the dorm where Rae herself slept. Underneath the central dome of the ceiling stood a canopied bed, its covers spilling onto the floor. Mirrors hung at strange places on the rose-patterned walls—some near the floor, some at the ceiling, and just one small one over the dressing table where Saonna's perfumes and creams stood uncapped. Big pink chairs were draped with lovely clothes: dresses of fur and velvet—Rae would have liked that material for theater costumes—lace underwear, sateen corsets, and long lambswool underwear for winter. Saonna never, ever put anything away. *Nobody* in the cult did, except Rae and the other children, who had to clean up the dorm rooms and the dining room every day.

This is the way it should be, Rae had thought, seizing a long yellow ribbon and twining it around her hair. *This way, you can see everything there is. All at once. Like it will be after we transcend.*

Waiting was the only way to live. She knew that. But the meditative slowness of all the adults around her, so frustrating when they imposed their deliberation on the madcap, aimless games with which the children filled their time, sometimes gave her a funny feeling of being not suspended, but caught up in an onrush of fleeting days. She cried every time she had a birthday. She didn't want to grow up. Because soon—Sister Flora said probably when Rae was in her early twenties—the Queen, the Last Queen of the Dynasty, was going to die far away in Kingsburg and all of humanity was going to come to an end.

The adults often discussed how it might happen: plague, black rain, the end of childbirth, floods. They spoke of these terrifying things quite calmly. They had even calculated how long it would take death to reach Plum Valley Domain, presupposing that it would spread outward from Kingsburg. They didn't know *how* it would come. All they knew was that it was coming. That much had been revealed to the Prince in a vision. It was why, long ago, he had joined the Dynasty.

Such was the stuff of myth among the children of his acolytes.

But the end of humanity wasn't a myth. It was a fact.

No more dress-up. No more sweet to suck clover. No more Daphne. No more Saonna. No more Rae.

Transcendence.

In her mother's bedroom, she shook herself, and throwing a robe of mangy leopard fur around her shoulders, pranced over to gaze in one of the mirrors. For three hours, while the cult convened for prayer and supper downstairs, she amused herself trying on Saonna's dresses and creaming her face, playing music hall. All the actors at real music halls were men, with short hair, wearing wigs and heels—so she couldn't quite manage to believe in herself. When Daphne was around, that didn't matter. But without her it wasn't as much fun.

And Saonna did not come. And it got to be Rae's bedtime. Through the ceiling, she could hear the other children talking and scuffling. Her eyes were sore with tiredness. She was usually a good girl; Sister Flora would turn a blind eye to her absence, since she didn't make a habit of it; yet she was appalled at her own temerity. She climbed onto Saonna's bed, crawled under the fluffy but rather matted covers, and curled up, breathing in the heady smell of Saonna mixed with the scent of must.

And she must have fallen asleep, because suddenly she was awake, and a big, heavy-breathing animal was crawling onto the bed, jerking the covers away from Rae, flopping down hard on the mattress. The room was horribly dark. Rae lay stiff and still.

"Mother?" she whispered. She never called Saonna that. "Mother?"

"Rae? Rae, is that *you*?"

"Motherrrr," Rae said. "Motherrrr! Will you light a candle?"

Saonna tossed. She groaned and sighed. It sounded as if the bed itself, that massive, rotting piece of furniture, were releasing air from the depths of its frame.

"Please!" Rae nearly screamed.

"You shouldn't be here," Saonna mumbled. Letting out soft cries as if in agony, she slithered head down off the edge of the mattress and crouched with a thump on the floor. Rae held her breath.

Steel scratched on flint. Yellow light flowered into the room, shaking up and down the walls as Saonna heaved herself back up onto the bed to sit facing Rae.

Her hair was tousled. She wore nothing but a grimy negligee. Under her daughter's open-mouthed stare, she twisted her head uncomfortably and gathered the filmy stuff close to her throat.

"Where *were* you?" Rae asked. She felt herself close to tears for the second time in one day. "I was waiting and waiting!"

"It's none of your business what I was doing." Saonna seemed to take charge of herself. "And I don't know what you and your little friends were playing at in here, but you can just leave now. I have to be up early. I have to feed the bloody hogs at dawn." She snapped her fingers. "Go on."

Rae wrung the cover desperately with her hands and tail, twisting it up around her like a nest. "Mother," she wailed, "I *love* you," and, bursting into tears, she threw herself across Saonna's lap.

"Oh, Queen," Saonna whispered. Distractedly, her hands rubbed Rae's back. It did not feel like a caress. Not like Daphne's arms and legs wrapping around her when they curled up in bed at night; not like Sister Flora's gruff one-armed embrace, that she gave you when she was pleased with you. A hard, embarrassed rubbing that rucked Rae's shirt up on her back. "By the Dynasty, how I wish your father was alive!"

Rae gulped. She knew her father had not made it out of Kirekune; she had never dared to try to find out why. "How—Mother, why is Father dead?"

"Don't call me that." But Saonna's voice sounded far away, as if she were thinking of something else. "There was a lot of snow. Far more than we expected. A blizzard hit us after we had entered the mountains, before we reached Khyzlme—the trading post. Our horses died. Our food was running out. Vashi forced me to eat the larger share of what we had left, so that I could nurse you." She laughed. "My family hated Vashi. My sister Saia was incivil to him. I was never able to convince her that he was a good man—that his affiliation with the Dynasty didn't mean he didn't love me. But Saia didn't understand him any more than she did me. I never belonged in Okimachi!"

"Why not?"

"Oh, Kirekunis like outpourings of emotion. They like fancy words and flamboyant clothes." Saonna's words dripped with distaste. Rae wondered what Saonna thought, then, of the gorgeous music-hall dresses Rae had tried on that evening. "They are so vulgar! One doesn't realize the full extent of it until one has lived in Ferupe. But it was—it was ironic that Vashi, by his self-sacrifice, should have proved Sayi so wrong, and never have got the satisfaction of seeing her eat her words. Not that he would have rubbed it in, anyway. That would have made him just like her."

Saonna had stopped rubbing Rae's back. Rae was afraid to remind her that she was there. Lying perfectly still, she whispered: "How did you—and—and me—get out of the snow?"

"What? Oh. A trader came by, eventually. He took us into Khyzlme. A horrid smudge of a place, stinking of meat and leather, with dogs running around in the snow. The wild men there couldn't believe we had entered the mountains without trading our horse and wagon for a dogsled. How were we supposed to know? We never met anyone who had come west across the pass. Only traders and peddlers travel *into* Kirekune, because there's nothing over there that would be of interest to anybody except a merchant. But to tear oneself *out* of Kirekune, now—that is noble! So many of our mansion had gone before us . . ." Saonna snorted. "And many more were planning to follow. I expect their bones lie under the snow. The Shards made it. So did you and I. So did the Greys and the Dirkes. And there are other Kirekuni families at other mansions. But we are just a fraction of those who tried."

Rae shivered. It took an effort of will for her to dispel the image of those frozen skeletons. "Why?" she whispered. "Why did they all want to leave Okimachi?"

It did not sound like such an unpleasant place to her. Surely people wouldn't make fun of you for being Kirekuni in a place where everybody was? She envisioned lots of mansions clustered together, their halls and ballrooms filled with people in bright-colored clothes, their black hair flowing, their long tails (tattooed like Saonna's) carried high behind them.

"Oh . . . the religious are persecuted there. Not that we aren't persecuted everywhere, in this degenerate century! But the presence of the Dynasty is so small there that it's frustrating. The Decadents of the East cult was growing more popular when I left—I suspect their conversion rate has overtaken ours by now. Posing imbeciles! They believe dancing in the streets will save them when the Queen dies!" Saonna tapped Rae eagerly. "Girl, one must be of a certain class to comprehend the doctrines of the Dynasty. That is how the survivors of the apocalypse will be self-selected. And an atmosphere of refinement can be quite pleasant when one has grown up the way I did, let me tell you! I shan't go into details, but . . . To speak truth, that was the greatest attraction the Dynasty held for me, before I became enlightened."

Rae did not understand her mother's allusions. She was fascinated with the idea of Kirekune—of Okimachi—a gaudy trader's city. Even the horrors it held would probably be delightful. But she didn't dare ask Saonna to explain. It was rare enough to hear anybody speak with passion, let alone her mother; let alone with her as audience. Apparently she had finally managed to catch Saonna at the right time. Conscious, as always, of the brief blinding torrent of days that lay ahead of them, she thought suddenly, *And it may well be the last time!*

She buried her nose in Saonna's musky negligee.

"Takashitsune Hone was the Prince under whom I first studied the doctrines of the Dynasty. He was great. But the most propitious Mansions of the Dynasty in the world are right here, in central Ferupe. Rae, we live in the Seventeenth Mansion of the Glorious Dynasty! The First Mansion is not three hundred miles from here! We are assured transcendence! Even in Okimachi, we knew that our best chance lay in coming to Ferupe. The sad thing is that we knew so little of the thousands of miles we would have to cross." She was silent for a long moment. "And there. Circumstances govern us all, even the Children of the Dynasty."

Another pause. Saonna straightened her back as if to push Rae off her lap. Rae tried desperately to think of some way to keep her talking.

"But Mo—Sister Saonna! I know the Dynasty is great, but why don't other people want to become part of it? I mean—in Greenberith—they call us culties—crazies—"

Saonna sighed. "Oh, Rae! I don't believe you've understood a word I've been saying. It takes a certain *purity of soul* to live in Waiting. I don't think they should allow you children to go into the town . . . it does nothing for your morals. As I said, the Dynasty is different from other cults. It is the first and truest. The Easterners of Okimachi, for example, will allow anybody off the street to come in and dance with them and meditate with them and partake of their food, as a result of which they've made themselves a public nuisance. It's a very Kirekuni approach to transcendence. We, on the other hand, are essentially

Ferupian—in the *old* sense—in that we don't make a show of our-selves. And so the degenerate don't understand us. It can be hard—but that's why we live here in the mansion. As you grow older, you'll find that it's in you to bear misunderstanding, and even take pride in it. You're a child of the Dynasty. You are of a certain class." She laughed wonderingly. "When I first came to the mansion in Okimachi, I couldn't even read and write! I could not speak any Ferupian. And even my Kirekuni was poor—I had such a new-city accent. Well, it took me a year, but I learned Ferupian. That was the only reason I survived the rest of the journey here, after Vashi died. One trader after another . . . and all of them wanted just one thing from me. You're lucky. You've been raised up right. *That's* what your father died for."

For no reason Rae found herself thinking about the music hall she had once gone to. That had been the best escapade of her life. She and some of the other cult children had stolen a lift into Salmesthwarth on a hay cart. They had worn their nicest clothes—though the hay hadn't done those much good. They had not let anyone know they were from the mansion. Maybe that was why they had been allowed to stay inside the theater, after they were discovered sneaking in through a storeroom door.

What little she understood of the bawdy songs and skits had both shocked and delighted her. At each fervent rendition of "Ferupe Loves Our Queen," she jumped up, put her hand to her chest and bawled out the words as lustily as any of the happy, drunken people around her. Only later—so much later that the music hall was ineradicably embed-ded in her memory as a paradise of glitz and glory—did Brother James happen to mention that those who frequented such places were low. Commoners.

She rolled onto her back and stared up at her mother's face. The commoners *had* looked at her tail; she remembered that now. She'd had it commented on more times in the space of that evening than ever before. Of course, that was before Daphne's pronouncement, before Rae got the thing of being Kirekuni stuck in her mind, like a burr in her hair.

At the music hall, she'd grinned and let anybody feel her tail who wanted to. But she'd only been seven. Stupid seven.

"Mother," she muttered, not trying to get Saonna's attention, just testing the word. "Mother."

Viewed from below, Saonna's face did not seem to belong to the person Rae covertly observed during the day: it looked haunted, tired. She was gazing out of the huge window. Even with the candle still guttering, Rae could see that dawn was coming, graying the tops of the trees around the mansion, bringing the fields that jostled higgledy-piggledy beyond into hazy silver focus.

Everybody else was going to die anyhow.

She packed her clay hard in her hands, rolling it, walloping it, thwacking it against the trunk of a sapling willow. *Splat. Thock.*

Everybody else was going to die anyhow.

The children of Greenberith who whispered behind her back, even when the tall beautiful Shard boys took her to walk between them. (She was in awe of the Shard boys. She was glad they were going to transcend.) The music-hall actors in Salmesthwarth. The farmers who wouldn't let the cult children play in their fields, and never gave them ripe plums, although the local bullies got theirs regularly at the start of the fruit-harvesting season. Squire Carathraw, who turned up every so often on the front doorstep of the mansion, half-drunk and ragged, pointing to the weeds that clogged the front drive and blubbering that the cult had ruined the land of his fathers. Well, it was his own fault, wasn't it, if he had been greedy enough to sell?

The Dynasty "did not deem modification of the physical world necessary." Brother James said that when the cult first bought the mansion from Squire Carathraw in 1855, all the lands which were now tangled forest had been a sculptured garden. Twenty or more locals had lived here just to take care of them, and of the daemon machines that mowed the lawns and clipped the topiary and burnished the windows. Those were now, mostly, fallen in glittering heaps beside the walls of the mansion. Some of those ex-servants, graying now, still turned up to accuse and beg, although unlike the squire, most of them had been reabsorbed into their own world. (The *condemned* world.)

The squire's world had not wanted him, Rae supposed.

Brother James said of course it hadn't. The vice of greed had brought Carathraw low. He was an example.

And it was his own fault. Only the worst kind of squire, those who valued cold sterling over the land their fathers had held for hundreds of years, would sell their houses—no matter how tempting the price. And the Dynasty offered very tempting prices! But eventually, inevitably, the money was spent and the firework flared to earth. The squire, by this time generally without his family, came crying home to his ancestral mansion. But the Prince who now ruled the mansion had to close the door in his face. The squire had sold, had he not? He was not the sort who would be able to profit from joining the Dynasty. He was an example for the rest of the people, some of whom would eventually grow in spirit enough to seek out the Dynasty.

Squire Carathraw's lips were loose and perpetually wet from sucking on the stone bottle he carried. He wore clothes that he seemed to have inherited from a much smaller, poorer man. All the children said he lived in a ditch, but he managed somehow to be as fat as a pig. Rae had nightmares in which she saw him standing over her, his mucky boots planted on the mattress, pointing with shaking fingers to the gilt cherubs around the ceiling of the dorm that were all flaked and falling down.

Every time his voice was heard in the drive, she and Daphne ran to hide, laughing hysterically with fear.

But he was going to die.

She worked her clay angrily.

The little stream gurgled like a baby. Rae, be happy! Rae, be hap-ap-appy!

This stream was better than any other in the whole hundred-mile-long Plum Valley because it had fish in it. (Culties did not kill anything to get their food, not even fish. They lived for the most part on rice from the eastern plains that came once a month in trucks.) When you went paddling in the big pool in the woods, you could feel trout and minnows and freshwater guppies slithering against your legs, and of course you had to scream louder than anyone else. If you tried to walk upstream from the pool, though, you found you had to get out of the water. The stream wound in a deep defile through the tangly woods that surrounded the mansion, now and again vanishing beneath the wall-like thickets that subdivided all the lands where the children were allowed to play. Rae and Daphne sometimes stood at the very edge of the trees, looking wistfully down over a sunny patchwork of fields and hedges. They never ventured out. Not two girls alone. Blond bully Colm had a scar on his shoulder that he showed off constantly. It was the place where a splinteron from Farmer Jelleby's daemon gun had had to be ripped off. Colm said he hadn't even cried. *Well, isn't that nice for you,* Rae would think, folding her arms and silently fuming. She knew that if she even *saw* Farmer Jelleby pointing his gun at her, she would cry.

Colm, nasty Colm, was going to transcend just because he belonged to the Dynasty. Was that *fair*? Rae wondered. She looked up. "Is that *fair*?" she said aloud to the trees.

"What?" came Daphne's laughing voice. "Is what fair, Rae-baby-oh?"

Rae whirled around, clutching her clay to her chest. She didn't see Daphne until the other girl waved. She was sitting in a tree a little way down the stream, her bare legs twined around the branch, her chin on her hands, her long reddish hair dangling.

All the members of the Dynasty, boys and girls, men and women, had long hair, but Rae's was the loveliest—second only to the Shard boys'. Because she was a Kirekuni. "How long have you been sitting there?" she shouted.

"Not long. I thought you were going to hear me climbing up, but you didn't." Daphne's voice vibrated with injury. "You weren't in bed last night. How am I supposed to know if you're all right, or what?"

Awww, Rae thought. She glanced at her heap of actors and material and decided to leave them for later. She stood up. "Okay, Daphne the Squirrel." She climbed to the top of the bank and pushed through the weeds and undergrowth to the bottom of Daphne's willow. It was so branchy Daphne had not been able to get very high. Rae stood on tiptoe and stretched up both her arms. She could almost grab Daphne's hair. "Come on down!"

Daphne held on, looking solemnly down out of her pinched brown face. She was darker-skinned than Rae, and shorter—but then, Rae was as tall as any of the twelve-year-olds. Sister Flora said that if she didn't stop growing, she would never become a consort.

"Where *were* you?"

Something clogged Rae's throat. She swallowed, hard. But she couldn't keep it from coming out. "Daphne, if I—I—if I ran away, would you come with me?"

"Tee hee," Daphne said loudly. "Tee hee!"

"I mean it!"

"You bloody well do not!" Decisively, Daphne swung off her branch and landed with a grunt on the earth. She picked herself up and brushed off her knees. She wore summer shorts cut from last winter's breeches, which before she inherited them had been the property of some hireling in the days of Squire Carathraw. They were belted around her flat chest with a piece of red ribbon. "Come on, dummy, don't you want anything to eat? I've got some honey in my cupboard in the ballroom. Brother James gave it me."

"Yummy yummy honey," Rae sang, right on cue, sadly.

"Oh, you're being *silly*!" Daphne shouted. *"Silly!"* She threw her arm around Rae's shoulders. They ducked to avoid a branch as they started through the woods. "Yummy honey. Ouch, my foot. Yummy yummy yummy, Rae-baby-baby . . ."

Rae joined in reluctantly. The song irked her, and after a moment she realized why: she was not a baby any more, not Sister Flora's, not Brother James's, not anybody else's. She thought she would be Daphne's a little longer, just to keep her happy. But it was not real.

if there are any heavens my mother will (all by herself) have
one. It will not be a pansy heaven nor
a fragile heaven of lilies-of-the-valley but
it will be a heaven of black-red roses . . .

—e.e. cummings

BOOK TWO

THE CATCH

The Open Air of the World

Jevanary 1893 A.D. *Ferupe: Lovoshire Domain*

Midwinter, just after the turn of the year. Smithrebel's Fabulous Aerial and Animal Show was in Lovoshire Domain, at the westernmost point of the grand itinerary that Saul Smithrebel had sketched anew on his map last year, rumbling slowly southward through the Apple Hills. Lovoshire was a domain renowned for nothing except its massive, millennia-long flirtation with the Wraithwaste, the daemon-infested forest that stretched for thousands of miles along Ferupe's western border, over which the war with Kirekune was being fought right now. The Wraithwaste had never really been part of Ferupe. It was alien, unknown, colonized only by trickster women. In the rest of the country, the name of Lovoshire evoked a dark glamour. Beyond Lovoshire lay only the trackless Waste, and the exotic glory of the war front, into whose brilliance all young soldiers vanished. And beyond that . . . Kirekune!

Here in the Apple Hills one often saw airplanes gliding high and silent overhead, on their way to the front from the air bases in Salzeim. But there were no bases in Lovoshire itself, nor (for some reason known only to the Queen) in any of the other heavily forested western domains. Here, the war might as well have been a thousand miles away. People's everyday business was quite different, and of a great deal of interest to Crispin: it was daemons. It had been years since the circus passed through daemon country. He had only been fifteen the last time around. So this time, Lovoshire held a special attraction for him, too.

It was an attraction, however, which vanished quickly when he remembered that in the Apple Hills, in Jevanary, it rained every day without fail. He and the other drivers muttered disloyally that it had been a mistake on Mr. Saul's part to come here in winter. What a fool the Old Gentleman was! The takings were unbelievably meager.

Last time, it had been Aout. High summer. The hills had been far greener than they were now. And the dark-haired people hadn't hidden in their wooden villages, putting their heads out when the musicians struck up, drawing them quickly back in when they glimpsed Missy, Charmer, and Two-Tails, the elephants. They had been so generous with themselves, so joyous, that the circus had not been able to do anything more than plug into their summer-long celebration, crystallizing the giddiness, synchronizing the overflowing energy into one glorious three-hour performance after another.

Even the Old Gentleman's chronic sense of lateness had abated. He had consented to do one show after another in the same location for as long as the appleseeds kept coming. Each clink of coin, to him, rang another note in the tune of a Ferris wheel. That had been his fixation ever since the daemon in the carousel died and they had had to sell it for scrap. A Ferris wheel! Prohibitively expensive, considering a twenty-foot daemon would be needed to power it—but maybe not! A tipsy-giggly-making chiming Ferris wheel from whose top you could see miles over the forest!

Crispin's mother had been dead three years when he was fifteen, but he'd only just succeeded in forgetting all the things she had used to tell him. He passed the summer in a daze of elderflower wine. The hills were the sort of place where young men ought to have been thin on the ground, most of them having been snapped up by the army; but in the west, for some reason, the recruiters were not so gung-ho, and the population of the appleseed towns was gloriously skewed in favor of the young. In every village, Crispin met up with the local boys and drank cider under haystacks. He sobered up only when he was due to perform. (Always on the verge of getting himself chucked out of the troupe, never quite crossing that line. Elise Valenta had threatened to eject him more than once—but he *knew* they couldn't do without him. How he'd capitalized on that knowledge!) And he'd had a fling with a different girl every night. As a rule western girls were more prudish than heartland, prairie, southern, or northerners, but they were also more beautiful. (So it had seemed to him.) When they got drunk, the usual taboos fell away like layers of confining garments, and the dubious looks that Crispin provoked in all strangers, female or male (to which he had, at fifteen, achieved a hard-won immunity) gave way to the smoldering immobility of attraction. Attraction they could not repress, and did not want to. At fifteen, he hadn't been immune to *that*.

"Best damn summer I remember," he said sourly, as he, Millsy, and Kiquat the snowman climbed down from their truck cabs. They surveyed the site.

"Bloody shithole." Kiquat flexed stiff fingers. "Here?"

The roughnecks were making so much noise unloading the trucks that the dense silence lingered only in negative. The Old Gentleman had given the signal to stop in a field at the top of a hill, where the road paused for a breather before plunging down again into another dizzying series of hairpin bends. It was apparently used as a travelers' rest, though what travelers passed through here with any regularity, Crispin couldn't imagine. Probably gypsies—though he hadn't seen any of that lot on the roads for ages, not since they got out of the southlands. On the trunks of the trees that leaned over the field, various symbols had been hacked. He'd peered at them as he parked Poppy 2. Most of the carvings looked as old as the hills themselves, and as meaningless. They were unlikely to be real writing: in Lovoshire, a schoolteacher would look as out of place as the elephants did. But Crispin wouldn't have known if they were. Like most circus people, he was illiterate, and he had no problem with that. Millsy said that knowing how to read and write caged you in. Millsy claimed to have had a Kingsburg education, and subsequently forgotten every letter, every equation, and the name of every constellation and flower he had ever learned. "Quite a feat," Crispin would say sarcastically whenever he mentioned it. They had been friends so long that Crispin wasn't fooled. Forgetting was not that easy. But everyone had to have his little secrets, and Crispin was not one to pry into things.

Kiquat wandered off to sleep somewhere. Droplets of dew gathered on the straggling ends of Millsy's beard as he listened to Crispin's recollections of that good summer. His bloodless lips were pursed, his head tipped on one side. Joining his thin hands together inside the sleeves of his overcoat, he nodded appreciatively whenever Crispin came to a salacious bit.

"Yes. Yes, I do remember. But I'm afraid you have it wrong, my young friend. That wasn't the Apple Hills, it was the Yellow Sweeps, as they call the lower hills of the Happy Mountains in Galashire. A westerly range—but more pleasantly situated than this Queen-forsaken place . . . This is the first time since you were born that we've taken the southward leg this close to the Wraithwaste." He shrugged sadly, his thin body swaying from top to toe. "And I hope it will be the last. Mr. Saul is not pleased with the takings. Not at all. He thinks it is due to the activity of cults around here. Those of the locals whom they have not drawn in, they have got under their sway . . ."

"Load of tripe," Crispin said. "If you ask me, the problem is there's so many daemons in the woods. They mess people up." He tapped his temple. "No one's going to go to the circus if they're sleepwalking half the time."

"I could be coaxed into agreement with you. But tell that to Smithrebel."

Crispin breathed slowly, watching his exhalations puff white in the air. *Last time the Old Gentleman was pleased with the takings,* he thought, *King Ethrew was on the throne in Kingsburg! He doesn't understand that altering the itinerary does nobody any good. What he needs to do is build us a better reputation. Visit the same places over and over. Over and over. Smithrebel's ought to be a name like Furey's, like Gazelle's, Murk & Nail's . . .*

Too tired . . .

The two months they had expected to spend in these muddy, slimy hills were nearly over. All anybody wanted to see now was the last, long downhill run which would carry them out of the fog and rain into the flat farmlands of Thrazen Domain. Sweeter than a girl's kiss to Crispin would have been the sight of the sun. And last night, while he was at the wheel of Sunflower 1, staring entranced at the headlights bouncing along the road, the Old Gentleman had crawled forward through the hatch from his quarters, and sitting forward with his hands on his kneecaps, regaled Crispin with long-winded anecdotes of his own boyhood in the circus.

Why? Crispin wondered. The Old Gentleman took an interest in him that was more than unusual, it was creepy. Crispin believed the Old Gentleman had a grudge against him—probably for some fucked-up reason to do with his mother—and was trying to kill him, but was too much of a coward, and too greasy a professional, to stain the circus annals with any "accidents." So he had to employ dirtier, subtler schemes.

It had been worse when Anuei was alive. Crispin had felt he had to protect her from the Old Gentleman. Saul was just not *good* enough for her! One time when he was ten he'd walked in on them. Grunting and bouncing in the dark of Daisy 3. The Old Gentleman wriggling like a white worm on top of Anuei's black bulk. Crispin had gasped and stiffened, and the red-eyed, growling beast inside him rose up and took a flying leap at the Old Gentleman and tried to rip him bodily off his mother.

That was the night he first knew, honest to the Queen knew, that he was strong. The Old Gentleman tried to hush the incident up, but of course people found out. You can't very well pretend a battered face, a swollen groin, and a broken arm are all the result of falling off a chair.

And not long after that had come the night when Mike Valenta's trapeze ripped loose from the rigging, dashing him to the mats thirty feet below. His back was broken in seven places. The Flying Valentas found themselves without a catcher, and Smithrebel's bereft of its star turn. It was then that the Old Gentleman interfered with Crispin more intrusively than any owner had a right to interfere with his performers' children. Despite Anuei's violent, silent disapproval, Crispin was made an aerialist.

Queen, how he had hated the Old Gentleman for forcing that wedge between him and his mother. Working with the Valentas was the first thing he had not been able to talk to Anuei about.

But since then . . .

Perhaps the Old Gentleman had not even *thought* about Crispin's probable unhappiness; perhaps that had merely been the egocentrism of a child, who traces everyone's motives back to himself. Perhaps it had just been the circus instincts bubbling to the top in Saul Smithrebel's dried-up, one-track brain. For Crispin turned out to be a good catcher. He would never have made a flier. He was just too tall and bulky. But his weight—he weighed less than Prettie herself—his big ugly hands, and his ability to swing head down for hours without getting dizzy, made him, Herve freely admitted, a better catcher than Mike had been. Rock-steady. It used to worry Crispin that Herve didn't know that was all just an act of will. Rock-steady! In truth, in those early days, Crispin had been racked by a paralyzing fear of heights.

But gradually he came to enjoy flying, even to believe he loved it. Days, days, and more days. Rehearsals and performances. Tape-wrapped wrists and ankles slapping into chalk-dusted palms. The tricks you learn to ensure that someone's life is safe in your hands, even when it looks to the audience as if a thousandth of a second's miscalculation means the flyer's death. It's all a matter of being on.

The Old Gentleman's interference, however, had more repercussions. While Crispin tried to juggle his responsibilities to his mother and to the Valentas, he ended up neglecting Millsy. Millsy was the only adult who had taken a real interest in him as a child. They were friends and playmates; and Millsy taught Crispin geography, history, and everything it was possible for a child to learn about daemons— all the knowledge he might have needed, in fact, except reading and writing, against which Millsy was violently prejudiced. To Millsy, and only to Millsy, Crispin had confessed that he still hated his mother's lover—that giving Smithrebel a broken arm hadn't made any difference—that every time the Old Gentleman tried to talk to him, he wanted to attack him again. If the Old Gentleman wouldn't leave Anuei, couldn't he at least leave *Crispin* alone?

There had once been an understanding that Crispin would become Millsy's apprentice, that their friendship would, so to speak, be legitimized. But neither of them ever mentioned it after Crispin started training with the Valentas. Their night meetings came to an end. And Crispin hated the Old Gentleman for that, too.

But even when he was rushing to practice tumbling with Herve at five in the morning, there had been the hot, seductive stink of daemon breath wafting out from under the hoods of the trucks; exhaust staining the night as the engines turned over; and prickly hints of *not-scent* around the cotton-candy machine, the carousel, the appliances in the cook tent. His defection to Millsy had been gradual but inevitable.

"Like it or stick it up your ass," he had said finally to Herve.

Herve and Elise had chosen to like it. But hot-tempered sour-tongued southerners that they were, they'd never managed to forgive him for choosing to be better with daemons than he was on the flying trapezes. He could insist until he turned blue in the face that when he'd joined the troupe, he'd been young enough to have become reasonably good at anything; that Smithrebel's couldn't afford for any adult to have less than two skills. But those were excuses, not explanations. Solely on the strength of his half-Lamaroon resistance to gravity, an advantage which far outweighed the drawback of his height, he could have become one of the best catchers in Ferupe. He could have been a mainstay of the Valenta troupe, instead of just a permanent adjunct. Perhaps, with his skill and Prettie's, the act could even have lifted out of Smithrebel's into the orbit of one of the really big circuses. A whole life spent sweating in the limelights.

But by the time he was sixteen, he was driving trucks, and it was too late. Every time he was late for a rehearsal, or showed signs of sleepiness—the curse of the daemon handler—Herve lashed out more bitterly than before. Gradually, the empathy necessary for a risk-free performance trickled away.

Thank the Queen—he thought now—Elise and Herve had found another boy to train. Fergus Philpotts, son of George, the elephant handler, and his wife. Fergus might not be a Lamaroon, but he was a circus baby. Pretty soon, Crispin knew, he himself would be relegated to back-up catcher and then phased out.

It sounded wonderful on the face of it; but it could easily turn out to be the worst thing that ever happened to him. While it had seemed that Crispin would fit neatly in with the Valentas, the Old Gentleman had left him pretty much alone. But now . . . He must know what was in the air; what did he have in mind for Crispin this time around? There wasn't a chance in hell he would let him just drive trucks. Smithrebel's invasion of the truck cab last night had been like the recurrence of a childhood disease of which you can't remember the symptoms, only the pain. Crispin had wanted to slouch in his seat and smoke and tip the ashes on the floor of the cab, spit out the window, sing dirty songs, shout that he wasn't having any of it, not this time. But he had only nodded and clenched his fists tighter around the wheel. Yes sir. No sir.

And he was worried about what Prettie might do when she was faced with the cessation of their working partnership. *That* had been over years ago. But the way she looked at him had never changed.

She and the Old Gentleman seemed to be boxing Crispin in, one on either side, pressing close, closer. He could refuse Prettie all right—that was horribly easy—but for obvious reasons, he could not refuse to take a new job, even though the Old Gentleman was likely to assign him heavy labor and long hours.

On the other hand, if he was honest with himself, he really did not know how much longer he could keep on like this. For four years he had been driving all night, every night, rehearsing every morning, and performing once, sometimes twice an evening. He was twenty years old. He needed some free time. He needed time to *think*. That was all there was to it.

Tired . . . The deep blue vistas of dreams were shedding their nighttime disguises of transparency, creeping up around him.

He hoped he wasn't swaying on his feet. When you are six feet eight and look as if you can move a mountain, you'd better not let anyone see otherwise.

Millsy grabbed his arm. "Ware, my friend."

The shambling figure of Donald Lloyd was coming across the field, dodging the roustabouts hauling rolls of canvas with a nimbleness that belied his long-limbed awkwardness.

Donald was the only clown in Smithrebel's whose bumbling ring-center persona did not change when he came back out through the red curtains. He had been badly affected by his years in the army. He never talked about them, or about his desertion, though unlike many, he freely admitted he had deserted. Had he been clownish all his life, and stumbled into his second profession by a happy accident? Or had he been a different person, a tolerable person, and changed after he took up clowning? One had to be careful of that.

"I thought I was *dead*," he shrilled as he drew up to Millsy and Crispin, staring at them in terror from under his hair. Crispin gazed stonily down at him. "She was groaning and wobbling every time I fucking downshifted! You gotta have a look at her, Cris."

"I got stuff to do." Crispin glanced across the lot. Lee and George Philpotts, the elephant-training brothers, were coaxing their animals out of Speedwell 11 to help raise the poles of the big top. Crispin had no responsibility for the elephants, but he was supposed to assist with the labor.

"I'm not getting behind the wheel tonight if you don't. Come on. *One* of you."

Millsy shrugged. He was like an empty overcoat hanging on a hanger, shivering as the truck swung around the bends. Movement without motivation. A human mannequin. Mills the Magnificent, who claimed to be the only male in six domains who could handle uncaged daemons. He was too young to have gray hair, and he talked like a quack doctor. He was unmarried. Once or twice Crispin had wondered, with a prickle of discomfort, if Millsy liked it *that* way—but he always dismissed the possibility. There were no men like that in Smithrebel's, except for Shuffling Will the high-wire performer, and everybody knew about *him*.

"S'pose I'd better check it out," he said. "Go on, then, Donald."

The big top, half up now, quaking as the elephants pulled at the ropes, covered most of the field, a vaguely octagonal expanse of grubby white canvas. The smaller black tops of the sideshows were scattered on the far side of the field in a haphazard midway. Anuei had performed her act, which Crispin had never, ever seen—he'd obeyed her request not to sneak in, because she'd never begged him for anything else—in one of those little stuffy tents.

The trucks resembled a circular stockade of children's blocks. The big top would abut onto the gap between Tulip 5 and Hollyhock 7, so that the performers could pass from the enclosure to the red curtains without being seen. All the tailgates were down. The panels of the menagerie trucks, Speedwell 11 and Pink 12, had been removed to let the cats, apes, and elephants smell fresh air. They were setting up a racket: couldn't wait for their cages to be set up on the grass. The sight of the flaking swirls of blue and yellow that covered the trucks, and their red silhouettes of dancing people, most of them cut comically in half where the shutters of the living quarters' windows were raised, always put the metallic taste of homesickness into Crispin's mouth.

Which was stupid, because he *was* home.

He set his toolbelt down on the squelching dead leaves and propped the gigantic, warped wooden hood of Lily 6 on its rods. Donald, for once, was right. The whole vehicle shuddered gently.

"Hold up," he shouted to the roustabouts who were unloading ring lino from the back of the truck. "Stand clear."

He gulped damp air into his lungs and ducked into the hot, reeking interior. As a handler, he could feel the stink of the daemon, a powerful, localized source of tension. It stung his nostrils and eyes. He wiped water away. "You stupid hog, Donald! Cotton candy for a brain. Poor old lady." He straightened up, took another breath of fresh air, and bent to gather hammer and pliers out of his toolbox. A daemon handler had two skills: the purely mechanical, which was just knowing the ins and outs of the transformation engines that power trucks, generators, and all the other machines that human ingenuity had devised to exploit daemons; and the daemonological. The interesting bit. Not dangerous, per se, for a celled daemon was a defanged daemon. And yet . . .

Taking a firm grip on the vibrating edge of the hood, Crispin slid back the hatch in the top of the cell anchored in the middle of the engine. The entire body of the truck jounced upward, and then sank on its wheels. Crispin held on. His bones shook.

Two thousand pounds' worth of fury glared up at him. The face pressed against the silver mesh under the hatch was just like a human child's, except that it was bright green. A silver collar gleamed, pinched cruelly tight around the daemon's neck, trapping most of her mane of black hair. She sat in the three-by-three-foot oak housing with her knees drawn up to her nose, her arms by her sides. The cage was too small to allow her to change position. Her lips moved as if she wanted to speak.

"Now, now," Crispin muttered. "Ugly little bitch, aren't you? Come on, calm down, soulless whore you are."

She seemed properly angry. Nothing wrong there. Starved to the point of madness, not misery. A fine balance. Supposedly, you could eke a powerful daemon out for fifty years with the right care and feeding, but Crispin had never heard of one that had lasted that long. Millsy asserted that *captivity* killed daemons. Crispin agreed. If you were cooped up in a cell too small to stand up or lie down in, and the touch of the walls irritated you beyond pain, driving you mad with the urge to escape, so that you pushed and pushed and pushed—just as you had been trained to do. . . .

Lily 6 shook as though she were going to fall apart any minute.

Whispering obscenities, Crispin tapped the sides of the cell with the hammer. Probably a loose join. Daemons could not stand oak, so that was what must be used for the cells, and every crack must be sealed with an alloy containing at least 70 percent silver. The catch, of course, was that silver is infuriatingly weak. He had just located the loose place, and was fishing in a pocket for silver nails, when someone wrapped a hand around his arm.

Concentration shattered. Black bubbles danced in front of his eyes. Swearing, he dived into the engine cavity to retrieve his hammer, and the daemon shot a tentacle of power out through the loose join and sent fierce shivers up and down his spine as his fingers closed around the handle. The lip of the engine cavity caught him in the stomach. He heard a faint shout and knew that Lily 6 was standing on her port wheels, her center of gravity tipping dangerously high.

Every last kink in his hair straightened on end as he banged the vital nail in.

A squelching thud shook the earth as the big truck dropped back onto all eighteen wheels. The daemon shuddered with misery.

Crispin slammed the hatch closed, hooked it shut, and spun around to see if the person who had wrecked a nice straightforward fixit was still in the vicinity. That lash had hurt. He would lambast—

Prettie Valenta stood in the muck, her head bowed, wringing her hands. Her little body was sheathed in one of the long pink dresses he'd once liked so much on her. "I'm sorry!" she said before he could speak. "I'm sorry! I didn't see you were . . ."

Why else would I have my head in the guts of a tractor, girl? What do you want?

But it was his own fault, and he knew it. *Can't you get it through your thick skull, Crispin, that just because it's there for the taking doesn't mean it comes free?* He had only made that mistake a few times, but the last had been very recent. He shook his head in anger.

She was smiling hopefully.

"You know never to interrupt me when I'm working with a daemon."

"But I—I have to tell you." She wasn't smiling anymore. "Last night—Father finally decided to tell us what he's been thinking. He says—oh, Crispin, he says Fergus is ready to perform. He's gotten good enough to catch me. Father wants to put him in the ring on alternate nights, and then permanently."

"Good," Crispin said. "Maybe I'll finally have time to give all of these old ladies a once-over." He flung his arm out to embrace the semicircle of trucks. "Queen knows they've been waiting for it long enough!"

Prettie's eyes glimmered like raindrops. She was so predictable! Crispin felt as if he would fly apart. He looked away from her, up into the sky. The dawn had given way to another misty, motionless winter morning, weeping clouds. He rubbed his back. It ached.

Hadn't he all the appearance of a man living in the open air of the world, indifferent to small considerations, caring only for truth and knowledge and . . . to . . . find at least some happiness in the search?

—Henry James

The
Lagoon

Crispin stood on the catcher's platform, halfway between the ring floor and the craze of rigging under the roof of the big top. Howard-the-lights, suspended in his high cradle, had all his glares turned on Prettie as she climbed artistically up the ladder to the flyer's platform thirty feet away, where Elise stood waiting to handle the bars for her. Crispin himself was in shadow; it was unlikely that anyone was looking at him. He wiped sweat off his face with a blue-sequined forearm. Herve stood behind him, fidgeting like one of Millsy's daemons when it was out of sorts. Crispin guessed that after they went off, Herve was planning to tell him about his demotion—he must not know that Prettie had let the cat out of the bag. Ugly little despot though he was, the Valenta patriarch couldn't be looking forward to that interview.

There had been a period of about two years when Herve had been the closest thing to a father Crispin had. A few vestiges of that relationship lingered. Crispin wasn't looking forward to the interview either.

Unsmiling white faces clustered below in the darkness. Elise had finished her turn, to the scattered clapping of sixty or seventy people, perhaps half a hundred of them smelly, blond-headed Apple Hills natives, the rest "seeds." Seeding was a technique that worked better in large towns, where everyone did not know each other by sight. Here, the audience wasn't taking well to being jollied along by strangers whose effort to dress like locals had resulted in some really bizarre outfits. Crispin suspected the crofters didn't really *understand* the circus: they were still trying to figure out what they had forked over their coin (or chicken, or fruit, or cheese) for. Unlike more sophisticated folk, they saw entertainment for nothing other than what it was, an elaborate method of scamming you out of your money.

But Prettie never noticed whether she had an audience or not. She was that rare creature, a circus artist who performed for the sheer love of it. She hoisted herself onto the top of her tower and flung her arms wide, her expression radiant.

But she was studiously not looking across the gap at Crispin.

As she swung out into the air to do her solo routine, her limbs coiling bonelessly around the ropes of her trapeze, his suspicions were confirmed. She wasn't really on. No prizes for guessing why. As a performer, she had a tendency to go wild, depending on luck and instinct rather than on concentration—tonight, she appeared to be flirting with the very concept of balance itself, constantly on the verge of making a fatal mistake. The audience couldn't look away, of course, though from the little screams and gasps coming from below, most of them were not so much fascinated as they were genuinely petrified.

Queen damn it! Crispin thought, clenching his teeth. He was the one who had to compensate for her lack of finesse. He was the one who had to ensure her safety. And she wasn't making it any easier.

She caught a rope, twined a foot in it, let the trapeze dart away to Elise's waiting hands and cast herself into a spin, head down, one hand on her heart, the other stretched out.

Eye contact.

Crispin stiffened.

Eye contact.

Her spin slowed.

Eye contact.

He felt unprofessional heat rising in his face as he swooped out to join her. Don't think about it. Jackknife. Flipping around the bar of the catcher's trapeze, he locked his knees on the padded supports, arching his back to get up speed.

She was building back-and-forth momentum. Wait. Wait. Now! At the highest point of her swing, she let go of the rope and soared toward him, her body arched like a fish's. Somebody in the audience screamed. Behind her the rope vanished into the roof. In her blue-feathered leotard, she looked lighter than a bird. Inch for inch, Crispin weighed even less; but no one would have guessed it. Effortlessly, he caught her wrists and lifted her, twisting her bodily around so that they were suspended face-to-face. Momentum carried them across to the flyer's platform, down, then up to the catcher's platform, so high that Crispin could have grabbed the railing. Candy-dank air swished past their ears; lime glares sizzled in silence. The audience ought to be clapping at this point—Smithrebel's seeds were making a valiant effort to start a hand of applause—but the poor locals were likely too frightened to make a sound.

One of her feet lost its hold. She promptly let go with the other, so that she curved away from him, like a branch splitting off from a tree trunk. Crispin tightened his grip. "In the name of the Queen, *concentrate!*" he muttered.

She radiated at him. Close up, it was a horrifying sight. Her heavy paint made her look thirty, and half-witted.

Until the finale of the act, nothing went too badly wrong. Herve had once been a catcher, and although now he couldn't swing head down for long without getting dizzy, for the last few routines he liked to join Crispin and Prettie in the air. It was an opportunity for Prettie to show off her flying skills, more than anything else; as she somersaulted between her father and her ex-lover, the limelights followed her like avid admirers. These routines were far less difficult for Crispin. Standard catching, nothing fancy.

Maybe he relaxed too soon. Maybe that was what happened.

But later that night, when he tried, sweating and shaking, to remember what he had done wrong, he could come up with nothing but the facts.

It happened when the act was nearly over, just as he reached the far point of his swing and swooped down again toward the center of the ring, his hands stretched out to Prettie, who was somersaulting toward him, dangerously off course. The big top exploded in flames. Sweat broke out all over his body. The scent of unfamiliar things burning filled his nose. It was a wonder he didn't lose his knee-lock on the trapeze. The animals—the audience—the trappings! *Everything* in a circus is flammable, even rain-soaked. *Danger! Danger!*

But in less than a second, or so it seemed, he realized that he was no longer in the big top at all.

There was no transition; it was just that the crash of sensations was so enormous and sudden that it took his brain a minute to process it.

He was standing in a street. It was night. He could feel the pavement under his boots, smell smoke in the air. There was a saliva-sweet taste in the back of his mouth, as if he had drunk a cup of bitter tea. All around him, people were running and screaming and crying and trying to establish order and failing. Their clothing billowed around them. Monstrously tall buildings huddled over the pavement, blocking out all but a thin orange strip of sky.

He could not distinguish even a word of what the people were shouting. The cadences sounded all wrong. Not like normal speech, nor yet like the Lamaroon his mother had spoken to him when he was little. The corners of Ferupe were different enough that they could seem like foreign countries. But this place was truly alien.

The people had tails. Long, pale rat-tails carried high behind them, which they used as third hands: holding bags and bundles aloft, lifting swaths of skirts, wrapped around children's wrists. Now he knew where he was. Kirekune.

A man turned to scream something at him, his face stretched blank with terror. Crispin didn't need to understand him to know what was meant. *It's getting closer!* The windows in the tops of the buildings flickered redly with the light coming over the roofs.

So why was he, Crispin, standing still? Why wasn't he afraid?

As if that flaw in the plausibility of the whole picture had shattered it, like a sheet of glass, he was no longer standing at all.

He was no longer himself. He was sensation without comprehension.

The night whistled blackly around him, windy and strangely warm. That warmth was of the air: the leaping orange glow that ringed the peak of the city-mountain before him, like a necklace of malignant orange crows. His cheeks stung with it and his eyes ran. The part of him that was still able to think wanted to shield his face, but he could not move his hands: he didn't even *have* hands. Didn't have a face. He was immaterial, swooping dizzily over a vast slum of shacks that crawled with people as tiny as ants fleeing a kicked anthill.

The face of the city-mountain loomed clifflike before him, honeycombed with black maws, lumpy with buttresses and built-up ledges. Round domes and needlelike spires pricked up like black hair all over the mountain's head.

Closer, closer, and he was swooping up to one of the maws, entering it. He was drawn, pulled along as if he were on a string. The floor of the tunnel had been paved, creating a wide street. Filthy stalactites thorned the roof. Gaslights cast a black pool of shadow around each piece of rubbish in the gutter. The tunnel was empty but for a few groups of fleeing people. They all had long black hair. The tails held gracefully behind them gave them an oddly toylike appearance. They might as well have been clockwork mice. They came scuttling from around the sharp bend ahead, and from little tunnels that opened halfway up the sides of the main tunnel. Many of these lesser tunnels had sentry booth–like structures at the entrances, and the tiniest had curtains.

But if they were all fleeing, then Crispin was flying in the wrong direction. Why was he going back into the city, when it was on fire?

And again, the obvious question shattered the stream of images. He was standing in an empty street of the same city. A different street. Here, there were no crowds, no screams of fear. Crispin did not recognize these buildings with their elaborate facades, nor the crossroads farther up the steep hill where vendors' stalls lay overturned, nor the still-lit gaslamps, to one of which a dog was chained.

The dog's terrified barking was the only noise apart from the ominous background roar. Orange light flickered over everything. Crispin could hear the flames crackling further down the hill. Close-up, he knew, a fire sounded like a cacophony of trees cracking and elephants screaming and glass breaking, all rolled into one. So it was a good long way off yet. But still—too near—

And if he was correct, the fire was no longer *above* him, as it had been in the last street where he stood, but *below* him. He was on the peak of the mountain.

A stranger stood in front of him. Crispin blinked. Why hadn't he seen the man before?

But before he could take in the details of the stranger's appearance, the whole scene—sight, sound, smell, feel, and taste—fell to pieces with a long, bright, painless tinkling. It was as if his failure to recognize the man instantly had been a mistake in all possible worlds, a fatal step off the high wire of continuity.

It was like going through the windshield in a truck wreck—if you were extremely light, like Crispin Kateralbin, and were able after somersaulting thirty feet through the air to land well enough on wet leaves that you didn't break anything worse than a shoulder. Cartwheeling disorientation took him through blackness, and redness, and heat, and cold, and nausea, and unbearable pain.

And left him, as limp as a dead rat, hanging on a trapeze under the wet, smelly big top on a rainy night in the Apple Hills, alone in the air, his swing gently slowing to a stop. Far below in the ring, people were standing in a circle around something blue. Many of the bleachers were overturned. (That reminded him of something. Something . . . What?) On the far side of the tent, a stream of locals were being shunted with some difficulty, like a herd of cows, out of the crowd flaps. Howard-the-lights' cradle swung empty, and his glares were no longer aimed center air. Their beams dotted the sides of the tent with white circles.

Crispin hauled himself up onto the bar. He peered down between his feet, holding lightly to the ropes. The combined weight of the performers and ringhands gathered in the ring was squeezing mud up between the squares of red-and-white-checked ring lino. Suddenly, yet without surprise, as if he had known all along (and that reminded him of something too . . . something . . . what was wrong with him?) he saw that it was Prettie lying in the center of the ring. Prettie sprawled unmoving in her blue leotard and tights. She must be badly hurt.

"Oh, shit," he murmured.

Flames . . .

Fading.

His first impulse—simply to let go of the trapeze and drop down to join them—passed like a breath. Slowly, feeling rather awful, since everyone seemed now to be looking up at him, he snapped his body into a swing, back and forth, back and forth. After building sufficient momentum, he released the trapeze and flew easily through the air to the catcher's tower. He could not help feeling a little pleased with himself as he made a perfect landing. But as he descended the ladder, back into reality, the ugly, vaguely accusatory expressions on the faces below told him what he had really known all along. Prettie wasn't just hurt. She was dead.

What had he done?

Flames . . .

He couldn't remember. It was like blinking awake at the wheel, only to find that in a moment of exhausted unconsciousness, you have driven off the road. He stumbled as gravity reclaimed him into the heavy, dreary world of Smithrebel's, where people parted to let him through and whispered as he passed, where nobody took the initiative to do anything, not even cover a dead girl's body, not even straighten her neck or close her eyes, until the Old Gentleman arrived. Here he came now, pushing through the curtains with a couple of ringhands behind him. He looked genuinely worried, as well he might, for Prettie was, had been, his star turn. Elise was crying. Herve was hugging his wife and staring at Crispin with a murderous eye. But Crispin himself could not take his eyes off the Old Gentleman. It was not Saul Smithrebel's fault that his white, jiggling jowls, compressed between the collar of his red ringmaster's coat and his top hat, looked overpainted, like a clown-face of sadness. But it was a truly remarkable sight, unprecedented in Crispin's memory.

Smithrebel shouted, "In the name of the Queen! Tell me you got the gulls out before she croaked!"

Rain plinked on the roof of Sunflower 1 and on the raised shutters of the windows. Crispin slouched on one of the Old Gentleman's tiny, hard chairs with his legs stretched halfway across the room. The Old Gentleman sat against the other wall of the truck, behind his shaky little desk, peering between stacks of papers as if over a siege wall. Everything about him suggested he was on the defensive—but this was his lair, this was his showdown, and Crispin refused to be drawn into participating. Even though, from the way the Old Gentleman was dragging out the showdown, that was what he seemed to be asking for. Even though part of Crispin wished he could say something which would really set the Old Gentleman on his ear. *That* would be a treasure to take away with him!

But on the other hand, what was there to say?

"Thanks very much, I'm sure, sir"?

He was fired. Sacked. Given the push.

"Of course, I don't expect you to leave now," the Old Gentleman said fussily. "Ridiculous to leave you stranded in the middle of these confounded hills, heh? No, you shall be my guest until we reach Weschess. Or Thrazen Domain. How does that sound?"

"Marvelous," Crispin said flatly.

He detected mingled irritation and uneasiness in the Old Gentleman's laughter. "Believe me, Crispin, I wouldn't do it if I didn't have to! But feelings are running high. At this point it's become a question of my authority."

"No need to apologize."

"I merely . . ." The Old Gentleman sighed. "Crispin, you have always been so reliable. I don't understand how you could suddenly—"

Crispin blinked. The Old Gentleman didn't think he had *meant* to kill Prettie. Did he?

"Nobody else understands either. That is part of the reasoning behind their outrage. The feeling is that Herve and Elise . . . and the boy . . ."

"Fergus."

"Yes. That they are suffering enough already. That it would be unforgivable of me to keep you here, constantly reminding them of their grief. As if I cared more for a half-breed daemon handler than for my star performers. Do you see? I have no choice."

You're lying to me, Crispin thought. *You know that everyone thinks I did it deliberately, because I was going to be let go from the troupe. Never mind that that makes no sense whatsoever. You're afraid that if you show favoritism to me, the Valentas'll pull out of the show. Then you'd really be up a creek, wouldn't you? But you know, Old Gentleman, you're the owner. You don't have to justify your whims. Nobody could force you to fire me if you didn't want to.*

"I was going to quit anyway," he said, wishing it did not sound so much like the false bravado of a punished child.

The Old Gentleman yelped with happiness. "But I understand! Of course you, too, are heartbroken . . . You and she . . . oh, yes, I know. Everybody knew. And I understand perfectly. I remember how I felt when your mother passed away."

Don't you drag her into it! Crispin thought.

He had not actually had time yet to consider his feelings. At first, shock had overwhelmed him. Later, curled in the driver's seat of Columbine 4, unable to face sleeping in the men's quarters, he'd been overwhelmed by guilt. Guilt that grabbed him by the throat and overpowered him. And it drove him wild that he could not recall what he had done wrong. When he had failed to twist close enough for Prettie to catch his wrists, when he had, as Millsy told him, gone limp on the trapeze, failing even to look up as she tumbled thirty feet to the checkered linoleum and the elephant shit, screaming at him, reaching vainly . . . in her last moments, she had lost the grace which all her life had lifted her out of the ordinary. And Crispin had not the vaguest recollection of it. In his memory, there was no gap between Prettie alive, flying, and Prettie dead.

He thought of Millsy, lying in his bunk in Hollyhock 7, out cold along with a dozen other men who on most nights could be found transfixed behind the wheel of a truck. Crispin, too, should be there. For a daemon handler, not even tragedy outweighed the lure of an unexpected full night's rest. The Old Gentleman would not usually let anything short of a fire stop Smithrebel's from tearing down on schedule, but he had allowed that the Valentas, now reduced to two, deserved their night of vigil. However, most of the circus seemed to be treating Prettie's death as a welcome excuse to suspend routine. The dripping night was dead silent but for a voice which Crispin recognized as Elise's, sobbing and throbbing and falling like a hoarse reed pipe. Even Crispin, shifting and scratching in the darkness, had been appalled to feel a sense of relief blanketing his mind. Questions and answers came gradually to seem less vital.

Finally sleep rolled over him. Then there was no more Prettie hovering on the edge of his vision, no more Prettie asking with her big eyes if she could ride with him in the cab (and snuggle up under his arm, and kiss his neck), no more dreadful responsibility every night that she flirted with death. All the strings tying him to the Valentas were cut by the scissors of oblivion.

Until he woke before dawn, grinding his teeth, his body prickly with sweat. He couldn't remember what he had been dreaming, even after it hounded him awake again and again. Drugged with exhaustion, for sleep had got its teeth properly into him, he dragged his coat over his head and allowed himself to be the subject of a tug-o'-war between exhaustion and the terror that lurked in sleep. Finally, when morning shone through Columbine 4's windows and the birds of the Apple Hills gave full, dolorous voice, he gave up the fight for rest and crawled out of the cab in search of breakfast, grumpy as a wild elephant, and sore-eyed.

Now the Old Gentleman stared at him thoughtfully, fingers laced beneath sagging jowls.

"In all honesty, Crispin, I'll be sorry to see you go. You are my last reminder of Anuei. In a way—though there were many women before and after—mmm?" He laughed, inviting Crispin to join in a masculine wink-wink-nudge-nudge. Crispin sat like a stone. The Old Gentleman shifted some papers from one side of the desk to the other. Why was he dragging this out?

"She was the love of my life, you know," Saul Smithrebel said at last, with the air of one making a great confession.

"Yes, well, we've all gotta get over our losses sometime," Crispin offered. "I mean, don't look back too often." From outside came the cranky roar of a lion, and an elephant's mournful trumpet, and the voices of the roughnecks. Now that Smithrebel's had finally started tearing down, it was proceeding at its usual whirlwind pace. Crispin shifted, thinking about all the things he ought to be doing. It had not quite hit him that he was no longer an employee of the circus; he would never again have to load trucks, feed daemons, hump rolls of canvas across a field, take down the cook tent. Never again.

The Old Gentleman stood up and came around his desk. Crispin did not stand; he would have had to bend his head—Sunflower 1, like all the trucks which had been made into living quarters, was partitioned horizontally as well as vertically, with the upper story reserved for storage. The ceiling was extremely low. Crispin looked up at the Old Gentleman with what he hoped was a pleasant grin (sunny boy holds no grudges). "Well, I suppose that's that, then?"

"I'm looking forward to heavy bookings in Thrazen," the Old Gentleman said. "It's farm country, and odd though it has always seemed to me, there is far more money for the populace in farming than there is in the daemon industry. Then, of course, there are the army bases around the Thrazen War Road." He paused.

Crispin had no desire to work on an army base. And if the Old Gentleman meant that he should join up . . . no, that would be unthinkable even from him.

"The point is, of course, that I shouldn't think you'll find it hard to get a job." The Old Gentleman coughed. "You can travel with us all the way through Thrazen, if you like, though of course I can't allow you to participate in the running of things as you have been. Then when we reach Thrandon, you'll get two months' severance pay. That seems to me the least I can do."

The thunderous cloud over the horizon lifted a fraction. One of the peculiarities of Crispin's affiliation with Smithrebel's was that he never received anything over room and board. He was not sure whether this was Anuei's legacy—she had been personally kept by the Old Gentleman, rather than receiving any regular salary—or whether it was simply the Old Gentleman's skinflint nature. At least, and this was a larger comfort than it should have been, he knew it was nothing to do with his Lamaroon blood: the two roughnecks who were Kirekunis, and Kiquat, and the Izte Kchebukaran, got paid the same salary as anyone else. It had taken quite a bit of guts to approach them and work around to finding this out. Circus might be lower-class entertainment, but Smithrebel's people, Crispin among them, considered themselves respectable and did not go around talking about money.

Millsy had no interest in money. This was another clue to his high-upper-end origins. He provided Crispin with beer coin whenever Crispin asked, but because one had one's pride, this was seldom.

Now he was about to receive the first handout of his life.

"Mmm?" the Old Gentleman said, tipping his nearly bald head on one side.

"Come to think of it, I don't know why I'd want to to hang around until we get to Thrazen Domain," Crispin said, grinning widely at the Old Gentleman. "I'll just slink off, shall I? I wouldn't want to make any unpleasantness worse. You know." He paused to let the Old Gentleman get the drift of things. "People might think you might be doing something for me that you wouldn't for anyone else."

Was it possible for the Old Gentleman to turn paler? Crispin seemed to have succeeded in touching a nerve, though he had been probing without much of an idea where to pinch.

"But, my dear boy . . . Of course, I understand that in that case you will need more than a few pounds."

"Deuce hands, maybe?" Crispin suggested pleasantly.

The Old Gentleman's throat bumped. "Yes. Yes." He fumbled in his pocket, and extracted crumpled pound notes one by one from handfuls of fluff, nuts, string balls, broken knife blades, and coins. Crispin could not take his eyes off the sorting process. There were fivers and tenners. Did anyone in the circus know that the Old Gentleman carried this kind of wealth on his person?

"Nine . . . ten. Let's make it eleven, shall we?"

"Thanks," Crispin said, pocketing the notes. He was vastly taken aback to see a gleam of what might have been tears in the cloudy blue eyes. He got slowly to his feet and unfolded his cap. Whatever was wrong with Smithrebel he wasn't about to give the money *back*!

The Old Gentleman stepped back a pace, birdlike, rubbing his papery fingers together. "This isn't right. This just isn't right. There's something . . . something I have always meant to tell you." He paused. "Your dear mother wouldn't have thought it right at all for me to send you off with nothing more than a few dry pound notes of your . . . your inheritance."

He did an odd little tap dance. Crispin noticed that the black patent leather of Smithrebel's shoes was scuffed and muddy. A thread of worry tugged at him. The slightest hint that the flabby little Ferupian might be more than a small-time circus monarch, destined to share the fate of all imperfectly competent monarchs—that is, to be the object of derision, flattery, and resentment in equal proportions—that he might, in fact, be a human being—had always unsettled him. Especially as the Old Gentleman tended to single him out to be the object of such hints. Crispin usually met the Old Gentleman's oblique pleas for pity with a stony face. But now the recklessness of the freed criminal prompted him to say, "My inheritance?"

He wouldn't put it past the Old Gentleman to have heisted some of Anuei's belongings after her death. Maybe he was having an attack of conscience. Relics from Lamaroon? More of the famous forbidden props, most of which Crispin himself, at the age of twelve, had burned without opening the boxes?

His heart quickened. He knew he would not have the fortitude to leave those boxes unopened this time.

The Old Gentleman looked up, his blue eyes hooded. He shook his head. "No. I . . . I apologize. That was unprofessional of me. Go your way."

Bullshit, Crispin thought. Frustration welled up inside him. He bowed sharply from the shoulders. "Well, then, in that case, thank you for your generous gift, Mr. Smithrebel, and farewell. It has been a pleasure working for you."

He turned on his heel and pushed out through the curtains. A dark passage led to the lowered rear door of the truck. Oblivious of the trappings being loaded, the elephants hooting, a toddler crying for its mother, he jumped down to the mud and turned his face up to the rain.

He had a cramp in his neck. For a minute he stood feeling the tension drain out of his muscles.

Then he jammed his cap firmly onto his head, fingered the soft old notes in his trousers pocket, and went to find Millsy.

Millsy accompanied him some distance down the road. Not southward. The last thing Crispin wanted was to be overtaken by the circus and have rude jokes shouted out of the truck cabs at him. They walked north, back toward the towns where Prettie had performed.

This was truly the last of it, this hilly road overhung by dripping trees. As they walked, Crispin felt himself overcome by a wave of sentiment. He glanced at Millsy: a wooden mannequin moving jerkily, his feet weighted down by wisdom as if by cement overshoes. A master of secrets Crispin could never understand even if he was given a chance. A friend.

Ever since Crispin had become as competent a handler as Millsy himself, there had been a distance between them. There had been a time when Millsy poured out his soul to Crispin, night after night. He told the boy things he had probably never told anyone else. Even though Crispin had been too young to understand the half of it, he could remember if he wanted to.

Only he didn't, particularly.

Only he couldn't help it.

There had been good times later on. No matter what Millsy's flaws, there was no one else in the circus worth arguing with. Sharing a bottle late at night, after a good show, when they were on a three- or four-night stand outside some big town where the Old Gentleman allowed they didn't have to move to draw a new audience the next day. Talking daemons. Talking about humanity and politics and the war—the questions that talking about daemons inevitably brought up. Getting worked up the way you can only do when you're drunk.

It had begun to rain again, and Millsy turned the collar of his coat up around his ears. Crispin stopped. There was a moment of awkward silence. The old handler said, "You ought, I think, to be able to make it back to Valestock in a couple of weeks if you go straight north. We came by an extremely circuitous route, after all."

Crispin nodded. "If I was you," he said, and paused as he remembered that the fates of Smithrebel's were no longer his business. What the hell. Good advice comes back in cowries—one of Anuei's sayings. "If I had Smithrebel's ear, the way you do, I'd tell him to cut some of the shows on the itinerary and head straight for Thrandon. There's no good dragging this out. The takings last show must've been shit."

"Yes, they were," Millsy said, gazing into the distance. "And we had to refund most of the entries after the accident. But you know how Mr. Saul is. I do not think I have a hope of changing his plans. All we can reasonably expect is that next time around, he will have learned his lesson with regard to the Apple Hills."

"And maybe next time he'll strike gold," Crispin said, remembering the summer of the Happy Mountains. "And maybe bloody not." He shifted his knapsack on his shoulder and looked down at his friend. "Why do you stay, Millsy?"

Millsy shook his head. "You mean, when I could have far better things? When I could be respectable, or rich, or both? I stay because I love the circus. I love it. You know that word, Crispin? *Love.*"

Suddenly Crispin was furious. How dare Millsy lie to him? Now that they were probably never going to see each other again, telling the truth had, paradoxically, become all-important. "That's crap. Nobody loves being an entertainer. They just love traveling, being out of reach of the law."

Millsy's eyes glinted like steel ball bearings in nests of wrinkles.

"You only think that because you yourself are not in love with the circus."

Automatically, Crispin started to protest, but Millsy held up his hand.

"I have been watching you since you were a toddler—I am afraid sometimes you forget the great differences in our ages, my friend—and I know you better, perhaps, than you know yourself. Your mother, Smithrebel, Herve, Elise, and even poor little Prettie, all of them tried to—to convert you to the circus, if I may use the word without vulgarity. I was guilty of the same crime myself. Do you remember when I tried to make you into a trickster?"

"Queen, yes!" Crispin grimaced, remembering badly bitten fingers, occult wounds that did not heal for half a year, fits of shivering that took him unexpectedly during that period. Millsy had, he remembered, been badly disappointed, though he was at pains to conceal it. But he had waxed philosophical about the whole thing. It required an extremely rare combination of qualities to trick uncollared daemons; all women had the raw potential, but almost none of them the will. Men had the will—that was why ninety-nine out of a hundred handlers of collared daemons were male—but the wrong chemicals in their bodies. Millsy was a biological freak.

"But I failed. All I succeeded in was making you into a competent daemon handler. Which by no means limits you to working as an entertainer. Daemon handlers are needed in every single field, whereas tricksters are not. In the same way, only a few people need to know how to make candles, but everybody needs to know how to light them. So it was lucky for you, really, that you did not have my blood." Ruefully, Millsy pinched his own thin forearm. "If you had followed in my footsteps, the circus would have had you for life. And I am convinced, now, that you would not have been content."

"And Prettie wouldn't be dead!"

Millsy winced. "Crispin, I do not know what happened. But she was courting Death. He would have come to her sooner rather than later, no matter what—it was just a stroke of bad luck that He chose you for His tool."

Crispin gritted his teeth. "How dare you try to fake me with philosophy?" Anger almost choked him. "Bad luck my foot. I fucked up."

"Does it gratify you to believe that?"

The rain drifted lightly through the trees.

"I'm gonna settle down," Crispin spat. "I told the Old Gentleman I was gonna quit anyway—and it was the truth! I've had enough of this. It's a mug's game. Maybe there's something *wrong* with me—born and raised in the circus, and all I can do is leave." He stared into Millsy's steely little eyes, trying to read him. "Come back through Lovoshire in five years and ask for me, I'll be living in a fine townhouse with servants of my own and girls on both knees!"

"Oh, Crispin," Millsy said with a catch in his voice.

"What? *What?*"

"You'll only be unhappy if you fix your heart on that kind of life."

"Can you read the future?"

"I know the ways of men!"

Crispin folded his arms. "You're being insufferably obscure," he said in Millsy's own, rather affected accents. But Millsy was too agitated to notice.

"People are . . . I have lived among settled folk, as you have not, and I feel it my duty to warn you!" The old handler rocked on the balls of his feet. "Your skin. Your height. Those are only the most superficial of your differences from the average Ferupian! And *those* are the differences they will notice. Those are the differences they will reject you for!" He laughed, but it was more of a bark. "Why couldn't you have waited to kill Prettie until we were in Kingsburg? There, there are other Lamaroons—you would have had a far easier time of it!"

Crispin gasped in disbelief. "Not you, too. Not you, too! Smithrebel thinks I did it—"

"On purpose, yes! He can scarcely help thinking that, and so do most of his employees, but not I. I trust you. You say you passed out in midair. I believe you. I only hope it was not the symptom of some illness which will return to plague you later in your life."

The possibility was a horrid one. It had not occurred to him.

"I so much want you to have a happy life!" Millsy insisted.

Crispin could imagine Anuei, if she were alive, saying that. But if Millsy felt *paternal* toward him, this was the first he'd heard of it. He hardened his voice. "Why don't you tell me what you're really getting at? You're warning me against a shitload of fake dangers. You're not usually paranoid."

Millsy shook, each segment of him trembling individually, as if his strings were being jerked by a great hand.

"You secretly want me to fail, don't you?" Crispin said. "Just like you failed. You don't stay with Smithrebel's because you love it, you stay for the same reasons the deserters do." He took a deep breath and deliberately dragged the squirming past into the present. "I know you got kicked out of the army, Millsy. I know you got kicked out of court. I bet there's a lot of people trying to catch up with you."

"You're wrong," Millsy said faintly.

"You told me all about it yourself. When I was little, and you'd come and get me at night, and—"

"No!" Millsy was shaking so violently now that Crispin feared for a second he would fall apart. "That's unfair! Crispin, I had thought *better* of you!"

Maybe it was unfair, at that. Millsy obviously thought Crispin held those long-ago nights against him. But there had not been anything sordid about it. Only after Crispin grew old enough to know right from wrong had he started to think of the incidents as perversions. In reality, Millsy could not have been gentler. And the day that Crispin had first expressed the slightest discomfort, Millsy had withdrawn and never touched him again.

How tightly had he been holding himself in check, all these years?

That's sickening! How can I think such things? To keep from dwelling on it, Crispin said loudly, "You told me all about your years at court! You told me how they plotted to kill you! You *had* to leave."

"I chose of my own accord—"

"Yeah. Just like I'm leaving *here* of my own accord. Yeah. I was only a kid, but I remember how Queen-damned bitter you were!" He stared at Millsy. "And you're not half as old as everybody thinks you are!"

"I have described the effects that tricking daemons can—"

"You're what? Forty-five? That means—I know what's wrong with you. You're jealous of me. Because I have another chance. And you don't." He gestured around at the silent trees. "This is all you're going to have. For the rest of your life." He made circles with his thumbs and forefingers and thrust them at Millsy. "Nothing. Zero. Zip."

Millsy whispered, "Galianis."

"What?" Crispin shouted, nearly at the end of his wits, because this was the last hour he would ever spend with his friend, and he was wasting it on recriminations. "What are you saying?"

The first shades of dark had begun to fall. It looked as if Millsy was stroking the air in front of him. Then, all at once, Crispin saw the thing like a small blue child clinging in the crook of his arm. Millsy must have had the daemon with him all along. Galianis wore child-size breeches and a woolly jumper, probably cadged from one of the circus mothers. It had been asleep when Millsy called it to materialize; at its name, it opened enormous eyes and cleared a shock of pale hair out of its face with one hand. "Guests always welcome," it piped. There was not a trace of intelligence in the saucer-sized orbs that fixed Crispin. "A budget imbalance will unfortunately be inevitable. Tastier than any other brand. Sweet yet spicy!"

Millsy rubbed the daemon's hair. It responded to the caress by smiling, practically purring. But so would a kitten. "Closed every second Tossday for inventory," it said, and hopped to the ground with the suddenness of a sparrow. Its stream of slogans, catchphrases, and overheard sentence fragments dropped to a mumble as it started to dig holes in the mud with its fingers.

That would get on my nerves inside five minutes, Crispin thought. *But Millsy loves them like children.* He sighed and drove his hands into his pockets.

Millsy looked up. His eyes were at once anxious, sad, and self-mocking. "What a mother hen I am," he said. "I suppose I was trying to warn you against every eventuality. Although that's not possible. I apologize."

"Well, if nothing else works out, there's always the army," Crispin said.

Millsy laughed. "Yes."

There was an awkward pause. The rain grew a little heavier. Crispin wondered where he was going to sleep that night; if he would even be able to sleep in the wet and the cold. Perhaps he should just keep walking. How long could he keep on going before he fell down? Or could he find shelter with the locals? A movement distracted him. Galianis had leaped back on Millsy's shoulder. Two pairs of eyes regarded Crispin: one flat and pale blue; one whose dark, sad gaze sent a pang through Crispin, deep inside where he had forgotten it could hurt.

"I'm sorry if I said anything to offend you," he said stiffly, formally.

"Oh," Millsy said, and coming alive all at once, made a move to hug Crispin. Crispin instinctively stepped back. Millsy said with a rueful smile, "You devil! Not even this once?" and moved toward him again.

"Get off!" Crispin said violently, and jerked away. Something of his horror must have shown on his face. Millsy's mouth quirked, but he did not try to hug Crispin again. "You can deny it to me, but not to yourself," he said.

"You sicken me!" Crispin shouted. "I've had enough!" His throat was full again. "I tried to patch things up, dammit, and you—you're still trying to sabotage me! Well, I've had enough!" He flung around and strode away into the gathering dark, feeling angry, stupid, and betrayed. Childishly, he kept expecting Millsy to come after him. Behind him was silence.

And after a moment: "Fresh every day. We don't need your sort around here. A position is open to an experienced scribe."

And it was too late to turn back, and Millsy was not coming after him. Crispin reached the top of the hill and risked a glance over his shoulder. Millsy stood in the confusion of their footprints—they had churned up the mud so much that it looked as if there had been a fight—his hands in his pockets, his overcoat flapping like a scare-the-crows' ragged garment in a wind which was apparently localized. The daemon had vanished again.

Crispin swore aloud, and turned his face north.

Even in the rainy twilight, the grass of the verges was a brilliant peacock green. Darkness closed down from the top of the sky, finally erasing even the faint redness above the western treetops which had signaled the sinking of the sun behind the Wraithwaste. Little black squirrels came out and chee-cheed in the trees, as loud as the tree monkeys of the southern forests.

Crispin figured he might never have a house, or servants. But all he needed was a place to stay and a job which brought him enough money to keep a girl who made no demands on him. That was all he needed. Was it too much to ask?

Right now it seemed that it was asking for the earth. Millsy had made it seem that way.

And the memory of *that moment* reverberated in his head like the sound of a plucked guywire. His steps squelched faster. He would not slacken his pace. This was the only way he was ever going to get somewhere.

If you shut your eyes and are a lucky one, you may see at times a shapeless pool of lovely pale colours suspended in the darkness; then if you squeeze your eyes tighter, the pool begins to take shape, and the colours become so vivid that with another squeeze they must go on fire. But just before they go on fire you see the lagoon.

—J.M. Barrie, *Peter Pan*

The Ugliest Shop
of All

Fessiery 1893 A.D. *Lovoshire: Valestock*

"**H**ey . . . up!" Crispin shouted. He bowed. "And now . . . for the most dangerous feat performed by jugglers of any stripe, in any of the twenty-one domains! Ladies and gentlemen, can I have a volunteer from the audience?"

The urchins giggled and crowded each other. The scattering of daemonmongers' wives with their black umbrellas, dresses which would have been able to stand up on their own, and wickerwork baskets in which they carried their excuses for going out to the shops—trifles (Crispin imagined) like thin slices of ham, little jars of goose-liver pâté wildly unseasonable hothouse berries—his mouth watered—ornate, remote creatures, they leaned their heads together and smiled disapprovingly. A week and a half of performing on the corner of Main Street had taught him that although they might linger longer than any others, only very rarely did coins come from those plump, suede-gloved fingers. Even the drab nannies who stopped occasionally to watch without visible sign of interest would occasionally send their charges over with tuppence to put in his cap.

He wondered if the mothers knew where their offspring had been when they kissed them good night. That type feared contamination worse than death. They were the same everywhere, whether their husbands' business was daemonmongering, shopkeeping, manufacturing, or farming. They were People of Consequence, men and women who lived penned in by the perceived necessity of leisure, who had imperceptibly overrun Ferupe sometime during the last hundred years. It was their prejudices, direct and indirect, that had prevented Crispin from making an honest living in Valestock.

That he should have sunk as low as the commonest gypsy!

Well, at least he was juggling on Main Street, not in the slums, or the music hall. But performing at all, anywhere, meant swallowing his pride. He had wanted to hide his background. He had spent all but a pound of the Old Gentleman's money on food, cigarettes, clothes, the bathhouse, and a haircut; then he had enquired after a job with every daemon handler in Valestock. Men at the waterworks, the fixit shops, the cell makers, the apprentice houses—and finally, after all those had turned him away, the daemonmongers themselves, though he was intimidated by the very sight of those well-kept shops that reeked subtly of money. Daemons were big business in Valestock, of course, as in all towns near the Wraithwaste, and all of the money was concentrated in the hands of Valestock's five or six bona fide daemonmongers. Though word said that even they were not the end of the chain, that the real money went to their masters in Kingsburg. Their truckers made forays into the forests to collect the goods from the trickster women. Other minions evaluated the daemons, celled them for travel, and shipped them out—mostly to Thrandon or Salzburg, and thence to the war, but also, of course, to the rest of the country.

No other country in the world was as rich in daemons as Ferupe. In Valestock, even the taverns had daemon glares hanging outside the doors!

The daemonmongers' shops were cloaked in vibrating auras that raised every hair on Crispin's body. These auras were so thick he couldn't believe the crowds flowed past the doors without noticing them. Inside were dark aisles of cells stacked to the ceiling, and shopboys dressed in yellow, whose hostility toward Crispin, like that of all the other men he had talked to, was unbelievable.

Every male over the age of twelve in this town worked in the industry. They made scarcely enough money to stay alive, and most of them would not see a daemon once in the year, but they were still insufferably proud. Maybe that was why Crispin could not find a job.

Perhaps the women, who here, even more than in the rest of

Ferupe, must of necessity stumble through life on their men's coat-tails, would have been easier nuts to crack. But he had not, and would not, sink to using sex to unlock doors. So he made the rounds of all the independent truckers who were currently in town. He wanted a secure position, and trucking on a haul-by-haul basis was anything but steady—but as it turned out, he might as well not have bothered, because the truckers stared at him with flat eyes and shook their heads. Crispin wondered what they had heard about him from the fixit men and the shopboys.

Finally, one driver-handler, sun-browned and kinder than the rest, had taken him to a slum eatery and, obviously thinking he was desti-tute, bought him two monstrous doorstep sandwiches. Over ale after-ward, the truth had come out. "Boy, I don't know why you gotta hear this from me," the man had said. "But the fact is, in this part of the country, no matter how much you know about trucking, you ain't gonna get hired. Now I'm from the east—Kythrepe—on the Cypean border—ever been there? I don't have anything against darkies myself."

Crispin held his tongue.

"My dispatcher's based in Galashire, domain north of here, and frankly, round here's the worst place in the country for people like you. Man wouldn't let me bring anyone in for an interview—and yeah, I can tell you've got experience—if he's . . ."

The trucker fell silent. After a moment, he reached out and touched Crispin's cheek. Crispin forced himself to sit still.

"Maybe you should go south. Be easier to find something down there."

"Yeah, that's what I wanna do," Crispin said carefully. "I'm sick fed up of this rain. But how the hell am I supposed to get down there without a rig?"

The trucker had shrugged helplessly and called for more ale. They ended up getting stumbling drunk; Crispin slept in a doorway. It wasn't so bad, so the next day, he removed his belongings from the rooming house (where, he now knew, he had not been imagining the proprietress's frowning disapproval) and carried his knapsack with him to the lumberyard, where he purchased blocks of light wood to carve juggling pins. That night, he slept on a corner. The street couldn't frown at you, or put you in the bunk with the wonky legs next to the door, or refuse to serve you breakfast on some flimsy pretext. And his remaining shillings were better spent, he told himself, making himself presentable in the bathhouse each morning.

Thus Valestock had slammed its doors in his face.

Now, by revealing his circus background to the dour crowds of the town, he had pretty well scotched any chance that those doors might crack open again. But what else could he do? Smithrebel's would be deep in Weschess Domain by now, a good two hundred miles away. He *couldn't* go back, even if he would.

His gaze roved around the crowd. He had already picked out a little boy who was hopping up and down hysterically beside his nanny. The kid had tried to be chosen to hold the juggling props every time. He deserved his chance, Crispin thought, since this would be the last routine of the day—even though from experience, he knew the eager kids tended to be cutups once they got any attention.

"You, kid!" He beckoned the little boy, who pulled away from his nanny with a squeak of joy. "All right, miss?" Crispin met the woman's eyes. She moved her heavy head up and down. "What's your name?"

Albert, as he introduced himself, was no exception to the eager rule. He danced around with the unlit torches, refusing to hand them to Crispin; he fell flat on his face, and when the crowd roared with indulgent laughter, he proceeded to do it again—and again, and again. A red-faced farmer came and handed him a shilling. A fellow in a grubby white coat, who had been watching for the last two performances, brought his meaty hands together for the first time. Finally Crispin had to shame Albert's nurse into hustling him away by making cracks about the excellent discipline she imposed on her charges.

After Albert's departure, the crowd lost interest. The respectable women lifted en masse, like a flock of gray parrots, and drifted away. Crispin went through his fire-juggling routine to the shrieks of the town urchins, whose fascination was gratifying, but not lucrative. At last he caught the torches, blew them out one by one, indulging for the kids' sake in a bit of slapstick, pretending the flames just wouldn't go out, and packed his props into his knapsack. Two small boys darted up to him and tugged his arm. "Show me, mister!" one of them squeaked. "I wanna be a juggler when I grow up! Why doncha get burned?"

Crispin grinned, tipped the takings into one hand, and stuffed his cap on his head. "Sorry, man. Trade secret."

"There were a circus," the other, younger, boy said. "They had jugglers."

"Yeah." Crispin rubbed the coins together in his fist, making a noise like crickets. The boys giggled. "That's where I learned. Everybody in the circus knows how to juggle—we all have to fill in sometimes, in spec."

"Low-down trash," the older boy said, without malice. "My dad says circus people aren't no better'n gypsies an' niggers."

"Circus people are the best," Crispin said.

"I bet I could learn to juggle better'n a circus kid! C'mon, mister!"

The younger boy's forehead wrinkled. "Yeah, but yer whole family went to see it," he objected. "And yer dad got drunk-as-a-dog an' went with some whore!"

"My dad don't go with whores! You shut that, take that back, Sykey, you bastard!"

Crispin winced as they flew at each other. When he was growing up, there had been no other children his age—Skeeze and Horace, Mrs. Beecorn the costumier's twin boys, were four years younger, and Anuei had impressed on him over and over again how necessary it was for him to be gentle when playing with them. That was why he had not learned his real strength until the night he almost killed Saul Smithrebel. And after that he'd been careful. These boys, by contrast, knew no such thing as restraint. By the time they grew up, they would be scrappers right through, just like their dads, every bone in their bodies broken and mended twice over. But there was no need for them to kill each other today, not here.

"Leave each other out of it." They writhed as he separated them.

"Circus trash!" the bigger boy squealed, and twisting, spat at Crispin. Crispin was so surprised he let them both go. They darted off into the crowds of Main Street.

"Damn," Crispin muttered. He jerked the straps of his knapsack closed and hoisted it onto a shoulder. "Pure gutter! What can you expect?"

Night was falling. The passersby had a determined air, slogging grimly along with their heads down, as if they were caught in a collective dream in which steaming, perfumed dishes of supper hung just beyond their noses. The doors of the baker's shop next to Crispin's pitch were closed. Through the little square panes of glass in the windows, Crispin could see the shopboy sweeping the floor, tossing leftover loaves into a sack for rebaking. Above the awnings, windows glowed with gaslight. Silhouetted figures danced their domestic waltz behind the curtains. It was starting to rain.

"All right, move it," a voice said.

Crispin swung around. It was the man in the white jacket who had been watching all afternoon.

"Can't have none of that circus nonsense here. You'll have to move along. *Ay'll* escort you back to wherever you're staying."

"Who are you?"

"Me?" The man seemed to puff up. "*Ay'm* Constable Carthower," he announced. "And Ay—"

"Can I see some proof of that?" Crispin asked. The man frowned, but his fat fingers dug in the breast pocket of the tight white coat. The garment was of a unique, peculiar design: round-collared, and tailored with panels so that it fitted like a second skin over Carthower's man-tits and prodigious belly, flaring over his sizable butt like the skirt of one of Prettie's leotards. Crispin vaguely remembered Kiquat—or somebody—speaking of provincial police as "white-coats"; but he had failed to make the connection when he saw Carthower in the crowd. He took pains to seem good-humored as he examined the constable's badge, nodding at the meaningless embossed letters.

All circus people had a deep dislike of law enforcers—a mistrust that conflicted not at all with their patriotism, but reinforced it. Millsy had often said that if anyone told the Queen how her country was actually run, the poor lady would swoon clean away. Crispin chewed his lip, pretending to examine the badge, playing for time. What if he was going to be jailed? They took everything you had, in jail. That was how they paid for their police stations and salaried their heavies. "So what's the problem, Constable?"

"You're the problem, boyo."

"Have I had charges brought against me?" This time, Crispin spoke with his best imitation-Millsy Kingsburg accent. He should have thought of it earlier. The constable was visibly disconcerted.

"You haven't," Carthower admitted reluctantly. But then his confidence in himself returned, and with it his threatening manner. "But you *will*, Ay can promise you that, if you don't remove your little act off of this street!"

"I'm afraid I don't quite understand, Constable," Crispin said. "Over there"—he gestured to the other side of Main Street—"a band of fiddlers were playing all afternoon. Isn't that more of a public disturbance than my humble sideshow?"

By now night had fallen. The constable's face was implacable in the faint illumination from the baker's windows, and red as an apple. "None of that," he said softly. Crispin's heart sank. The constable knew that he was putting it on. Carthower ran a fat tongue around his lips, as if barely able to control the desire to do unspeakable things to Crispin. "Listen—boyo—Ay get paid to keep the streets habitable. Take your act out on the eastern road. Be my guest. But we've had your kind dawdling here before—*darkies*—" He almost spat out the word. *Do I look like a damned gypsy to you?* Crispin thought. "And although we are always ready to give anyone a chance, in the past our goodwill has been abused. Yes! Abused! And Ay am afraid we can no longer tolerate your sort in this upstanding town. Providing a spectacle for gentle ladies. Corrupting the youngsters, too."

Carthower was Law: he clearly knew himself, in hassling Crispin, to be well within the boundaries of his directive. If he had no charges now, Crispin knew he would have produced some by tomorrow. It was useless to protest. Yet that very realization drove him to argue. "I'm not doing any harm! If I wasn't entertaining those kids, they'd be off nicking shit from your precious *upstanding citizens*!"

"Would they indeed," Carthower said. "Well, you'd know all about that, wouldn't you—" He paused, and said deliberately, "Nigger."

Crispin hissed. If it had come from anyone else he could have taken it in stride, but from this grease-pated, red-cheeked fellow, this scum of a scummy hamlet—Dropping his knapsack, he pulled back to swing at Carthower.

The constable stood quite still. His lips were curved in the ghost of a smile.

"*Oh*. Assaulting a police officer," Crispin said. "*That's* what you want to pin on me, is it! I bet it works most of the time, too—anybody would want to punch your mug in just so they don't have to look at it! Did they hire you specially for the job of filling up the jail every night?"

A lock rattled, and a tantalizing scent of bread wafted into the damp night. The baker's boy gaped fearfully at Crispin and the constable as he sidled out of the shop and locked up. Carthower stared back with the same red implacability he used on Crispin. The boy scuttled off into the night with comical speed.

Carthower said softly, "How'd you like to become Valestock County Recruit number sixty-seven, nigger? We're having a bit of trouble meeting our quota this year."

Crispin sensed that the policeman, in speaking of the war, had broken a personal taboo. It showed in the way he licked his lips. People in Valestock liked to pretend the war didn't exist. And it was possible to do so, because here, the Wraithwaste served as an absolute wall between Civilization and Chaos. Only the airplanes in the distant sky might remind Valestock of Ferupe's other business, which was not daemons. An unpatriotic thought flashed across Crispin's mind: the Queen, in forbearing to establish army bases in Lovoshire, Weschess, or Galashire, seemed to be collaborating in the effort to spare the deep west any knowledge of the war on the other side of the forests. What had being wrapped in cotton wool like that done to this part of the world?

Crispin picked up his knapsack and narrowed his eyes at Carthower, trying to hide how frightened he was. "Thanks so much for the offer, Constable," he said sarcastically. "But I'm afraid I won't be able to help you with your quota. You won't be seeing me around much longer, in any case. Go home and jack off, now; you've been having fun, but I'm afraid I shan't be able to satisfy you. Not until you have charges to bring against me. And I can't provide those either at the moment."

He turned and moved away down Braselane Street. There was not a sound behind him. His spine crawled. Finally, as he turned the corner, he heard the constable's measured steps move off.

"Asshole," Crispin said, and forced himself to grin. He felt sick.

In the rest of the country, police-enforced draft quotas were rare. The sons and brothers of landed squires took officers' commissions; and as for the rest, a certain type of citizen, though of course not the best, thought the army as honest a trade as whatever their fathers did, and a good deal more glamorous. But in the west, there were few squires: daemonmongers were the only nobility; and towns like Valestock needed all their able-bodied men to keep the wheels of the industry turning. No one *wanted* to join the army. Obviously, the police had got into the habit of killing two birds with one stone by filling their quotas from their black books.

Crispin had no real idea where he was walking to.

The "good" section of town lay mostly on the flat. As he crossed the bridge over the Applewater, all signs of affluence had vanished as suddenly as if they had been an optical illusion. Now he was in the slums, which the proliferation of the daemon trade had long ago caused to spread back up into the crevices of the hills. The windows of the little houses were redly lit by hearth fires. Only a few had gaslights. None had daemon glares.

Reluctant to ascend any farther, he turned, his boots sloshing in the mud that had replaced the cobbles underfoot, and started back toward the river.

He came on it suddenly as he entered River Street: a building shaped like a haybarn, painted colors no farmer would know the names of, twice the height of the houses that pressed against it on either side. Little colored daemon glares blinked fast around its open doors. People spilled outside, smoking, swilling ale from earthen mugs, laughing raucously.

The Old Linny Palace of Delights. (Thus he had heard Valestock's citizens call the town's only music hall, with varying degrees of approval.) Like all circus people, he disapproved of music halls on principle; and the few times he had gone slumming with Millsy or Prettie in other towns, to see for himself, the quality of the entertainment in the so-called Palaces and Pleasure Houses had been poor enough to reassure him that there was really no competition. But since Valestock's respectable folk were such paragons of righteousness and virtue, perhaps even the homegrown song and dance of their servants, adjuncts, and parasites would be superior to that of the rest of the country, morally, if not artistically.

Ought to be good for a snigger, he thought rather desperately.

I had a girl an she was Prettie

Crispin started, then sank back.

She was the apple a Valestock city
When I took er to the music hall she wore erself out

Larfin an swillin ale and callin out—
All praise the Queen!

The band revved up with a wheeze of brass and crashed into the all-too-familiar chorus with excruciating vigor, as if they expected sheer decibels would somehow disguise the fact that they were off tempo and off-key.

Crispin sighed. Now if only they could manage to disguise the singer's nasal tenor, too.

The chief aim of all the singers was, of course, to invent as many new riffs on Ferupe's scores of national anthems as possible. The most interesting feature of the evening was the inhuman speed with which colored lights flickered over stage, pit, and gallery. Crispin stood and placed his hand on his chest, singing along with the sixty or so men and women in the hall:

All praise the Queen
Our hearts beat with hers
Slander the Queen
That is Ferupe you curse
Let me some day
Be graced by the sight

(exaggerated emphasis on the high note, a heavy-handed drumroll— Smithrebel's band could play anthems far more evocatively, Crispin thought)

Of my Queen in the light
Of her virtue and might!

Grinning at each other, delighted with the power of their own lungs, the music-hall patrons flopped back down onto their chairs. Strange, Crispin thought, that such fervent patriotism could be coupled with ignorance of the war. He was having more trouble than he had anticipated forgetting Constable Carthower's threats: the draft quota weighed on his mind; and now he thought life in the infantry could hardly be worse than this.

The tenor, his duty to the Queen discharged, swung back into a succession of bawdy couplets. No one was listening—in fact, they were making so much noise it was difficult to hear the singer—but that was the point, wasn't it? Money meant so little that you didn't even feel the need to watch the entertainment you had paid for. Ale slopped. Chairs crashed. In a corner near the door, a fight broke out. Sweaty-faced girls shimmied between the tables, platters of sausages and fried apples held over their heads.

Crispin clenched his fists under the table. He had no right to feel superior to these animals! Every last one of them had something he didn't: work!

It was easy to tell the town men apart from the farmers. The farmers' jackets hung raggedly on their big frames, their voices were less discreet than the townies'; they were accompanied not by shrill girls but by stout wives and children. Crispin would starve rather than sink to farming. These were not the prosperous tenant farmers of the heartlands; these were men and women whose only inheritance from their ancestors was a scrap of forest, who saw no better way to live than to scrabble a meager harvest of fruit from it. They led lives of dirt, poor food, and animal procreation. To become one of them would be the ultimate loss of face.

Yet he couldn't even get a job sawing oak for daemon cells! Was he going to end up like this? Weather-beaten, alcoholic, unaware of the desperacy of his own situation? Not an intelligent thought left in his head, his only consolation an occasional drunken lark? Better the army!

It seemed as though the very lowest walks of life were the only ones open to him. The circus had left its mark on him. From the height of the flying trapeze or the truck cab, the gap between performers and patrons had seemed unbridgeable—but now here he was, lumped with poor souls who had worked around daemons all their lives, yet never felt the slightest curiosity about them.

The waitress he ordered an ale from looked at him distrustfully. She pocketed his coin with an insolent snap of the wrist, not speaking, and glanced at him over her shoulder as she moved away. He *didn't* belong here. At least, not in her eyes. That was relieving, in an odd way.

The brew was foul. Thinleaf smoke thickened the air to fog. It smelled stomach-turningly sour. Crispin pulled out his own tobacco cigarettes and lit one, ignoring the glares of men who clearly thought he should offer them around.

His chair was so far over to the right of the pit that he could see straight into the left wings. People carrying assorted props rushed to and fro at a frantic rate. Craning backwards, he could see up behind the piece of scenery—whatever they called it—painted with a gigantic face of the Queen that depended from the roof at the front of the stage. Whenever the music went up, the rack of daemon glares installed behind the scenery swung into action, sweeping the hall, bathing center stage in a flood of color, the hoods that covered first one, then another snapping back with audible thocks. The main hall was lit only by gas hoods; the stagelights were far more complex. They swiveled and hopped with a life of their own, an array of mechanical chorus boys far better choreographed than anything on stage. Levers and gears extended up into the darkness of the roof. That pointed undeniably to the presence of a demogorgon here, in the Old Linny.

The show was almost over. Shouts of "T'morrer, moocher!" and "Love to yer lady!" echoed from the door. The tenor with the Prettie girlfriend had been replaced onstage by six reedy boys dressed in red ball gowns—a delegation from the Valestock Tap-dancing School for Young Ladies, according to the harassed master of ceremonies. Even before the first tap, there were shouts of "Back to th' schoolroom!" Unobtrusively, Crispin put his ale mug on the floor and went backstage.

In the maze of steps and doors into which he found his way, the bustle seemed only now to be reaching fever pitch. No circus spirit here; this was *work*. People rushed past him, sometimes twice or three times in different outfits, without sparing him a glance. A few narrowed their eyes suspiciously in response to his "Pardon me . . ." and hurried on. It was becoming more and more of an effort to sustain a polite tone, when finally a harried-looking girl with her arms full of the Tap-dancing School's furbelowed red dresses stopped and turned to look at him. "Yes, can I . . ."

Her eyes widened. *Go on, girl, scream!*

But she did not even fall back. Not that that was possible, really, in the narrow corridor. She clutched her armload of cheap and slithery red stuff closer to her breast. "Can I help you?"

"I'm looking for Mister—I've forgotten his name, for the daemon handler who works here—"

She wore her black hair scraped back from her face in a bun, the way Prettie used to wear it; she had Prettie's neat features. But her body was not like Prettie's at all. She was unusually tall. Though small-hipped, she had generous breasts, crushed together in a low-necked bodice, and the shadowed cleft between them sank so deep that it practically invited a man to plunge his fingers down . . .

In the name of the Queen, Crispin told himself, *this isn't a girl you check out at your leisure, you openmouthed fool!* She was already frowning. He favored her with a full-power grin, the one that never failed. "The man who handles the daemon," he said as if he had never paused. "I'm afraid I've misplaced his name but . . ."

"Rutridge," she said. "Yes, he's in the roof." She shifted the costumes into her right arm so that she could gesture with the left. It was slim, the hand nearly as white as her breasts, the nails clipped short. "Go there, that way, then right, then there's a door with a no-go cross on it, and you'll see the stairs up." She looked back at Crispin, hesitated a moment, and her smile flickered. She had bad teeth. It was the perfect touch. It placed her firmly in an age bracket, older than the nubile adolescent she had first seemed, but none of her teeth were gone; she couldn't be over, say, twenty . . . "He's in a cranky mood; if it was me I wouldn't disturb him at his work—but I suppose he sent for you . . ."

"Of course," Crispin lied. "Thank you, miss—"

But she was already gone, whisking away along the corridor and into a door, the red material flying behind her like wings. He memorized which door she'd gone into. Then, slowly, he started toward the corner she'd indicated, resigning himself to kiss ass and flatter ego and demonstrate intelligence and generally prostrate himself like a dog in the name of the great, the miragelike Position. She had one. If even a girl could get honest work, why couldn't he?

Constable Carthower had told him why, even more bluntly than the trucker from Galashire had. But Crispin refused to believe them, despite the evidence, before giving the thing one more go. And after that . . . ? An insidious little voice asked him. After that, one more? And one more?

Go to hell, he told it. He ascended the ladderlike steps, careful not to make a sound that might disturb the man hunched into a niche of a vast wheel-and-lever apparatus that seemed to have dropped roots into the rafters like a skeleton creeper, glimmering metallic in the darkness.

Is this it?

Bloody well better be.

He wanted to bang loudly on the door, to release the frustration which had bubbled higher every minute he spoke with the daemon handler, but he just rapped with the unbruised knuckles of his left hand.

Backstage was silent. The gaslights which hung at the turnings of the corridors had mostly been switched off. Crispin had escorted the old handler out into the drizzle, nodding pleasantly at the litany of complaints and abuse issuing from the gray beard, which seemed not so much directed at Crispin as at the whole world, and specifically the vile intransigence of daemons. Rutridge did not question Crispin's remaining inside the hall, where surely he had no right to be. He shuffled furiously off into the damp night, cursing. As Crispin closed the door, the smile dropped off his face faster than a broken clown-mask, and he found himself punching the doorjamb so hard it was a wonder he did not break his hand. He rested his forehead against the ancient wood and remained there for a few minutes, unmoving.

Then he went back inside.

He knocked again on the door.

But of course she had gone home long ago. The only people left in the Old Linny were the men sweeping out front, and the girls cleaning the kitchen and the bar.

Crispin glanced in both directions, then laid his ear to the door. It sounded as though somebody were inside . . . but it was probably just rats. Well, maybe he could sleep here tonight, provided he woke early enough to escape unseen. Better than the corner outside the daemon-monger's, anyway! He laid his hand on the handle.

The door opened. Crispin jerked upright so fast he dizzied himself.

The girl showed no sign of having noticed anything out of the ordinary. "Yes?"

"You told me where to find Rutridge," Crispin said. "Remember? I wanted to tell you you were right. He's a piss-mouthed old bastard."

"Were you looking for a job? Mr. Knight's the one you ought to have talked to, although I don't think—"

Crispin pulled a face. "Not just *any* job. I'm a daemon handler."

The girl nodded. "I see." She held on to the side of the door. Behind her, Crispin saw a small, grimy room equipped with a full-length mirror and a ratty yellow velvet armchair in which she had been sitting; her sewing lay over its arm, the needle glimmering in the gaslight. She was only a slavey, he thought, left to finish her work after the costume mistress had gone home. There were lines of tiredness under her eyes.

But they were still amazingly beautiful eyes. And those *breasts*!

She was looking up at him wearily, without a trace of curiosity. He could not stand it any longer.

"I'm going for supper. Do you want to come?" He knew full well his rude tone made the invitation sound more like a proposition than any respectable girl would stand for. She drew a sharp breath and flinched upright. He growled, "Well?"

"It's too late," she said nervously. "Nothing's open."

"Oh, yes it is," Crispin said. "Place called Slimey's. It's across the river. Truckers go there mostly. But some women, too. You won't feel out of place." He did not mention what type of women they were—or that it was almost certainly not her sort of place. Dammit, he needed to treat himself to a bit of pleasure after a long, hard day of failures. On a not entirely conscious level, he needed to prove that the power he'd once exerted over women still existed. He needed to give as little as possible, and in return get everything she had to offer.

"Do come," he said in his best persuasive tone. "You've been working hard all night. I can see that. And it'll be on me."

She nodded slowly, considering the idea. Then she smiled brilliantly. It was like a blow in the face, a slap that stung as if he were meeting her for the first time, all over again. He saw stars.

"All right. Do you mind waiting while I change?"

Without waiting for an answer, she whisked around. The door closed behind her.

Left alone in the corridor, Crispin grinned hugely. "Fuck you, Rutridge," he murmured. "Yeah, and you, daemonmonger sir, and you, madam landlady—yeah, and you, too, and all, Millsy—"

Another girl came around the corner. Her eyes flicked from the door to Crispin's face. "Who are you?"

"I was about to ask you that," Crispin said with a grin. Her lips were painted carmine red; she had rough skin and a figure that would have been an hourglass if she'd had much of a waist. She had been in the act of pulling the pins out of her pile of brown hair, but the front pieces still framed her face in greased loops.

"Doll," she said. "Doll Henley." She came closer to Crispin. "You trying to get some out of Rae, darlin'?" she whispered. "She's a one, she is. Only been here a year. And strange, oh my!"

"Miss Rae and I are going for a late supper," Crispin said in quenchingly aristocratic tones, staring down at her.

"Auggh," she whispered, and tossed her head coyly. More brown locks slid down around her shoulders. "I can tell you're looking for a tumble. There's girls here who'll give it to you. And girls who think they're too good. See what I mean?"

"I believe so," Crispin said. "You know, there's a proverb about that. Girls that kiss, their chances miss; girls that tarry—"

"Oh!" She stepped back. Now, he knew, she would milk the insult for all it was worth. "Oh! You damned bastard—you—"

The door opened and Crispin's supper partner stepped out. She wore a dress that had probably once been black, but was now a strange shade of violet-gray. It was tailored to fit her body from hips to throat, so that her neck rose like a stamen out of a trumpet of carefully stitched ruffles; the skirt swished in folds about her booted calves. When she saw Doll, she seemed to shrink a little.

"Well, if it isn't the young lady herself," Doll said.

"Come on," Crispin said, pushing Doll firmly aside and taking her arm. "I've just been having a nice chat with your friend here. Miss Henley. Let's go." He led her past. As they moved away, Doll caught her arm, and Crispin heard her hissing vituperatively in her ear. Then Doll flung away so hard that the other girl staggered.

As he opened the backstage door, Crispin asked, "What did she say to you?"

Outside, the rain had stopped.

"Do you really want to know?" The girl—Rae—made a face. "She said I was a whore who puts a spell on all the best men and don't let no one else get a look in."

Crispin said, "Well, it's nice to know she has such a high opinion of me." Best to warn her now, perhaps. "Though if she judges men by their pockets, she was wrong as all he—out and out wrong."

"She's a fucking tart," Rae said, as they picked their way along the side alley. Her language shocked him. "A tart. That's what they all are. Scheming whores'd fall apart like corpses if they didn't lace themselves up so tight! Sleep with one of 'em, it's a fucking death sentence!"

They came out onto River Street. No one was left about. The lights still blinked their colored patterns on the mud. The Applewater crawled beside the street, five feet down, black and silent, chopping at its banks with little waves.

As they made their way through the silent streets, Crispin realized the mood had been spoiled. Tension shivered between them. In the dim light from upstairs windows, he saw her worrying her lip; he felt vaguely guilty. *It's not your fault, girl.*

He'd pay for her supper, take her home, and find somewhere to kip down. And tomorrow was another day. Although he had no idea what it might hold.

Slimey's was hidden in a cellar, even farther from Main Street than the Old Linney—but in the other direction, out toward the eastern road, by which most traffic entered and left Valestock. There was an eighteen-wheeler parked in the street outside, but all the same, unless you knew, you'd never have thought to knock on the plain green door beside the tinware shop. At the bottom of a flight of stairs, the eatery served endless variations on bread, eggs, and pork, and endless ale. Tonight most of the tables jammed into the dark little cave were empty. Crispin had come here three times since the trucker from Galashire had first shown it to him. It was cheap (although to buy this meal, he had to spend his very last pennies, leaving only a pound note in his pocket) and nobody tried to talk to you if they didn't like your looks. The only lights hung behind the counter. The dark *did* make the whores look better, although Crispin never had need of them. Not yet.

As the ugly waiter set down their plates, Rae finally broke the silence. "I'm afraid I don't even know your name, sir," she said lightly.

As they came in, everybody in the place, men and women, even the group of four brawny, drunken heartlands truckers, had stared at them. This had seemed to cheer Rae up. Her voice was bright with vitality now. But the quickness and grace with which she set down her cup of tea, curled herself on the stool, and sipped, head on one side, were not natural.

Crispin took a bite of eggs. "Crispin Kateralbin. And Miss Chester said your name was—"

"Rae."

"Rae . . ."

"Clothwri—" Then she stopped, and shrugged. "Rae nothing in particular."

"Then what am I to call you?"

"Why not just Rae?"

All right, whatever!

After a minute, stirring her tea, Rae said, "So what did Rutridge say to you?"

He called me a worthless sap, an insult to his profession, a satanic instrument of the apocalyptic cults, and other things that would have made me laugh if he hadn't been so deadly serious.

But Crispin could not repeat the language Rutridge had used, even though Rae herself had a foul mouth. Besides, he did not believe Rutridge had meant to *insult* him. The man was simply so battered in his soul that he no longer had a thought to spare for courtesy or consideration. Long years of daemon handling could do that— Millsy had often implied—especially if a man was without boon companions.

"He told me a lot of things," Crispin said. "I didn't get a chance to say I was looking for a job. As soon as he noticed me, he started railing about his own problems. Apparently his wife drinks, and he has to support her habit."

The men at the next table were eavesdropping attentively. Rae threw them a poisonous look. Then she turned back to Crispin with a smile. "Yes, that's right. We all know about Mrs. Rutridge at the Linny. And he does tend to go on, and nobody lets themselves get button-holed any more. So he's starved for an audience."

Crispin put down his fork. "He didn't understand a thing I was trying to tell him! That music hall really has possibilities! He's not an innovator, he just puts his old daemon through its paces; but with that mechanism up there, you could do fantastic things! You could combine the colors, you could make designs on a backdrop—I'm on thin ice here, but I expect you could even *write* in lights—"

"Yes, I've thought of that."

"I bet you could even get the fine folks down there to see something like that!"

"I wouldn't count on—"

"I told him it wouldn't cost anything to revamp the sequences; you'd probably even save money by cutting a couple of those crap acts you have out there now and putting on light shows instead. I told him I'd do it for room and board—"

"Look, I can see you're not from around here—"

Crispin drew a breath.

"I'm sorry," she said quickly. "I didn't mean it that way." She stretched out a hand as if to touch his cheek, as the trucker from Galashire had done, sitting at this very table or one of the ones next to it, but before the movement was half-completed she drew back. Crispin had in that split second prepared himself for the brush of her fingers. As he watched her hand drop as if in slow motion back to the tabletop, he had to restrain himself from catching it up.

There was a moment of silence, and then Rae said anxiously, "If it comes to that, I'm not from around here myself."

"I didn't think you were." Crispin favored her with a smile.

"I feel as if I ought to apologize for Rutridge. *And* me! But I—"

"No need," Crispin said. "Let's play confessions. Where do you come from? Until a little while ago I was with a circus. Smithrebel's Fabulous Aerial and Animal Show."

He had tried her with it to see how she would react—like testing a sore muscle—but she only nodded. Her long, pale, perfectly sculpted face was serious.

"Miss Henley told me you'd only been at the old Linny a year," Crispin said.

Without warning, her face crumpled. She sipped her tea distractedly. "Oh, don't ask me!"

"Why? Are you ashamed of your background? Can't be much more of an embarrassment than mine."

She took a gulp of her tea. Then she fiddled with the buttons of her dress. She was flushing. "Come on," Crispin wheedled. Taking the hand that lay on the table, he looked into her eyes. "Whatever it is—"

"Oh, yes it can be more of an embarrassment!" she said miserably. But she did not take her hand away. Her palm was soft and hot. He could feel the pulse in her wrist. "Do you want me to lie?"

"If you can make it really, really good . . ." He stroked her wrist gently with his thumb.

She jerked away and sat upright. The men at the next table turned away, disappointed. Crispin saw her throat move inside the buttoned trumpet of her collar. "Please. No. Let's talk about you."

"We have been."

"Oh, *don't* go all masculine on me! I thought you weren't that way—that's why I came—"

Crispin could not help laughing out loud. "Then you're a lot more naive than you look!"

After a second, she smiled hesitantly and took a ladylike sip of his chicory coffee; her mouth twisted, but she put the mug down quickly as if she hoped he wouldn't notice. When she saw him watching with interest, she broke down in giggles and hid her face in her hands. "Oh, my!"

"Quite all right," Crispin said, with as much of a bow as he could manage from a sitting position. "It'll make it taste even sweeter." He took a deep breath. He felt oddly exhilarated. It was a sensation he had never experienced before—except maybe, if he wasn't deceiving himself, with Prettie, back in the early days, when they used to talk about flying . . .

Rae didn't look so much like poor, dead Prettie any more. She was older, sadder, more worldly. If she was a flyer, Crispin thought, she would practice for hours a day to get every last little movement down right. But she'd never make a flyer. She was far too tall, and she had too good a figure. He did not try to continue the conversation. Slowly, she grew nervous.

"Daemon handling seems to mean a lot to you," she said at last.

"That is, it means a lot to almost every man in this town. But you're different, you don't have a job! Do you want to tell me why? Or is it something else I wouldn't understand?"

Crispin laughed. This time, he had to wipe his eyes with the edge of his sleeve. "Rae, if you haven't joined the trickster women by the age of what, twenty . . ."

"Eighteen."

"You look older."

"I know."

"Then there's no way I could make you understand. Do you know that's the first time any female has ever asked me about daemons! Blessed Queen. Most girls couldn't care less—even around here, with all their dads and brothers in the business. Even though, without dae-mons, they wouldn't have gaslights, water, cloth for their dresses, gold for their jewelry, there wouldn't be any trucks, so there'd be no trade, for Queen's sake you'd have to eat apples all year round! . . ." He was getting carried away. He laughed, and filled his mouth with eggs.

Rae was looking at him with interest. "Daemons are in everything, aren't they? I've always thought that. Ever since I was a kid—the gar-den of my—house—was full of them. But nobody here cares."

"Then think how much less they care in the rest of the country! It's absolutely bloody scandalous."

"Yes." She paused. "Still, for me it's neither really here nor there. All I ever wanted to do was design costumes. Gorgeous costumes."

He nearly laughed until he saw the look in her eyes.

"But I don't have a hope of ever getting to be wardrobe designer at the Old Linny. Madame Fourrière works us like dogs."

"You've been in music hall all your life, I suppose."

"I worked my way across half of Ferupe with a traveling fairday act. The Fattest Man In The World—and he really was! I got so tired of sewing on buttons . . ."

She had been with a traveling act. And she had found a perma-nent job. Crispin felt his face getting hot. "So what's the difference between town fairs and the circus? No offense, Rae, but no one in the circus I come from would be caught dead in a music hall! And yet"—he banged his fork on the table—"and yet I'd be willing to bet my last farthing I couldn't get a job sweeping the damn floors at your damn Old Linny! What's the catch? Can you tell me what is the catch?"

"Oh, Queen," she said. She reached out and squeezed his hand.

Instantly he disliked himself for playing on her sympathy. No matter how genuine either of their feelings, it was a cadge. He pulled away.

"Mr. Kateralbin, I know how you feel. I—"

The bouncer stood over them. Crispin gave him a slow, stony look.

"Finished?" The man gestured to their empty plates. "You'll 'ave to leave. We're closin'. Police rules, you know."

"But look at all these people," Rae said childishly.

The bouncer snapped his fingers. "You stay, you pay."

Crispin rose to his feet, picked up his knapsack, and took Rae's arm. Sometimes it was pleasant to tower over other men. He took a joy in the fear that fleeted across the bouncer's face. "As a matter of fact we were just leaving." He pulled Rae against his side, pleased that she was so beautiful, her face luminous as a candle flame in the gloom. "We have business elsewhere."

The bouncer's silent fury and frustration followed them like a miasma up the stairs, mixed with the sharp smell of newly hammered metal coming through the wall from the tinware shop.

"Wouldn't sweep their damn floors," Crispin muttered.

"I wouldn't want you to," Rae said.

Crispin escorted her back to her lodging, which were on Main Street, in the attic of a lodging house beside an armorer's shop. Again, they did not speak a word as they walked; but the tension was gone, replaced by a comfortable silence.

Rae put her key in the door of the lodging house, and turned. "Will you be at the Old Linny tomorrow night?"

The question hung in the air.

"Maybe," Crispin said, although he did not intend it. "You never can tell. Go on, now. Go to bed."

Crooked teeth flashed. She turned and ran quietly up the stairs, her dress swirling around her boots. Crispin caught the door and closed it gently behind her.

Then he turned and walked off down Main Street toward Cranzelow, the daemonmonger's corner, toward his hard cold nest in the doorway.

Head pillowed on his knapsack, he fell asleep almost instantly—
and was wakened not by the nightmares which he could not recall,
could never recall, but by the sound of running feet and voices, and
the clanging of a bell, and—nightmare—no, *reality*—oh, Queen—the
crackle of flames.

I can't abear a Butcher,
I can't abide his meat;
The ugliest shop of all is his,
The ugliest in the street;
Bakers' are warm, cobblers' dark,
Chemists' burn watery lights;
But oh, the sawdust butcher's shop,
That ugliest of sights!

—Walter de la Mare

Slide

The disturbance was coming from Main Street. Crispin thought about going back to sleep. In this town they probably called the fire brigade when something spilled on the kitchen range.

But in the small hours of the morning? No. It had to be a real fire. Queen—in this damp, it couldn't even be that!

He sat up.

When it had been raining for months, a fire couldn't start unless it got a *lot* of help. The police of Valestock weren't stupid enough that they would fail to figure that out. Arson! A real turnup for the books. If Constable Carthower and his colleagues weren't already infesting the streets, they would be soon. Crispin stood, slinging his knapsack over his shoulder, and was about to put distance between himself and Main Street when a thought struck him.

Rae.

Every muscle in his body went rigid.

"You've got a death wish, Kateralbin," he said aloud, and spun and loped in the direction of the fire.

As he slid along Draper toward Main Street, his worst suspicions were confirmed. The arsonist had known what he was doing: the blaze had evidently started in the armorer's shop. Crispin couldn't tell whether the barrels of daemons in the back of the shop had gone up yet, though small explosions, irregularly spaced, sent the firemen staggering back from the flames, their boots skidding on the glass that had fallen from the windowpanes. Puffs of black smoke lifted into the

❈ 115 ❈

night. Neither sand nor water hoses seemed to be having much effect: the fire had already spread to the lower floors of the lodging houses on either side of the armorer's. A crowd of escapees huddled in the shadows on the other side of the street. More were being carried or dragged down the stairs, shrouded in wet blankets. Crispin could not see Rae anywhere.

Three white-coats stood behind the firemen's rumbling daemon pump, guarding a second huddle of refugees. Crispin pressed deeper into the shadows.

Carthower was shifting from foot to foot, worrying his lower lip. *Coward,* Crispin thought with hatred. Then he saw that the refugees— five or six men, so badly burned that their clothes hung in singed rags—were chained with their arms behind their backs, faces outward, in a painfully tight circle. They were singing. The sound was barely distinguishable over the noise of the fire and the pump; the words were impossible to make out. Crispin couldn't even hear the tallest policeman shouting "Shut up!", though when he struck one of the prisoners an open-handed blow across the mouth, the implication became clear.

Crispin blinked, and flitted across Draper Street to join the larger crowd of refugees. The inhabitants of nearby houses were pouring out, some gathering to scream unhelpfully at the firemen and policemen, some mingling with the blanket-wrapped, shivering refugees, searching for relatives, neighbors, friends. Crispin moved through the crowd, unobtrusively examining sooty faces, until he saw Rae.

She was standing alone in front of a dress shop a little way down the street. Flames danced luridly in the window behind her. Her face was pink with heat. She still wore the violet dress, with a man's coat over it: a tough, waterproofed affair bunched in by a drawstring at the hem. Her hair was coming down around her face in silky strands.

He touched her arm. In the circumstances, it didn't seem at all unusual that she sagged against him. Anyone else would have done, he thought as he held her carefully close. And why *hadn't* anyone else come to offer her refuge from the night and the destruction? Heartless. They were all without heart.

"What happened?" he said in her ear.

She was shivering. "Oh, Queen! I'm so glad you're here! I can hardly believe it. I don't know what happened. Yes, I do. Culties—

culties set it in the armorer's. They probably planned to burn themselves to death. Anticipation of the End Of Humanity. That's what they call it when they do something like this. They'll kill themselves now, first chance they get, because they got rescued before they could burn to death."

"Didn't know there was much of that around here," Crispin said, though he was remembering what Millsy had told him to the contrary.

"Yes, Apocalypists. They live outside town. Nobody pays any attention—I could have told them—Apocalypists have no class, absolutely no class." She laughed, with a note of hysteria. "They'll blame the Dynasty, because it's the best known cult, but only Apocalypists would do something like this. They haven't had any revelations—they just steal other people's ideas. They're pathetic. That's why they pull stunts like this. They're afraid to wait for the end of the Dynasty, so they think they'll cheat death by killing themselves—they're crazy, they're fucked up—"

"It's all right," Crispin said, although it wasn't. "All right. Stay calm."

His only firsthand experience of culties was the "Royal Dance Troupe" of Smithrebel's, who swore up and down that they were charlatans. *Real* culties didn't visit the circus. Of course everybody knew they were nihilists, and a disgrace, and ought to be outlawed—but if you thought about it, the only crime against society of which they were actually *accused*—the buying up of tracts of land for monstrous prices—seemed quite innocuous. And that was just as much the fault of whoever owned the land in the first place.

But if *this* was the kind of thing that went on, in the night, in isolated towns . . .

If it was a dry season, half of Main Street would be in flames right now. Crispin understood why a town would not want to have the news of such vulnerability noised about.

"But they've got them all now!" he murmured. "Do you want to get a better look?"

"No!—Yes—"

As they eased through the crowd, there was a tremendous boom. Redness flared almost to white; heat hit them like a wall. People cried out.

Cautiously, Crispin took his fingers away from his eyes.

The daemons had gone up. The armorer's was a fireball, burning with the white brilliance of a glare. Flames licked out of the top windows of the house where Rae had lived. The firemen and policemen were pulling back, wheeling their equipment, chivvying the manacled culties along with them. As they were kicked away from the flames, the men tipped back their heads, singing. "What! Ho! Blow a kiss! To the birds of the apo-ca-lypse!"

One of them jerked his chin at Crispin and Rae in a beckoning gesture. A grin studded with black teeth split his stubbly beard. He looked as though he were laughing. "I see you, sister!" he shouted through his companions' song. Rae froze.

"Pay no attention," Crispin muttered, "come on, we'll go—"

Within a minute all six culties had changed their tune. This time they shouted the words so loudly they were audible even over the din of the fire.

"It was late last night / When the flames broke out / And downstairs ran my lady-o / Her brothers dear / Did await her there / With a kiss, and a Bonnie Bonnie Biscay Oh!"

Rae screamed. All three policemen turned toward her and Crispin. Carthower's eyes narrowed.

"She did it," the first man shouted, and all six took up the chorus. "*She* did it! *She* did it!"

The policemen ignored them. Heads together, they were staring at Crispin and Rae. Carthower gestured emphatically; Crispin could guess what he was saying. Why had he been such a fool as to come anywhere near the police a second time?

"*She* did it! *She* did it!"

"You're hurting me," Rae sobbed, and Crispin realized he was gripping her wrist.

"Sorry." He relaxed his grip. "But I think we're going to have to run for it."

And as Carthower launched himself on a winding path through the crowd, randomly starting and stopping as if he were playing a game of Red Light, Green Light with Crispin, as if he thought Crispin did not see him approaching, it started to rain again. The noise of the skies hitting the fire was that of water being poured onto a piping-hot griddle the size of the big top. Even the townsfolk's screams of gladness could scarcely be heard. The culties put their heads back and gnashed their teeth, shaking chained wrists. Crispin dragged Rae away down a side street. The rain was so loud that he couldn't tell whether or not they were being pursued. Their boots skidded on the wet cobbles. Once they fell, in a tangle of wet limbs. Crispin dragged her to her feet. "Can't you go any faster?" he shouted.

"No," she gasped. "You're killing me! Leave me behind!"

Suddenly his assumption that she was coming with him struck him as ludicrous, even frightening. Had her proximity *worked* on him somehow? That was what the cleverest kind of daemon did when they were trying to get you to fall asleep at the wheel. He stared into her face. She looked wretched with fear; her hair clung in black snakes to her cheeks. The rain trickled off her onto his hands. His instincts screamed at him to go, get out, leave her. "I can't leave you! Come on!"

She sobbed. "You have to go, they'll catch you. They'll pin the whole thing on you."

"Queen, *I* know what to do," he muttered, and pulled her protesting around, in the direction of Slimey's, where the bartenders were probably even now stuffing padding under the upstairs door to stop the joint from flooding.

In this end of town, the windows of the houses were dark. It seemed nobody had noticed Main Street going up in flames. Rain slopped off the roofs and gurgled along in the gutters. The eighteen-wheeler was still parked outside Slimey's. Crispin closed his eyes for a moment as they slowed to a walk. A long-haul cross-country rig with the Wesson & Sons logo on her grille (he recognized the monogram as you might a face), sixty feet from fender to fender, over Lovoshire regulation weight for unarticulated vehicles. That was why she had not been parked in the depots outside Valestock. Bringing her into the streets made even less sense, but rules were rules, after all.

The tires came up to his waist. His mouth watered at the thought of the traction in those finger-deep treads. Fantastic for hills. No good for winding roads; but she'd be able to hit sixty miles an hour on the straight.

Smithrebel's had had a Wesson & Sons for the animals when Crispin was a child, but it had turned out not to be economical. They'd switched to Boltons. The Wesson daemon was so large it gobbled food like there was no tomorrow. His heart quickened at the very thought.

"Stand guard." Leaving Rae facing the door of Slimey's, he went to crouch by the front grille.

Daemon price tags increased exponentially according to the size of the beast. And daemons that came from the Wraithwaste, instead of the smaller forests scattered throughout the rest of the country, where commercially owned trickster women captured tiny, short-lived daemons by the dozen, were dearer yet. Wraithwaste daemons were commoner now than they had been when Crispin was little; but because the demands of industry were increasing even faster, and factory owners bought as many as their daemonbrokers could get them, trucking companies had to pay top dollar to get their fingers in the Wraithwaste pie. The daemon in the Wesson & Sons was an ancient, strong beast, top of the line. He could feel its aura emanating out through the grille at him. A wave of shivery heat. Like standing over a pit of embers.

"I know you're in there, you loathly spotty creature! You sweet road-eater. Do you hear me?"

Heat caressed his cheeks, dried the rain on his eyelashes. He rested his forehead on the wooden fender.

Anger. Pain. Must get away will get away will push and push and push and push as soon as I see the least little opening through which it is just possible I might be able to escape; hunger. Fury. Hunger. Fury. Hunger.

He flexed his fingers and stood up. He walked back around the truck to where Rae was standing. "You're coming then, are you?" He squinted at the door to see whether there was an alarm.

"I suppose you plan to take—to take *this*." She gestured at the monstrous length of the truck. "You know that's a jailing offense. At least."

There was no alarm mechanism that he could see. "Not taking it. Borrowing it."

"I don't suppose you plan to bring it back!"

"That constable's got it in for me. If I don't get out of here, it'll be a jailing offense. It can't get much worse."

"No," she said with an odd little catch of her breath, "it can't. Everything I owned was in that room. Granted it wasn't much."

He couldn't leave her to her destitution. On the other hand, there was nothing more irritating than women who felt they had been coerced into doing something against their will—they would rub it in your face twenty-four hours a day.

He jumped up onto the lowest step, balanced there wrestling with the door for a minute, and then slid into the cab, throwing his knapsack in ahead of him.

She heard him cursing as he fiddled with the controls of the truck. Her eyes were prickling. Inside her head she heard the fire bells ringing again, and knew: *It's happening. Just as I always used to fear. They've found out where I am. They've come to punish me.*

She was drenched through and through. She did not have a penny in the world. She still had her job but nowhere to live, and would she be any unhappier if she went on the road again, in the company of the first person she had met in months who did not seem to hate her?

She couldn't find it in herself to fear the man. Caution didn't matter anymore. *Nothing* mattered anymore. Nothing. She caught hold of the rearview mirror and pulled herself up onto the lowest step: not difficult because she was taller than most men, as well as limber from filling in for the boys who performed at the Old Linny. The Negro leaned over and pushed the door open with his fingertips. She clambered in and settled into the nest of blankets that covered the hard wooden seat. For a moment, as he did not look at her or speak, she wanted to scramble back down, out of the cab, away, but then she saw he was *concentrating*, like Madame Fourrière concentrated when she was thinking about a new costume, like Rae herself often had to concentrate on not thinking about home, and the truck snarled alive beneath them. She choked a scream. Her teeth rattled.

A grin transformed the Negro's face. With one of his huge hands he gripped the wheel, with the other a cable that went straight down, vibrating, into the dashboard. It was wrapped so tight around his fist that it cut into the flesh. "Now now, my darling," he was whispering, "come on my shit-eating lovely, my lipsmacker of miles . . ."

The whole great vehicle seemed to rear back, and with a plunge, they took the corner of Mandall and Applewater at a good twenty miles an hour. Behind them, someone was shouting. They did not slow down.

The rain splattered on the windshield. With a surge of delight, Rae realized that they were making for the western road.

When a woman take the blues,
She tuck her head and cry.
But when a man catch the blues,
He grab his shoes and slide.

—Quoted by Shirley Williams

Book Three

The Trap

Prophet and Priest

Fessiery 1893 A.D. *Lovoshire: Western Route 2*

Darkness, and the rumble of the wheels. The dynamo headlights of the big rig cast cones of yellow light over the gravel road. In the fog, Crispin could not see more than twenty yards ahead.

As flatlands gave way to forest, he slipped into the familiar half-trance of travel. His instincts responded to each dip in the road, letting his mind drift free. His body, physically linked to the daemon via the whipcord, tingled in a state of mild arousal, tempering languor with excitement and a tinge of self-satisfaction.

Exhilarating to know that in two months he hadn't lost the knack. Over daemons, at least, he could still triumph. This one was bigger and more wayward than any he had driven before: its owners, whom he remembered seeing in Slimey's, were muscular giants, taller than him, and there had been at least two of them. He suspected they were not particularly good handlers. The Wraithwaste daemon responded poorly to the steering, and it kept trying to slack off speed. But he had it pinned down now, doing his bidding.

Easy. Easy as falling asleep.

Millsy would have been blown over backwards.

"Mmm, yeah," Crispin whispered. Keeping his eyes on the road, he fished out a cigarette and lit it one-handed.

The trees peeled away into the darkness on either side of the road. The rain had stopped and it was a still, foggy night.

He exhaled slowly. He had stolen a truck. Stolen it. This would put him on the wrong side of the white-coats for a good long time. "Borrowing . . . !" He had known he was sealing his fate the moment he jimmied the door of the cab.

The settled life was exactly what it had seemed from the outside. And that was the awful thing. It had never been any use for him to try to fit in. Now he knew what it would take, and that he didn't have it. Worse: no matter how much money he had, he would never have been able to do as he liked. The expropriated society of elephants, clowns, aerialists, and foreigners was the only world in which he belonged at all.

A shudder of loneliness turned the marrow of his bones to air. He pressed his foot down on the clutch, shifting up into sixth. The smooth clicking of gears and the daemon's shudder of protest made him smile. Escape seemed to be the thing he was best at. A dubious distinction!

He had forgotten the girl asleep beside him on the seat.

Rae woke to the cold, gray light of late afternoon, with a bad taste in her mouth and a cramp in her neck. For a minute she wanted to go back to sleep, as she had done several times already; then she realized the truck had stopped. She rubbed her eyes, shivering as she untangled herself from the inadequate blankets. "Where—where are we?"

Crispin sat behind the wheel, as immobile as the music hall's Living Statues, whose specialty was not to move no matter what the audience threw at them.

She started to speak again and then thought better of it. She had had ample opportunity to examine his profile while the miles rumbled away—she had not liked to break his concentration, even when he slumped and muttered to himself, and she wondered, frozen with fear, what on earth could be keeping the truck on the road? But his face still fascinated her, to the point that it forbade questions. When she first met him she had thought he was all Negro, but now she wasn't sure. That aquiline nose. The high, intelligent forehead. The prominent lips. He wasn't black, but sort of yellow-brown. His eyelashes were even longer and thicker than Rae's own.

Right now the eyelashes rested on the cheeks. The head drooped lower and lower on the chest. One of the massive hands fumbled almost vaguely with the cord that led down into the dash. Had he fallen asleep?

She touched his shoulder.

A mistake! Oh, oh, Queen! She felt his whole body tense, then relax, and he expelled a long, slow breath. "Bloody useless daemon!"

"What's wrong?"

He turned to her, opened his eyes, and for a moment his forehead rumpled as if he was trying to remember who she was. "The daemon's acting up. It's hungry."

She knew less than nothing about daemons. "Isn't there anything to give it?"

"In the circus we used to feed ours on chicken, salt pork, even bread, scraps. But boys like the ones who own this shit feed their daemons on little tiny *other* daemons. Splinterons, is what they're called. Better performance, but the gorgons get used to it and then they won't eat anything else, they'll starve first. If there was any, they'd be here." He slapped the middle of the seat. "Holding cell. But it's empty. Look." He lifted up the seat and slid back the wooden hatch underneath. "Nothing! They must've been planning to load up in Valestock."

"What's *that*?" Rae could see something glimmering deep inside the wooden box.

Crispin bent to peer in. "What? Oh, *that*. How can you—A tiddler. Wonder if I could—" His hand slid stealthily as a snake down into the cell. Rae watched him cup his fingers around something that looked almost like a toy soldier, except that it was luminescent blue, and naked, and wriggled on the palm of his hand—

And then was nothing.

She shivered, feeling something pass like an intangible wind through her, out of the cab.

He shook his hand as if it had been burned. "Wouldn't even have whetted this pampered motherfucker's—'scuse my Kirekuni— wouldn't even have whetted its appetite." Using his other hand, he slid the hatch closed and let the seat bang down on top of it. "Used to getting all the eats it wants. Should *never* let a daemon get used to having its own way. Otherwise, it'll choose to stop, just stop, and nothing short of a trickster can make it go again."

Rae scowled. Outside the windows of the cab, trees rubbed wetly together, massed like patchy brown-and-green costumes hanging from the clouds. Ahead, the road was no more than a gap in the forest.

Crispin shook himself and smiled lopsidedly at her. "Cheer up! We'll just have to go on shanks' mare."

"You haven't told me where we are going," she said, with an effort at a coquettish laugh.

"That's because I don't know, do I?"

"Oh." She felt an almost physical longing for her little room on the fifth floor of the lodging house: her mirror, her pallet, the curtain behind which her dresses hung: all burnt now, black dust the engraving of the Queen and the bowlegged dressing table she'd bought for a song. How she had tried to anchor herself in the real world. And she had been punished.

Crispin said reluctantly, "If you want me to escort you back to Valestock, I will. That's the least I can do in fact. I shouldn't have brought you this far."

"It's all right," she said forlornly. "I don't have anything left. Nowhere to go. I—I'm in your hands."

She waited for him to respond. He would have to look after her, of course. One of the strictest rules of the road was that men cared for women, no matter what. But it seemed vitally important to know if he was pleased with the prospect. When he didn't speak, she tried the laugh again and said, "Well, then—where are we?"

"Somewhere on the western road. Not that it's been a road for quite a while. More of a rut." A trace of satisfaction crept into his voice. "I'd say we could give Valestock seventy or eighty miles right now."

Oh, by the Queen!

She sat still, biting her fingers, trying to keep the tears from her eyes.

Once, maybe, she would have forgotten herself and begged him to take her deeper into the forest. West! To Kirekune! But last night's craziness had abandoned her.

"Mmm. I'm hungry, too." He slouched back in the seat. "You?"

She could not answer. She was crying. She didn't know what was wrong with her. Stress—loss—hunger—all of those, triggering something else. *Don't—oh, please don't—let him see—*

Kirekune!

Ferupe had killed both her parents. They had not lived to see the end of the Dynasty. After Saonna died, Rae had felt herself called to reclaim the heritage her parents had forsaken. She had lain awake at night, heart beating fast, planning her glorious mission into the west. At the age of eleven she ran away from the Seventeenth Mansion. It wasn't long before she fell in with a company of patriotic playactors; they'd treated her badly but she'd been lucky, she knew now, that they had found her before someone worse did. For years she wandered, switching from one lot of travelers to another whenever the first lot headed south. She crossed half of Ferupe, tending northward, drawn to the snowy pass Saonna had described, and the vision of that glittering city where she might belong.

But adult comprehension led her to realize that because of what she'd done to herself, even if she made it across the pass where her father had died, she would be just another freak. And anyway she was not free to go. Despite everything, she was still a child of the Dynasty. Her upbringing bound her to Ferupe. The knowledge of transcendence returned to her fantasy-dazzled mind like a razor-pinioned bird returning to a glade. The bird settled on a bough, bending it nearly to the ground. It clacked its iron feathers and sang to her, an eerie tune in a minor key.

She gave up trying to get to the northern pass and signed on with Tom, The World's Fattest Man, Music Hall Prodigy. Wherever the show went, she went, without a backward glance. And once again, she cried at night, because she knew that she alone, out of all the ignorant illiterate Ferupians around her, was burdened with knowledge.

By the time she reached Valestock, she wanted only to settle down, to find a measure of happiness before transcendence wiped all such things from the face of the world. She knew it made her weak and materialistic, but she couldn't help it. The deep west was the last place she wanted to settle down in; but it was in Valestock that she was offered a real job. Making actual costumes for the stage, with Madame Fourrière.

She had said good-bye to The World's Fattest Man and by the time she realized her mistake, it was too late. Her life in the Dynasty and in traveling shows had sheltered her from the real world to a degree that she did not appreciate at the time. Getting enough to eat had never been a problem on the road: a pretty young girl could, if hunger pinched badly enough, always sit herself on someone's lap and share his dinner in return for allowing him to fondle her. Men tended to give you food anyway, in the same way they would give a pet dog scraps. It was what they expected to get in return that became the problem. One realized the value of one's virtue very quickly. Protecting it had been a full-time job for Rae, on top of her other duties. She had quickly developed her own brand of coquetry.

But shortly before Valestock, she had reached the age where her refusal to be bedded was an actual insult to the men around her. None of them even thought of marrying her; she wouldn't have taken them if they had; and she wasn't going to find anybody else as long as she kept traveling.

So she stopped.

What she did not know was that in Valestock, society had many different layers, like a sandwich cake. When she took a job at the Old Linny, she buried herself at the very bottom, in the crumbs. And no one was there to help her up. On River Street, one was either a married woman or a never-to-be-married woman; there was no in-between ground, much as Rae tried to create it. She did not see why she could not step smoothly into the part of young lady, alone in the world, but quite respectable, and oh so *marriageable*! So, in the face of her landlady's clear disapproval, and aware that she was being charged a special "entertainer's rate"—she knew what that meant: a whore's rate—she rented rooms on Main Street. Doll and the other girls at the Old Linny hated her for it. Didn't they understand that all she wanted was a good name? She wept in secret, and hated them back. By the time she realized that, in fact, they understood her snobbishness better than she did, she had ruined her chances of being accepted among them.

After that, what could one do but wear the gown they had given her?

She started taking up with men deliberately. It was easy to heat them to boiling point, have them quivering at her feet, and then let them fall on their faces for the other girls to pick up. And it made her feel, briefly, powerful. Although she knew that they would all hate her, every one, if she let them find out her secret.

She wanted someone who wouldn't hate her. She wanted a husband, an income, a house—or even just rented rooms—she wanted in-laws who would help a young couple get on their feet.

But she had finally come to face the fact that working for Madame Fourrière would not help her find any of these things. Madame was a genius, exiled from the Kingsburg Ballet because of a vendetta on the part of the principal ballerina—so she said. The costumes that she and Molly, the other assistant, codesigned were magical. But Madame Fourrière and Molly used Rae like a slave. She would stand among the racks of clothes at night, when she should have been mending, fingering the sateens and velvets, breathing in the smell of camphor and old sweat. It was the only time she got to handle the clothes.

Scurrying through the stinking corridors of the Old Linny late at night, quiet as a house mouse so that the maintenance men would not hear, she wished for her tail back, so that she could flick it gracefully, perfecting the picture. And when she peered out of her mousehole, the future was bleak. She could remain in Valestock, or she could go on the road again. Either way, she had not enough years remaining to grow old. Her "affectations" would never become manageable "eccentricities." The saddest thing in the world was that she would not have anyone to hold her when death started spreading from the capital. She would die young, and she would die alone.

Maybe it was this sensation of black-glass pincers closing on her, closing, closing, that had prompted her to ask the Negro that question she had never asked anyone before: *Will I see you tomorrow?*

She had not known that he would take her west. The possibility of getting to Kirekune this way, through the Wraithwaste, through the war, terrified her. But last night in the truckers' eatery, she had not even been thinking about Kirekune. She had liked Crispin for a reason she did not understand—the very opposite of physical, to put it one way. She had thought, Maybe—maybe—

And then the fire.

She saw with sudden terror that he had seen the wetness on her cheeks. His face wrinkled. He put an arm around her shoulders and patted her. The asexuality of the touch was like a slap. She found herself crying harder.

"Girl! By the Queen—Look, if you want to go home, tell me."

"I don't think you understand," she said, sobbing. "I have no home. All I have in the world is the clothes on my back."

"But if you keep on crying, I won't know what to think! I'll think you want to go back to Valestock. And I know I said I'd take you, but to be quite honest, I think we'd both get arrested!"

"Anywhere but Valestock," she said at last, when she had herself under control. Her voice quavered. She despised herself for it. "It's—it's up to you!"

"Anywhere but Valestock." Crispin rubbed his eyes. "Yeah, well, I have a few ideas. The way I see it, we've burned our bridges behind us; there's really only one place to . . . no. No, no. I won't tell you yet. I've got to think about it for a while. But I promise everything's going to be okay." He grinned. His smile was almost as good as a fire, warming her. Not a raging fire *(smoke creeping under her ill-fitting door, the reek of burning oil: PANIC PANIC PANIC)* but a comforting hearth-fire.

"Are you hungry?" he asked.

She admitted she was.

"I'm going to go see what's in the trailer. The back wheels aren't coming down heavily, so if there's a load, it's really light. But you never know."

"*I'll* go look," she said, suddenly needing to get clear of him for a minute, and, kicking her feet free of the blankets, she wrestled with the door handle and jumped to the ground. It was much farther down than she remembered from last night. Luckily, the mud flung aside by the truck was soft.

"But, oh," she whispered, picking herself up, "oh, my best dress!"

She was gone before he could stop her. He sagged back. The daylight scratched his sore eyes. He rolled down the window, rested his elbows on the edge, put his chin on his hands, and closed his eyes. The drips from the trees on his head were cool and regularly paced.

Sleep took him from the inside outward, suffusing his body with a warm heaviness that made him not want to move ever again. He hadn't experienced this degree of exhaustion since mornings in Smithrebel's, when he would sit in the cab of whatever rig he'd been driving, sleeping yet at the same time listening to the familiar sounds that told him the big top was about to go up and it was time for him to stir about.

"Empty boxes," Rae's voice said from below.

He opened his eyes. She was standing under the window of the cab, looking up. Beautiful, yes beautiful, even covered with mud and soot, her eyes puffy from crying. (*Please,* Queen, let her not make a habit of it!) She was smiling waterily. Her arms were filled with an assortment of little wooden boxes which he recognized as transport cells for daemons.

That night he lay on his back beside a tower of cartons that he had erected in the middle of the trailer to give her some privacy. Outside, a light rain was falling. He could hear her turning restlessly on the other side of the stacked boxes. So she couldn't sleep either.

A heavy meal of bread and cheese sat uncomfortably in his stomach. Living by one's wits seemed to be a quagmire into which one sank deeper not through inertia, but through struggling. Ransacking the truck for edibles, he and Rae had discovered only carton upon carton of daemon cells: "Product of Fewman and Fewman, Valestock, Lovoshire Domain," she had read on them (confirming Crispin's guess that she was far better educated than she had a right to be), but no daemons inside with which Crispin might have placated the rebellious gorgon. And nothing humans could eat, either. But Crispin still had that pound note in his pocket, and he said to her, "There've got to be people around here we can buy food from. Come on."

Oh, the naiveté of the morning.

Sure enough, walking back along the road, they had come to a set of little turnoffs into the woods, just wide enough for, say, an oxcart. They chose one at random. As they followed it the forests gave way to many little apple orchards separated by unruly hedges. "Oh, how lovely," Rae said, clasping her hands to her breast. "I was beginning to think we'd left civilization behind altogether."

Most of the trees were bare, but one large orchard was planted with a different species. Heavy, glossy, white apples bowed down the branches. Five or six dark-haired boys, wrapped against the cold in shapeless layers of rags, moved slowly from tree to tree, pulling a great wheeled basket with them. When they saw Crispin and Rae, they gaped.

"Eh," shouted the boy at the bottom of the ladder, after a minute. "Traders?"

"We're looking for your parents," Crispin called across the orchard. "Where d'you live?"

After a minute, the child jerked his chin in the direction they were going. "'Tisn't much farther."

"I'm so hungry," Rae whispered to Crispin. She stepped onto the grass and closed her hand around a low-hanging apple. "May I?" she called out.

One of the children seemed agitated, and pulled his brother's smock. The brother shook his head and wrenched away. "Go on, lady!" he said, then bent his head and said to the smaller child, his rough voice carrying clearly between the trees, "Go youse, tell Mam traders coming."

The little boy trotted off, looking fearfully over his shoulder.

Crispin watched Rae eating her apple as they continued down the path. From time to time, she picked threads of dark hair from between her lips. Something about the shape of those long, long thin fingers—the boniness, the sallow hue of the knuckles—reminded him of something . . . something . . .

The road opened onto an earthen clearing in the trees, bisected by a broad, muddy stream. On either side of the ford clustered log houses and outbuildings on low stilts. Hollyhocks grew tangledy around the feet of the stilts. Geese, hobbled pigs, and small children wandered along the stream. The women appearing in the doorways looked unfriendly.

Crispin squared his shoulders and marched up to the nearest woman, conscious of Rae lingering behind him, her apple core concealed in her hand.

Oh, Queen.

In the turpentine-smelling darkness of the trailer, he sighed.

What a *disaster*!

Rae was breathing deeply, peacefully now.

He had started off on the wrong foot by offering the women money. It was no good. They recognized the pound note, but they would have none of it. And, of course, it would be of little use to them, seventy miles from Valestock. Over and over, they had stubbornly repeated that the traders always brought barter goods; where were the barter goods?

"We have some nice little boxes," Rae ventured timidly.

"Shush," Crispin whispered. The women wanted knives, tanning chemicals, rennet, cloth, thread. They would have no use for wooden boxes with slogans on.

And then the women's voices became suspicious. It was the wrong time of year for traders, anyway. What was Crispin doing here? Did he have a truck? Where was it? He would have to talk with their men. The men were off in the wildwood, hunting. He could come back at night.

It was then that Crispin realized he had made a mistake. He took Rae's hand, and they backed away, smiling apologies. Crispin watched the tiny glassless windows of the house for movement. Eyes showed in the darkness, and his heart quickened, but it was only a toddler pressing his nose to the sill.

When they were out of sight around a curve, he grabbed Rae's hand and doubled back into the woods. Rae said, "What?" but he dragged her along.

"I'm not going to take that shit. You'll see."

The sogginess of the earth enabled them to move soundlessly. When they had circled back within sound of the hamlet, they scrambled up a tree to wait. Rae complained in whispers about the state of her dress. "I haven't another—"

Crispin grinned and twitched the sleeve of her man's coat. She was clinging to a slightly lower branch. Her face, foreshortened, looked childishly young. "I'll cut down one of my shirts for you. Should reach your ankles. You'll be proper." When her face fell, he laughed softly. For a moment she looked hurt, then she saw the joke, and joined in.

Night fell slowly, almost imperceptibly. The bark of the tree had a musty, bready odor. Crispin leaned his cheek on the trunk and fought tiredness, listening to the hamlet settle down for the night, geese being chased into their house, pigs into theirs, children being put to sleep.

When the occasional song of birds stopped, yellow spots of light appeared through the trees—candles in the windows of the huts. The stream burbled on in the night, talking of loneliness and constant motion. Rae fell into a doze, clinging on her branch. When the last candle had been extinguished, Crispin woke her.

They approached the hamlet with as much stealth as if they were tracking a daemon. Once, back before Crispin was handling, the daemon of Hollyhock 9 had somehow escaped its cell. Collared but not celled: that was the most dangerous sort of daemon of all. It had fled like a whirlwind between the tents. Luckily, the circus was only just setting up, and there were no townies on the lot. Gibbering, it stunned every living thing in its path, desperate to escape the silver collar which kept it from dematerializing. It had not intelligence enough to scrape the silver against a sharp edge, or to dash out into the desert. Millsy took command calmly and naturally. It wasn't his daemon—his were uncollared—but he was Smithrebel's authority on all things occult. He sent everyone into cover, and then produced a five-foot-square piece of silver lamé from his sack and hid between two blacktops. (Twelve-year-old Crispin goggled from a nearby truck.) Two of Millsy's own daemons materialized, dressed in their little sweaters and breeches, and ran after the escaped one, herding it like a runaway bull, driving it eventually into the gap. Then Millsy simply dropped the lamé over it, anchoring it to the ground.

It had been that incident that pushed Crispin toward Millsy for the second time. Calm bravery in the face of danger was a side of Millsy he had not seen before, an aspect of daemon handling he had not really known about. He was twelve. Anuei had been dead two months, and he had been apprenticed to the Valentas for a year.

It had all been circumstances, the way it ended up, hadn't it? If the daemon hadn't escaped, Crispin might not have become a handler. If he hadn't been a handler, he could have become a better aerialist, and Prettie would not be dead. Looking back at his childhood, he sometimes thought he could have been good at nearly anything; unfortunately, Millsy's flattery had seemed more agreeable than Herve's system of punishment and discipline, and so it had been handling.

Not that he would give up daemons for the world.

Slipping through the wet woods with Rae's hand in his, he thought that he should have been more than one person. In order to accommodate all the conflicting impulses and abilities and weaknesses that came of being a half-breed, he should have been a whole set of tall brown brothers and sisters.

But his father had died. Joe Kateralbin. The man Anuei had told him so many stories about.

They slid quietly into the clearing. Not a soul stirred in the darkened

houses as Crispin pulled Rae toward the little outbuilding he had earlier marked out as the pantry-storehouse for the huts on this side of
the stream. It did not take long for them to slide the bolt back, fill
one sack with loaves and another with cheeses and dried fruit, and
tiptoe out again. They couldn't hear a sound over the rippling song of
the brook. But his skin crawled as if with worms, and until they got
well away into the orchards he expected to feel dogs barking and
voices behind him. He even fantasized the crack of a gun, and a
starved daemon hitting between his shoulder blades. Except for the
truck—which had felt as though it *wanted* to be his—he had never
stolen anything before.

When they reached the road proper, he saw Rae's face gray and
stretched in the moonlight that filtered through the clouds. She was
gnawing on a hunk of cheese.

"Here." Suddenly ashamed of himself, he nudged her. "Give us
some."

Sitting on tarpaulins in the half-empty trailer, they shared the food
in silence. Rae's hands moved languidly, and her eyes were unfo-
cused, as if she were thinking about something else altogether.
Strangely enough, she did not seem bothered in the least by their
crime.

For the umpteenth time, he turned on his side, trying to get comfortable. He had given her both the blankets. He pictured her curled in
a snug ball, breathing deeply.

The circus existed outside conventional law. To settled folk,
Crispin had never been more than an untrustworthy darky. What was
so wrong with finally fulfilling their expectations?

Moral compromise glimmered very near. On either side of the way
he would have to walk—he could see the way clearly in the darkness,
a jeweled aisle like a peep show floating in the air—people mouthed
and danced silently. Some he recognized, and some he didn't.
Daemons curved in and out around all of their feet.

He turned over, and the picture vanished. It wasn't doing him any
good to lie here worrying!

Rae sighed in her sleep.

The clarity of that vision had unnerved him more than he cared to
think about. He could not lie here any longer. Damned if he
wouldn't—damned if he wouldn't—

He uncurled to his feet and stepped around the partition. "Rae?" he whispered. "Are you asleep?"

No answer. He bent down and touched the blanket-shrouded figure. Her hair spilled like black oil, tributaries diverging over the lanolin-slick wool. She did not move.

Damned if he wouldn't—

He knelt and touched her hair, smoothing it back from her temple. Her eyelashes cast a dark shadow on her cheek and the side of her nose. Her mouth twitched. She was sleeping soundly.

He brushed her lips with his own. No response. But already the fire was starting. Want fueled need. Need to lie beside her, to embrace every inch of her. Not to take her, but just to touch her. And Queen, how he needed to feel her soft hands touching him, caressing him with the ardor Prettie had never seemed to realize was possible. For Prettie, passivity had been the height of compliance. It had taken a southern prostitute to awaken Crispin to the delights that lovemaking could, and should, hold. And Rae wasn't a whore, she was a townie, and Crispin was convinced that at some point in the past, she had been gentry. It lent her an allure that made the prospect of getting into bed with her absolutely irresistible.

He was shivering. He kissed her again, a little bit harder. This time he wasn't imagining it, her breathing did check. And her mouth held his for a moment. He rested his elbow on the blanket, then lay down, still kissing her. Her eyelashes didn't move, but she turned slightly onto her back, opening her arms. When he slid under the blanket, and found her clothed in long underwear under her petticoat, her kisses became sweeter, deeper. Her hands came up and held his: she allowed him to touch her breasts, but not any lower.

That was all right. It was enough. Languidly kissing her gave him a feeling of being adrift in a blue-green sea. He could have cried with gladness that she had not pushed him away. Her embrace was the temperature of the hottest, sweetest-perfumed bath. There was no such thing as time, or cold, or urgency.

In the darkness, her eyes were pitch-black slits.

"Rae," he whispered. "It's me. I'm here."

"I thought you were a dream," she said sarcastically. Then she was kissing him again, and her hands ran all over his body. She was undoing the catches of his shirt, running her fingers down his stomach. He couldn't stand it anymore; he thrust his hand down behind her, over her buttocks, and her laughter became a sudden gasp of terror, and she grabbed his hand and pulled it away—but it was already too late.

He wrenched away from her as if he had been shocked by a daemon. Sitting up, "Rae?!"

She hunched into a ball, dragging the blankets tight around herself. "Go away!"

"No. I don't know—what the hell—" Anger and incomprehension beat redly behind his eyes. His first thought had been that somehow she was a *man*—but *behind* her—no, it was ridiculous, nothing else about her was masculine, it must be a deformity! In that case he needed to know what it was. A deformity wasn't so bad. He needed to know. Suppressing the turmoil in his mind, he held her down and systematically unwound the blankets, then lifted up her petticoat. Ignoring her dry-eyed sobbing and flailing against him, he felt the protrusion at the bottom of her spine through her underwear. It was about the length of his index finger. It was mushy soft, but it definitely had a bone. It ended in a fleshy flap.

She had stopped threshing. She lay on her face, her petticoats up around her shoulders, crying into the tarpaulin.

Finally it hit him. The "deformity" was the amputated stump of a tail.

She was—or had been at one point—a Kirekuni.

"And I'm surprised you didn't guess it before!"

Crispin realized he must have spoken aloud.

"You pig-stupid imbeciles. I hate all of you. You can't see what's in front of your noses! Go away. Go away."

He scarcely heard her. He sat on his heels, gazing at her in disbelief.

A Kirekuni!

So much for sweet mystery. Oh, if only one thing would turn out how it seemed—

"I've ruined everything," she sobbed quietly. "Now you hate me. I knew it would be like this."

"I didn't guess," Crispin said dully. "Your hair—skin—I *should* have guessed. Why do you hide it?"

"I have to!" She sat up and grabbed for her dress. Her face was wet and pink with tears. She buttoned the faded poplin feverishly over her petticoat, yanked her hair free and shook it out. "How would I get any work without pretending?"

"In the circus where I—"

"Oh, the *circus*. Yes, I could have been a freak! And I don't know about you, but I'd rather conceal what I am than have everybody staring at me!"

"The way they stare at me?"

She sunk her face into her hands. "You don't understand the littlest thing about me!"

"Ah," Crispin said. "But I *know*. I know about you. What are you going to do now?"

He watched her cry without reaching out to comfort her. The thought of touching her was repugnant now. But he would have to be kind. He had promised. The shock was no excuse. Of all peoples, the Kirekunis had the worst reputation for their lack of compassion, their blind obedience to their rulers, and their decadent sexual mores. If Rae came of *that* place, it explained a lot of her mystery. But her nature itself wasn't what horrified him the worst. It was the fact that she had *hidden* it—the physical violence that she'd done to herself, or had someone else do to her. He felt betrayed and sick.

"Can I stay with you, Crispin? Please don't send me away." She took his hand, and remembering the caresses those same fingers had delivered a few minutes ago, he couldn't help pulling away. "Just take me with you. I won't be trouble. Please—"

"Why would you want to keep company with a *freak* like me?" he said angrily.

Hot tears dropped on his fingers as she kissed them. "We're both freaks. We neither of us have any business in this country!"

"Why did you do it to yourself?"

"You understand. You *must* understand. How nice it would be if other people thought you belonged in this country. How nice it'd be if you could really, honestly believe it yourself, even if it was only for a little while." Her hair fell down to hide her face. "You have tremendous physical courage, and if it'd been possible, you would've done the same as I did. So don't even bother pretending to be disgusted."

He forced himself to breathe evenly. "My mother told me never to slug anybody for calling me nigger," he said. "Hell of a woman, my mother, she was as black as the bottom of a river. Words didn't bother *her*. She had other ways of getting her point across. Apparently in Lamaroon they sing, and so on. So it wasn't because of that that she was so quiet. It was because she was a stranger here."

Rae stared down at her crossed ankles. "*My* mother *loved* words. She had me come and read to her when she was dying."

"Is that why you ran away?" From where? Not Kirekune? He could not figure it out.

"She died when I was ten. I ran away when I was eleven."

He could not prevent his eyes from going to her skirts. Her ankles peeked out from under the ruffled hem. If he did not know, he would never have guessed. He *hadn't* guessed. "But *why*?" he asked again. *"Why?"*

She closed her eyes. "Have you ever been angry? With somebody? Enough to hurt them?"

"Course I—"

"And did you?"

Crispin shrugged. "Yes." He was remembering Saul Smithrebel.

"Well, I wasn't ever strong enough to hurt anybody. Except myself." She shrugged.

Bile rose in Crispin's throat. It was too ghastly. The knowledge that this fragile girl had been capable of such terrible self-mutilation made him wary of touching her.

"Queen," he said, standing up. "I—"

Outside, a bird squawked. Another joined in. Crispin stood frozen as the noise spread throughout the immediate forest: twitters, tweets, hoots, and brief burbles of song, a symphony of alarm.

"Someone's coming!"

The rain had stopped. The birds slowly quieted.

"What's going on?" Rae scrambled to her feet.

"Sssh." His straining ears caught the unmistakable noise of a branch pushed out of someone's way, whisking back into wet under-growth. "Yes." Quietly, he swept the blankets and tarps together on the floor, knotting them into an unwieldy bundle. "Quick quick quick now."

Himself, twelve years old, two months after his mother died, standing stiff and straight beside Poppy 2. Red Bob and Kiquat and

Grouser and Harry stood like shadows at their stations around the outside of the circled trucks. The circus was traveling north, along the Cypean border. Local prejudice against "westlanders" had necessitated night-long sentry shifts. You never knew which of the quiet, white-blond, sun-darkened people streaming out after the show might be coming back that night. Once they tried to steal a truck. Other times, it was circus children. In the inner domains, it was believed that gypsies stole babies; that might be right, but Crispin had never seen evidence of it. In his experience it was in the infertile, red and open east, where necessity had crowded out compassion as weeds crowd out flowers, where people would do anything for fat, dark-haired children to raise alongside their own hollow-chested offspring.

Crispin's own father had been an easterner who, sick of his desert home, had taken to the road with Smithrebel's thirteen years ago. So Anuei had said. Every night during the show Crispin could not help searching the upturned faces, looking for those few he would recognize: his relatives.

The gun lay heavy and oil-smelling in his arm. The night was empty, purple-shadowed.

He remembered the way you *knew* when that noise in the sagebrush wasn't a dragonet, or a fox.

Rae laced her boots. The tears had dried on her face. A Kirekuni. "Let's go, Crispin. Let's get out. I don't want them to find us."

Crispin agreed wholeheartedly. But he was not so worried about being caught out in his theft of the food as he was about the *other* dangers he had scented in the hamlet. What was his little bit of thievery, if that was, as he suspected, a village of thieves? Did they perceive themselves as governed by the law at all, these people who lived out on the edge of nowhere? Crispin slid to the rear of the trailer. The tailgate would have to be dropped; there was no other way of escape. He listened with all his body to the small noises of the night.

It was the sibilants of their whispered speech that gave the approaching men away. He beckoned Rae. She was doing better than he'd expected. She slid her feet soundlessly along the planking, and when he passed her the bundle of blankets and food her arms trembled only a little. If she was afraid, she was also in control of herself.

From right behind the tailgate, barely two feet away, a whisper: *"Give us that here—"*

Just as Crispin's hand was about to close on the big latch, he felt something sharp prick the heel of his thumb. He flinched back. Rae stifled a gasp. A piece of metal had been introduced underneath the latch and it was being fiddled about from outside.

All in one instant, Crispin grabbed Rae's wrist, flicked the latch open, and launched himself against the tailgate, intending to smash the intruders to the ground. But the resistance he had counted on was not there. As the heavy wooden slab crashed to the earth, he staggered and lost Rae. Something lashed the back of his neck. As he rolled to his feet he saw Rae being clutched close by a heavy, fair-haired man in a leather jerkin, roughly the size and shape of a boulder. The man's teeth and dagger glinted. The clouds had scattered and the moon rode high in a black-violet sky, shedding a light onto the road which seemed preternaturally strong after months of pitch-black, wet nights. There was another man behind Crispin. Crispin spun and punched him in the diaphragm. As the man's knees buckled, his knife fell, and Crispin snatched it up out of a rut. His own dagger was out of reach in his knapsack—in Valestock he had not worn it because of city rules, and he had not thought to put it back on. *Rae,* girl!—the boulder-man was yammering something about traders—

The third man came around the side of the truck. When he saw Crispin, his expression changed from disgruntlement to shock. In the moment before his hand moved to his dagger sheath, Crispin calculated the risks of turning his back on the boulder-man, decided to go for it, and charged the other would-be thief, slamming him against the side of the truck so hard that he could *feel* the daemon in its cell wake and shiver up some tension in the braced wood of the chassis. " . . . garg," said the man. His mouth was open, and his fingers scrabbled at Crispin's wrists, but Crispin was not thinking clearly, and he did not slacken his grip. *Rae!* He shook the man by the shoulders, so that his head cracked against the wood, and wheeled again to face the boulder.

In the moonlight the man's face was like a big gnarl of wood, split by a smile. Steel hovered at Rae's stomach. Not her throat. *There* was a mark of cruelty and cowardice. *Thank Queen,* he thought inarticulately, too poor for guns—no chance if a daemon gun—

"False pretenses," Rae choked. "He says we come here under false pretenses!"

"The hell is that to do with—"

"I've told him there's nothing in the truck that he might want! He won't believe me!"

The boulder's voice was surprisingly high, with a tone of injured righteousness. "Impostors! Youse enticed our women and left nothing to show, no gifts, not even no name!"

"Entice your *women*?" Crispin exclaimed. "That what they told you? Got my own woman, haven't I? No need for your whores, have I?"

"*Crispin,*" Rae sobbed. She had been holding up well before, but now she seemed understandably terrified. She screeched as the boulder-man's knife pricked her abdomen.

Crispin weighed the second man's knife in his hand. Its owner tried to rise. Absently, Crispin kicked him in the throat. It was not a good blade. He bounced it, trying to find the balance. The boulder's voice became oilier. "But why are youse here? Looking to do a little business, maybe, were youse? Wrong time of year for apples, but—"

"Same kind of business *your* women do when the traders come?" Crispin retorted. "Oh, yes, I'm sure!"

"Youse be a gypsy!" the boulder shot back. "Youse always ready to—"

Without even really thinking about it, Crispin threw the knife. It caught the big man in his right eye and entered an inch and a half before stopping. Some of Rae's hair was caught in the wound; she screamed without stopping as she wrenched out of the suddenly stiff arms. The big man staggered backwards, flailing.

"Oh, hell," Crispin said under his breath, and pulled her past him into the forest at the side of the road, just as the third man stirred and began to wake.

The forest smelled ever crisper and greener as they plunged desperately into the night. Crispin heard the boulder's death gurgles behind them for longer than he would have thought possible.

"Where—are we going?" Rae gasped.

"Dunno," Crispin told her. The wet earth gave squelchily under their feet. They would be leaving a clear trail: their only hope was to get far enough away that the hamleters would not bother coming after them. "Somewhere it won't matter."

She did not ask again. As she hurried along, she pushed her hair out of her face, disentangling it roughly from her eyelashes and lips. It was nerve-wracking how she seemed to trust him. Had he not insulted her? *Why* should she trust him?

"Here, you'll wear yourself out," he told her. "Slow down."

> *For both prophet and priest ply their trade through the land, and have no knowledge.*

>   —Jeremiah 14:18

A Fortunate
Fellow

Fessiery 1893 A.D. / *1209th Year of the Lizard.*
The Raw: 52° N Sector: 3,000 feet

Yoshitaro Achino felt the bullets plow into *Miss Drybones*'s undercarriage. The knowledge that he'd been hit pierced the sweating frenzy of battle. Half a second later Ju's voice came through the speaking tube. "Daemon!"

Yoshi's stomach clenched. For a second he forgot about the other Gorgonette in his sights, and in that moment the Ferupian banked and dived away to safety, leaving the immediate sky empty. The deafening roar of *Miss Drybones*'s daemon engine died away in a matter of seconds, leaving Yoshi with his hands trembling on the stick and the whipcord, Ju shouting incoherently in his ear as the wind boomed over the cockpit. Screamers, fired from the Ferupian antiaircraft guns below, streaked blue, red, and green around the plane. Yoshi dodged the hail of little daemons instinctively. He was in a blue funk.

The KE-111, a two-man biplane, had only one engine, and now the daemon that powered it was dead, eaten by an enemy screamer that had somehow gotten inside the cell housing. All the instruments read zero. They were gliding.

"Going to make a forced landing." Yoshi pushed the stick forward, and they swooped down. Below, no-man's-land sparkled with starved screamers.

"He's still on our tail," Ju barked. "Hold her steady."

In the horrible silence of the dead plane, Yoshi *heard* the tracer bullets leave the rear gun turret.

"Got him," Ju said in exactly the same voice. In his mirrors Yoshi could see the Ferupian kite staggering, its pilot fighting desperately to hold the machine level. The Gorgonette's rudder had been damaged, but its daemon cell was evidently not ruptured, since the propellers were still blurring round. Yoshi held *Miss Drybones* to her glide, and Ju fired again, this time with deadly accuracy, and the Gorgonette wallowed in the air as a blade of its right propeller went spinning.

They had sunk out of the dogfight, and no one was chasing them, even though *Miss Drybones* was a sitting duck: the Ferupians all had enough to do to keep the rest of Yoshi's Wedge off their tails. But Yoshi himself had not the ghost of a chance. He was too far from the Kirekuni lines even to think about swinging back toward home. The mission had been to ground-strafe the Ferupian 83 Squadron's base, to which, scouts' reports said, the 83 had too recently to have moved installed ack-ack guns; so his Wedge had piled out of Anno Ma on a fine winter morning, and all had been going smoothly until they had the bad luck to meet up with a patrol crew of Gorgonettees over no-man's-land. To bring a Queensdog down on top of his own men and fry them behind their barricades was a highly praised achievement—not least because it was so difficult to make a kill while simultaneously dodging ack-ack. Both sets of lines, separated by about two hundred yards, were equipped with antiaircraft guns, so you were just as likely to get riddled with bullets by your own side as to get screamer-infested by the enemy. Nonetheless, each Wedge of Ishigonara's 20th fought over no-man's-land at least once a month.

The unholy din of screamers had faded now, but that was only because *Miss Drybones*'s descent had taken them behind the Ferupian lines. Ju was shouting in Yoshi's ear, berating him, demanding why the hell he couldn't try to bring them down in no-man's-land, where Kirekuni troops might find them, and if not them, then the plane with its valuable instruments and guns. Pilots were dispensable; aircraft less so. Yoshi didn't answer. A cold clarity had come over him. He had felt it a few times before in his life, and he knew what it was. *He did not want to die.* Therefore, he was not going to take a single risk which might lessen his chances of getting out of this alive.

He knew he was a coward, and he didn't care. Flight Command

could sing for their kite parts. He had seen the survival statistics for pilots shot down in no-man's-land. There wasn't ten feet of unrutted ground. Landing was impossible. You ended up in *flames.*

On the other hand, nobody shot down behind the Ferupian lines was ever heard of again. *But* (thought Yoshi desperately, at twenty-five hundred feet, with sweat drenching his pullover and jacket) that didn't mean the captured pilots weren't sitting in a cosy prison somewhere in the land of the Queen, dicing and writing their memoirs! Not a half-bad way to spend the rest of your term!

He banked, conserving height. Below, the front lines were a hilly tone-on-tone morass of rock and soil, almost white in the winter sun, netted with ramparts and jeep tracks and barracks. But it must thin out soon. In the hazy east he could see flat ground: the desertified Raw under Ferupian control.

"What it comes down to is that you're a fucking awful pilot, Achino," he muttered, poking his head out into the slipstream, his eyes watering, to scan the ground below. (Ju agreed, loudly, through the speaking tube.) The terrain was getting worse. There was nowhere to land. Now the ramparts had been replaced by sprawling wooden ordinance dumps—favorite ground-strafing targets of the SAF command, and therefore equipped with screamer guns, which opened up as Yoshi glided over. He must have been the easiest target that ever waltzed into their sights. He made the sluggish *Miss Drybones* dance to the best of her ability, but inevitably, he felt a series of thunks on his port wing, and Ju shouted through the tube:

"We're hit! You son of a whore!" His voice was thick with fear and fury. Explosions deafened Yoshi as Ju used his revolver to pick off the slavering, multilegged daemons scrambling up the wing. "Bastard dog, no-balls coward, incompetent—"

Yoshi reached up with his tail and ripped the speaking tube off his helmet. The wind cocooned him in its voiceless roar.

Miss Drybones's nose propeller had slowed almost to a stop. The dials were all dead, but he estimated he was at about four hundred feet. At least he'd gotten past that lot of screamers. He supposed he could try to land on the sand, fuck the tree stumps, right here where new ramparts were being constructed in readiness for the day when the Ferupian troops at the front would be pushed back this far. The men on the ground had seen him; they were shouting and running.

Even in the middle of his calculations of crosswind and speed and how much distance he'd need to taxi, Yoshi got a certain pleasure from scaring the shit out of them. It was true, Ferupians were all cowards.

At least, he believed so until he saw them dragging some kind of a wheeled firearm into position. Pale orange flared at its breech. An F-99—a ground-based long-distance flamethrower. One of the few weapons the Ferupians possessed that fired something other than daemons. And one of their least pleasant.

Ju was thumping on *Miss Drybones*'s fuselage, trying to alert Yoshi to the danger. Yoshi nodded. They had to put down. Just had to put down and prove they were harmless. Then they would put the F-99 up. *How am I doing, Commander Ishigonara? If you saw me now, you'd really have reason to call me* miki-noko!

Then Ju opened up *Miss Drybones*'s rear guns, and in an instant all was confusion, and the rattle of bullets, and barbarian voices yelling as fire arced across *Miss Drybones*'s nose. As Yoshi made his second pass and came in to land, he felt heat on the back of his neck and realized that the tail was burning. So *that* was why the rudder hadn't been responding! Significant! Ju might be burned alive. "Fuck," he said aloud, and brought her down fast. Touch; bump; touch; taxi. The terrain was impossible. It was all he could do, dragging at the stick, to keep her from yawing over. For a couple of minutes, while the fire crackled behind him, he thought he was actually going to make it. And then she was over on her nose in the sandy soil, and there was a terrific crunching of wood and metal, and something that looked suspiciously like the rudder sailed past the cockpit, and despite the restraining grip of his harness he lurched forward, cracking his head on the metal sights apparatus. He scarcely even felt frantic fingers unfastening his harness. He scarcely heard Ju grunting curses as he dragged him clear.

He woke on hard ground with fire shooting through his back. He struggled upright and nearly screamed. Then he choked it down. Disciples didn't scream!

As he got to his feet he realized that only a moment had passed. *Miss Drybones* lay with her tail in the air and her nose in a half-constructed rampart, burning yellowly in the brilliant sun. Men swarmed as close as they could get to her, heaving buckets of sand and earth at the flames. KE-111s were constructed almost completely of metal, of which the Ferupians were desperately short; of course they wanted to salvage her. Where was Ju? Had he escaped? Yoshi swung around, stumbling dizzily, to see whether it would be possible to make a getaway.

A semicircle of uniforms watched him from a distance of about five feet. One of them was holding Ju by both arms. "Game's up," Ju said, his face twisted with pain. "We've got to die honorably. Now, before they take you! I'm bound—I can't do it—do it, do it now—"

One of the Ferupians stepped toward Yoshi and barked something unintelligible. Yoshi shook his head, his mind ticking at high speed. He was a pilot and a Wedgehead: technically he was Ju's superior, so it was his duty to command Ju to commit suicide, and then he, Yoshi, must in his turn draw his knife and stab himself through the heart before they could reach him. But in the *unofficial* hierarchy of Ishigonara's 20th, Jumone Fray, by virtue of his swaggering pride and boastful manner, was far superior to Yoshi, though he wore only a gunner's wings. So Yoshi must obey Ju and kill both of them now, before they were captured and forced to tell everything they knew.

But what, even under torture, could they say that the Ferupians might find of use? That Ishigonara's 20th Flight, out of Anno Ma, was so high in the esteem of SAF command that Yoshi had always been miserably aware he was a disgrace to it? That Ishigonara took a vastly unfair amount of credit for his flight's successes—that he was really just a career bureaucrat irascible with arthritis and heartburn, trying to hold on until the 20th was rotated out of the combat zone? That the madam of Anno Marono Chadou was called Amita? That there had been a brawl between SAF officers and SAPpers last week which resulted in two men dead and thirty confined to base? What could the Enemy conceivably do with that kind of information? Neither Yoshi nor Ju, in their years of active duty, had ever gone farther from Base 20 than Anno Marono. They knew no more than that of the Great Problem. *Yoshi's* war was the combat pilot's exhausting routine of takeoffs, landings, kite checks, and daemon coddling, with death pressing stiflingly close on all sides, all the time: the death of opponents, the death of friends. Win or lose, it mattered not in the least. All a Disciple had to do was keep going to the best of his ability. And two years of thrice-weekly forays, occasionally relieved by a bout of pitch-black sex with whoever wanted it badly enough to approach him, had tired Yoshi to the bone. He was tired of being a Disciple.

But not tired enough to die like this.

The Ferupian sergeant shouted at him again and gestured. The Ferupians were all tanned, heavily muscled fellows, squat as trolls. Next to them brawny Ju looked tall and willowy.

Disciples don't scream!

His hand drifted almost of its own volition down toward his thigh knife.

Two of the Ferupians grabbed him by the arms. "Oh, by the Significant," he said in relief. He sagged in their grip.

Ju's face contorted with thwarted passion. "Have you never done anything honorable in your life, *miki*?" he shouted. As the rest of the Ferupians closed in around him, he threw himself from side to side, thrashing free. The commanding sergeant whirled around, yelling. For a moment Yoshi could not see Ju. Then Ju lolled ungracefully to the ground, hair fluttering into wide-open eyes. His helmet rolled clear. Yoshi smelled fresh blood, and saw it, spreading down Ju's chest, blackening the tan leather jacket which the gunner had cleaned with such care.

And instead of being punished for acting out of turn, the private who had knifed Ju was being *congratulated*. Was it possible? Smiles broke like sunlight over the Ferupians' faces. They kicked Ju's body, grinning at Yoshi and pointing to it. One man even strode up to him, grabbed his face, and turned it in the right direction to make sure he saw.

The sergeant shouted at Yoshi, trying to direct his attention to the still-burning *Miss Drybones*. What did he *want*? Yoshi said loudly, "I don't speak Ferupian. But I surrender."

With some difficulty, he lifted his hands above his head. The men gripping his wrists held on tightly. "I surrender," he said, looking first at one of them, then at the other. "I surrender." Their expressions were blank. He shouted at all of the squinting, red, ugly faces. "I surrender! Do you understand? *Surrender!* Give up! Pax!"

When he joined up, back in Okimachi, he had taken the standard oath that he would commit suicide before he let himself fall into the hands of the Enemy. But even then, he had known he didn't mean it. Without even having looked into the guns of a Gorgonette, he had known that he was a coward.

"My name is Yoshi Achino! I'm an officer in Ishigonara's 20th flight of the fifty-two north sector of the SAF, and *I am surrendering*!"

The sergeant looked at him. Yoshi had the feeling he was really seeing him for the first time. Behind him, the construction detail was finally succeeding in smothering the flames on *Miss Drybones*'s wings and fuselage. Ju's body lay still, ignored now.

"Honorable surrender taken," the sergeant said then in halting but comprehensible Okimachi dialect. His eyes were the same bluish shade as whey, like a ghost's. Yoshi could see the tiredness in them. "If officer waits—apology, guard necessary—jeep take him to place of translators. Safety assured. Ferupians understand Kirekuni officer's oath same as life."

The sun beat down. Yoshi could smell daemon smoke from the demogorgon he had soothed every night, that had already been dead when it burned with *Miss Drybones*. He laughed aloud.

"Apologies, explain amusement, apologies," said the sergeant suspiciously.

"I'm a deserter. Do you know what that means for a Disciple? I've heard that your soldiers break their contracts quite regularly and suffer no consequences. But for us it's different. Among us, a soldier who deserts is mourned as a dead soldier. And if he's found, he *will* be a dead soldier."

In another life, that was what he said. In real life, he just smiled the brilliant smile that had made him the darling of his mother's whorehouse. "Pardon me. I was just laughing at the awful terribleness of your Kirekuni."

By the time the jeep came and took him to the "place of translators," Yoshi was nearly delirious with pain and thirst. Ju—brave Ju—had wrenched his shoulders in dragging him out of the cockpit, and the bulge where his skull had crunched with the inside of his helmet was too tender to touch. He'd had to throw away his helmet because his hands were chained, and he could neither wear nor carry it. The chains were "for honor only," as the sergeant had assured him. Yoshi had never heard of there being honor in getting your arms fastened behind your back, but with Ferupians, everything was different. Unable to resort to sign language, he hadn't been able to make either of his guards see that he wanted a drink. They passed a bottle back and forth in the front seat of the jeep, laughing loudly and ignoring their captive, even when he did foolish, gurgling imitations of a man enjoying a drink of water. Before the jeep had got very deep into Ferupian territory, he knew that they did understand he was thirsty, but they were ignoring him because they despised him.

Oddly, he felt slightly better when he realized that. By now the fact of his desertion was hitting him hard. It meant that even if the Ferupians did not kill him he would never be able to go home again. His mother and sisters would reject him. They might even turn him in. That possibility required consideration, at some future date. But contempt was what he expected from the soldiers. It was what he, in their place, would have felt. He had failed to live up to the soldiers' concept of the way a pilot should act. If they showed him anything other than dislike—*then* he would know he was done for.

The Ferupian Raw was rolling and barren, dotted with trees and ancient-looking wooden structures.

Yoshi tried to distract himself from his parched throat by speculating about the uses to which the Ferupians were putting their territory. This was very different from the Raw he knew. The Army of the Significant did things properly: as they inched forward across the plain, they razed everything and erected new towns, villages, and irrigation systems. They then imported plains people—the Chadou—and set them to work catering to the needs of the army. It was called extending the empire. By contrast, the Ferupian Raw looked like a wasteland. Yet he suspected that many of the firebombed buildings were secretly in use, and that the Ferupians tore nothing down for strategic reasons. He saw the point, and admired it, though it showed that they had a pitiful lack of confidence in their air force's ability to defend their territory. Commander Ishigonara liked to say: *They don't make Ferupians the way they used to, boys! When was the last time a sortie came into our airspace? One could nearly feel out of sorts on their behalf!*

We're winning, we really are, Yoshi thought exultantly. *Look at how empty this place is.*

Then his stomach did a sickening flip-flop.

They're winning.

Whatever they chose to do with him, his fortunes were those of the Queensdogs now.

After perhaps two hours, during which Yoshi estimated they covered twenty to thirty miles, the jeep stopped outside a heavily strafed tower within sight of more trees in one place than he had seen in his entire life. Ordinarily he would have stared in fascination. Now the—*forest*?—barely registered on his thirsty misery. Yet relief was not far off. The man whose office was sunk three flights of stairs into the ground beneath the tower, who wore three multicolored bars on either side of his wide gray chest, said, by way of a haggard Kirekuni translator: "My boy, you look half-dead and filthy. After we talk, a hot bath, perhaps?"

Automatically Yoshi's hand went to his thigh. But they had taken his knife. The office was a box-shaped cavern hewn out of the ground rock, as large and gray as its inhabitant, lit shadowless by lights brighter than Yoshi had ever seen except in the houses of nobles on the old-city hill. The floor was uneven, but the corners of walls and ceiling formed perfect right angles. A decorative waterfall tinkled through an arrangement of copper pipes in one corner. The place was not like anywhere Yoshi had ever seen in Kirekune. Were the Ferupians poor? Or did they just not believe in beauty? Yoshi, the gray man, and the Kirekuni woman all sat on hard wooden chairs. Guards stood to attention by the door curtains.

"What would you like to drink?" the translator said. She spoke nearly simultaneously with the gray man. Yoshi had no idea how she did it. He blinked and tried to smile.

"Uh—wine. I'd really like a glass of wine."

The gray man laughed, it seemed for an unwarrantedly long time, and shook his head. The translator said in her soft, dead voice: "You are in Ferupe. We drink ale. I will have a mug of southern brew brought."

Yoshi bobbed his head politely. The gray man laughed again.

"I find the manners of Kirekunis most amusing," the woman translated. "Tonight you will sleep under this tower, in a deluxe suite.

This is Chressamo, the headquarters of Intelligence for the Lovoshire Parallel. You are not a prisoner. You are an officer and my guest."

"May I know your name, sir?" Yoshi asked the gray man, remembering to look at him and not at the translator.

This time it seemed as if the man would explode with laughter. He shook, his eyes ran, and he clamped his hands on his large knees, straightening up only when a servant's footsteps rang on the stone and glasses of foaming golden beer were placed on the small round table between them. "Ahhh." He grinned, winked at Yoshi, and drank deeply. Yoshi followed suit, closing his eyes for a moment in relief.

"There is absolutely no reason for you to know my name," the translator said. No beer had been brought for her. She held her elbows out from her sides, her hands in her lap, like a bird's wings. "After today you will never see me again. I am sending you a hundred miles north of here to 80 Squadron. They have had experience with Kirekuni traitors . . . drink, drink!" Her voice was low and expressionless, where the gray man's tone was genial. The contrast was eerie. "You're not drinking!"

Yoshi startled. Obediently, he raised the glass to his mouth and swigged the bitter liquid.

"Isn't the ale excellent? As I was saying, they have seen men like you before. Chissa—" the translator stopped and listened for a moment. She answered the gray man in harsh, glottal Ferupian, then turned back to Yoshi and said, "Eighty Squadron had a Kirekuni on their rosters for six years before he was killed. You won't find it difficult to fit in."

"Was he killed in action, sir?" Yoshi said warily.

"No. In a fight with other men of the squadron. Over a matter of a girl. I believe his balls were kicked to a pulp and his tail torn off. You would do well to be careful." The gray man watched Yoshi, obviously anticipating a reaction.

Yoshi drank again. The alcohol made him bolder. He leaned forward and looked into the translator's eyes, making it clear he was speaking to her and not *through* her. "Mademoiselle, please. Is he telling the truth? Am I to be spared, to fight on Ferupe's side?"

Something like pity flickered in her eyes. "Your life is yours to defend, Disciple," she said. Her voice sounded even fainter without the rumble of Ferupian behind it. "You have no one but yourself to blame for your defection."

"If they are recruiting prisoners of war they must be very short of trained pilots. Is that so?"

The gray man's eyes narrowed. "I'm tired of you," the translator said in a frightened voice. "Out." She added hurriedly, "He's only a sergeant, Disciple. This isn't his office. It's mine." *But there's nothing Kirekuni in the place!* Yoshi thought. "And I answer only to Sostairs— the colonel of this place. All the officers interview their prisoners in my office, for the effect of the thing. He doesn't have the *authority* to kill anyone. It's not like it is in the field." Her mouth worked.

The guards descended on Yoshi. He judged it wisest to cooperate. As he was frog-marched across the cavern, out of the corner of his eye he saw the gray man yank the translator out of her chair and pull her onto his lap. As she sank down Yoshi saw that her dress fell in a clean line. She had amputated her tail. Or had it amputated for her.

That night he slept dreamlessly for fifteen hours between linen sheets, beneath the ground. The next day he spent beneath the sun in the back of an open truck. As darkness fell they were still rumbling north. Screamers traced patterns like fireworks on the horizon. Yoshi drowsed, trying not to fall against any of the other men, Ferupians all, who sat blanket-wrapped along the sides of the truck. Vivid images swam in his mind: the women of his childhood, his mother's "girls," with their eyes like black olives and tails wrapped in bright ribbon. Snatches of their voices came so loudly in his head that each phrase nearly woke him up. After them came the parade of men who had each so briefly held a place in his heart, after he chose the worst possible way of escaping that world of bonbons and chamber music and purse-lipped penny-pinching. He hadn't wanted to become a workhorse, a benign unprotesting butt for the women's jokes like his uncle June. So at the age of eighteen he had entered the Disciples. He was now twenty-one, and he had not gone one day without regretting that decision.

Since his posting to Ishigonara's 20th, he had come close to resigning himself to dying in combat. Now, however, after this latest disaster, cowardice throbbed like energy in him.

He was wide-awake and he did not want to die. His fingers and toes tingled in the moonlight and all of the sleeping Ferupian soldiers were handsome, especially the fair ones.

> *Oh, the animals I saw every day from that cockpit! . . .*
> *What a fortunate fellow I am, I kept telling myself.*
> *Nobody has ever had such a lovely time as this!*

—Roald Dahl

The Farthest Darkness

Marout 1893 A.D. *The Wraithwaste*

"I think we're lost," Crispin said, chewing his lump of cheese slowly. "I don't know why we didn't turn back when we had the chance. I must have been out of my mind."

Waiting for Rae to reply, he squinted up through the thickety undergrowth, searching for some break in the flat gray clouds. There was none. If only he had a compass! He could not remember when the green fertility of the Apple Hills forest had given way to this living graveyard. It must have happened very slowly—or maybe all at once, overnight, while he was asleep. The forest smelled dusty, as if nothing had lived here for millennia—and during the day it was as silent as a desert. Not a single bird gave tongue, though they sang at night. They were ordinary birds, he had seen them, but they sounded like boys and girls. Their voices meandered over the snortings and crashings of wild animals in the pines, an orchestra of wildness. The stink of daemons clogged the air. He felt daemon claws on his skin all the time, curious talons of power brushing his neck, and it took all he had not to blow up at Rae. She wasn't the reason they were in such a fix. In fact she had practically nothing to do with it. It was all his fault.

Most of the pines looked dead. Shocks of brown needles fell into pieces at a touch. Crispin had given up trying to get the splinters out of his clothes and hair. Rae, on the other hand, tended her appearance industriously, braiding her hair into long shiny ropes and winding them onto the back of her head, all ready to be dusted over again until it looked like an unglazed coil pot. Since losing her hairpins in the flight from the truck, she had been using twigs.

She was combing her hair now, kneeling on a mossy stone at the edge of the stream. The black curtain of it swayed over the water. The stream was a ribbon of greenery and life winding through the pines, full of fish that were absurdly difficult to catch. Crispin and Rae made their bivouac beside a different stream every night. The nights were the worst he had ever experienced. When he was walking, he didn't have to think. But at night, his worries sat like hunger in his stomach, keeping him from sleep. Where was he going? Where he was taking Rae, who had given herself so completely into his care? It had only been eleven days—they *couldn't* have gone very far—yet he had not seen any signs of civilization since they entered the pines. Once, six biplanes, laden low with supplies for the troops at the war front, had glided west beneath the clouds. He had stared after them, knowing it would be futile to shout.

The road along which they had come from Valestock must continue somewhere in the forest, and Crispin presumed it led to the war front. At this stage, even that would be better than nothing. But they had left the road at a tangent, and no amount of zigzagging had helped them recover it.

And there was something else, which he did not think Rae had noticed, even though she had glimpsed the splinteron in the holding cell, something few girls would have seen. Certain trees shimmered as if they were surrounded by a ring of heat. It was not so much that the effect jumped out at you, as the way it *didn't*. On a couple of occasions he had gotten a fix on these illusions and tried to approach them, but somehow he found himself turning aside, and before he knew what was happening the place would be far behind him, a flicker as if of movement among the trees. At such times he always felt *watched*. Of course it was nonsense: he *was* being watched, yes indeed, by invisible daemons, hundreds of them, but not by anything else. Yet he could not stop looking for human footprints in the dead needles, or blazes like the ones he himself made on the tree trunks to ensure they did not go in circles, carved by the hands of strangers, woods-folk.

He was almost grateful at night when the daemons crept close to him, crawling over his skin, drawn by his bodily warmth nearly to materialize, because it distracted him from his worries. Uncollared daemons could be dangerous—but unlike collared ones, only if provoked. He had to concentrate on fighting the impulse to brush them off.

It might have been easier if he had been able to talk to Rae. But she was even more of a mystery now than she had been the night they first met at the Old Linny. The fact that she was Kirekuni explained her not at all. She had not cried since they entered the Wraithwaste. Her cheery unflappability, her refusal to listen to his worries—it was all an act, he knew it, but he could not tell what was underneath. Looking at her now, voluptuous in the shirt and trousers he had loaned her, he could not believe he had ever touched her. Neither of them ever made reference to what happened between them before the men from the hamlet broached the truck. Crispin had constantly to search for signs of her Kirekuni heritage in her face to remind himself of his stupefying discovery.

Now she said, "You know we can't go back. You're a murderer, Cris. They'd string you up. Anywhere in the western domains."

"At least in jail I'd get regular meals. I'd be willing to die for one real meal, I think." He swallowed the last of the cheese and rubbed his stomach regretfully. The hunger pangs were arrows of pain. Aware that they had to conserve their provisions, he pulled a dried apple out of his knapsack and bit into it. The texture was that of old leather, but it filled his mouth with sweetness. "I don't understand why you're not more worried."

She shrugged. "I trust you."

"You don't understand how stupid that is. I keep trying to tell you."

She merely gave a tinkling laugh. The ends of her hair caught up drops from the surface of the stream. The liquid speech of water and stones made up for her silence: she was a creature of the morning, she could not be expected to answer in human speech.

It may have been at that moment that Crispin fell in love. He knew in some corner of himself what was happening. Shaking his head to clear it, he reached into the bag for another dried apple.

Then he stopped. "There's a demogorgon right behind me. Quite a large one. Can you see it?"

"A kind of shimmering?"

"Yeah, it would be." Crispin shuddered and, all in one movement, stood up and spun around to confront nothing.

Downstream, where the black water curved into the trees, a fish jumped. The daemon vanished into the air with a tumult of power.

The exact nature of daemons' relations with the visible world was unclear to him, Millsy had said sometime long ago. Unmaterialized, did they exist in the air? On another plane altogether? In physical places, like earth, or water, or the bodies of animals? No doubt there were trickster women who knew the answers, who could dispel the myths that made daemon handling far more difficult, no doubt, than it needed to be. But such secrets were not for the heads of men.

Crispin's scalp tingled. He bit into the apple and drove his fingers through his hair, scratching.

"Are we still in Ferupe, do you think?" Rae asked. She shook back her hair and started to plait it.

"Hurry up," Crispin said. "Course we are."

But suddenly he was not sure. If they were no longer in Ferupe, that could explain a good deal. The Wraithwaste . . . at what point did it stop being Ferupian? Those places in the trees at which you could not look, no matter how you tried . . . "The Wraithwaste is Ferupian. That's why we're at war."

"Some places don't have any nationality. Some places just are."

"Oh, now you're talking through your hat," Crispin said.

She lifted her hands behind her head, looping her braid around itself. "No, I'm not," she said around a mouthful of twigs. She never had had much of a sense of humor, and recently she seemed to have none. "I'm saying what I think. And now I'll say some more. This place is stranger than anywhere I've ever been. And, Crispin, there are people here. I know it. It's just that they haven't let us see them."

"You're crazy."

"I think we're getting near a place of trickster women."

Crispin sighed. "The trickster women. Yes, of course! That's exactly who I want to approach with my hat in my hand! Take us in! Care for us! Feed us! I know you're kindly old girls—"

"Oh, shut up," Rae said violently. "Let's see you come up with a better idea, then!"

"I don't think trickster women even *exist*. They're a story you females cooked up to try and prove something."

"Where do daemons come from, then?"

"How should I know? Maybe daemons don't exist, either—maybe they're a mass hallucination! Maybe *civilization* is a mass hallucination, maybe Ferupe and Kirekune and the war is all a dream you and I had last night! We think we remember having pasts! We think we remember being apart! But in fact this is all there's ever been, we're gonna be alone here forever and ever—"

Reflexively, both of them looked around at the impenetrable mossy thickets.

After a moment Rae said, "I never thought there could be a place without people. I never . . . Maybe I was wrong."

The brook sang softly to itself. Somehow the sound did not lessen the endless silence of the forest, but emphasized it, as lettering points up the whiteness of a piece of paper. Rae's fingers had stopped moving in her hair. She looked frightened. It tore at Crispin's heart.

"Of course there're people here," he said, less confidently than he had meant to. "All we have to do is find them. And we're wasting time right now." He picked their bags up and snapped his fingers. "Come on. Your hair looks just as good down."

"Does it really? I'll leave it down, then."

He stood impassively as she shook her head a couple of times, freeing the braids, then rolled up the trousers he had lent her and splashed across the stream to join him.

They walked in silence. The air was cold and dry, but Crispin grew hot from walking and tied his coat around his waist. The pines stood far enough apart that it was not necessary to force a path through them. Their trunks were practically branchless for twenty or thirty feet—like flaky pillars holding up a ceiling of interlaced boughs. Soft dead needles carpeted the ground, and brambles and puffball mushrooms grew around the bases of the trees. Little collections of skeletons lay half-concealed by fungi-encrusted fallen trunks. In some places, the green-stained bones were piled into knee-high cairns: the refuse collections of the largest and most fastidious daemons. Crispin walked a few paces behind Rae. He had heard too many stories of travelers losing each other in broad daylight in places like this to let her out of his sight. Apparently she had heard some of the same stories, for she never stopped glancing over her shoulder at him. The fifth or sixth time he caught her looking, he made a face at her.

She burst into nervous laughter. "Oh, by the Queen, Cris. Don't do that!"

He crossed his eyes and let his jaw hang.

"Aaaah!" She sagged against a tree trunk. "I can't help thinking something's got into you when you do that!"

There was a note of real fear in her voice. He returned his face to normal. "Well, we can't stop now; it isn't even the middle of the morning."

"Yes . . ." She did not move. "Crispin, I'm afraid. There's nobody. And there's so many daemons. I know you think I can't feel them, but I can. And you . . . you . . ."

Her head was buried in the arm that rested against the tree trunk; her shoulders quivered. She seemed to be inviting his touch.

"Girl. I'm doing the best I can. What do you want?"

"I want—" She gasped. "I don't know what I want. But I do know it's pointless to go on. There's no end to this waste. We'll never reach Kirekune. And yet we can't stop, can't stop—"

If they were trying to reach Kirekune, this was the first Crispin had heard of it. He suppressed the slur that leapt to his tongue. "So we won't go on! We'll try and turn back, although I doubt—"

"No! No! You don't understand. We're both going to die anyway. Why did I leave Valestock? We're all going to die."

Alarms went off in Crispin's head. Never since he had known her had she confessed to weakness. This was what he had dreaded most, all these days. He said robustly: "While there's life there's hope."

"I'm not holding you responsible, Crispin! You've been wonderful. Absolutely wonderful. But—but . . . I just don't think I can go on any farther."

Crispin went to her. "Are you sick? Are you tired? We'll stop right here for a day, maybe two, you can rest. I'll try and kill a rabbit for us—I used to be pretty good with the throwing knife—"

She laughed a trifle hysterically. "You still are! But rabbits aren't such easy targets as men!" She lifted her head, her long hair spilling back. "I can go on, of course I can! Oh, Queen, I've been playing the part of a silly female for so long that I can't stop, but I can't help feeling it's pointless, because there's really only one important thing in all the world, *one* thing. Do you understand?"

He could not make her go on in this state. He made her sit down on the ground, in the pine needles, with her back against the tree on which she had been leaning. The brown musk of crushed puffballs rose. She coughed. Crispin dropped his knapsack and sat down opposite her. "It's all right, I promise. We'll have a rest, and then you'll—"

"No, let me explain! I have to explain!"

He closed his eyes. "Explain what?"

"Queen . . . There're certain things I've known ever since I was a child. I used to try and tell people sometimes. It's called evangelizing. But you can't help it, really. You want so badly to tell someone else, so they know, too. I left off when I realized nobody understands. But you—I feel like I can't go any longer . . ." Her words trailed off. "Since I left the Mansion . . ."

"A mansion," Crispin said. "So you *are* nobility. You never would tell me your family name."

"I'm *not* nobility! That's not it at all!"

He touched her hand, silencing her. "Start at the beginning."

"All right." She drew a deep breath. "All right. My aunt owned a whorehouse in Okimachi—she may still, for all I know. That's where my mother grew up. My father was the son of merchants. My name is Achino—in Kirekuni that's *ash*, not the tree, but what's left over from a fire. Rae Ash. I've been going by Clothwright for years, but I—I didn't want to lie to you."

"But you did lie to me," Crispin said, suppressing the high note of unreason that threatened to creep into his voice. "You didn't tell me you grew up in a cult."

"How do you—"

"It's true, isn't it? Just say yes."

"You're not as stupid as you look, Crispin Kateralbin!" Then she seemed to crumple. "Or is it that obvious?"

"Just putting two and two together," Crispin said. "They tend to add up to four." His voice fell flat and loud on the silence of the forest. Once again he had the feeling of being watched. He could barely keep from twisting around.

"All right. It's true," Rae said.

"*Which* cult? The Nihilists? The Apocalypists? Did you help them set that fire in Valestock? Have I been your dupe all along?"

"I wouldn't set foot in an Apocalypist house if they *paid* me! I'm a child of the Dynasty."

"Can't say I've heard of them."

"The *Glorious* Dynasty. It's the only cult that receives true revelations. That's why they don't need to advertise, like the Apocalypists do. See here, Crispin. This is how I was taught it." Like a schoolchild, she folded her hands in her lap. "Everyone in the civilized lands—Ferupe, Kirekune, Cype, Izte Kchebuk'ara, the Mim, Eo Ioria, the Pacific islands—is descended from your Royals. As the Ferupian influence expanded over the centuries, the webs of kinship that lead, by however circuitous a path, back to the Monarch, spread, too—through rape, *droit de seigneur*, polygamy, miscegenation. The Significant Lizards of Kirekune are also related to the Ferupian Royal family, and intermarriage continued until the beginning of the war. When, around the tenth century, the Kirekunis began to expand *their* empire, history repeated itself on the other side of the continent. By the end of the eighteenth century, if not earlier, both the western and eastern hemispheres were infected with Royal blood. You and I, and everyone in the world, are distantly related to each other and to the Queen. To be human is to be Royal."

She paused for breath.

"Thus, anything which affects the Queen affects us to a lesser degree, just as a tug on a knot makes all the threads leading out of it vibrate. This is evidenced by the way in which in the last century, as the monarchy declined, society has also declined, giving rise to decadent customs, widespread fear of the future, and, simultaneously, the rapid development of new and hideous twists on daemon technology, which in their turn cause the war to escalate further. All this can have but one result: the death of the Queen."

Crispin started. Her singsong voice had almost hypnotized him, but that jerked him out of his trance. "That's the most unpatriotic, traitorous thing—"

"But death—death has no lesser degree. Death is simply death." Her voice quivered. "And so when the Queen dies—as must inevitably happen—and she has no direct descendant who can inherit her responsibilities at the center of the knot of humanity—why, then, we must all die with her. No one knows what shape the apocalypse will come in. All that has been revealed to us is that it will come."

"But—" Crispin spluttered. "Why is the Queen the knot? Why not the Lizard Significant? You said they were related—it makes no sense—"

"Because the Queen is directly descended from Thraziaow, the first King ever! Because—because that's the way it is, do you hear! The way it is!"

Crispin could not take his eyes off her.

"The war has already rendered the Queen unable to bear a child. It will kill her soon. Maybe we have twenty years; maybe ten; maybe two." Rae's evident belief in what she was saying made each of her words ring with conviction, like Millsy's when he spoke of daemons. And why shouldn't they? She, too, was speaking of what she knew. Only in her voice there was an element of despair. "Maybe she'll die tomorrow. I'm not privy to the secrets of the court. And that's why I can't—anymore. I just can't. I had to tell you."

To Crispin it seemed impossible, absurd, that she should start to cry now. He almost laughed. He caught her in his arms and held her close. "Oh, Rae. Oh, Rae, Rae. Is that all. Is that all it ever was? It's not true. Culties are crazy. It sounds slick, but it isn't based on anything, anything at all. And to think you've been plagued by lies like that ever since you were a kid!"

"But it isn't lies." She was crying in his arms, but not holding onto him. "I can't make anyone understand, not even you. I don't know the right *words*!"

He lifted her up, looked into her tear-stained face. He wanted to kiss her and comfort her; but that would be unforgivably irresponsible. Any sympathy at all would be an implicit agreement with her crazy cultie theory. It would be a validation of her baseless despair. He pushed her upright and said roughly, "Stop it. It's your nerves. And if you *know* it's your nerves, you're all right, see what I mean?" He mopped off her face with the edge of his sleeve. She did not resist. "Used to happen to me all the time. Waiting in the performers' entrance, when I was just beginning on the flying trapezes. I'd think about how easy it would be to fuck up and break my neck, and all of a sudden I couldn't go on. I'd just start bawling. Well, I was only a kid. It was lucky for me I had Herve, that was my old man, to knock me into shape. First he'd slap me on both cheeks—*pow, pow*—and it'd be such a shock I'd stop. The audience couldn't hear anything because of the band out front. Then he'd say 'Hold still, child,' and put some powder on my nose. If I only had some powder, I'd fix your face, too." He looked at her, narrowing his eyes. "See what I mean? See what I mean? Circus and music hall aren't that different, are they?"

Her whole body shook with a sigh. "No, they're not."

"There, see? You're all right now." He stood up and pulled her to her feet. She would not look at him. "We have a long way to go. Come on."

"But to where?" she murmured as she buttoned up her coat. "To where?"

"Rae—"

"No. I'm sorry. Sorry about that. I think you're right, this place *is* getting to me!"

"Could happen to anyone."

She unbuttoned her coat all the way down again. "But it doesn't happen to you! I wish I was like you! You're so steady! You're so confident!" She bit her nails. Crispin felt flabbergasted. Finally, he slapped her gently on the back.

"We really do have to get going."

She was silent, her head bowed, as they started to walk.

And dozens of miles of haphazardly crowded pines and winding streams amplified the silence between them. Crispin's boot crushed through a fox's scoured skull. The faint sonic whine of an airplane made him look up.

Ten days later. The end of Marout. The Wraithwaste

"Oh, the lovelies!" Rae breathed.

Crispin could not speak. For the first time since entering the Wraithwaste—indeed, for the first time in his life—he was seeing daemons materialize in their natural habitat. The ground fell away suddenly from the place where they stood concealed in the trees. A stream poured down over exposed rocks to form the pool below, then, wider and darker, flowed out of the other side of the dell. Bright sparks of color flittered over the surface of the pool. On the banks there were snowberry bushes and holly, white berries and red mingling so closely they seemed to grow from the same branches. Small pink flowers misted the rocks around the fall. Around the pool grew yellow flags.

And the daemons!

Some lounged in the grass, looking like families having their Sunday picnic in the park, except that none of them stood more than two feet high, and all were naked. They yammered in their curious language of odd phrases and advertising slogans, served each other little delicacies on plates made of woven pine needles, finger-combed each other's hair. These more human daemons fascinated Crispin, yet repelled him, like Millsy's pets, whom the sentimental old trickster had dressed in children's clothes. Other, smaller ones sat on the branches of the pines, picking termites out of the bark with long, monkeylike fingers. And those that darted and hummed over the water, aimless as mayflies, but the size of crows—those made him want to echo Rae: "Oh, the lovelies!" They had iridescent wings. They had bodies like adult men and women. Unlike the daemons on the banks, who were mostly dull in color, the fliers came in all the hues of the rainbow. Their voices were like the chimes of tiny bells. He had never seen such daemons in captivity; he supposed they were not strong enough to be used in transformation engines. One could probably use them to feed large daemons, or burn in daemon glares. The economics of it would have to be worked out.

Smiling, he glanced at Rae. She had clasped her hands between her breasts in that theatrical yet wholly unself-conscious gesture she used.

"I wonder what draws them here," he whispered. "They don't generally materialize like this."

"They're beauties. I think beauty will last. Only humanity has to come to an end. Because people are like a canker in the world. But these—these are *natural*."

"Oh, Rae, not *that* again!" It was torn from him. Mistakenly, perhaps, he had thought the matter resolved days ago. "I thought you'd—"

"The Easterners, and the Apocalypists, say the whole world will be destroyed—not just humanity—but I don't think that can be true. After all, these little creatures haven't done anyone any harm. It's people who have done *them* harm."

Below, a daemon shrilled in a voice of alarm: "Twice the range of the F-98! New top-of-the-line model! Ten gallons of oil shipped with each item!"

Crispin spun back toward the clearing. His skin prickled, and his hair stood on end. "Sssh!"

Down below, the daemons were exclaiming loudly, grabbing each other's hands and vanishing. Something larger was coming. Crispin closed his hand on Rae's arm, ready to drag her away, because it was coming from *behind* them, but before he could move he felt it pass, sweeping down into the grotto, and there came a noisy bubbling from the pool, as if masses of water had been suddenly displaced. For a moment all was silent, the surface flat. A small daemon on a branch gibbered with fear. Then the big daemon reared a glistening white head out of the pool and sighed pale flames that hissed on contact with the water.

On the other side of the pool, a forearm ten feet long snaked out of the water and a hand the size of an umbrella curled around a clump of flags near the bank, crunching them off.

"Stay back," Crispin whispered.

"Will it come after us?"

"I dunno. Never seen one this big. It's not a daemon, it's a demogorgon. This's the kind of beast they use in municipal water-works. Factories. Places like that. *Thousands* of dp."

Without warning the daemon shot its other arm up out of the water and grabbed the little brown daemon on the tree branch. There was a flurry of movement too fast to be seen and then the hideous, all-too-human face sank beneath the water. Severed bits of the brown daemon rose to the surface of the water and bobbed on the ripples.

"Shit, I'd like to have those bits," Crispin whispered.

"No." Rae grabbed his arm. "Don't go down there. Don't you dare!"

He shook her off. The prospect of possessing the remains of an occult beast was too good to miss. Who *knew* what uses the bones might have! Calling daemons—repelling daemons—

Quietly, he scrambled down the steep ground beside the waterfall, keeping behind the bushes. Unobtrusiveness was the thing. Luckily the grass on the floor of the dell was tall enough that he could eel through it on his stomach. As he approached the pool he put his hand on a small daemon. It jerked away, and he felt the sting of it throughout his body. For a moment his vision went black. But when he recovered he could see the water before him, and he eased forward another foot or so, sliding his hand down toward a finger that floated within reach. Then a hank of black hair. Stuff them in a pocket. Another—

There was a smell of burning that he could not identify. It crossed his mind that it might be the smell of burnt water—an occult stink, if ever there was one!—and Rae's voice pealed out, high and desperate. "Crispin! *Behind you!*"

He rolled over, throwing his arms up in front of his face. All he saw was a confusion of brown robes—and faces, faces, faces. Though he realized afterward there could not have been more than two of them, they moved so fast they seemed half a dozen. A girl's voice. "What are you doing here!" Another: "Sally, look out, the daemon!" And all the water exploded upward out of the pool, drenching Crispin, blinding him, and a whiplash of light cracked across his eyes.

He woke to feel hard, cold ground under his cheek. This was nothing unusual, and at first he thought it was simply the beginning of another day of walking; then he opened his eyes.

It was night. Slowly, he got to his feet. The blood rushed to his head and he almost fell over. Staggering, he caught onto a bush, then hummed softly in pain as he extracted the prickles from his palm. The waterfall gushed noisily. All around he felt the dancing urgent presences of daemons. Now he could see a little. So he had not gone blind.

"Rae!"

His voice was weak. And his eyes hurt. His fingers found blood crusted in his brows and the creases of his eyelids. The strangers had struck him across the face after the big daemon stunned him, he guessed, but though they had had him at their mercy, they had left him lying. Had he been of so little importance to them? Common sense told him they would probably be coming back.

"Rae!"

Slipping and cursing in the dark, he clambered back up beside the waterfall to the spot where they had stood to watch the daemons at play. Astonishingly, the knapsack and blankets were still there, and he seized on them with a grunt of relief. But a haphazard search of the vicinity revealed no signs of Rae, nor of a struggle.

In his dazed state the emergency was unquestionable. Swearing softly to himself, he recovered his coat, put it on, and slung their belongings across his shoulders, then plowed upstream through the thickets until he could cross the fast-flowing stream easily. "Rae," he murmured to himself as he pushed on through the forest. "Rae, Rae, Rae." The sound of his own voice comforted him, as did the fact that his throat appeared not to be as badly damaged as he had thought. "Rae, Rae."

He searched for her for what seemed an infinitely long time, as often as not half-asleep on his feet. On the branches overhead, avian virtuosos sang solos. The trills crawled down his spine like drops of ice water. At some point he realized that the footing had got a lot easier, and that he was no longer having to avoid trees. Tiredness dulled the delight which came of the sudden knowledge that he had hit the road again.

It wound like a river of pine needles through the forest. He followed willingly, stumbling from time to time on the hacked-off tree stumps hidden under the sharp carpet. He was not too far gone to note that none of the curves were too tight for a truck. The branches of the overhanging trees had also been lopped off. Nobody except the driver of a big rig would have had that done. Could it be that he had not left civilization at all? That the Wraithwaste had seemed a wilderness just because he did not have a map?

Stopping in mid-stride, he put his head back and gazed at a strip of solid, midnight blue sky. Though the clouds obstructed the stars, it had been a long time since he had seen any open sky at all.

The road forked in two. By this time he had nearly given up hope of finding where the strangers had taken Rae, but in a final bid for lit windows, he chose the narrower road. It ended in an empty clearing where a gigantic, peeling pine thrust out of the bare earth. Nothing moved. There were strange objects hanging from the high branches of the pine, and peering up through the dark, he thought he made out carcasses. The song of night birds pierced his ears as loudly as a crescendo from a trained choir. A light flared behind him and in its brief, hallucinatory glare he saw that the bark of the pine was crawling as if it were covered with ants.

He swung to see where the light had come from, and the ground gave way under his boots and he fell, bumping and rolling over sharp corners, into blackness.

It seemed only an instant later that he woke to find a face hanging over him which he decided must be a dream, or perhaps, because of its clarity, a vision: the face of a child no more than six years old, possessed of dark brown skin on which two ripe black eyes showed purple and yellow. The child's lips worked soundlessly. Crispin tried to sit up, banged his head on a tree root hanging overhead, and rolled over, moaning.

"Get *up*," the little boy said, pulling at him. "He wants to talk to you. Come on, darky."

The word on the child's lips carried no sting. Crispin twisted himself around in the root-roofed crevice, wincing at the pain of new bruises, and stood up. Even when he stumbled into the middle of the room he had to bend his head. It was a low, brightly lit cavern, the worst pigsty he had seen in a long time.

"His name is Orphan," said the old hermit. He pronounced it strangely, as he did everything—Or*paan*. Crispin nodded, eating as fast as he could. The stew the little boy had served him was extraordinarily delicious. He was aware that there were far more important things to do than eat, but his body was rebelling: it refused to let him ignore its cries. Maybe the stew was poisoned. He didn't care. At least he wouldn't die hungry. "*My* name is—" The hermit paused, contorting his wrinkled apple of a face. "Call me the old gentleman." He sniggered.

Crispin stopped with his spoon halfway to his mouth. "Old Gentleman?"

The hermit nodded eagerly.

Crispin's moniker for Saul Smithrebel, a lifetime ago, had been "Old Gentleman." It had been born as a childish attempt at sarcasm, but by the end it had become a token of grudging deference to the ringmaster. Calling this strange Wraithwaste hermit by Smithrebel's title would be like classifying a skunk with a venomous asp. "I used to know someone else called that."

Bad move. An expression of wrath grew on the hermit's face.

"No offense," Crispin said hastily, putting down his wooden bowl and readying himself to spring back—though there was practically nowhere to spring back *to* in the junk-jammed cave. "No offense, I'm sure."

The little boy, who had been silent since he delivered Crispin to the hermit, pushed himself between the old fellow's knees and, placing a hand on either bony thigh in a curiously adult gesture, turned to face Crispin. Crispin nearly laughed out loud at the sudden resemblance of the composition to pictures he had seen of the young Queen with her father, King Ethrew. "His name is *Jacithrew Humdroner,*" the little boy announced emphatically.

"And what about you," Crispin said with a smile, ignoring the hermit's frown.

The child turned his face away and put his thumb in his mouth. "'M Orpaan," he mumbled indistinctly. "Mum 'n da got kilt bee sojers."

The impulse which must have been building in the hermit's brain for a good minute and a half finally reached fruition. He howled and smacked the little boy in the side of the head. Orpaan flew past Crispin, across the cave, and pushed himself under the low-hanging roots as if he were trying to burrow into the earth. That he did not cry out struck Crispin as terrible. Growling, he seized Jacithrew Humdroner's bony wrists, jerking the old man to his feet. The red beast cavorted inside his head. He gulped, and blinked several times to clear his brain. It was only necessary to make a point, not to do murder. He placed his left hand ostentatiously in his lap and squeezed Jacithrew's wrists in the other until bones rubbed together. "Don't ever hit him again," he said between his teeth. "All right? Hear me?"

"Let me go!" Jacithrew gibbered. "I'll tell you lovely things, true things, things you'll never ever ever know if you hurt me!"

"Huh!" Crispin considered the old man. Liquid eyes stared up in terror through tangled gray dreadlocks. For the first time, he noticed that though Jacithrew's face was as wrinkled as a pug dog's behind the forest of beard, his skin was a good three shades darker than Crispin's. Like Orpaan's. How did that come to be? Some daemons were dark-skinned, too. Was the old fellow a weird kind of intelligent daemon, half-human perhaps, neither fish nor fowl? Or was he merely an eccentric hermit? And in any case, what was he doing in the middle of nowhere with a child?

Jacithrew gave a sudden great heave. Crispin tightened his grip. The room was lit by daemon glares nailed to the plunging taproot in its center. In the real world, outside the western domains anyway, daemon glares were luxuries, but in the Waste things were obviously different. A radiance far brighter than gaslight emanated from the silver cages. Each object in the cave, from the logs piled beside the fire hood to the thread-roots hanging from the ceiling to the wooden machine fragments—some as large as beds, some smaller than a man's hand, some half-cannibalized for parts—cast shadows like black paper cutouts.

He felt a tentative tap on his arm. It was the child. "Please let Jacithrew go," Orpaan whispered. "Please please please. He's me new dadda see, since me mum and me real dadda got kilt. He tends after me, please. I tend after him. See."

It was impossible to refuse such a request. Crispin let Jacithrew go; the old man flopped back onto his three-legged stool with a shriek. Orpaan, to Crispin's astonishment, climbed onto Crispin's knee and sucked his thumb feverishly, all the time keeping an eye on Jacithrew as if he were afraid the hermit might hit him again.

Without warning, Jacithrew leaned forward and said clearly, "The orphan takes to you. You are one of us."

"What? One of who?"

"Your skin, your eyes! You are one of the ancient folk, the masters of daemons! Had you been one of the pale folk"— Jacithrew made a surprisingly swift chopping motion with one hand—"I would have gulletted you as you lay at my mercy. But now I am convinced of your heritage!"

He *was* mad.

"I had not thought there were any more of us left. There is Hannah, of course. But she is different." He plucked at Crispin's arm. "And you are so strong—so healthy!"

As mad as a Marout hare. The old man's ravings nearly topped Rae's carefully worked-out future history for a tall tale.

On the other hand, if Crispin humored him, he might just get a second bowl of stew out of the bargain. Soon he would be strong enough to start searching for Rae in earnest. He settled the little boy more securely on his knee, mindful of the child's bruises. "Jacithrew, huh?" he said to the old man. "How'd you get a name like that? Sounds like a noble. A squire, anyhow. But I've already been wrong about that once, and I swear if you're a noble, I'll eat my hat."

They soar by the ponds of Heaven,
go sporting to the farthest darkness,
showing what it means to have a body but no desires,
to keep living on and on to the end of time.

—Mu Hua

Secret
Signs

Rae did not know what to say. To her intense frustration, she suspected she was going to cry. They wanted her to tell them all about herself, and there was no way, of course not, so why couldn't she come up with any lies? Her mind was blank of everything except fear. And a shriek that echoed silently: *Crispin* . . .

She couldn't stand them all staring at her like this. The *pity* in their eyes—

She rested her forehead on her blanket-wrapped knees and shuddered. She remembered stumbling through the naked woods yesterday morning, hanging on the blond girls' shoulders, into sudden shocking greenness, past an earthy enclosure where chickens, ducks, and turkeys gabbled to each other across a pond, into the house where the girls lived. There had been something wrong with her, she still did not know what. Her body had tingled all over as if all her limbs were asleep and would not wake up, she had scarcely been able to form a coherent thought, and when she tried to speak, her words staggered drunkenly. They had led her to this attic bedroom, they had plumped up the goose-down pillows and folded down the patchwork coverlet and told her to go to sleep. Since the door was locked, and her head was woozy, and every time she touched the window catch a shock of occult pain went through her, she had gone to sleep. When she awoke it was night. She had slept at least twelve hours.

She had barely had her eyes open for a minute when they had all pushed into the room, skirts swinging, hair flying indecently, a nightmare of loose femininity. "She's awake! She's awake!" In with them wafted a strange, prickling *not-scent* that made Rae's eyes sting. They gathered round the bed and wanted to know her name, where she came from, what she had been doing in their daemon dell.

"I don't know where I am," she said, raising her head. "Who are you?"

"Oh, the poor child." Their voices rang with concern.

"Poor girl. Rae, that's her name, isn't it? Rae."

"She's a Kirekuni, you know."

Panic swelled in Rae's throat. What supernatural perception did they possess? Then she remembered that they had undressed her. Her skin was bare under the soft woolen nightgown they had put her into. "You already know about me. What more do you want?"

"Her nationality matters not at all, Millie," said another, severely. "A woman is a woman." It was the oldest one who spoke, the crone with the beautiful face. Rae longed to pin up the silver hair that straggled over her shoulders—then the aristocratic cheekbones and high forehead would be done justice. She'd have to get rid of that sack of a dress, too. Give her a gown of pale mauve linen, with a trumpet hem, and pearls at her neck . . .

Rae's terror was slowly subsiding.

The old woman rested an authoritative hand on the shoulder of the dark-skinned one who knelt close by the bed, her black eyes fixed on Rae's face. "I am Anthea," the old woman said. Her brown-spotted fingers closed a little tighter on the dark one's shoulder.

"Hannah," said the dark one.

"Liesl," said the tall, freckle-faced woman standing at the foot of Rae's bed.

"Sally. Millie. We're so happy you're here, Rae," said the two blond girls, speaking with a simultaneity that would have earned applause from a music-hall audience. They giggled, as if appreciative of their own comic effect. Rae guessed they were only a couple of years older than herself.

The freckled woman—Liesl—turned on them with sudden fierceness. "What are you two doing up here, anyway? You ought to be watching Mother! Go on! Get out!"

The taller twin—Sally, Rae thought—yelped and brushed at her arm, though nothing had touched her. Without a backward glance, they piled out the door. "Impossible," Liesl muttered. She folded her hands on the foot of the bed, glancing defiantly at Anthea.

"We are not giving Rae a very happy introduction to our sister-hood, Liesl," Anthea said. She smiled sadly at Rae. "I'm sorry. But we *are* glad to have you here. I hope we did not give you the impression we were not." She moved slowly over to the dresser and took a pile of clothes out of the drawer. "Hannah, you may go. Liesl—mmm—you may go to the menagerie and pick out a daemon for her to practice on when I show her our first tricks. She may as well start finding out what we do here."

"She hasn't even told us where she comes from!" Liesl said in a low voice. "Did you notice that, Anthea? Or has she bewitched you, as Sarah did? And she hasn't told us why she was with a Wraith! She might be planted by the culties, like Sarah, to sabotage us! Or by the lizards—seeing as she *is* one! How can you talk of showing her our tricks?"

Anthea's old gaze rested on Liesl. "Have I been wrong yet in the matter of a girl, sister? We will keep this one."

Rae started upright in bed. "Your ladyships! I'm afraid there has been a misunderstanding—"

"Sssh."

Liesl laughed. "Welcome to Holstead House."

"No call for sarcasm, Liesl," Anthea said, her voice taking on an edge. "Out."

And before Rae realized what was happening, the door had closed after Hannah and Liesl.

Anthea let out a sigh. Then she smiled and held out the folded clothes to Rae. Fine wool. Rae fingered it. Her mouth watered. It felt like Anchain cashmere from the south. But how could it be, here?

Perhaps the women—the *trickster* women—were not cut off from civilization at all. Just because Rae and Crispin had been walking for days did not mean they had come very far. But where had they come? And where was Crispin? What had the women done to him, when they left him lying on the grass of the daemon dell?

"Get dressed, my dear." Anthea lowered herself with a sigh onto the foot of the bed. "Please, give no thought to their hostility. Things are strange these days; no one from Ferupe can be trusted. We have had to become cynical. That is why Liesl was rude. But she should not have questioned my judgment." She shook her head. "Are you hungry?"

"No," Rae said. She was starving, but she would not have eaten anything the trickster women offered her unless she was at death's door. To think she had suggested that she and Crispin throw themselves on these women's mercy! There was no mercy here: she could feel it in the way they treated each other.

"Then we shall go down to the menagerie." The older woman smiled. "I am so excited. I know you weren't planning to come to our house, Rae. You've made that clear enough. I hope that someday you will tell us where you were going. Not many travelers come this far into the Wraithwaste, unless they're coming to us! And none of them ever leave. I should not like to see you end *that* way. However, I am convinced you will not. Once you see what our life is like here, you will no longer want to leave."

Rae stripped her nightgown off. "You're trickster women," she said.

"That is what they call us in Ferupe. But we have no tricks that a girl of ten couldn't learn." Anthea laughed, and Rae found herself smiling, too. "We are just 'working girls'." The meticulous way she used the slang term pointed up her old age. "You are a 'working girl,' too, aren't you? You have a look of independence about you."

"I'm a costume designer," Rae said, unable to keep a trace of pride out of her voice.

"Wonderful! But you are not *completely* independent, are you? You are part of a network the size of a town or a city, without which you are nothing." Anthea's voice was so gentle that for a minute Rae did not realize the trickster woman had utterly dismissed Rae's passion. Anthea went on, with that edge creeping into her voice again: "We, on the other hand, have complete autonomy. We have all of the Wraithwaste for our domicile. The only people within two hundred miles are others like us." She smiled. "Other 'working girls'."

Rae was getting an increasingly bad feeling about the nature of this place. To hide her confusion, she fastened the tiny wooden buttons up the front of the dress. She was disconcerted to discover that the garment was completely shapeless. Her breasts pushed it out into a shelf, and from there the fabric fell straight to the middle of her calves, without a flare in sight. Her waist was disguised. There was a slit in the back enabling her to walk, but that was all. "Your lady-ship?" She plucked at the excess fabric. "I don't think this quite fits . . ."

"It fits perfectly," Anthea said. "And—by the way—there are no ladies here. Call me Anthea, as if I were your sister." She hopped up, very sprightly for a woman of her age, and took Rae's hand. Her fingers were bony and dry. Rae smelled that strange, nostril-prickling *not-scent*. "Because I *am* your sister. And I should like you to meet our Mother."

Holstead House was built in the sprawling, organic style of farmhouses. It must have been at least five hundred years old, probably more. Rae could not get rid of the feeling that she had been here before; but that was probably only because she had been in so many similar houses during her days with traveling shows, when they were frequently reduced to singing to gentlemen farmers for their supper. The kitchen had whitewashed walls and stone flags. Tabbies dozed around the hearth that smoldered in one wall. Pointing to a closed door next to the hearth, Anthea said that it led to the drawing room. "We only use that room when one of the Freeman brothers, Jethro or Alfred—they are our agents—comes. That is, once in a blue moon. When we are alone we prefer to be comfortable rather than to observe the formalities. Beyond the drawing room there is a dairy and pantry, which open only to the outdoors."

Rae nodded. After the unnatural brightness of the bedroom, the firelight was soothing. Around the kitchen walls hung a wealth of peppers, onions, garlic, and squash, braided into ropes. From the look of the wooden sink, the house had running water. Running water! The provenance of those wealthier than Rae ever hoped to be. Her mouth watered at the sight of half a loaf lying in its crumbs on the kitchen table. But she was strangely convinced that she must not eat anything here, that it would be laced with mind-altering poisons.

Anthea drew her back into the high, dark entrance hall that

would not have seemed out of place in the Seventeenth Mansion. But they did not go out into the front garden, though Rae would have liked to see all that greenness again, even in the dark—just to know that it had been real. The back door was even more massive than the front. Anthea beckoned Rae out into the night. "Around here. We have no doors between the house and the menagerie. It is safer this way."

Rae had forgotten how cold it was outside. Gasping, she crowded into the door that Anthea opened. The brilliance made her eyes hurt. Anthea reached over her and slammed the door shut.

Rafters arched to a roof as high as that of a music hall. Whippy, naked branches and serpentine creepers twined up the walls. In a farmhouse, this would have been the byre—or in a wealthier establishment, servants' quarters. Here it was a tropical garden, lit by a hundred unmoving suns.

Anthea turned to her, smiling broadly.

"Where's all this light coming from?" Rae whispered.

"Daemon glares." Anthea pointed up. The suns were only ceiling lights, as bright as the overhead stagelights in the Old Linny, except white, not colored. And because they were everywhere—on the walls, on the trees, even half-buried in the earth—neither the trees, nor the flowers, nor Anthea or Rae themselves cast any defined shadow. It was what gave the uncanny impression of daylight.

She picked up one foot. A shapeless puddle of blackness shrank beneath it.

She looked up. Anthea was watching her with a strange expression on her face: not hostility, or dissimulation, but joy and pride and the desire to impress. Rae had readied her defenses for everything conceivable except this naked *want*. It was her instinct to recoil. She carefully kept her face immobile.

Faint insect sounds swelled around them. Nothing moved.

"Pssst!" Anthea hissed, rising on her tiptoes, looking up. "Sssst!" She stripped the sleeve back from one wrinkled arm with expert speed.

"Sssst! Here, baby, here, dear one! Adorable Fanimus!"

An especially large flower fell slowly from the branch of the dogwood to which it had clung, twisting and turning (though the air was preternaturally still), its tiger-striped petals fluttering like streamers. It landed asprawl on Anthea's thin arm, dusting her skin with pollen, and though it could not have weighed more than a few ounces, Anthea staggered under the impact. "Fanimus," she murmured caressingly. And the flower became a tiger-striped baby of perhaps a year. It clung to Anthea's arm with an un-babylike strength.

"I love you," it said in a high voice, crawling to her shoulder. "Is the bread ready? Eleven dozen head, that'll be 242,000 pounds—shall we send it to be deposited as usual?"

"In the name of transcendence," Rae said, watching Anthea play with the daemon. "You can do that. My—my friend—would be so envious."

"Your friend?" Anthea said absently, caressing the daemon. "Liesl and Hannah went back to the dell to look for him, earlier tonight, but he was gone."

Rae did not like to think about what the trickster women would do to Crispin if they caught him. She chewed her lip. *Will he come? He's probably twenty miles away by now. But he has to come. He can't leave me here! I don't know how to escape! Crispin . . .*

Nights of watching him sleep sprawled on his face, watching his broad back rise and fall. Mornings of going stubbornly through her toilette, ignoring his pleas to come on, come *on*, the sweet awareness of his gaze resting on her body and hair. The impossible, absurd longing to touch him, just once, to close her fingers on his forearm. She *knew* the warmth of his skin. She *knew* the prickle of his body hair. She *remembered* . . . She would not let herself remember how his arousal had felt, pressed against her leg, in the heat of those last few moments before he discovered what she was.

Anthea said, still in that abstracted voice: "Are you watching closely, Rae? You have probably never seen a daemon materialized. Or if you have, it was celled in the bowels of some machine with a collar round its throat. Daemons are invisible, except when they choose to materialize, and they materialize only when they feed."

"What—what do they eat?" Rae forced herself to pay attention.

"Each other. And trees, plants, any vegetable growth. Animal life, if necessary. That is why the Wraithwaste is a waste. Nothing is alive here, except where we've forced it to live again by clearing out the daemons. There's threads of sap running through the pines, keeping them from rotting where they stand, and that's all. Most of the animals have been gone for at least fifty years, eaten by the daemons, or driven out."

"But wasn't it always like this?"

Rae could not imagine the silent forest through which she and Crispin had wandered ever having been green. Death was so thick in the air that it seemed the desuetude must have lasted a thousand years.

"Not always." Anthea leaned against the lower branches of the tree from which the daemon baby had fallen. Rae blinked, seeing the tangled, naked trunks shift to accept her weight, linking themselves in a kind of cradle. The baby scrambled off her arm, up to one of the topmost twigs, and gradually turned into a flower again. Anthea looked wistfully up at it, rubbing her arm.

"The Waste has only been dead for, perhaps, fifty years. Although in trickster years, of course, that is more than two lifetimes . . . It has to do with the war. How much do you know about the war?"

Rae shook her head.

"The degree to which the reality of Ferupe's distress is kept from her citizens is appalling. I'll explain later, or maybe Hannah will. The war is her specialty, you see." Anthea laughed. "The long and the short of it is that soon we will be no more. I'll leave the rest to her. But there is a bright side of which I do find it pleasant to speak: our task is far easier now than it was for our sisters a hundred years ago. Tricking used to be a difficult art. Now the daemons are so numerous that it is like picking up apples from under a tree. It is a joke really, a joke on the daemonmongers. They do not know that we catch more daemons more easily than our predecessors did, so they pay us the same per-capita prices, leaving us with far more money than we have any use for. We invest it in the Kingsburg banks. Of course, the more daemons there are in Ferupe, the more likely a disaster becomes, so one could say that we are being irresponsible; but to look at it another way, it is now necessary for us to provide Ferupe with enough daemons to last for eternity. And when the war finally reaches us, my sisters and I do not intend to be caught in the screamer factories. Rather, we will leave the Waste. But we will not starve."

Rae could follow none of what Anthea was saying. Wars, daemons, disasters; none of it seemed particularly relevant to the bright stillness of the menagerie. She looked around, wondering where the rest of the daemons were. "But how exactly do you catch them?" she asked when Anthea paused for breath.

"Oh, my dear, forgive me! There is so much to tell you . . . When daemons feed, they materialize. We create an ambiance where they like to come to feed. The smallest ones eat grass and berries, and they lure the bigger ones. Anything the size of Fanimus or larger we lure back to the house. Some trickster women, myself among them, hold, too, that the big ones get bored, and curious about anything they do not encounter in the normal run of their existence. They have minds; did you know that? At least, before they are collared."

"How do you lure them back here? Isn't it dangerous?" Rae remembered the huge, spider-limbed water daemon which had stunned Crispin, and which had stunned her, too, before it rushed back up the waterfall. *That* was what had been wrong with her on the walk back from the dell; that was how Sally and Millie had caught her so easily. That numbness, that inability to think. Daemon shock.

Anthea smiled. "It *is* dangerous. But only if it is done wrong. And no girl who does it wrong lasts very long here." She patted the cradle of branches beside her. "Come sit with me. Exarces is very comfortable."

Rae bit her lip. Anthea's words sounded ominous. Uncertainly, she walked over to the cradle of branches and sat beside Anthea. The creepers on the roof kissed and separated, twining, parting. Rae blinked. It was as if she were watching them grow through a kinetoscope, speeded up, jerky from the motion of the hand crank. For the first time since entering the menagerie she became aware of the *not-scent*. It was so strong that it was no longer so much a scent as a texture in the air. The row of sunflowers against the wall of the farmhouse shimmered as if heat were rising from the clotted earth.

"Is *everything* in here a daemon?" she asked suddenly. "I mean, the trees—everything?"

Anthea smiled with girlish delight. "I wasn't sure whether you'd guess."

It seemed obvious now. Rae ran her hand along the smooth, dappled bark of the tree. "What did this look like when it was—" She had been going to say *alive*. "When it was a daemon?"

"This is its quiescent state. It's how we store them until the traders come. This is really a warehouse, not a menagerie; but in this line of work euphemisms are necessary. When they're quiescent"—Anthea circled a branch in her thumb and forefinger—"it's much easier to put collars on them."

"But why don't they dematerialize?"

"Maybe you noticed that the door is flanged with silver? The keyhole is silver, too. So is every single nail and rivet in the walls." Anthea shook her head, glancing up at the roof. "And every beam is oak. Even if they could dematerialize, they could not escape without doing themselves an injury."

This place must have cost a fortune, Rae thought. *Who built it?* For all Anthea's rather ostentatious talk of investments, the trickster women seemed too out of touch ever to have had any initiative. It had probably been the daemonmongers, their masters, who had set them up here. The house seemed several hundred years old. Had there been daemonmongers hundreds of years ago? Of course there had. After all, there had always been daemons.

Anthea was looking at her closely. "My dear, I don't want to pry. But have you family members in the business? You are so perceptive, I'm starting to wonder whether you *did* mean to come here after all, you mysterious little thing."

"No." Rae shook her head quickly. "Where I grew up, we were never allowed near daemons." The Dynasty's policy of noninterference had meant that the exploitation of daemons was frowned upon severely. And for some reason, that was one of the few Dynasty edicts which the Prince of the Seventeenth Mansion did not let his disciples contradict in their everyday life. There had not been a single daemon in Carathraw House since the Dynasty bought it. "But I ran away," Rae said sadly. The temptation was too much for her: she was tired, and hot, and alone, and Anthea was nothing if not sympathetic.

"You ran away?" Anthea said. "From where?"

Rae shook her head. "Plum Valley Domain," she said, biting her lip. She knew she had to resist the temptation; it was this same craving to share the things that tormented her which had led her, against her better instincts, to try to convert Crispin. Now she was convinced that she could not speak of the Dynasty without trying to convert her listener. The force of her belief seized precedence over her more oblique, delicately shaded needs. That was why she dared not start confessing her past to Anthea. On the other hand, Crispin had never been kind to her as this woman was. She could not remember anyone except Sister Flora, at the Seventeenth Mansion, ever being this kind to her.

Anthea started forward. "Look! There's Mother!"

Rae looked up. She had not thought "Mother" really existed. But sure enough, a tiny white-headed figure with a yellow imp on either shoulder glided between two trees at the other end of the menagerie.

"She blends in well, doesn't she?"

Rae nodded.

"I hope the twins are somewhere about. Mother cannot be trusted not to leave the door open when she comes back upstairs."

"Anthea, ma'am," Rae gasped. She could not stop herself any more. "I'm sorry. I ran away. I don't know where I'm going. I don't—"

Anthea pulled her into her arms. Rae, her cheek pressed against cashmere, tried desperately not to cry. "You poor child! I've tired you, haven't I? Yes, I have! I'm always too eager to show off the beauty of our life here! I forget that you have come through the Waste, and the first thing you need to do is recuperate! I shall have a thing or two to say to Hannah and Liesl for forgetting to remind me! There now. There now." She stood up, still holding Rae close. "Mother! Sal! Mil!" she shouted angrily, shattering the quiet of the garden.

Rae heard the twins' footsteps. She pulled away from Anthea to face them.

"Girls, I'm leaving you in charge of Mother," Anthea said breathlessly.

"That's where we've been," a twin who could have been Millie said.

"Watching her."

"And watching you."

"For the last three hours."

Three hours? Rae thought.

"We think it's time for Mother to go to bed."

"When she's ready to go," Anthea said evenly, "you may."

"Then we're going to be up all night."

"You pamper her too much, Anthea," the other twin said sulkily. "She's old. She doesn't know what she's doing. I can't imagine why you bother."

Anthea did not answer, but Rae could see her trembling as the twins sauntered away, arms round each other's waists. Sally extended her free arm above her head and dropped her head onto her sister's shoulder. Now that Rae knew what the other girl was doing, she watched with fascination, not confusion. "Sssst!" It was a shrill, wet noise, like the sound a furious cat makes in its mouth. "Here, here, come—"

The daemon pushed up out of the ground and crawled up Sally's body, red-skinned, with an enormous bald cranium and fingers tipped with long yellow claws. Rae watched all the humanity drain out of the girl's face as the daemon wrapped itself around her arm and sucked her fingers, one after the other, lovingly. Her sister stood as steady as a rock, supporting her.

"Anthea!"

Liesl stood behind them, stolid, red-haired, angry. Muted by the undergrowth came the sound of the door slamming. "What are you doing? I thought I told you to give her some time to prove herself before you took her in here! Now she's seen things we can never let her get away with!"

"You forget that we're keeping this one, sister," Anthea said. She took Rae's hand and pulled her past Liesl.

"Her man is staying with Jacithrew!" the red-haired woman said. "He's one of them—a Wraith! Just as the girls said! In circumstances like these . . . I can tell you, Anthea, you may as well forget about her!"

Anthea's fingers clamped down on Rae's wrist, and she pulled her through the trees to the door. Rae felt nervous and excited. It was like being a child again, thumbing her nose at Daphne from the safety of Sister Flora's skirts. She had *forgotten* Daphne! When was the last time she had thought of her—with regret, with love, at all? *How* could she have forgotten?

The oaken door slammed behind them. The cold air rushed into her lungs like water. She almost choked.

The black-and-silver shapes of pines surrounded them, jagged cones made of broken mirrors. Tears of cold filled her eyes.

"Anthea, could you—could you show me the front garden?" She tugged the older woman's sleeve, half-laughing, half-crying. "Look, the moon's come out—"

I see that woman's "bite several mouthfuls out of you," the laughter of those green-faced, long-toothed people and the tenant's story the other day are obviously secret signs.

—Lu Hsun

Daemons!

The next day, Orpaan showed Crispin the trickster women's house. It was about three miles down the road, and if Crispin had kept going that night, he couldn't have missed it. It was like an estate house straight out of the heartland, complete with a garden greener than anything else in the Wraithwaste. Orpaan insisted that the trickster women would know if they entered the barrier of oaks around the garden; Crispin was willing to risk it, to see if Rae was there, to get her back, but with Orpaan at his side, he dared not. They slunk all the way around the house and garden, keeping to the pines. No one came out or went in. But the presence of daemons was so concentrated that sometimes Crispin could hardly see for the shimmering of the air. The house gave off an aura of impregnability completely at odds with its comfortable, affluent appearance. Without having so much as glimpsed a trickster woman, Crispin knew they were horribly dangerous.

And they had Rae . . . !

Still, there was nothing further he could do now, and the day was only half-gone. In gratitude to Orpaan, he offered to take him fishing. Unbelievably, the child—the Wraith, as he and Jacithrew called themselves—did not know what fishing was. Crispin took him to the brook—to a spot well upstream from the daemon dell—and showed him, with string and bent thorns. They had to talk in whispers so as not to disturb the demogorgons that lived in the water. Crispin winced to think how often he and Rae had splashed unheedingly through the Wraithwaste streams.

They caught nothing, but it did not dampen Crispin's spirits. Now that he had seen the house of trickery, he knew his enemy, and he felt that rescuing Rae might after all be within the realm of possibility. He tried not to think about spending another night with Jacithrew Humdroner in the claustrophobia-inducing underground house.

Orpaan too seemed content. As they walked back in the twilight, he grabbed Crispin's hand and grinned. Crispin felt a surge of liking for the boy. It was Orpaan who had put Crispin to bed and brought him food; it was Orpaan who had answered his questions and showed him the house of trickery. What could Crispin ever do to reciprocate? Since he was already planning one rescue, perhaps he could just make it wholesale, and carry Orpaan off, too. Jacithrew was as dangerous as the trickster women in his own way.

But when they entered the clearing, all such thoughts were driven out of his mind by the sight of the old Wraith out in the open, upended inside a chaotic mass of wood and leather like a duck feeding on the bottom of a river. Clankings, tappings, and swears replaced the usual silence.

Crispin gaped, his suspicion that the old man was dotty becoming a certainty. He began to grow angry. What did the old loon think he was *doing*? All the bits of machinery that had lain about the root room were now arranged on the ground in the center of a stubby framework pod. Its leather wings stretched all the way across the clearing. Jacithrew was banging about with a hammer, singing to himself, as happy as a sandboy. When he heard their steps he bobbed upright, beaming. "See!" he shouted. "See my flying machine!"

"Hannah helped him get the bits we couldn't make," Orpaan whispered, tugging at Crispin. "He says we're going to fly away from here. He says we're going to fly far, far away from the trickster women. But I thought he forgot. He hasn't worked on it in ages."

* * *

"It'll never work!" Crispin said later, after he had persuaded the old man to leave his engineering for the night and come below ground for something to eat. He felt like a father to both of them. That should have been amusing, but it wasn't. "You're madder than a blue jay!"

The old hermit cackled. Inside his beard, his lower lip was poochy and soft. "You shall see yourself proved wrong-oh-wrong-oh, my boy! Tomorrow is the time! I am delighted"—from his seat on a tree stump stool, he made a bow—"to have a larger audience for my maiden flight than I anticipated."

Crispin stared. "When you want to, you can talk like a fucking scholar."

Jacithrew's eyes were cloudy. He reached down, scrabbled in the pan of roasted hazelnuts, and stuffed several into his mouth. The pair's food was left by Hannah, one of the trickster women, at the fork of the road. It was better than any Crispin had ever eaten. When he saw chicken soup and hazelnuts, his estimation of the trickster women had risen several notches. It had taken a great deal of self-restraint not to finish off the nuts as soon as he took them out of the fire. *Courtesy! Courtesy!* he thought, watching crumb-filled saliva drool down Jacithrew's beard.

Jacithrew seemed to have decided that Crispin was worth talking to. Or perhaps—more likely—he did not know who he was talking to. On and on he went. On and on. Nine-tenths of his ramblings were pure nonsense; but he did not seem to mind argument. He even seemed to enjoy it. And even though the old Wraith was mad, Crispin could not resist challenging his absurd theories.

"My machine is of the soundest construction," Jacithrew said proudly. "It will bear me up. I am light. And my daemons are as strong as any the pale bitches can catch."

He waved a hand at the corner of the room, where the low-hanging roots shimmered in the bright light of the daemon glares. At least three very powerful daemons were squatting there, invisible. Another—Kankeris—guarded the door in the tree overhead. Seeing that one briefly materialize had given Crispin an understanding of the "shimmering trees" which he had noticed elsewhere in the Wraithwaste. Under each of those trees, he guessed now, had been a root room, the home of Wraiths.

Hopefully, better balanced Wraiths than these. Crispin did not like to think that Jacithrew and Orpaan were representational of their race—that living in the Waste was enough to drive even the natives mad.

The fire cast a feverish red light on Jacithrew's face. Given the heating power of the daemon glares, Crispin could not see why Jacithrew had insisted on lighting the hearth. Orpaan huddled at Crispin's feet, arms wrapped around his leg, thumb in mouth.

"I shall fly over the tops of the trees," Jacithrew said. "I shall fly all the way south to the land of the Painted Nomads."

"The *Red* Nomads," Crispin said. "Izte Kchebuk'ara."

"Yes, Kchebuk'ara. Yes, that's it. I can't stay here any longer! A Wraith does not live on charity from pale people."

Crispin ate another hazelnut. "You'll kill yourself. I examined your machine, and it *looks* all right—I mean, it has wings and everything—but it can't *work*!"

Jacithrew pouted.

"I don't know anything about airplanes, but I know you can't just jump off a tree and expect to fly," Crispin said relentlessly. "It doesn't make the least bit of sense. If that was the way it worked, *everyone* would be flying instead of walking!"

"Ah," Jacithrew said with a big smile. "But everyone does not have my daemons. Have you seen my daemons? Sueras!" He clapped his hands. "Amanse! Gelfitus! Fremis!"

They materialized as they came to him, shambling hand over hand through the clutter like skinny apes. The largest, Fremis, which had crimson-and-cream-dappled skin, would have been fifteen feet tall if it had been able to stand up under the low ceiling. Amanse was a female with green hair. They filled the room with their long limbs, draping themselves over Jacithrew's lap, over his shoulders, knotting themselves around his feet, chittering nonsense. Crispin froze, terrified that one of them would touch him. His skin prickled all over with anticipation of the shock.

Jacithrew grinned, his face framed by a circle of blue arm. Orpaan sleepily cuddled Amanse's green-tressed head. She licked the child's arm with a pink tongue, and Crispin wanted to sweep him out of danger.

How did the Wraiths do it? In their natural state daemons were wild, dangerous creatures—but these were as tame as dogs! And they were uncollared! Millsy's beasts had been child-sized; these were giants; and the Wraiths weren't even tricksters! Crispin's old daemon bites, from the time Millsy had tried to make him a trickster, ached hellishly.

The ability is in the blood, Millsy had said. It's in the blood.

Did Wraiths have trickster blood, one and all, men and women? How could that be?

Jacithrew called the daemons' names aloud again, sending them back to their corner. Crispin breathed out.

"You're mad!" he said to Jacithrew. "Mad, mad, mad! And you talk nonsense! You're so arrogant! If it weren't for the trickster women you wouldn't even be *alive*! I don't see *your* people keeping you in food and necessities."

Jacithrew sat up straighter. "You think the pale bitches do it for me? They do it for the child."

"Can't argue with that!"

"I'm not a fool, you know," Jacithrew said with a crafty gleam in his eyes. "There's a reason I keep the brat around! If he were older, they'd have left us both to die in the wilderness. Pale women care nothing for Wraiths."

"Wraiths, it seems, care less!"

"My people are *dying*," Jacithrew said faintly. Crispin thought he was going to cry. "They have destroyed us. It has taken ten thousand years, but they have finally accomplished their goal. Ah!" He sat up straight. "But when the bells toll, they will die! All of them, as one!"

Is he a cultie? Crispin thought disbelievingly. "Where did he hear that?" he muttered to Orpaan.

"There was a girl said it," Orpaan whispered back. "A girl with the tricky ladies that came to visit us. Her name was Sarah."

"Where is she now?"

"Buried in the forest. We buried her."

"What?"

"She died. She was all eaten." Orpaan scowled.

Crispin thumped Jacithrew on the knee. "Old man! Old man! Have the—the pale bitches—ever threatened you and Orpaan? You see, my girl—" He had not yet mentioned Rae to Jacithrew. But if the old man hated the trickster women as much as he said he did, perhaps he would help Crispin against them. "They have her—"

But Jacithrew had not heard a word. As was his habit, he had slowly worked himself up to an outburst, and now there would be no stopping him. He spat freely as he talked. "Ferupians have ruined my people. Anything they offer us now is no more than an insult. They have pushed us back and back. Ah! My people are living all on top of each other among the dead trees. Our tribes have been torn apart. We have forgotten everything we once knew. We flee from their armies, and die at the hands of their common folk if we try to leave the Waste. Useless! Therefore, I say: we were born in the Waste, and we will die with the Waste. Ferupe has been our death, but we will be Ferupe's death when the bells toll. Ah!"

"If you hate all Ferupians that much, why don't you hate me?" Crispin asked angrily. Orpaan moaned.

Jacithrew wiped his mouth. Saliva gleamed on his chin. "You are not Ferupian!"

"Not Ferupian? My father was a native of Linhe Domain. An Easterner. Easterners are snow-white under their tans, and their hair is as pale as the sun—I'm a bit of a mishap, all right, but I'm as Ferupian as they come."

Jacithrew laughed. He reached out and traced a wet trail on Crispin's arm with his finger. "That is what you think. Let me tell you a secret, boy-oh boy-oh! Pale people hate dark ones. You can't trust them. Have you made the mistake of trusting them before? I see you have. But I know about the outside world. Hannah told me. And she is dark, too, she is! She knows! The Ferupians and the Kirekunis have carved the world into halves between them. Ravening white monsters, they are as heartless as the wind! And you have made the mistake of trusting them!"

Crispin rubbed between his eyes. When he was six years old, Anuei had said to him in a moment of anger: *If I could do one thing for you, my son, I would take my blood out of your veins.* Crispin had never forgotten that. The words echoed in his mind, and his mother's face gave way to the faces of girls from the east, the west, the north, the south, the heartlands, the capital. *Blood out of my veins.* Plump and slender, fair-haired and dark, tanned faces and winter-pale, and all of them white as the insides of figs underneath their clothes. Limbs intertwining with his. *Blood in my veins.*

He hadn't made love to a stranger since his early teens. With

Prettie's eyes on him, it wouldn't have felt right. Now Prettie was dead, and all of those girls melded into the only other girl, into Rae. It had been pitch-black night the only time they touched. But in memory he could see her breasts lolling from her dress and taste her tiny nipples.

He opened his eyes. Madness shone in Jacithrew's black-currant pupils.

"If you knew what I know, you'd be the happiest man alive," Crispin said, smiling.

Jacithrew let out a strangulated shriek and launched himself off his stool. Crispin had to stop himself from laughing as he fended the old man off. The only danger was that Jacithrew would call his daemons, and he was clearly too confused and angry now to do that. "Fly now," Crispin taunted. "Fly! Fly through the roof, why don't you!"

Love and hate. Dark and fair. Rae!

In his struggles Jacithrew kicked the fire. It collapsed, and a rain of sparks flew up into the wall. Orpaan cried miserably, "No, no, no," and hit at Crispin's legs. Crispin let go of Jacithrew. Propelled by his own momentum, the old Wraith staggered halfway across the root room, stumbled on the base of the central ladder, and collapsed. Crispin wrapped an arm around Orpaan. "It's all right! All right! He's not hurt!"

Orpaan clung to him, weeping frantically. Jacithrew lay prone, fingering the bottom rung of the ladder. Suddenly he bounced upright. Tears mixed with smiles on his face. "Come on! Bring the child! We can get my flying machine up into the tree!"

"No!" Crispin said.

Orpaan tugged frantically at him. "We've got to do what he says! Got to! Come on!"

Suddenly Crispin felt exhausted. "Suit yourself then. All right." He passed his hand over his face. *What's to be done?*

Jacithrew was already halfway up the ladder. "Ropes!" he shrilled. "They're in my bed! Find the ropes! Bring them! Quickly, quickly!"

Searching in Jacithrew's bed, which was in the brightest part of the dazzling room, Crispin thought: *I can't stay here any longer. Gonna rescue her and get out of this ferret hole. He may knife me in my sleep tonight, not because he remembers we quarreled, but just because he thinks for a moment that I'm someone else! How many people has he really been talking to, all the time I thought he was talking to me?*

From above, Jacithrew shouted shrilly. "Come on, my children! What are you waiting for?"

"Please," Orpaan whispered.

Crispin saw tears shining on the boy's cheeks. He was crying soundlessly. In the daemon glares, his face looked like a carving of wet teak.

Crispin scooped him into his arms. "Your head!" Orpaan sobbed, too late. A root-knot caught Crispin in the top of the skull, and he saw stars.

"Help me find those ropes," he said over the ringing in his ears. "We don't want your dadda to do himself in trying to climb that tree."

"He's *not* my dadda," Orpaan sobbed. "My dadda's dead!"

Fresh air! Fresh air! Crispin thought desperately as they rooted in Jacithrew's reeking blankets. *Fresh air!* The night outside was cold and clear and dizzy with daemons snapping, darting, chasing each other, filling the space between the earth and the stars with their own particular brand of terminal confusion. *What's to be done?*

A frost had struck the forest during the night. The front garden looked as though it had been coated with sugar.

Rae stood under a yew, holding a cup of hot tea, watching Sally and Millie, on the other side of the bare potato patch, yank winter artichoke roots out of the earth. She had offered her help, but they had refused. They were talking so softly that although the garden was as quiet as the rest of the Waste (the trickster women apparently hadn't bothered to entice birds and animals to inhabit their patch of reclaimed flora) Rae could only just hear the buzz of their voices. She knew they were talking about her.

All around the potato patch, boughs rustled in the hint of a breeze. She shivered and thanked the Queen that she had not been sleeping outside. After only a few days in Holstead House, the ordeal of the past couple of weeks was coming to seem more and more like a nightmare. And indeed, her nights were full of memories. The blood spurting out of her rude captor's eye mingled with the flames spurting from the windows of her room. The murdered man's shriek became the voice of an Apocalypist calling to her. *Sister . . . sister . . .* And then it was Crispin calling while she fled from him, weeping, guilty, through the forest. *Rae, where is my ray of light?*

It had all happened. But it seemed implausible that it had happened to her. She, Rae Ash (not Rae Clothwright, not anymore) wasn't made of such resilient stuff. Look how readily she had trusted her life to Crispin. A complete stranger! If she had been stronger, she would have taken responsibility for herself. Look how he had deserted her at the first sign of difficulty—as all her road companions had, all her life. No man could be depended on. Yet she had kept hoping, to the point of risking her life. What if he'd decided to leave her stranded in the middle of the Waste? What if Anthea, Liesl, Hannah, Mother, and the twins hadn't been there to save her?

But perhaps she had been *guided* here. Perhaps transcendence had finally pushed her to a place where she could have the peace she needed if enlightenment were to blossom in her. The trickster women did not flaunt their wealth, but they were as well-heeled as Valestock's richest daemonmongers. The Fewman brothers; Riddlebird; Gurrey; they, and perhaps three others, were each worth more than any heartlands squire. So, apparently, were the trickster women. The sheer numbers of priceless objects laid out haphazardly in the dusty drawing room told Rae that here she would not have to worry about making a living. Anthea's "working girls" were ladies, or as good as, after all.

And—her frivolous side briefly reasserted itself—it stood to reason that there must be a few bolts of good material somewhere in the house. Perhaps she would even be able to do something about the women's lackadaisical style of dress. Just because you were not on parade before hundreds every day was no reason to neglect your appearance! (Rae herself had spent an hour before the mirror this morning. After two weeks without soap, the state of her hair and skin was deplorable. She longed for rouge and hair oil.)

How would she dress them? For Anthea, dusty pastel hues. For Hannah—it would be a challenge to find colors that would set off her dark skin, and Rae hadn't seen enough of her to know what jewelry would suit, but she would love to get the chance to make her over. She could be beautiful. For Liesl—dark colors, certainly; but what material? Velvet, perhaps. For the twins—

She looked across at the winter artichoke bed, where the two fair girls were dawdling over their task.

Chance would be a fine thing!

Well, it's no business of theirs whether I gather artichokes or not—

She sauntered around the potato patch, and feeling their eyes on her, got down on her knees and started systematically digging the knobbly roots out of the clods of earth.

"Here."

Millie, who was slightly taller and had a scattering of acne on her chin, tossed a trowel across the fallen stems.

"Thanks." Rae smiled. Without looking up, she knew the twins were watching her, unmoving.

"You've done this before, haven't you? Most people don't know what to look for. They get stones in with the 'chokes." Sally's voice held the hint of a sneer.

Rae sat back on her heels. "Where I grew up, we children had to do the gardening. We were the only ones who did any work."

"Where did you grow up?"

"Plum Valley Domain."

"That's a long way from here."

Rae tossed a double handful of artichokes into the bucket.

"You're spoiling your dress," Millie remarked after a moment. "You'll have to wash it yourself, you know."

"I'm pretty familiar with the way things are done here, I think," Rae said amicably.

"That's what you think," Sally sniggered.

"'Choke sap is so hard to get out," Millie said.

Rae brushed earth off the brown wool. Its serviceableness frustrated her beyond words. "I'll manage."

"You talk like a Wraith," Millie said.

"What's a Wraith?" Rae asked.

"No," Sally said. "She talks like a *man*."

"Oh, my, that's what it is!"

Both of them laughed. Rae winced. She was no match for the two of them. The only way she knew how to meet sniping was with silence, and she did so.

"You know what's going to happen to you, don't you," Millie said suddenly.

"No, I don't." Rae looked up, alarms ringing inside her head.

"Huh. Just as I thought. We were different; we guessed. That's why we didn't—"

Sally elbowed her twin.

Millie flushed. "Me and Sal grew up on a farm. Near Valestock. That was before we ran away."

"Why?"

"We were different. We always knew that."

I always knew that, too, Rae thought with sudden bitterness.

"The thing that makes us different, it's a kind of—of—"

"Strength," Sally said.

"Yes. You have to have it. To do what Liesl and Anthea and Hannah do. You can't be one of us unless you have it."

The obvious implication was that Rae didn't. She felt bruised. Why did they hate her? She had tried to be friendly. Her nails were packed full of dirt. She picked up a broken bit of stem and scraped. The silence of the garden, which for all its greenness contained no living things except insects, was unbearable. "How old were you when you ran away?" she asked them. It seemed the most innocuous question possible.

When Sally spoke there was wariness in her voice. "What do you want to know *that* for?"

"I—I don't know."

"Because we aren't telling you!" They held on to each other's arms, shaking. "We can't tell you that, so stop asking!"

Why are they afraid? Rae wondered in confusion.

"Girls."

Rae had never been so relieved to hear Liesl's deep voice. She stumbled to her feet, dropping the trowel and her lapful of 'chokes, and turned. Liesl was holding something that looked like two yards of expensive silver lamé scrunched up in one hand. It would have made an attractive bodice, though there wasn't enough for a whole dress. She jerked her head. "Rae. Come with me."

Rae cast a glance around the potato patch. She felt like a wild deer brought to bay: no way to escape.

Liesl frowned. "Don't be afraid. I'm giving you a chance at the real thing. Whatever Anthea has shown you, it was just pussyfooting around. I know she hasn't taken you into the Waste."

Where *was* Anthea? Rae's protector, the only one of them who stood wholeheartedly behind her—

"If you refuse . . . It's a responsibility," Liesl said. "Some of us can handle it. The rest"—she looked at the twins and smiled unexpectedly—"let their prey get away, and have to stay home and dig the garden."

"Oh, *Liesl*," Millie said, and laughed. "That's not fair!" After a minute Sally joined in, giggling hysterically. They clung to each other.

"Go on, take her then!"

"We don't want her!"

"Leave us alone!"

"You're so *mean*, Leeze!"

Liesl laughed and blew them a kiss. She started off across the potato patch, then looked back impatiently at Rae. "I thought you were coming?"

Rae gulped and followed her, stumbling across the potato rows.

Women are truer, they never accept you on face value, the way men do, she thought desperately. *They see deeper, straight to your weaknesses, and before they accept you they've got to make you feel like* nothing, *like a child! Oh, I pray I'm not wrong about them, I pray it's worth it in the end to be humiliated like this—*

Tears pricked her eyes. *Was* she wrong? Did Liesl, Sally, and Millie really hate her? But if Liesl hated her, why was she "giving her a chance at the real thing"?

"Hurry *up*," Liesl said from the blinding, blurry greenness ahead.

Liesl and Rae came through the Waste to the daemons' dell in a matter of twenty minutes. Today there were no daemons picnicking on the grass; in fact the place was nearly deserted. Liesl lowered herself cross-legged to the ground, hid her piece of silver cloth inside her coat, and buttoned it. Her eyes were the color of blue chalk. Red holly berries glowed like frozen fireworks over her head, only a little brighter than her hair. "There's a good-sized one in the water. A Jaseras. Go look."

Rae moved cautiously to the edge of the pool. The surface was like smooth black rock. Tiny daemons circled above the water, slowed down by the cold, their wings layered veils. "I don't see it."

"It's lying low. It's eaten. That's why everything is so quiet. The little ones won't come back out until it's gone. That makes your task easier."

"Couldn't you show me how it's done first?" Rae said desperately. "And then I'll do it? I mean, I've never seen—"

"Daemons are not like fancywork, girl," Liesl snapped. "One chance is all you get. There's no unpicking."

"I don't even know how to begin!"

"Right, then!" Liesl folded her hands on her crossed ankles. "You have to *listen* for it. You'd never have got this far into the forest unless you had some kind of an affinity for them. They'd have driven you mad otherwise. But now you have to listen with your whole self, not just your ears. That's important. When you hear a red, round, oily *mmm* like a Jaseras, call to it by name. Jaseras . . . Jaseras . . . like that." Liesl's voice was meandering. "And summon it. Summon it. Summon it."

"How do you know its name?"

"Practice."

"But—but—I mean—why do they even have names?"

"They *are* their names. You'll hear. You'll see. In a better world we would merely be witnesses to their names . . ."

She fell silent. Her lips moved as if she was chewing. She looked suddenly old.

Rae shivered and knelt on the bank.

"Jaseras?" she said, with a feeling that she was making herself ridiculous by taking part in this game. "Jaseras! Are you there?"

It all happened in the space of a few seconds, and afterward, she was not the same person ever again. Such moments of personal flux are rare, and it is even rarer to know them as they happen. Rae did. She smelled the scent you got in a smithy where men were forging iron, and knew the world had changed forever. The air crackled. Tiny fingers tugged her hair. Small daemons were gathering around her head, diaphanous wings drifting across her vision. She had no attention to spare to brush them away. "Slow smooth powerful one," she whispered, the words coming from she knew not where. "Jaseras. Body of beauty."

She *knew*, as if she could see into the water (but the knowledge had nothing to do with sight) that the daemon had thrust himself out of his rock cranny under the bank, unlidding his dark eyes, that he was paddling toward the surface, responding to the sound of his name. As he came closer, her world loosened at the seams, and opened up. There was a genuine connection between daemons and humans, something stranger and stronger by far than the connection between friends, or between man and woman, a resonance of blood, a forgotten instinct—and she had just remembered it. It was like feeling the person you loved most in the world coming toward you. Patterns of fiery light formed in her skull, burning so bright that the world before her eyes paled: tendrils of light reaching toward each other, melding. When she joined with the daemon she would no longer have to endure the distractions and demands with which her body constantly assailed her. She would dematerialize.

Nothing life offered could be so sweet as that freedom. Who would be human?

Jaseras sounded.

The tiny daemons scattered, chittering, as his sleek head thrust through the surface. He must have been at least ten feet tall when he stood on solid ground. His face was more beautiful than any man's, his hair floated on the water like black weed, his spine was finned like a trout's, his skin was the color of red rose petals. She wanted to touch him.

Slowly, so slowly that the moment seemed to last hours, he reached out of the water and took her hand. His skin was wet but not slimy, soft but not clammy. Her hand was completely hidden in his fingers.

"Now get up," she heard Liesl saying, from a great distance. "Stand up, girl! Make him follow you!"

How did Liesl expect her to move? She knew instinctively that movement would shatter the communion. Jaseras's power pulsed through her, an electrical, sexual buzz that came in waves as he rested his elbow on the bank and rubbed his cheek against her arm. She couldn't have moved for the life of her.

"Rae!"

That wasn't Liesl, was it?

"Hist! Rae! Up here!"

A familiar voice. Whispering. Rae suspected she wouldn't have been able to hear it if not for the daemon. Physically connected to Jaseras's power, her senses were sharpened tenfold.

With a great effort, she focused on the woods at the top of the other side of the dell.

Nothing moved.

"*Now*, Rae! Here!" Liesl shouted, and Rae felt the length of silver lamé hitting her back and sliding to the ground. Jaseras flinched. She kissed his fingers, she would swallow him whole if that would make him stay with her—

"Rae, I'm here! Dammit, girl! Just give me some kind of signal! I'll deal with *her*, but I—I have to know if you're on her side! If you are—you're not, are you? You're not!?"

"This is the hard part, Rae!" Liesl's voice had taken on an oddly pleading tone.

"Rae, in the name of the Queen! Give me a *sign*—" Crispin was pleading with her, too, in the only way he knew how, with anger. He must not think she could hear him. Was he readying himself to attack Liesl even now? He must not do that.

She sat back on her heels. "Crispin, where are you? I can't see you!" Her voice was as loud as a child's cry, and wavery, petulant. The connection with Jaseras broke. She clapped her hand over her mouth.

She was back in her own body, huge, awkward, cold. Physical sensation roared through her, destroying the fine points to which Jaseras had tuned her senses. Her feet had gone to sleep. She opened her eyes and found that she had sprawled over into the grass. Liesl was standing above her. "Get away!" she shouted at the forest. "This is not your place, Wraith! Jaseras!"

The big daemon splashed out of the water in a rainbow of transformation. His legs split into a fan of feathers. His arms stretched into wings of translucent skin. His face elongated and stiffened into a beak. He rose into the air and dived between the pines, shrieking gloriously.

Rae screamed, "Jaseras! Oh, my love!"

And the daemon faltered, reeled through the air, and fell in a muddle next to her. He smelled of burnt leather. Liesl choked and staggered back. Up in the pines, there was the noise of somebody—actually, it sounded like two or three somebodies—getting away. Rae gathered Jaseras into her arms. She did not have even to try for communion with him, not this time—he sucked her in. His power pulse boomed like thunder, terrifyingly erratic. *Crispin. Jaseras. Cris. Jaseras. Jasercris—*

Silence descended on the dell.

Liesl pulled Rae roughly to her feet. "How I hate them!" Her low voice was trembly with loathing. "Forever interfering in our business! The Waste is *ours*, not theirs! All they know how to do is destroy our work, the sly, black shadows!" She shook her fist at the brown face of the forest above the waterfall. Her voice cracked. "You have *never*, not *once*, done anything which might encourage me to respect you!"

Rae gathered Jaseras to her breasts, trying to support his trailing wings and his water-slick body. He was transforming into human-form again, slowly, as if invisible hands were remolding his body from the outside. He was very heavy. She couldn't feel the pulse of his power anymore.

"Leave it," Liesl said. "He's dead."

Revulsion washed through Rae. She dropped the demogorgon and scrambled backward.

"Yes, I know." Roughly, Liesl pulled her to her feet, well away from the corpse. It was as corporeal as any dead bird, though no one could have mistaken it for a bird.

"We have to bury him," Rae said shakily. "Don't we? Shouldn't we do *something*?"

Liesl pulled her to her feet. "No. There's nothing we can do. It's best to leave them for the carrion-eating daemons. That way, their deaths are of *some* use."

"Don't you *care*?" Rae heard her voice scaling toward hysteria.

Liesl stuck her hands into the pockets of her coat. "I know what you're thinking, Rae. There are far too many of them, and nonetheless one could mourn each one as a lover. But if you think grief is intolerable, try guilt. We ship out hundreds of them every year, and each one that goes into captivity would be better off dead."

"I don't understand why he died. He flew up—and then—"

"The Wraiths killed him out of sheer spite. They are no better than wild beasts."

Liesl spoke as if she knew Jaseras's killers from long experience. Yet it had definitely been Crispin up in the pines. Then, Liesl could not know it had been he. Logic helped Rae regain a little self-control.

"Who are they? The Wraiths?"

Without warning Liesl started toward the edge of the dell. Rae scurried after her.

"They lived in this forest before it was ever part of Ferupe. Before there *was* a Ferupe. They have daemon blood. A lot of it, even today. It's possible to civilize them, but even then you can't trust them." They started up the side of the dell. Rae's feet slipped on the exposed roots; her dress hampered her movement. "Our sister Hannah is a Wraith," Liesl said. "You must remember that. Don't treat her the way you would treat anyone else, because she'll take advantage of you. That's how they are."

They were walking through the dead pines now. Liesl held a broken branch out of Rae's way.

"You didn't do too badly," she said abruptly. "Even if the Wraiths hadn't come, I would have had to step in—you weren't in any condition to follow through on your initial overture to him. But you established communion in such a way as to make me think that you have talent."

Rae's heart swelled. In the back of her mind, she was appalled that so qualified an approval, from one she mistrusted, could make her happy. But she had forgotten what it was like to be approved of. The word *encouragement* had not been part of Madame Fourrière's vocabulary.

"Thank you," she stammered.

Liesl laughed. "You don't trust me. You're wise. But listen now"—her face went serious—"you would do well not to trust Anthea, either. She may act like your own mother, but she's a daemon in disguise."

"What?"

"Oh, not literally." Liesl's mouth quirked. "I mean that she is extremely charismatic, in such a way as to deceive the unwary. When a new girl comes to the house, Anthea isn't straight with her, the way I'm being with you now—she tries to draw her in by making this seem a far nicer place than it is. You'd think she would know better after the number of failures we've had. But in fact she doesn't have the wisdom which comes with age. She's much younger than she looks. How old do you think she is?"

"Sixty?" Rae hazarded. "Seventy?"

"She's a year younger than I am. I'll be twenty-eight this summer. There's no such thing as an ancient trickster woman, Rae. Mother is only forty. The twins are thirteen. You'd never have guessed that, would you? But some of us have aged faster than others. Like Anthea."

There was no way Anthea could be only nine years older than Rae. It was impossible. The sun of her success with Jaseras went in. "You're just trying to get me on your side!" she blurted. "You and Anthea hate each other! That's obvious! Why should I believe a word you say?"

"Why should you believe a word *she* says? In the name of the Queen, follow through, Rae," Liesl said irritably. "Of course I want to get you on my side. For your own good. I don't hate Anthea, in fact I love her dearly, I'm merely trying to tell you the truth about her. She's afraid of losing her authority. But in fact she never had any. There's no use in looking to her for protection. The rules are the rules, and none of us have any say in *that* matter. Anthea did at one time, but she couldn't hold out long enough to make the rest of us accept her as Mother's successor. And for years now Mother has been too much lost in her mind to enforce her will."

Rae shuddered. Up ahead, greenness glimmered through the denuded pines. They crossed the road, a sandy strip like a winding slot in the pines, into the garden.

"Is it all too much for you? There are traders coming from Valestock next week," Liesl said. "You still have the option of leaving with them."

Back to Valestock? Never. *Crispin . . .* He had come for her, he had *come*, as she had feared he would not. But she was no longer sure she wanted to leave to go with him.

Her communion with Jaseras had changed her outlook entirely, coloring everything a slightly different shade. Certain things, such as communing with daemons again, had taken on new importance. Other things no longer had much importance to her at all. Her gratitude to the trickster women had been replaced by the need to root through their secrets and extract anything else that might be as wonderful as what she had experienced this afternoon (no matter how badly it had ended). Liesl's apparent straightforwardness made her perversely eager to find out what the red-haired woman was still hiding. "I'd rather stay," she said definitely.

"Very well," Liesl said. "Maybe you'll change your mind."

* * *

Gingerly, Crispin touched the bite on his arm. "Fuck. Fuck. Fuck."

He and Orpaan sat with their backs against a pine from which the bark was peeling in long, threadlike pieces. Orpaan was weaving the threads into triangular mats. "He'll like these," he said. "He might be able to use them for the flying machine. To make it more comfy."

When Orpaan said he, he meant one person: the madman Jacithrew. Crispin did not answer. He had had all he could stomach of Jacithrew and the flying machine. His arm burned as if a hundred fire ants had all stung him in the same spot. Oil and salt. That helped, he remembered. If he only had some. And the foul smell of the daemon's death clung to his clothes and skin; only a good wash would get rid of that, and washing was a forgotten luxury.

He looked over at Orpaan. Even if the child, like Jacithrew, could trick daemons, how was it that he could *kill* them? Millsy had not been able to do that, nor had he implied that *any* tricksters could. Orpaan hadn't even struck out at the daemon, just slithered in front of Crispin and stood his ground, his little fists clenched.

Crispin closed his hand over the child's fluffy head and turned Orpaan's face gently upward. The small fingers fell still on the bark weaving. Eyes empty of deception met Crispin's. "Orpie," Crispin said. "It's important. Please tell me. How did you make that daemon stop attacking us?"

"Because you didn't." Orpaan blinked. His eyelids were almost purple. With his skinny body he bore a resemblance to a naked bird.

"I said how, not why," Crispin said.

"You were fighting it all wrong. If I hadn't been there, you would've got hurt." Orpaan spoke fast, but Crispin was coming to understand his oddly stressed accents. "I had to."

"I couldn't've done what you did, Orpie. No way. Who taught you?"

"Nobody taught me. 'M a Wraith. Wraiths know daemons."

"Am *I* a Wraith?"

"No! *He* thinks so, but you're not!"

"Could you teach me to do what you did?"

Orpaan appeared to think deeply. "Maybe," he allowed at last. "But your blood's probably wrong." Crispin held his breath.

Trickery was in the blood. And blood could not be changed. But mightn't there be a chance? Everything was different in the Waste. Anything could happen.

"One time, Hannah told me—she told me if I wanted, me and her could share our blood with her sisters, and make them stronger. I don't like them. I didn't want to. I s'pose—maybe—I like you. I could do it for *you*."

"*Could* you?"

"Maybe! I dunno! She said it would hurt!"

Orpaan was avoiding Crispin's eyes and fiddling furiously with his pine bark. Nevertheless, Crispin couldn't help pressing him. The pain in his arm needled at his patience.

"Orpie. Where are the rest of the Wraiths? I haven't seen any shimmer-trees anywhere around here."

"Cause there aren't any around here. Too close to the tricky ladies!"

"Then why do you and Jacithrew live here, on your own?"

"Just cause—cause—cause they give us stuff. Stuff for me. They're sorry for me!"

But not sorry enough to take you to live with them! Crispin thought. *Not even Hannah, although she's one of you!*

He had disliked the trickster women without even meeting them. Now he had seen one, and it had done nothing to improve his opinion of them. The redhead had looked like a farmwife in that sack of a dress, with her man's boots. And she'd dressed Rae the same way! Jacithrew had implied that the trickster women had as much money as minor royalty—so why didn't they use it? Crispin had always envisioned trickster women—when he'd envisioned them at all—as dryadlike creatures scarcely dressed at all in veils and jewels, speaking in lovely flutelike voices, floating through the trees with daemons trailing behind them like lovesick troubadours. The reality was not only less appealing, it was downright distasteful. And the way she had been speaking to Rae . . . ! Crispin had nearly plunged down into the dell. Only Orpaan's urgent warnings held him back.

She's got daemons! the little boy had hissed, his eyes showing white around the irises. *She could kill you! Just like that!*

But there were so many invisible daemons in the dell, thick as feathers from a burst pillow. Which of them "belonged" to the red-haired woman? Millsy's tame daemons couldn't have killed anyone. How much stronger were hers?

When he saw that big one rise from the water and transform into a bird, he knew. He had tried to fend it off with his knife, but it just dematerialized wherever he touched it. He couldn't fight air. Meanwhile it had pecked him badly. If Orpaan hadn't done whatever he had done, Crispin would undoubtedly have been killed.

"Stop messing with my hair!" Orpaan shouted, wrenching away.

"Sorry." Crispin sighed, and stood up. There were no explanations. There never were. "Let's take you home."

Maybe he should just forget about Rae! Better forget her than die trying to rescue her! It was becoming harder and harder to remember the world outside the Waste. If he didn't move on soon, his mind might warp like Jacithrew's.

Orpaan tugged at him. "*Will* get your girl back," he promised. "They're trying to make her tricky, but we won't let them! We'll get her!"

His voice was sad as only an eight-year-old's can be, vibrating so much with misery that it was almost comical. But he wasn't playing for effect. A child raised in isolation has no sense of theater. Crispin knew Orpaan would be deeply hurt if he laughed. Instead, he bent and swept the little boy into his arms. Orpaan made a small noise and buried his head in Crispin's shoulder.

"You know what, squire," Crispin said. "I could use your help when I go to get her. You're more of a match for those bitches than I am."

What he really wanted to say was: *I'm not going to leave you. Not ever.*

"Yeah. I'll help." Orpaan sighed and dug his fingers into Crispin's neck. "Carry me."

"Wriggle round, then. Piggyback. Ouch, fuck, don't grab my arm like that! Shit. Are you holding on?" He felt Orpaan nodding. "Here we go then!"

It was a walk of perhaps three miles through the forest to the clearing where Jacithrew's pine stood. Crispin was wearier than he thought, and his arm ached. He had to put Orpaan down before they had gone half a mile. Neither of them suggested using the road. Even in the company of a child who was a "native" of the Wraithwaste in every sense of the word, Crispin felt as if he were sneaking through enemy territory, surreptitiously observed.

Daemons according to the Greek idiom, signify either Angels or the Souls of Men . . . the Souls of Saints, and Spirits of Angels.

—H. More

The Heart of Light

Icy rain spattered on the window of Rae's room. She sat on the bed, fully dressed, stroking the marmalade cat which she'd found asleep on her stomach when she woke half an hour earlier. The daemon-trapping disaster had worn her out more than she realized. When she and Liesl returned, Anthea had professed not to have been told Rae was being taken to the dell. Scandalized, she had fussed over Rae and sent her to lie down. Rae had slept through to night.

Her room was overbright, as usual, and hot, lit sharp-shadowed by the daemon glares affixed to the ceiling. The bright ozonic *notscent* permeated the air. A few minutes ago Rae had discovered that if she looked at the glares from above, she could see a shadowy, multi-legged shape in each one, writhing in its hardwood dish. She guessed that before long she would wish she knew how to turn them off.

She looked out the window into the lashing dark. Somewhere a few miles away Crispin was sleeping in the cold and the wet. Or probably not sleeping: no one could sleep in this. She visualized him huddled in the shelter of a thicket, smoking the last of his vile cigarettes to try and keep warm.

A key rattled in the lock. Rae turned. It was Hannah. The Wraith woman balanced the tray of food she carried on one knee while she closed the door behind her.

"Anthea told me to bring you this." She set the tray down on the bedside table. As always, Rae was taken off guard by the light ironic tone of her voice, so at odds with the perpetually sullen look on her face. "She said you hadn't eaten since breakfast."

"I haven't! Thank you." The scrambled eggs looked delicious. Rae reached for the mug of hot milk and sipped, savoring the faint taste of spices. It would be rude to start eating until Hannah left.

Hannah sat down on the foot of the bed. "You went to the dell with Liesl today?"

"Is Anthea still angry about that?"

Hannah shook her head. "But I ought to warn you about Liesl. She's not what she seems."

It's the same thing all over again, Rae thought in frustration. The endless, thinly veiled backbiting which seemed designed for no higher purpose than to turn her around and around until she didn't know whether to trust any of them! Then of course there was the possibility that they were all in it together, and meant to confuse her! Whatever the case, she was sick, sick, sick of it. "If all you're going to do is criticize her, please don't bother," she said shakily.

Hannah looked at her with a smile hovering around her mouth. "You wouldn't speak like that to me if I were any of the others," she said. "You're lucky I don't hold it against you. Do you know why I don't intend to? You're a Kirekuni, and I'm a Wraith; we are neither of us like them. They would speak to you differently, too, if you hadn't . . ." She made a small chopping motion with her fingers.

Rae found herself disliking Hannah even more. She fought to keep her face stony.

The Wraith woman folded her hands demurely in her lap. "But to be fair, you can trust Liesl, Rae. Underneath, she's kindhearted. Kinder than Anthea. Anthea is constrained by the responsibilities of her authority—or her *perceived* authority."

"It was Liesl who told me you were a Wraith. I didn't know what you were."

"Not even Liesl would be able to resist bringing that up," Hannah said bitterly.

"Are you—?"

"I just told you so. Look at me." Hannah tugged a strand of wavy black hair. "I was born not ten miles from here."

"But you look nothing like Crispin!" Rae bit her tongue. Whatever

Crispin's parentage, he hadn't got a drop of blood in common with Hannah. "What is a Wraith?"

"Oh, Queen." Hannah tossed her head. "There aren't as many of us as there once were. I haven't spoken to another one in ten years—except for an old man who lives near here with his adopted son. I've taken them up as a sort of a cause, in lieu, I suppose, of doing anything more for my people. They're helpless, they can't fend for themselves."

"I haven't seen them."

"Of course I don't allow them to come wandering around the house." Hannah must have read Rae's expression as accusatory. "There's no need to look at me like that. The extinction of a people is a dreadful thing. Can you blame me for not choosing to be extinguished along with them?"

"No, of course not!" *Did you deliberately abandon your people?* Rae was wondering. *Or were you caught, compelled, coaxed into abandoning them?* She did not want to follow that line of reasoning too far. "But what do you mean, they're being extinguished?" she asked. "I don't understand! Are we in danger, too?"

"In the name of the Queen, girl!" Hannah picked up her feet and laced her fingers around her ankles. "Of course we're in danger! Have you never heard of the war?"

"Oh," Rae said. "You mean the soldiers are killing your people?"

"Not precisely. Well, not in a consistent fashion. *We* aren't Ferupe's enemy." The daemon glares cast shadows on Hannah's face that twisted as she moved, disguising her expression. "Maybe we were, thousands of years ago, but now the army pretends we don't exist. It's easier for everyone that way."

Rae imagined the kind of persecution she and the other children of the Dynasty had endured, magnified to include the carnage she vaguely associated with the war. "How can you say such a thing?"

Hannah's face did not change. "Because we really don't exist anymore, as a people." She sighed. "All right. I'll tell you a story. The story of the Wraiths."

Rae glanced involuntarily at her supper tray, then returned her gaze to Hannah's face. The last thing she needed was to offend yet another of them.

"Before history began, say twenty-five centuries ago, the Wraiths owned the Wraithwaste. They didn't have palaces or treasures, but they had all they needed. They had slaves to labor for them: the daemons, who at that time were not crazed beasts, but another race. The catastrophe of the present day began—this is all in the history books which you'll be shown if you stay here long enough—when Thraziaow, Wraith King, took his great entourage of Wraiths and daemons out of the Waste to join forces with a people who had more potential for greatness. The Ferupians."

As a child, Rae had been made to repeat litanies: endless lists of Kings and Queens who at one time or another had held all humanity bound up in their hearts. Lists which began with the name of Thraziaow. No one had ever said he was a Wraith.

"One can only suppose that the King's aim was to unite the Waste with Ferupe, and create a power that could not be stopped. And his descendants, though they soon became fat, white, and inbred, were more successful than he could have dreamed. When the Wraiths first came out of the Waste, the Ferupians were little more than crofters ruled by petty nobles; but over the course of a thousand years, Ferupe expanded its borders to Cype in the east, Izte Kchebuk'ara in the south, and the snowlands in the north. The Wraithwaste remained its western border. Not *of* Ferupe, yet the most treasured possession of the Kings, because of the daemons."

"My teachers said that Thraziaow had revelations," Rae said. "They never said he was a Wraith, though. I never heard of Wraiths."

"I'm surprised you were even taught of him! Ferupians don't like to remember that their empire blossomed under the tutelage of Wraiths—even Wraiths who had a healthy share of that desire for personal advancement which is such a cherished part of the Ferupian mentality. As for the revelations, your teachers were right. Wraiths used to be prophets, it came from their constant proximity to daemons. The gift has almost vanished now. I think it was concentrated in the ruling dynasty, and when Thraziaow left the Waste, he took it with him, just as he took the secrets of daemon mastery. Did your teachers tell you that?"

Rae did not want Hannah to ask any more questions about her teachers. The trickster women's tolerance might extend to Kirekunis, but it certainly did not embrace culties. "What were the secrets of daemon mastery?"

"That's the kind of thing I should be talking to you about." Hannah gave an obviously forced smile. "Mastery was the talent of the Wraiths. Trickery is women's business, and it has all but replaced mastery. The Queen, and her relatives, are probably the only masters of daemons left. Then there's handling, which is the specialty of men. It's a very fine balance, and everyone distrusts everyone else—especially the daemons, who resent all of humanity. *Resent* isn't a strong enough word. They hate us. They would destroy us all if they could."

"They hate us? How can they hate us? They're just—just daemons . . ." As Rae spoke, she remembered communing with Jaseras. For the first time in her life, she had felt herself in the presence of a kindred soul.

Hannah shook her head. "We should never have let Anthea take you under her wing. She forgets how little common people know about daemons. She forgets that most people, and especially women, take them for granted, like food and air. Listen. Daemons were *people* once. Human, you understand. A race native to the Waste. Like the Wraiths. But not as clever as they were strong, and plagued with mutation. After millennia of enslavement by Wraiths and Ferupians, for all intents and purposes they have stopped being human. All they have left now is the desire to rebel and kill."

"So why don't they?"

"Because ninety percent of the daemons currently in use across the world are just splinterons. You won't have heard that term before. Handlers tend to use it to mean tiny feed daemons. But in reality, a splinteron is a daemon collared by trickster women in the Echre Domain forests, say, or the Southern Wylde. Over the centuries daemons have escaped, or been deliberately freed, in woodlands all over the world. The descendants of those daemons are like farmbred tigers: just as dangerous as any Wraithwaste daemon, but passive, and easier to trick. A Waste daemon can bend hundreds of splinterons to its will, given a chance, and in fact that's how people are running the newest factories—the human overseer-handlers control the Wraith daemons, which in turn control the lesser daemons.

"Splinterons come of isolated branches of the Wraithwaste blood strain. Centuries of inbreeding have weakened their—their ability to *conduct*. Every handler knows that a Waste daemon is the most powerful, but, just like a man, he thinks that that's because it's bigger. On the contrary. Waste daemons generally *are* bigger, but that has little to do with it." She was ticking off points on her fingers, looking closely at Rae. "The daemon race is structured in a different way from humanity. Each human being has his own life, his own soul. But daemons all over the world have what might be termed a collective life thread. Each one, from splinterons to ancient Wraithwaste daemons, draws on the strength of all the others. Splinterons are only lesser because they're not such good conduits of the occult."

She's describing the daemon race sort of the same way Sister Flora and Brother James used to describe the human race, Rae thought. *All linked together.* It made sense, a dire, horrible kind of sense. She just could not quite pin it down—

"Wraithwaste daemons can provide thousands of dp without exerting themselves. For heavy industry, they're the only ones which will do. And that is why the war started." Hannah took a breath. Rae twisted her hands in her lap. Anthea had said Hannah would tell her about the war, that it was the Wraith woman's specialty. But it wasn't what she wanted to hear about. Transcendence had guided her; she felt herself on the verge of truth. *Tell me more about the collective life thread! Who holds the end of it? Where is the knot?*

Yet she did not dare interrupt Hannah, especially now that the Wraith woman was leaning forward, speaking with passion. At any moment she might say something that would rip the curtain off the picture of apocalypse that had until now hung in shadow in the central room of Rae's mind.

"The Kirekuni Empire is far younger than the Ferupian Empire." Rae knew this. When she was younger, she'd had to memorize history backward and forward. "Some say that the first Significants were cousins of the Ferupian Kings—that the Lizard Significant, unlike his subjects, has no tail. That's as it may be. But the histories are definite on the fact that in the beginning, the Kirekunis were isolated between their rivers, rich in metal, but ignorant of industry and technology. It was through contact with the by-then-full-grown Ferupian Empire, and trade by sea and across the northern pass, that the Kirekunis learned how to handle daemons. They instantly applied daemonology to warfare, as the Ferupians never had, and the Significant Empire grew to greatness, dominating the whole western side of the continent. In hindsight, we can blame the Dynasty for failing to see that if they taught the Kirekunis all the tricks of daemon manipulation, the Kirekunis would come to envy the Ferupians their possession of the greatest daemon source in the world. It must have become clear quite quickly that the Kirekunis had far more drive than the Wraith Kings, or at any rate their descendants, ever had. In building their empire, they didn't just per-suade dozens of scattered domains to unite under a single monarch—a relatively peaceful undertaking—but they marched out-ward from their homes on the plains and conquered thousands of miles of desert and steppe. They built Okimachi. But even there, daemons have always been scarce. I have heard that in Kirekune, it would be unheard of to burn a daemon for light." Hannah gestured to the daemon glares. "In all the lands that they conquered, the Kirekunis did not find one source of daemons as rich as the Wraithwaste. And even today, they depend on splinterons from the daemons that Ferupe once sent them in friendship, and later traded for metal. That's why they mounted the war: to capture the Waste, which Ferupe had never allowed them to colonize as we do." She shook her head. "We *should* have anticipated it! After all, every other time the Significants have wanted something, they have just rolled out their legions and taken it.

"But this time they were met with resistance. Unlike the barbarian peoples, Ferupe had the resources to fight back. And I do not think it will ever stop fighting until the whole Wraithwaste is destroyed, and there's nothing left to fight for."

Rae shuddered. Questions were bubbling in her mind, but she could not ask them. She could not let Hannah see how much she knew already.

"That's the irony of it!" Hannah said violently. "The Lizards are destroying the very thing they're fighting for! They are settling the lands over which their soldiers have advanced. There are no more daemons there."

"But—but then—when the Waste is all cleared, there won't be any more daemons at all, will there?" Rae grabbed at a thread of hope. "If they have a collective life thread, they'll all just die, won't they?"

"No—no! *That* isn't the risk—" For the first time since she'd begun speaking, Hannah checked herself. She shook her head, pressed her lips together, and turned away.

Rae wanted to weep with frustration. A light was glowing in

that room of apocalypse, but as yet it was too dim to see by. She had never imagined that a revelation might be stimulated by someone else; she'd always imagined it as a visitation, a swoon of lights and flutes. Yet everything was always far more mundane than one expected, wasn't it? On a rainy winter night in a farmhouse in the middle of a dead forest, the world lights up and hangs dripping.

"You can't start explaining and then just stop!"

"Can't I?" Hannah laughed bitterly.

"Everybody's always told me half-truths. Even my teachers, when I was little, told me half-truths. They didn't know the whole story. You know the other half. You've got to tell me! You and I are alike, aren't we?" She used Hannah's own argument against her. "Telling me isn't like telling anyone else!"

"I can't help wondering why you want to know so badly."

Rae forced herself to meet Hannah's gaze. "I communed with a daemon today," she said, knowing that for Hannah, that would explain everything, and anything.

Hannah smiled. The light in her face took Rae's breath away. "It's a unique experience, isn't it? It stretched your mind wide open. You realized that the definition of humanity is at once broader and narrower than you had been led to believe. . . . But I am a Wraith, and perhaps it was different for you. For me, communing with a daemon under Liesl's guidance was just a little bit different from what I'd been doing most of my life—just enough different that everything that had been unrelated clicked into place."

"You've described it exactly," Rae said delightedly. "I always wanted to make my living in the theater, the *real* theater, not the music hall—"

Hannah's smile died. "Rae, I'm not talking about playacting. I'm an unnatural creature. I'm a result of things that happened decades, centuries, before I was born. I need to talk about those things. I have to talk about them. Liesl doesn't—" She shook her head.

"The Wraiths are the key, aren't they?"

"The key to what?"

"To daemons!"

Hannah shrugged. "You could say that." Her dark eyes gleamed starlike under luxuriant fringes of lash. *Peach chiffon,* Rae thought wildly. *Layers and layers of handkerchief-pointed hems. A sleeveless bodice with detail of glass beads dyed to match the fabric . . .*

"There's nothing more to say about the Wraiths apart from the fact that we will soon be no more." Hannah spoke absently. Yet her eyes did not leave Rae's face. "For the first few hundred years we were left in peace. But as the Ferupian Empire expanded, daemon machines were developed, and the demand for daemons increased exponentially. In the last century, industries have sprung up all over the country. As far back as the tenth century, Ferupian women were sent into the Waste, first to learn from the Wraiths, then to oust them from the houses they had built with the Royal guilt money." Hannah waved her hand around the room. Rae shivered. "All the tricks that my sisters and I know were once second nature to the Wraiths, both men and women."

"They haven't forgotten *everything*, though, have they?"

Jaseras had fallen at her feet in a rain of feathers. There had been no sound of a blow, and no marks on the corpse. The demogorgon had simply been extinguished. By a Wraith?

Hannah shrugged. "All we have left is our instincts. The tribes are all split and gone. Before the war started, we had at least our dignity, and the underground homes we built when our houses were seized by the trickster women. Now we are no better than animals. And by the time the war is over we will be no more. The Ferupian army, as it is pushed east, is cutting down the trees rather than relinquish the daemon spawning grounds to the Kirekunis. And when the last acres are cleared, the last Wraiths will die, too. Unlike the daemons, who cling to the Waste only out of animal habit, we are bound here by our hearts. Me, for example. I am Ferupian in all but skin, but even I haven't left."

Rae wanted to say, *The war will never end. There's no need to be bitter. Everyone is going to die at the same time.*

Tears prickled her eyes.

"It's funny how you would have no idea there's a war going on," she said in a voice that trembled, looking out of the window at the rain-shot blackness. "Apart from the planes, I mean."

"Well, it isn't a rout. Or rather, it is, but on such a grand scale that it doesn't seem like one. In my lifetime the Lovoshire Parallel has moved back twice. It's about fifty miles west of here now. Since the war is supposedly being fought to preserve the daemon industry, King Athrenault decreed ninety years ago that we trickster women must not be distracted from our real business in order to provide for the army. And his son Ethrew and his granddaughter Lithrea have upheld the decree. The sparing of the Wraithwaste—of all the western domains, in fact—the entire slice of country between the Thavon War Route and the Salzeim War Route—is the only aim of the Ferupian war effort which has been accomplished. And yet if this house were fifty miles farther west, we'd be the slaves of the army! All rules fall by the wayside once you actually get within sight and sound of the war. I've seen it with my own eyes. There'd be officers quartered in Holstead House. All our daemons would be commandeered by the air force. If we were still there when the soldiers arrived, we'd be pressed into manufacturing screamer daemons. That's what's been happening to trickster women for almost a hundred years."

"But what will *happen* when the Waste is completely cleared?" Rae asked, maintaining a casual tone with a huge effort. "To the daemons, I mean? When there are no more Wraiths, and all the trickster women are in the employ of the army?"

"Well. This is what all of us at Holstead House think," Hannah said, still looking into Rae's face. Her gaze was so steady that it was eerie. "There are just as many daemons as ever there were. More. But the Wraiths are almost gone. Old Jacithrew, down the road—his family was killed by the army, and he went half-mad after the experience, and forgot everything he ever knew. More or less the same thing happened to his child, I believe. And the Wraiths are—how shall I put it? We're the chain that binds the daemons. How shall I put it?"

"The knot in the center of the strings," Rae said.

"That's good, kitten!" Hannah's voice was soft, meditative. "It has nothing to do with the actual Waste. Trees are just trees, after all. It has to do with the fragile balance between masters and slaves. A global balance of blood. For now the knot holds. But when the Wraiths are gone, it will unravel. The daemons that were once of the Waste will ooze out across the world, voiding their hate, killing one person here, one there, ten over there. And their freedom will coax the enslaved daemons out of their cells. It's not silver, or oak, that *really* holds them, but something more occult." *It's the Queen,* Rae thought. *Who is descended from Wraiths.* Comprehension was coming to her. "And when the slaves are free, the destruction will *really* start. Because people have been spreading splinterons across the whole world for two thousand years, it will not be localized. Everywhere that humans are, daemons will kill. Have you noticed that smell which follows Liesl and Anthea around? It's the smell of their pet daemons. It would poison you if you were exposed to it for long enough. It's what causes trickster women to age faster than ordinary people. And it's not even a taste of what dematerialized daemons could do if they put what is left of their minds to it." Hannah tucked her feet under her, getting comfortable.

Rae, frozen, could not move.

"Humans are defenseless against the kind of hate that kills with a touch. That's how we fear it will be. But it probably won't happen within our lifetimes. And it may never happen at all. It is merely trickster speculation. And we are notorious pessimists." Hannah giggled.

The light had been coming up slowly and steadily all the time Hannah spoke, and now it burned bright in the middle of Rae's mind, hollowing it out, erasing everything except the words which constituted the other half of the story, the last piece of the jigsaw. (Hannah lacked it. That was why she and the rest of the trickster women were really just as ignorant as the man in the street. They could and did fall back on *it-may-never-happen* patriotism. Rae did not have that option.)

The Queen is the knot.

The cutting of the knot would not cause plague or floods. Just the slow rebellion of the lower classes—the *real* lower classes, whom too few even factored into the balance, as a result of which all their prognostications were tragically flawed.

The reversal of the equation, she thought wildly. *There's nothing of justice about it. It's just the law of ebb and flow, the law that caused the Kirekunis to make war on Ferupe, that makes barbarians fight settled people, that makes a ferret bite its owner, that makes a netful of fish pour out and kill the fisherman when the net tears. The law of retribution.* She strove to hide her shudders. She was not the same person anymore. She had not been since this morning. The razor-pinioned bird was flapping to and fro across the inside of her mind, obscuring her vision. And yet there were circumstances. A dead forest, a farmhouse, a rainy night. A woman sitting on the foot of her bed. The existence of the bed. The existence of her body. These things meant she was still Rae Ash, and had to behave accordingly.

She bent her mind to the concerns of her "self" with a tremendous effort—and realized that if she tried to act as though nothing had happened, she would scream. She needed time to think. She needed—

"I'm really sorry," she said, and was surprised at the steadiness of her voice. "But—but do you think I could go to sleep now? All this history has worn me out."

Hannah stood up. There was something of anger in her brusque movement. It was as if she were trying to control disappointment. "Yes. Forgive me for my volubility. You probably weren't counting on such a long lecture! But you won't hear it from anyone else here—they like to dole out secrets slowly, over the course of years, whereas I feel that as a woman who is not Ferupian, not exactly, you deserve to know the other side of the story immediately. That way, you can choose whether to stay or go."

"But it's not the other side of the story." Rae lay back on her pillows, stifling an urge to yawn. Exhaustion battled despair and nameless need. Hannah stood over her, her face in shadow. "There isn't any other side," Rae said tiredly. "There are only lies. And truth."

"Very perspicacious," Hannah said. "And you haven't even eaten your supper. You really must forgive me. Do you want it now?"

"No. It's all right," Rae said. The daemon glares blurred together into a band of light around the tops of the walls.

"Poor child." Hannah stooped over her, smelling deliciously of newly washed hair and *not-scent*. One still took care of oneself, didn't one? There were certain standards that had to be maintained. That was why Rae had had to leave the Dynasty. They went too far. Their neglect of the standards around the maintenance of which day-to-day life was based had killed Saonna and it had been going to kill Rae, too. You *still* had to live, even if you were going to die tomorrow. You had to live *as though* you were going to die tomorrow.

"I've tired you. There you are . . . let me tuck you in . . . poor thing!"

Rae buried her face in the pillow. Blessed sleep. Hannah was stroking her hair.

"The truth is that no one knows much about the war," Hannah said. *No,* Rae thought: *I can't stand it, I can't bear to hear any more.* "The fact that the army is being pushed back is a well-kept secret, even outside the west. The soldiers who are invalided home are brainwashed into describing it as a series of strategic retreats. What a strategy! The Wraiths here know about the retreats—they know all too well—but they don't have a clue as to the whys of it. They are just carried along like rag dolls on a river. And when the river goes over the cliff—"

Hannah snapped her fingers.

Rae turned onto her back and looked up. Hannah's face was very close. "Did you learn all this from the trickster women? Or from your own people? Is that why you can't talk about it with the others?"

"Sweetheart, I learned *nothing* from my people. My mother barely had time to bear me before she died. Although I am of the Waste, I am not one-tenth so much Wraith as I am trickster woman. The difference between me and the others, if you will, is that they refuse to talk about these things—and I need to. I have to. That's why you must forgive me. I used you." It was said lightly, with a rueful smile.

Rae yawned. "At least you're honest about it. The others aren't. And they tell me it's for my good."

"Oh, honey," Hannah said, and suddenly, startlingly, bent and brushed her lips against Rae's forehead. "Don't be grateful. Don't be grateful for *anything* you're told here. If you only knew!"

Rae struggled to raise herself on her elbows. "If I only knew? Is there *more*? If I only knew what?"

But Hannah had moved away from the bed. One by one, she was extinguishing the daemon glares. She might have been blowing on them—Rae could not see—or doing something else. As each daemon flared out, the Wraith woman dropped a pinch of something that looked like dried herbs into the bowl-like bottom of its cage. There was a smell of soot. Blessed darkness descended on the room. From near the ceiling came a faint scrabbling noise—like mice in the rafters—and Rae knew it was the sound of the half-dead daemons feeding.

"Sleep now," Hannah said.

"But," Rae said in confused desperation. "But—"

The currents of sleep wrapped around her like wavelets of warm water.

"Sleep while you can. The traders will be here in a few days and we'll all be busy little bees."

Hannah moved to the door. A crack of light appeared, silhouetting her. "Anthea and Liesl are in conference, my sweet Kirekuni. They're close to making a decision about you. Why do you think Anthea didn't come herself tonight? She runs hot and cold, and tonight she's running cold. Now do you see why you must forgive me?"

"Hannah," Rae whispered. She felt as if she had been drugged. *Had* she? She would not put anything past them. "*Hannah* . . . do you mean I'm not going to be allowed to stay? Is that why you spoke to me? To get your own back on them by giving away their secrets to someone who doesn't matter anyway?"

"No." The door knocked shut, and all at once Hannah was bending over her, giving her another kiss. Without really thinking about it, Rae parted her lips. She felt Hannah's tongue meet her own and circle it, entering Rae's mouth. During the course of a long, sweet moment a simple kiss became an exquisitely sexual probing. Rae wrapped her arms around Hannah's neck. But the other woman pulled away. Her dry, callused fingers lingered for a moment on Rae's hair. Rae savored the taste of her mouth. "The most important thing is that you get a good night's sleep."

"Hannah . . ."

The door closed.

Rae was asleep almost before the daemons had stopped feeding.

And next morning she was surprised to find that she had dreamed not of Hannah, not of Crispin, not of death or destruction, but of the rolling, patchwork hills of Plum Valley Domain. Only now there were no crops in the fields, no orchards, but lengths of material that undulated like seaweed in the currents of the ocean, brushing seductively against her face and bare arms. The tops of the lengths grew much higher than her head. She was lost.

Every length was silk or velvet. There must have been a king's ransom growing in those fields. And they were brighter colors than Rae had ever seen, each length shaded from violet at the root through blue and green to yellow and orange, with brilliant red at the top, where the flower ought to be. A legion of little rainbows sunk into the earth. She pushed between the cloths, her shoes sinking into soft, fertile earth, calling out desperately for help. She could not hear her own voice. She didn't know who she was calling for. When she woke, she believed herself for a moment back in the Seventeenth Mansion.

I could not
Speak, and my eyes failed, I was neither
Living nor dead, and I knew nothing,
Looking into the heart of light, the silence.
Oed' und leer das Meer.

—T.S. Eliot, *The Wasteland*

Say the
Words!

The traders arrived in the afternoon. It was dry and chilly. They were late. The women of Holstead House were in an evil mood; they had sat up all night waiting for the trucks to rumble down the road. More than once one of the twins, excitable with anticipation, had mistaken the sound of a plane overhead for wheels. Lunch had been a silent, sorry affair. But Rae thought the trickster women hid their bad humor quite effectively as they hurried toward the trucks and embraced the dismounting men, kissing cheeks, asking after wives and children.

Of course any visitor would be a cause of excitement, she told herself, lingering in the edge of the trees, breaking a twig into pieces. Man or woman. Look at the attention they had lavished on Rae herself! (Although Liesl and Anthea had both been markedly colder since the night she spoke with Hannah, and there had been no more invitations to the daemon dell.)

Their behavior toward the traders seemed out of keeping with the fathomless woman-bond which manifested itself in their obsession with testing each other's weak points and their habitual disparagement of the male half of the daemon industry. In their flirting, she saw confirmed what she had guessed: the traders played a far more important role in their lives than they had admitted. Sex was almost certainly the key to the puzzle. It was depressing.

But the razor-pinioned bird fluttered around her head. This morning at breakfast, Hannah, who apparently thought she and Rae were allies (and did not seem quite so overjoyed as the others about the arrival of the traders) had commented on her silence. Rae could only shake her head mutely, causing everyone at the table to laugh. It was not pleasant laughter.

With a man on each arm, Anthea tripped back toward the green garden and pretended to catch sight of Rae for the first time. She fluted, "Darling! Come meet Mr. Hepplewhite and Mr. Ellary!"

Rae shook the traders' hands. To her dismay, she found she could not keep her eyes off them. Her sensibilities seemed to have realigned themselves without her knowledge. How long had she been at Holstead House? Only a few days. But already she could not accept the men as natural beings. Their heavy shoulders and stubbled chins fascinated her: they were unnatural, monstrous. She had always, she realized, thought of women as senselessly lumpy variations on human form. Now the men seemed the odd ones out, rough-hewn, unfinished variants on woman.

She shook the younger trader's hand and said in her most sincere voice, "Hello. Rae. I'm very happy to make your acquaintance."

A huge smile broke out on the man's face. "Jem Ellary. Delighted."

His voice was like farm bread, soda-harsh with the accents of Valestock.

"Isn't she a darling," Anthea trilled. "Now you must let me take you up to the house. You'll want to wash before supper. You haven't said how many nights you'll be staying; of course, you're welcome here for as long . . ."

"Long as it takes us to load up," Rae heard the grim-faced Hepplewhite saying as the trio moved into the trees. "Three trucks this time, see. Increased demand from bases. Hate to 'pose on you, Anthea, but—"

Anthea's answer was girlish laughter. Rae really believed, for the first time, that the trickster woman was not yet thirty.

She gazed at the trucks which hulked in the road. How many daemons would they hold? Would the menagerie be empty after they left? Did they plan to stay three days or three weeks? Everybody seemed to think she was acquainted with the logistics of these things. She wasn't a trickster, only a costumier's assistant; although she wasn't even that anymore. The razor-pinioned bird had taken it away from her for good and for all. The trucks stood about twenty feet apart, their trailers bending the branches aside—green on one side of the road, brown on the other. Chewed ruts followed them to their parking places.

She looked again. *One* of the trucks . . .

It couldn't be. Could it?

Liesl, Sally, and Millie were talking with the remaining truckers between two of the vehicles. (Hannah had not elected to join the greeting party.) One of the men was eagerly unfastening a tailgate to display the supplies they had brought Holstead from Valestock. Same game, same two-step that people danced everywhere.

Rae slipped out of the trees and around the back of the last truck. Quietly, she examined the main latch of the tailgate. In the daylight, the scratches were obvious. She tiptoed around the far side of the vehicle. Not obvious unless you were looking for it, but there was the dent where Crispin had smashed the would-be thief's head into the truck. She could even make out a trace of something dark. That night rushed back to her in a storm of dizziness and confusion. She leaned against the truck. The knowledge that she was going to die tasted like blood. Splinters dug into her fingertips.

The conversation around the front of the truck subsided into an incomprehensible buzz. Her ears rang. She put her hand to her mouth.

When she had got some of her composure back she ventured up to the tractor. Even without climbing up, she could see where Crispin had jimmied the passenger-side lock. She scrambled on the step—awkwardly, her dress hampering her legs—and peered into the cab. The blankets in which she had slept were gone, and the dashboard fittings looked new, but there was no question that it was the same vehicle.

"Hey, hey," a voice said softly behind her. "What're you looking at, lady?"

Rae yelped and lost her balance. For a sickening moment she teetered. Then big, warm hands fastened around her waist, and she found herself lowered to the ground, feetfirst, like a kitten in the grip of a child.

"Can't remember seeing *you* last time I was here."

He was at least thirty, over six feet, with a pitted face and deep-set blue eyes. He smiled.

"And I think I'dve remembered."

Rae was annoyed to find herself flushing. "I'm new."

"Baird Glassman."

"Rae. I'm happy to meet you."

"You aren't acting it."

"I didn't want to make a fuss." She bit her lip, prettily, not taking her eyes off his face. "I—I'm sorry. I just wanted to see—"

"Never seen a truck before, have you? Country girl? You've got that fresh skin."

"Only once. It's a *monster*!"

"Been making this run for a good few years. I remember when Sal and Mil were as wide-eyed as you. 'Course they were a bit younger. Not that they look it now!" He clapped her on the shoulder in a fatherly way, which almost allayed her bad feelings about him. "It's a hard life, this is, Rae, young lady. Sure you're ready for it? Might be things they haven't told you yet." As they came around the seven-foot hood of the truck and joined the others, he added softly: "Might be things no one knows. Not to discourage you! Just tryin'a make sure you hear both sides of the story. 'Course I don't know you or nothin'. You might think I'm being presumptious."

She wanted to ask: *Where did you get this truck?* After reliving the terror of that night, she found herself looking for Crispin. She couldn't believe he was not somewhere close by. Her eyes skidded over the animated faces of the others as if they had been a bunch of white stones. Suddenly she wanted him so badly that she pulled the trader's arm down and began, "Sir—Baird—I think I've seen—"

But Millie cut her off. "Oh, Baird," she chirped. "Ernie was showing me some of the traveling cells you brought! They're so *little* and *clever*! But do you really think you can fit our daemons into them?"

The youngest man covered a smile. Sally poked her twin, and Millie's face and neck went cherry red. She tried to cover her unintentional innuendo by holding out her hands to Rae and gabbling, "Rae, sweetheart, we haven't introduced you! Baird, have you—"

"Yes," Baird said. "We've met." He gave Rae a half smile, with one eyelid drooped. She returned it, inwardly cringing.

Liesl stirred herself smoothly to cover the silence. "It's getting late." She twined her arm through that of the tall trader. "I think we should make you unload at least one truck before dark, so we can begin packing the daemons first thing tomorrow, don't you? Have you brought hand trucks, Baird? It makes everything so much easier . . ."

Baird Glassman seemed overcome by the flow of her conversation. He nodded again and again, like a clockwork toy, as she led him away. The others followed, as good as hypnotized, the way Rae had seen daemons follow at Liesl's heels, like big ugly dogs. Liesl was not that pretty! But of course it wasn't always the pretty ones who snared the men. Liesl had that certain something else which Rae herself had longed for countless times, whenever she saw a ring on another girl's finger. As she stood looking after them, she found herself suddenly sandwiched between Sally and Millie. Sharp fingernails dug into her arm. The twins were wearing scent: the floral bouquet choked her nostrils. Millie's face was still pink, no doubt with the memory of her gaffe, and for once she let Sally do the talking. "Now, while they're all distracted," Sally hissed. "You have to come to the menagerie!"

Rae tried to fight. Her hair got in her face. They were both holding her. "I'm not going anywhere with you."

"Shut up." Sally pinched Rae so hard that tears welled up in her eyes. "Liesl made Anthea give you as long as she could! And we begged her, too! It's not our fault if you didn't make any use of the time! Now they're *here*, you can't just sit around like a lump any longer. Anthea's waiting."

"I didn't do anything," Rae protested in a whisper, not wanting to make a scene, as they dragged her along behind Liesl and her coterie of men.

"Exactly!" Millie hissed. "You just sat around accepting our hospitality, while we were on our feet night and day, getting ready for them! You haven't been in the menagerie *once* since Anthea showed you around!"

"But I was tired," Rae said, trying to keep her voice level. "All I could do was sleep. I mean it. I couldn't help it. There's something in the air—"

"Of course there is. You're in the Wraithwaste!"

"That's what we meant when we told you you'd have to be strong!"

Branches whipped Rae's cheeks. She could not free her hands, only turn her face to one side or the other, and on each side there was a twin.

"We tried to warn you!" Sally said righteously.

"We told you you need strength to survive!"

"The air is *thick* with daemons. You're breathing them right now. You can't help it."

"But you thought you were too good to listen to us."

"You didn't pay any attention."

"Now you'll be sorry!" Millie said viciously.

But there was a catch in her voice, and the scent of sweat filtered through her heavy perfume. Rae looked from her to Sally. These young girls, with the premature lines around their eyes and mouths and their skeletal, purple-veined hands, were no less upset by what was happening to Rae than she was. But that didn't mean they were going to let her go. "Come on," Sally said, and jerked her arm so that she stumbled.

But when they left her alone with Anthea in the bright stillness of the menagerie, what had seemed almost like a kidnapping took on quite a different aspect. Anthea bubbled with laughter when Rae spilled out the story of how the twins had accosted her.

"Those two! Their social skills are so poor! They are completely unaware of how frightening they can be. It's a pity they can't be exposed to strangers more often—they came to us so young . . . Now of course for you things will be different. You are already experienced." Anthea chuckled. "No, all this is—is a little test which we give our new girls. I wanted to get it over with earlier, before the men arrived, but I just couldn't find time. It's too bad of me, I know."

What about yesterday? Rae thought. *What about this morning, while you waited, and I dozed with my head on the table? You were watching me like you were trying to decide to have me on toast or on a sweet cake. I bet the twins were telling the truth, and Liesl pressured you to hold off as long as possible. To give me a little longer—for what? What have I done?*

"Have you been in here much during the past few days?"

Anthea asked offhandedly, stroking the furry leaves of a giant geranium. "I haven't been paying as much attention to you as I should. Forgive me."

Something snapped in Rae. "You keep asking me to forgive you. All of you. You and Liesl and Hannah. I don't understand."

"Oh, my dear," Anthea said, her voice sad. "My dear." Then her mouth hardened into a smile again. "Now, here's what I want you to do. The traders are all daemon handlers, but they can't do anything with our poor darlings until they're collared. We don't collar them before the traders arrive because they start to deteriorate as soon as they feel the touch of silver. And they go all helpless. It's awful to see. We'd have to feed them ourselves, by hand, instead of letting them just get along on their own in the menagerie. It's been tried, and it's just not practical . . . So we have a very busy few weeks ahead of us. We work in pairs—one of us collars a daemon and one of them cells it. We can only do about two or three dozen a day; it's very tiring work."

"There are six of them," Rae said, her heart sinking. "Does even Mother come down to help?"

"Yes, she does. Of course."

"Then why—"

"There is always the possibility. . . . Let me be honest." Anthea's face was serious. "Mother is old." It was true. Though Mother was only in her forties, she had the body of a nonagenarian. "And she has always worked with Baird Glassman, who is not a man to compromise the speed he deems necessary to make a profit. Therefore, you may have to step in for her. So I need to know that you can do what's needed. That's all." She smiled. "There's really nothing to be nervous about."

Rae took a deep breath. She could not see any way out. "What do I have to do?"

Anthea pointed to the center of the menagerie. Bushy geraniums grew in a mound around the base of one of the tall, whippy, bare trees which were the most puissant demogorgons. They were fifty feet tall, Liesl had said, in human form. Anthea circled a geranium stem with her fingers. "This one. I'm making it as easy as possible for you! Put your arms around it. Speak to it. Do whatever you have to. It will change into its human form. Then, when you have it close and trusting, slip *this* around its neck." She reached into her dress pocket and tossed Rae a silver band, no bigger than a child's bracelet, hinged in the middle. "There's a hook-and-pin closure. If it was a larger daemon it would be a spring strip, and we'd solder it closed, but this will do for a Nemanes. Maybe you'd better practice."

Rae snapped the band shut a few times. "Isn't it too small?"

"*I* caught this daemon. I chose this collar for it the same day. Look inside."

Scratched on the inside of the band, in beautiful copperplate script, Rae read *Nemanes*. She knelt in the earth by the geranium and tentatively stroked its stem. *Not-scent* wafted into her nostrils. She looked over her shoulder at Anthea. "You're not going to . . . watch?"

"How else will I know whether you have succeeded?"

Rae turned back to the plant and opened her eyes as wide as she could, trying not to cry. "Nemanes," she whispered shakily. She wanted to absorb herself in the daemon's greenness to the exclusion of the rest of the world. She rubbed her cheek against the furry, prickly leaves. "Oh, Nemanes. Be my friend. I'm yours. Trust me, Nemanes, I won't hurt you!"

"No good!" Anthea said. "No good at all!"

Rae visualized the daemon as a little green child who would grin and stretch and hop onto her lap and not mind at all having a collar fastened around his neck.

"I thought she had the gift for sweet talk! I'm never wrong!" Anthea murmured to herself. Rae's concentration almost shattered, but she forced herself not to give up.

And after a moment or two the leaves went away from between her fingers, as if they had turned to vapor. She could not open her eyes. The scent made her so dizzy that her head came off her neck and floated. *Something* hovered still before and above her. It was fantastically powerful, and she knew that if she looked up she would die, for its power lay not in any killing blow, though it was certainly capable of striking her if it wished, but in the sheer intensity of its presence. It was pungently masculine. It was ancient. All of its considerable energy was concentrated without movement or speech into waiting.

Waiting for her to speak words she had forgotten.

Waiting.

With a flash of fear so strong she could taste it, she identified the sensation: it was her tenth birthday again and she was being presented to the Prince. She had seen him every day of her life, of course, leading the evening prayers, but never this close up. Never in his own apartments. All the best furnishings of the Carathraw mansion had long ago been collected into the master bedroom. When Rae walked in, flanked by two of the Consorts (one of them Saonna), her spine dripping with fear, the unexpected riot of riches nearly shocked her into breaking her respectful shuffle. She kept her head down, though she longed to look around. The musty perfume of the place made her heart beat as quickly as it had that time she and Daphne and Colm stole buns from the baker in Greenberith.

The walls seemed to tower forever into the darkness; there was no ceiling. Only a few streaks of day penetrated between the heavy, unswagged curtains. The twilight gave the clutter of furniture a gloomy majesty akin to that of a glade of huge trees come on unexpectedly just before dawn. It was as if the furniture had been walking clumsily across the floor, and had only just frozen the moment Rae entered: as if the worm-eaten hearts of the sofas and beds and tables were still racing deep inside. Their draperies created a dusty spiderweb that obstructed all but one way into the room.

The Prince reposed high up, on a throne of stacked beds draped with fabrics that Rae wanted to run her fingers over and wrap around her shoulders and hide beneath.

She couldn't look at him. She couldn't do anything except stumble to her knees.

The Prince shone like a sun below the horizon. Behind her, her mother wavered, as insignificant as the setting moon. Rae knew just as certainly as if she had turned around that Saonna was biting her lip with worry. Rae had been supposed to say the words the minute she knelt.

What were the words?

What were they?

Trembling all over, she shrieked faintly, "Oh, Prince, I salute you with my soul, and I wait in ecstatic silence until the moment when you shall enfold me in the wing of your royal spirit and lift me above the nameless destruction that shall attend the death of the Queen to the place that is not a place, the safety that is not safety, the existence that is not existence, that is transcendence!" Her child-sized lungs were empty, and she gasped aloud. But she had done it, she had *remembered,* she had not disgraced Saonna!

"In the name of the Queen, girl," a furious female voice said. "Get out of the way!"

Rae felt herself toppling over. She could not make her hands obey her to break her fall. Her face pressed into the earth. She sneezed, shuddered, and sat up. Her knees and shoulders ached. Her mouth tasted like sleep.

Anthea straightened up from between the geraniums, wincing like an old woman and rubbing her back with her free hand. She looked haggard. Under one arm she held a squawling little leprechaun which was almost exactly as Rae had imagined it, except that it wasn't green. It was bright pink—the same color as the flowers on the geraniums. A silver collar encircled its candy-floss-colored neck.

Rae got slowly to her feet. "How long was I . . ."

Anthea's expression made her look down in shame. It was the same look she had seen on Saonna's face when the Third Consort caught Rae and Colm kissing down by the wading pool. It made Rae feel hateful, ungrateful, ugly inside her skin. That was the year Rae was ten: later that year Saonna would die, and in spring Rae would run away from the Seventeenth Mansion.

"You were under for about four hours." With tired sarcasm: "You didn't expect me to wait any longer than that, did you?"

Rae looked wildly about. The menagerie breathed and swayed. Overhead the daemon glares hummed. On a low branch of Exarces balanced a food-stained plate with a fork, knife, and water glass.

Four hours!

"You—you—"

"You weren't asleep," Anthea said over the meowling of the daemon. "You were in communion with Nemanes." She stepped out of the geranium mound, straightened her wool wrap, refastened the pin on her shoulder, and did something to the collar around Nemanes's neck. At once the daemon quieted. Its legs and head dangled. Except for its bright, blinking eyes, it looked catatonic. "It's such a small daemon I really don't know how you managed to get lost so deeply. But people drown in six inches of water. It happens."

"Anthea," Rae begged. Everything was happening too fast. *What* had happened? *Four hours*—"What did I do wrong?"

"Oh, nothing, nothing!" Anthea's voice was as sharp as pieces of a broken mirror. "Come on, everybody's outside! You've kept us in here long enough!"

She brushed past, wreathed in scent. Rae hurried after her. A newly risen wind slammed the door behind her. Anthea was making for a bonfire that had been lit behind the house, about a hundred feet into the dead forest. Rae had wondered before about the blackened clearing in the pines back there: it must have been created for this purpose. The scent of woodsmoke gusted on the wind, evoking her childhood as everything else did tonight. Camping out in the tangled grounds of the mansion with the other kids (nobody ever told the Children of the Dynasty not to do things which other children were only able to dream about), burning her fingers on potatoes roasted in a fire which only the Queen, surely, had prevented from burning down everything within a hundred miles, lying on her back on the bare ground after everyone had quieted down, Daphne cool and softly asleep on her shoulder, looking up into the star-filled night.

Could she really only have been six? It felt like yesterday.

Oh, Daphne! Where are you now?

Carried on the woodsmoke was another, darker scent, incense perhaps that the traders had brought.

Rae saw Anthea reach the clearing. She laughed back at the voices that greeted her, sounding young and wildly excitable. There was a shout from the watchers, and a terrified human scream, and then the fire burned bright and white as a giant fireball, its fingertips straining above the tops of the trees. With a shock of disbelief Rae understood that Anthea had thrown Nemanes into it. The trickster woman stood with her hands empty, looking into the fireball, a dark girlish silhouette against the glare. Then she spun around, laughing, her hair flying out in a slow corona.

Rae was clutching a tree so tightly that it hurt. Baird Glassman said behind her, in a pleasant, slightly slurred voice, "Have a sip of this, young Rae. I recommend the brew." A mug came over her shoulder and slid along her cheek, ice-cold, beaded with water. Without looking around, she took it and drank deeply.

* * *

But she *couldn't* just run away. It was out of the question. The very thought of venturing into the wind-tumbled forest unnerved her. Baird's arm lay on her neck, and he kept making small motions that meant he would like to take her somewhere private. But though she was afraid of being on her own, she was more afraid of what he might do if he got her alone. Safety lay in the leaping light of the fire, just as when she went out with her admirers in Valestock, safety had lain in public places where there was no danger of hands slipping underneath clothes.

Two of the other traders, young Ellary and a gangling fellow named Frazier, sat beside them, making desultory conversation and replenishing each other's mugs. Rae had counted on their talk to save her from the awfulness of her thoughts, but they were making it obvious through winks and innuendo that they weren't going to butt in on whatever she and Baird supposedly had going.

She couldn't reject his attentions. It was impossible. Now that Crispin had deserted her, and the trickster women had proved false, Baird was her only hope, though he did not know it. Anthea, Liesl, and even Hannah had all gone over to the other side. They threatened her like a row of red queens across the chessboard, promising certain destruction before the game was up. Baird remained on her side, an unlikely white knight with a wife and children in Valestock.

But she could not surrender to him!

Would he be repulsed? Like Crispin? Or would he laugh tenderly, dispelling the fears of nineteen years, and kiss her poor pale stump just as he was kissing her neck, with expert tongue-tip teases? It seemed inevitable that she would find out. But her courage was insufficient to overcome her fear. And a voice inside her cried, *Crispin . . .*

He was probably a hundred miles away by now. He had given up on her. And who could blame him? She had deserted him, that day in the daemon dell.

But back then she hadn't known how this was going to end! Transcendence had not played her false. But circumstances had. *And there, circumstances govern us all, even the Children of the Dynasty—*

When Baird first led her into the clearing, all the trickster women, even Mother, had presented brilliant smiles to her and pressed mugs of ale into her hand, and she had wondered if maybe it did not matter after all, if she had been wrong, if they were going to give her another chance. But then Sally and Millie had drawn her aside and told her it was no good.

"You'd better leave."

They both started to cry as Millie said it. Their tears shone red as blood in the firelight.

"They've made their decision."

"But how do you know? Where can I go?" Rae was panicking.

"Away!"

"Away from here."

"Tonight."

"Rae, we don't want anything bad to happen to you!"

"What?" Rae said. They had pulled her away from the fire, into the cold, crunchy forest. The three of them huddled together like refugees trying to console each other over some terrible loss. The darkness disguised the lines on the twins' wet faces. For once their youth was obvious. "What's going to happen to me?"

Sally wiped her nose. "Same thing happened to Sarah from the cult, and Anna from the south, and our cousin Jillie, when she wanted to be a trickster woman! We told her she should come, we planned it for months, we sent her secret letters, but when she got here it was no good, she wasn't strong like us . . . Oh Rae, we're trying to *warn* you, you didn't listen to us before, but if you know what's good for you, you'd better listen now! We could *show* you what's going to happen to you, we have scars you wouldn't *believe*—"

I'm in danger of my life, Rae thought, *because I made the mistake of trusting them, because they seemed kind! How naive can I be?!*

But the illusion was shattered for good now. She remembered what Anthea had said to her that first night, when she, Rae, had been deaf with tiredness: *Not many travelers come this far into the Wraithwaste, unless they're coming to us! And none of them ever leave.*

When the three of them returned to the fire she saw very clearly that the bright chatter Anthea, Liesl, and Hannah directed at her was no more sincere than the patter of shopgirls. They *seemed* interested in nothing but the traders they had hypnotized. But Rae did not miss the darting, snakelike glances that they directed at Sally and Millie, who had gone, barely controlling their sniffles, to sit with Mother.

Rae had excused herself from the three in a shaky voice. She had gone to the other side of the fire and sank down, grateful for Baird's ready embrace.

What was going to happen to her now? She dared not move from his side in case they meant to dispose of her right here, in front of everyone, though in that case she didn't know what he could do to protect her, anyhow. The way Anthea had disposed of Nemanes convinced Rae that death was the most likely probability.

But Baird would save her. He *had* to.

Fear sat like a lump of snow in her belly, melted only a little by mug after mug of ale.

And it was late, late, and nothing had happened, and Hannah and Liesl had retired, leaving Mother, and the twins, and Anthea, the most dangerous of the three. There were loud, sporadic cracklings in the forest, and Rae was certain that from time to time she saw eyes gleaming in the trees. She mentioned it half-jokingly to Baird, and he muttered something about the Wraiths coming when they smelt alcohol.

Thank transcendence I didn't make a run for it, then! Hannah had told her, both in words and in the language which did not lie, how much the Wraiths hated Ferupians. And what could be more Ferupian than this drinking party? It was a release from the obsessive austerities that governed Holstead House during the day. And like the parties that had happened occasionally at the Seventeenth Mansion, it was going to end with everyone pairing off. Would the Wraiths take advantage of Holstead House's vulnerability then? Or were they too much diminished to be anything but spectators at the feast? Rae felt in her heart that they were not half as toothless as Hannah had tried to make them sound.

The wind moaned like a storm in the branches overhead.

On the far side of the clearing, Anthea and her paramour Hepplewhite were snuggling, their bodies making a spider that twitched its great legs in the light of the dying flames. Sally, Millie, and Mother sat with two young traders, Greengate and Puriss, who seemed hypnotized by the twins. They had danced attendance on them all night and were only now, with respectful restraint, claiming their property: a hand on a thigh, another stroking flaxen hair. The twins sat passive under their caresses, like show horses being groomed by their trainers. Mother gazed off into the distance with a smile on her face, rocking back and forth, apparently unaware of the courtship taking place on either side of her.

"*Someone's* gonna have fun tonight," Ellary said for the fourth or fifth time, and drained his mug.

Frazier stared morosely at the fire. Suddenly he tossed his mug into the embers, where it burst, and stood up, stretching his long limbs. "C'mon, Jem. Time for you and me to hit the sack. Got a busy day coming up."

"Wasn't hired to be no stockboy," Jem Ellary muttered without malice. Staggering upright, he slapped Baird on the shoulder. "What 'bout you, fella?"

Rae closed her hand over Baird's. "I'll look after him." She smiled at Ellary, crinkling her eyes to suggest that the two of them had a private joke. "I don't think he's going to be good for much tomorrow morning, though."

Frazier and Ellary chuckled drunkenly. Ellary said, swaying and hiccuping, "Don't worry 'bout it. Always happens like this. We plan on starting to unload the minute we get here, and we end up drinkin' all night. Witches. They're witches. They do it to us, oh, what do they do to us?" he began to sing mournfully.

"Shut it," Frazier said, and wrapping his arm around the stumbling man, led him off. "Night."

"Night," Rae called, somewhat taken aback.

The clearing was quiet now but for the crackling of the fire and the surreptitious noises in the forest. Baird's kisses moved from Rae's neck to her mouth. Hardly knowing what she was doing, she let herself go. His tongue entered her mouth. He drew back and whispered, "Where? Where can we go?"

Danger seemed far away, and at the same time she felt its breath on her face. Her head was spinning. She could not face the forest, or the house: for all she knew, the bones of Sarah, Anna, and Jillie, who had also failed the trickster women's tests, were boarded up in the walls. By comparison, the scene of this evening's humiliation seemed attractive.

"The menagerie," she murmured, letting her hands fly over his shoulders, inside his coat.

She had never had an admirer who was this much older than she—or at any rate never encouraged one. She had always had more attractive offers. Not that Baird wasn't attractive, of course (and in the dark, you couldn't see his blue eyes, those blank spots in the pale face that reminded her of uncurtained windows onto an empty room). "Do you know the way?"

He pulled her to her feet. They meandered back toward the house, stopping every now and then to kiss. To distract herself from the flickers in the corners of her eyes, Rae asked Baird about the truck she had recognized.

"Stolen," he grunted. "Taken possession of by Fewman and Fewman. Believed to be original property of Lemonde Daemon Dealers of Cherry Hills." That was a domain near Plum Valley. The heartlands were home to the richest companies in Ferupe—heartlanders had more business sense than westerners, who were handed wealth on a platter every day, but did not know enough to hold on to it. "Compensation paid to Lemonde, minus costs of repairs."

"But how does anyone steal a truck?" she asked.

"Not that difficult if you know daemons." Baird pressed kisses into her ear. "Why?"

"I'm—I'm just curious." She twisted to avoid getting a tree branch in her ribs. "Everything you do interests me, Baird!"

He laughed indulgently. "Follow this then! Darky traveler stole the truck from outside of an eatery in Valestock, same night there was a fire in the armory on Main Street, all the police distracted. Rain washed away traces of escape. Truck later discovered stripped of fittings, primary daemon gone, contents of trailer missing, near a hamlet on the edge of the Wraithwaste, about a hundred miles from Valestock. Nigger never seen again. Most of missing fittings discovered on search of nearby hamlet. Daemon lost; peasants have no idea what's really valuable, they just like bright, shiny metal. Thieving magpies!" He laughed uproariously. "Boys taught 'em a lesson they won't forget!"

"Hilarious!" Rae laughed. "The Negro stole it, and then had it stolen from him! And later, the girl he had rescued from the fire deserted him without so much as a thank-you, and a daemon was set on him, and if he isn't dead by now I expect he's halfway to the war front! And I'll never see him again. I can't bear it. I'll never see him again—"

"What're you blathering about? You a storyteller or somethin? You a gypsy? No, no." Baird pinched her cheek, then kissed her hard on the mouth. "Too fair, too daisy daisy pretty—"

"I'm a little drunk, I think," Rae said meekly. Her heart was pounding inside her chest. "Oh, Baird!" They were at the door. The heavy slab of oak swung inward and they moved into a warm night that smelled of flowers. Rae was too grateful for the dark to question it; only in the back of her mind she thought, *Should close the door . . . should close . . .*

They came on Liesl and Hannah in the darkest corner of the menagerie, where tiny daemons grew like grass. Liesl's pale body shone in the night; Hannah was her shadow come to life. Her lips suckled greedily at Liesl's small breasts. Liesl's fingers clenched spasmodically on Hannah's buttocks. Despite her shock and disgust, Rae felt something twitching deep inside her at the sight. Baird clapped a hand over her mouth and pulled her away, crashing through the daemon growths. The two women were too absorbed in each other to notice the intrusion, or the noisy retreat. Nonetheless, to Rae, it would have been the worst breach of decorum to stay a moment longer in the menagerie. But Baird seemed to have been set on fire by the scene they had witnessed. Growling softly, he pulled her down near the door and started undoing her dress. Rae tried to push him away, but it was no good; she could not resist muscles that could keep a sixty-ton truck on the road for hours on end. He forced her back down onto the soil.

She imagined she could feel the rhythm of Hannah and Liesl's lovemaking pulsing through the earth. She had never guessed that that was what lay between the pair. Although really, she should have; she had seen the same kind of thing in similar circumstances, and it explained a good deal.

A warm wind blew over her, tickling her face as if it were thick with dust. It was going in the wrong direction. Not into the menagerie, but out. What was wrong? She could not think, could not act. She caressed Baird's hair. Now that it had started she did not want it to stop even for a moment. She did not want to think about what she was doing. Kneeling between her thighs, Baird pulled off his coat and shirt. His chest was soft with ginger curls. He squeezed her breasts, flicking the nipples expertly with his index fingers. The sweet disability of surrender washed over her. She dug her fingers into his shoulders, pulling him down on top of her, kissing him.

And rearing up, he shuddered and went limp, crashing facefirst into the earth beside her. For one absurd moment she thought he had finished, and he *couldn't* have yet, not a man in the prime of his life—but then she sat up and shook him, and he did not move, and there was a knife hilt standing out of his back, and she screamed. It came out as a whimper.

"Get away from him!" It was Crispin, standing huge and solid and black in the doorway. There was—could it be?—a *child* behind him, peering around his legs. "I think I've killed him. Queen!" He came forward and collected his knife, kneeling to wipe it on the daemon grass. "You're bloody lucky I came when I did!" He peered into her face. "He looks a real bastard!"

He had come. He would save her. But her mind was empty of all but the sweeping waves of blackness that were the wings of the razor-pinioned bird. She crouched transfixed. Intermittently, stars replaced the roof, and replaced Crispin's face, replaced the doorway. But the black wings beat even faster. Soon the wings would come close enough to slash her. She whimpered again, not in relief but terror.

"Say the words!" repeated the voice. Cuddlepie was stiff with fear. He couldn't remember one word, yet he had said them over and over all the way. "Too late! Eat him!" shouted the voice fiercely.

—May Gibbs, *The Complete Adventures of Snugglepot and Cuddlepie*

Undone

Earlier that evening, Crispin had seen Jacithrew Humdroner break his neck. There was no gore, no screaming or thrashing. Only the body in the wreckage of the flying machine, rearranged into the shape of a dead, twisted thing.

Orpaan had been too hysterical to do anything except curl up and scream. Crispin straightened out the corpse as best he could, carried it off into the Waste, and laid it under the pines, on a bier which he made by ripping apart the flying machine. As he turned to leave, his hair stood on end. The twilit air looked empty, but shadows danced and scudded across the carpet of fallen needles. Scavenger daemons were gathering.

It was a stupid death which could easily have been avoided. Crispin himself could have prevented it from happening, had he believed for one moment that the madman was *really* going to jump off the top of the big pine. But rationality made him stand and watch, sneering, until the very last moment, when it was too late, and he scrambled for the rope ladder. The flying machine did not go anywhere at all, though the daemons in it roared mightily. It plummeted straight down, crashed into the earth, and kept going through the roof of the root room, coming to rest in a jumble of soil and furniture.

Crispin, who had seen several fatal falls—most recently Prettie's—was less shaken by the death than he was by Orpaan's hysteria. The child howled and screamed for three hours straight, seemingly inconsolable, until Crispin, growing desperate, slapped him in the face. After that, the boy clung to him and would not let go. Hitting him was probably exactly what Jacithrew would have done.

The moment when, looking up, Crispin had thought, *Strike me, he's really going to*—the moment of the fall—neither one replayed itself in his mind as he led Orpaan through the woods. Instead, he could not forget what Jacithrew had said as he started up the rope ladder. The words had not really registered on Crispin's mind until after the old hermit was dead. Jacithrew's manic grin never left his face, but, interspersed with gibberish about the south, Crispin heard distinctly: "Look after my orphan, boy! He's a good child, and you'll be a better guardian for him than I was. At least"— Jacithrew sniggered— "he won't have to live on charity any longer—"

Jacithrew had cared for Orpaan, but not enough to keep on living for his sake. Crispin wondered if he had known the flying machine wouldn't work. If, like an old soldier, having lost sight of everything except his own inflated notions of pride and honor, he had planned his own grand tragedy.

But, no, he had been mad. What must have happened was that Crispin's arrival had liberated Jacithrew from his responsibility to the child, freeing him to take the risks he must have known testing the flying machine involved. And indeed, although Jacithrew could have completed the machine at any time over the past five years or so, he had only started working on it in earnest after Crispin stumbled through the roof trap.

A trap, indeed!

Crispin had not known he was becoming an accomplice to the old man's death. But that didn't mean he wasn't responsible for its consequences.

What with one thing and another, he and Orpaan did not leave the ruin of the root room until much later than he had intended. It must have been nearly 5 A.M. by the time they set out. There had been a high wind most of the night, though the air was bone-dry: it would be a fair dawn. But the sky was still tarry. Crispin gripped Orpaan's wrist tightly as they slipped through the roaring trees toward Holstead House. In his mind he was going over the things he would say to Rae once he found her. *Of course all that structure and tradition and shit seems pretty damn attractive—I know what a hard life you've led, even if you won't tell me anything about it—but how can you choose it over what I'm offering you? How can you?*

The funny thing was that his heart was beating so fast in his throat with the anticipated pleasure of seeing her again, he didn't know whether he'd even be able to get the words out.

Orpaan was exhausted, hiccuping softly with the last of his tears. He stumbled and nearly fell. Crispin forgot Rae. He lifted Orpaan into his arms. The child was a little lighter than Crispin himself.

Orpaan's eyes were wide. "Cris, the Wraiths are here," he whispered, looking around big-eyed, as if he was afraid they were being watched. "They want to get me. I have to go away."

Crispin could not help glancing around in his turn, but the pines seemed empty. In fact, ominously so. Though it was full dark by now, he could not hear a single night bird. "How do you know?"

"I can feel 'em. Can't you feel 'em?" Orpaan shuddered. "Some things I *know*! Cris, let's please not stop here!"

Crispin shook his head tiredly. "Sometimes you act like a tetchy old man. But all right." He surprised himself by planting a kiss on Orpaan's cheek. The boy grimaced and swiped at the spot. "I'm gonna carry you for now, but you'll have to climb down when we get there, cause we're gonna have to be real maneuverable. You know what that means? Maneuverable?"

Orpaan did not answer. His whole body was trembling. Crispin suppressed a pang of worry.

That afternoon, returning from reconnaissance at Holstead House, having witnessed the arrival of the daemonmongers' men, his head abuzz with plans, he had found Jacithrew tinkering again with the flying machine. The old man was evidently keyed up into a mood of giddy delight. As soon as he saw Crispin, he hailed him, and began to conduct a one-sided conversation so rambling Crispin wasn't sure whether Jacithrew was talking to him or to himself. His mood was a complete change from his usual dour scurryings to and fro. And this was no rabid outburst, such as he sometimes indulged in. Crispin was completely at a loss. When Orpaan handed Jacithrew a wrench instead of a hammer, and the old Wraith hit the child open-handed, leaving bleeding scratches on his face, it would normally have been all Crispin could do not to wring Jacithrew's neck; but today the incident just contributed to his growing sense of bewilderment. He had no idea how to deal with Jacithrew in this mood. He washed the blood off Orpaan's face, took him downstairs (hardly noticing that the guard daemon was gone and the door clearly visible in the pine trunk), lit the fire, and sat Orpaan down by it. Then, unable to suppress his curiosity, he brewed himself a mug of acorn tea and leaned against the pine to watch the machine take shape.

As the twilight gathered, and Jacithrew's loud, shrill monologue stopped making the least bit of sense, the machine grew and grew. The last of the parts that had lain about the downstairs room assumed their rightful identities. Three more pairs of wings, held apart by wooden struts, were layered on top of those that Jacithrew had already attached to the contraption. A carrying cradle developed on the chassis, and a propeller appeared on what Crispin could not help thinking of as the front grille, though there was no grille in sight. Finally, Jacithrew hopped out onto the ground and circled the machine, tittering with pleasure. "Help me raise it!" he ordered Crispin. Crispin jumped; he hadn't realized Jacithrew knew he was there. And as always when he had underestimated the old man, wariness made him decide to humor him, for risk of offending him.

Can't do any harm, anyway, he thought, as he climbed the tree, unlooped the bunches of ropes he'd put there before, and knotted them around the machine. Then, using a branch as a fulcrum, he hoisted the machine all the way up to the peak of the pine, anchored the ropes to the ground, and let it sway there, cradled by dozens of little branches. Jacithrew had suceeded in making it very light for its size. Every time Crispin brushed against it, his skin prickled with the presence of daemons.

He's just gotta get this craze out of his system, he thought as he climbed down. *He's been obsessed for days. It'll work itself out if I go along with him—*

"Oh, I will escape now!" Jacithrew caroled, prancing round and round. Crispin saw Orpaan looking out of the door in the tree and mouthed, *Go back inside.* "Yes, I will fly and fly and fly away from this dead place, to a land where all is life, I will fly south to Izte Kchebuk'ara, where the sun shines all day and there are beautiful redskinned women, where there is wine to be drunk beside a sparkling sea, where there is hope for an old man!"

At that moment they heard an airplane in the distance. Its advent cast a spell of silence on all three of them. When it was directly over-head, Jacithrew broke the quiet. He cantered back and forth, waving his arms and shouting, "Halloo! Halloooo! Storky-porky! Wild goose, bend your neck, wild swan, dip down!" He coughed. "Down, down! Dip down!"

The noise of the aircraft's great daemon engine grew fainter as it passed into the west. For a second Crispin, squinting upward, thought he saw a pale spot like a face appear on the fuselage. Then there was a faint whine and something hit the forest, about a mile away, with a long ripping crash. A flock of birds rose into the sky like dust from a beaten carpet.

Jacithrew stopped shouting.

Crispin followed the birds with his eyes.

Jacithrew shot a glance around, like a naughty child who finds himself momentarily unobserved, then made a dash for the rope lad-der and began to climb.

Rae didn't move. She was on her knees staring at the dead man. Crispin had to drag her to her feet. "Pull yourself together!" he hissed in her ear. He had to act confident. It wouldn't do to let her see that his plan had already been shot to pieces. The plan hadn't included killing anyone, let alone a man who was innocent, even if he *had* been trying to rape her. Crispin hadn't meant to throw the knife: it had just *hap-pened*, the same way it had happened back on that Lovoshire road. But this time the red beast had not done it. Killing the trader had not been an act of rage, but of some deeper, more difficult logic than Crispin used every day.

Orpaan stood in the doorway with his back to them, a small ragged figure with ridiculously big ears. Sueras and Fremis stood on either side of him, immensely tall and thin and crooked, their hands resting on Orpaan's shoulders. Daemons were sweeping over them and out into the night. But Orpaan did not move, and neither did his two demogorgons. It was they who had put the old woman and the lovebirds in the bonfire clearing out of commission. The five had sim-ply fallen silent and slumped against each other; Orpaan said they were stunned. That was when Crispin's plan had started going off course. What was it in the Wraiths' racial mentality? he wondered wildly. A passivity, an inability to think in terms of the long range, which combined with the accident of their dark skin made them perfect targets for the Ferupian patriotic spirit? It was incomprehensible how, with power like this at their disposal, they could have allowed themselves to be exploited for so long!

The sensation of all the daemons fleeting past Crispin was halfway between total pain and the feeling of swimming naked in a waterfall. He recognized the onset of a trance state and shook himself. *In the name of the Queen!*

He grabbed Rae and shoved past Orpaan out of the house. The wind had dropped. It was so quiet now that he could hear the crackling of the last of the bonfire, two hundred feet into the woods. The pines seemed to have marched closer to the walls. The cold wormed its way into his bones.

"It's the daemons," Rae gasped suddenly. "Can't you see them? They're up on the roof! They're all around the house! Anthea—Liesl—Hannah—I'm *sorry*—" She hid her face in his chest. Her body heaved violently. She wasn't crying, she was having hysterics. He could tell she had been holding it in for a long time, but all the same! "Orpaan!" he hissed.

The child, still staring into the daemon house, was pacing slowly backwards onto the bare earth. His daemons had become invisible again.

"Orpaan—"

Two women, one dark and small, one fair and tall, appeared on the threshold. Their clothes looked hastily put on. They stared disbelievingly at Rae, seeming scarcely to see Orpaan, though the child stood directly in front of her. Every alarm in Crispin's mind shrilled. He stared at them, trying to make eye contact, make them notice him. *We can settle this . . . we can still settle this . . .*

The fair woman met his gaze. Her lip curled. The humming of the daemons which had gathered into a cone over the house grew slowly louder. Crispin's skin itched as if it were being pulled taut over his face and scalp.

Rae wrenched away from him. He saw her mouth opening in a scream he could not hear, felt her shaking him. Her tear-slimed face wavered like a reflection in a warped mirror. Suddenly the odd pulling sensation ceased. There was a smell of burning hair. Crispin staggered, nearly blacking out as blood rushed to his head.

The fair woman slumped against the jamb of the door and slid to the ground. The dark-skinned woman let out a cry and stooped for a moment over her friend; then she rose and there was a terrible expression on her face. Orpaan still had not moved.

Daemon winds swirled down from the top of the house, cutting through Crispin's body like sweet-edged knife blades. Orpaan staggered back, then recovered. Rae wrung her hands. "Don't worry, darling," Crispin shouted inanely. "Don't worry!" What he wanted to communicate to her was that the Wraith woman was getting the worst of it. Her face had creased into lines of pain, and an unnatural light danced over her scalp, as if she had doused her hair in a bucket of cold fire.

"That's what she did to you!" Rae wept, tugging at his arm. "It's a Wraith trick that the trickster women stole, but she's a Wraith, too, and she's really good at it, and he's *killing* her! What is he, a daemon? I don't—*oh*—" Her voice changed. "Fineas, Sumannin, Tsuricus—"

The dark woman fell to her knees, retching. Horror cracked the daemon-induced glaze over Crispin's mind. He had not meant to kill anyone, and yet Jacithrew lay dead in the forest, and another dead man lay in the house, and the fair woman slumped dead in the doorway, and the five around the bonfire were probably dead as well, and all of it was his fault! If Orpaan died, too, for nothing, it would become insupportable. He lurched forward, swept Orpaan off the ground, and turned to run, the child writhing feebly in his grasp.

Which way? Which way? There were people in the pines, old, young, male, female. In the first gray light of the dawn, which was just touching the sky, they looked like creatures of tree roots, coated with ash. A stone's throw away, they were looting the pockets of the five Ferupians around the bonfire's embers. Crispin swung around again to grab Rae, who seemed incapable of moving, and froze as he saw the daemons avalanching up into the sky like an upside-down waterfall of jewels. They were invisible, of course, but he could feel each beast so strongly he knew them like pieces of his own body that were being washed off into the air. "Oh, Crispin," Rae sobbed, clinging to him. "Hurry hurry hurry! Oh, Queen, I knew it, I knew something like this would happen! Let's go, oh, please—"

The daemons stung their heels like thrown stones as they made their escape. Behind them the dark woman sobbed unheedingly over her dead friend. The trucks stood like skeletons in the road, their tarp-roofed trailers ribbed and shadowed. Later Crispin would be surprised that he did not think of stealing one. For that morning, carrying Orpaan, leading Rae, he must have walked twenty miles around curves and swerves, through ruts and sand hills, under thorns and creepers, over fox spoor and daemon bones, past the weed-blurred end of the road into the forest, before exhaustion finally got the better of fear and he muttered to Rae that he was going to lie down and sleep even if all the daemons in the Wraithwaste descended on them when he closed his eyes.

Her earlier hysteria had been replaced by a kind of pliant cooperativeness. She nodded, her lips bloodless, eyes swimming red. It was still deadly cold but the sun had come out, a fuzzy white circle at the top of the sky.

Avril 1893 A.D. The Wraithwaste

After the road ended, all was daemons. During the day, naked pines clawed at cold gray skies, or were lashed into a semblance of life by dry winds; at night, the throbbing darkness worked on Crispin's ears until he could no longer tell whether the buzzing was inside or outside his head.

They had come away from the destruction of Holstead House with nothing. Crispin had to struggle so hard just to keep himself, Rae, and Orpaan alive that he had little time to think about the change that had come over Rae. She had stopped resisting his advances, seeming finally to have accepted his rescue as proof of his love for her—a love he no longer understood himself. Her submissiveness might, of course, just be a by-product of their extreme circumstances. But when he had time to think about it, he felt not. It was as if their separation and reunion had produced a bond deeper than friendship, deeper than his responsibility for her, deeper than the physical lust which she now allowed him to satisfy in her body. If tempers flared, or hunger deadened speech, that bond remained. He could tell by her eyes when she was thinking about him.

"A Kirekuni," he muttered to himself sometimes.

But it didn't matter anymore. The love he felt for her when she allowed him to sleep in her arms with Orpaan curled between them or snugged around one of their backs, when she let him kiss her lips and breasts and even fondle the poor stump of her tail—it was not like anything he remembered. Occasionally he wished Orpaan weren't there. But even if Jacithrew had not laid it on him, he could not have deserted the boy. The other Wraiths hadn't taken Orpaan in before; they were not likely to now. And if the daemonmongers' men had found him, at the very most they would have shipped him back to a Lovoshire orphanage to spend his childhood in misery. Crispin wouldn't have subjected a mongrel puppy, let alone Orpaan, to life in Lovoshire. Privately, he assumed all of the responsibility for the atrocities Orpaan had committed—and this bond, which the child did not know about, was almost stronger than his love for Rae.

Bad enough even with both of them here! Stumbling through the Waste, his future drained of possibilities, his past an unrecoverable idyll, his sleep plagued by visions of cities.

He was in a city now, all right—the deserted city of the Wraiths. More than once the three of them had crashed through the roof of a weather-weakened root home, and as they sprawled in the soil, skeins of daemons had risen like smoke.

Here where daemons were the only living beasts, they materialized almost at random, fearing nothing at all. Though once they might have fed on the flora and fauna of the forest, now they lived off each other. The cairns of bones Crispin and Rae had noticed before, which marked big daemons' territory, had become as common as mushrooms—and they ranged from knee height to the size of a small hill.

Crispin had given up his attempts to hail the airplanes that droned with increasing frequency across the sky. But without telling Rae, he was doggedly tracking them westward. Their only hope of survival lay in making for the war front. Queen knew what would happen to Rae and Orpaan once they got there. War offered financial rewards to men, but only death to children and disgrace to women. Crispin's experiences in the Wraithwaste had given him confidence that he himself would be all right. But Orpaan and Rae . . .

He was feeling the pinch of having others dependent on him.

Orpaan, too, had changed. The night of the killings at Holstead House had been the last time he displayed any sort of fortitude. Perhaps it was the aftereffects of Jacithrew's death. Or perhaps he understood that he and his daemons had killed six people—Crispin had tried to explain it all away, but he did not seem to understand. At any rate, although Sueras, Fremis, and Amanse were still keeping company with the party, Orpaan had not materialized them since the night at the house of trickery. He seemed completely cowed. No longer did he offer suggestions and advice as if he was another adult. He merely trailed along, holding Crispin's hand, his thumb in his mouth. Although in their circumstances the very thought was so petty as to be ridiculous, Crispin feared he was jealous of Rae.

Orpaan made a constant, conscious effort to understand things. His recent string of failures to do so frightened him and made him miserable. He had thought he understood Jacithrew; but Jacithrew had died. He had thought he understood his daemons; but his daemons had powers he had never even guessed at. (He didn't even want to *remember* that.) Nonetheless, now that Crispin was always talking to Rae, not to him, Orpaan spent most of his time in silent communication with Amanse, Sueras, and Fremis. They comforted him when he remembered Jacithrew. *We're still here anyway,* they said, *even if those rotten devils Kankeris and Gelfitus cut out. The sleazes. But we love love love you! We're not gonna leave!*

And being in the "fuzzy" state of communion made the Waste look less stark—like it could be the forest near Holstead House, which was equally barren but somehow friendlier. It made him forget how hungry he was. Communion also kept him from remembering other things. If he remembered some of the stuff that had happened to him in his seven and a half years, he would start screaming. He knew. It had happened before.

But you couldn't talk to daemons all the time; it stopped being pleasant and got annoying, like having your head patted too much, the way Jacithrew used to do, except Orpaan had never dared to pull away from him. And when he started thinking about Jacithrew, he wished he had never helped him with the flying machine. Because no matter what Crispin said, it had been all his fault. All his fault that it was no good, not like the airplanes that flew overhead like beautiful jeweled darts. His fault that it had been a clunky toy that could no more fly than could a wooden plank. And because it hadn't flown, Jacithrew—Dadda, though he wasn't really Dadda—had *died*.

And now Orpaan was afraid Crispin and Rae, who he'd thought might be his new *new* Dadda and Mama, were going to die, too. Because there wasn't any food.

When Orpaan let himself come out of the fuzzy-happy trance, he knew this part of the forest. It was horribly similar to the place where he had been born. Only Wraiths could squeeze a living from this wilderness! If he had known Crispin was going to come here, he would have tried to explain about everything being dead, and then maybe Crispin would have changed his mind. But now it was too late.

Too late. Nothing to do, nothing to say. He could only try to keep up with them.

More than anything, he was scared of getting lost.

And he was worried about Rae. Crispin's girl. Her skin was so dull, her hair tangled, and she'd cut her dress up the front so she could walk. It didn't look right. Not like Hannah's dress. Hannah had always looked right; but Hannah, too, was now a part of the past. The only thing about Rae that still shone was her lips, because she was always licking them.

And Orpaan was worried about Crispin. Rae didn't watch him when they were eating, but Orpaan did, and Crispin *never ate anything*. But Orpaan didn't dare mention it, he didn't dare say anything that might get on Crispin's nerves, because sometimes, usually when he thought he was alone, Crispin would get angry, and there was the chance he might turn that fury on Orpaan. He was like Orpaan's nearly forgotten Dadda, like that. At night, when he thought Rae and Orpaan were sleeping, Crispin would get up and walk a little way away, and curse and kick and punch trees, and then lean his head against a tree trunk, and Orpaan knew he was crying. That was when he wanted to run out and hug him and say, *It's okay, fella, cause I love love love you!* Just the way his daemons said it to him.

But he did not dare.

Rae was far more open. She cried while they were walking, silently. There was never any warning when she was going to start, her mouth would just wobble, and water, invaluable water, would drip out of her eyes.

Orpaan liked to lie in between them at night, so that he could stuff his hands down his sides, one next to each of their chests, and monitor their breathing. Sometimes he didn't sleep all night himself, he was so busy keeping watch over them.

And day followed hungry day, and he was always thirsty no matter how much water he drank, and Amanse and Sueras and Fremis hissed in chorus to him at night in a way which they mistakenly believed to be soothing. Perhaps it would have been soothing to daemon kids. It kept *him* awake. But Orpaan knew they meant well, so he did not like to disillusion them.

What really *was* soothing, although he had not wanted it to be at first, was the way Rae hugged him and talked to him. Orpaan guessed that she used him to avoid talking to Crispin sometimes, and he felt bad for taking sides—but when she held him, he couldn't possibly pull away. When she wanted, she was kinder than any other woman he had ever known, even his *real* mama. "It's a good thing you didn't stay with Hannah and the rest of the tricky ladies," he told her once, when he felt like talking. "You're much too nice!"

Crispin was leaning against a tree watching them. His laughter sounded bad. "Hear that? Even he agrees with me!"

Rae hid her face in Orpaan's hair. "At least I would have lived to see my nineteenth birthday. I had such plans, Crispin! Not like you. Which is ironic, considering what I believe in." Her voice had gone small and sad. She shook herself—and Orpaan—and went on, "You're always in a rush to get somewhere better, but you have no idea where that is. And look where you've got us now!"

"I work things out as I go along," Crispin said. "And I know one thing: *I* would never sell myself into slavery for the price of a bed and a meal!"

"That just proves how little you know of the world," Rae said. She started to cry. Through her sobs, she hiccuped, "It wouldn't have been *slavery*, anyway! They *loved* each other! And now they're dead! Liesl, Mother, the twins, Anthea—"

The anger vanished from Crispin's face. He came toward them, and Orpaan reveled in the crush of bodies as he wrapped his arms around both of them. Crispin smelled of sweat, a good, familiar smell that brought back ancient memories. "Not as much as I love you. *Nobody* could ever love you as much as I do."

And Rae allowed herself to be calmed. It was always easy for Crispin to calm her. Orpaan sometimes thought he provoked her to anger deliberately, just so he could calm her again. But it was none of Orpaan's business. While Crispin was kissing her tears dry, Orpaan wriggled unobtrusively away and went to look for pine cones that still had the kernels in them.

When he had gathered a pile he knelt on the ground to pick the nuts out. He was astonished, and horrified, to feel warm wetness splashing on his knee. He looked around to see if either of them had noticed; but they were still wrapped around each other. He wiped his eyes hard. If they saw him crying, they might think he wasn't happy. And he *was*. He was hungry, but he was happier than he had ever been in his life.

The only time Crispin ever felt himself getting impatient with Rae was when she refused to speculate about where they were going, or how much longer they could last. Instead she would push her emaciated face into his neck and kiss him, sucking his skin as if she thought she could get some nourishment from it. The forest had become so sere and juiceless that even clean running water was precious; they were living on roots and keeping their spirits up with talk of banquets. At least, Crispin was. Rae would just keep walking, her face a blank, and he had the uncomfortable impression that her mind was somewhere else altogether, and his voice ran on, unheard.

He thanked the Queen that he had been born half-Lamaroon, constructed of air and muscle, needing only a few bites of food a day to keep walking. But in the mirror of a puddle, the morning after one of the Wraithwaste's infrequent rainstorms battered the land, he saw that his cheeks had hollowed to caverns and the bones beneath his eyes stuck out like crags. Rae had told him before that the eyes themselves glowed "like ripe cherries." He'd been pleased, because he thought she was joining in his running dark joke in which he compared everything around them to edibles; but now he saw what she meant. Appalled, he sat back on his heels.

Rae and Orpaan were around the other side of the ruin in which they had sheltered last night, digging in the long-abandoned vegetable garden. By some freak of fate, just as the storm hit, they had had their first piece of luck since fleeing from Holstead House: a deserted farmhouse, complete with menagerie and overgrown potato patch, which had certainly once been a house of trickery. Within the walls of what had once been the kitchen, stone flags underlay dead brambles, and the incessant throb of crowded, seething, self-devouring daemonkind faded to a buzz. It was like coming in out of cold which has numbed your flesh. The rain drummed on the broken-in roof. They had woken early and hurried outside into sunshine. Rae's excitement at the possibility of finding potatoes in the garden made her seem as young as Orpaan.

Strangely enough, the bleaker their situation became, the oftener Orpaan was coming out of his trance state. He had shown Crispin and Rae how to kill daemons that he materialized, and cook and eat them. He liked the furry ones; he said they were "softer." But even the flesh of "soft" daemons was so mouth-parchingly sour that you could only stomach tiny amounts of it before you vomited, with the result that they were all constantly nauseated. On the other hand, it was definitely better than nothing at all.

The sun shone brilliantly. Water dripped down Crispin's neck from the dead-creeper-swathed branches of the pines. The crashing of the invisible sea of daemons was so loud that he could hardly hear Rae and Orpaan chattering. With the clarity of a hallucination, he imagined what the air would look like if he could see them: millions of naked sprites of all shapes and sizes, pursuing and devouring each other with the frenzy of a hundred piranhas caught in three feet of water. And the world, Millsy had once told him, *was* like water to them, with no demarcation between air and earth and tree and man—the daemons could move through them all as smoothly as ghosts, and their passing left no mark. Only oak trees stopped them, as did silver, and there wasn't much of either around here. The daemons were a river rolling and curling back on itself, trapped behind a dam. But where was the dam? And when would it break?

Rae said that the Wraithwaste had been shrinking for hundreds of years. Soon it must reach its critical minimum area. Crispin could feel the imminence of that critical moment more and more clearly, the harder he concentrated on the subsonic noise of the daemons.

Danger! Danger! Danger! rang the alarms, as he slid imperceptibly into a trance.

Wearily, he forced his eyes open. He pushed his hands into his hair. It felt like a bird's nest. Rae had fallen into the habit of occupying her evenings, once they were too tired to walk any more, in separating his hair into dozens of fat, matted worms. She never smiled or talked as she worked. It was as if her life depended on keeping her hands occupied, and nothing else.

Overhead the sky was a pale winter blue. To the west, planes glinted in the sunshine like silver insects, circling as lazily as the flies that waltzed beneath tent roofs in summer. As a child, between shows, Crispin had sat alone in a corner of the women's dressing-room tent and stared at the flies, wondering without wanting to know what his mother was doing in her black top outside which the queue of men was often five or ten long.

Exotic dancing. Giving 'em tattoos where they want them.

Balloon Lady. Lovely lady.

Every now and then, near the horizon, one of the airplanes tumbled out of the sky. Crispin had never seen such a thing in days of watching them. He narrowed his eyes. Was this how they *landed*? There were twenty-two planes—then another faraway bluebottle spiraled down.

"Twenty-one," he said aloud, decisively. He stood up, ignoring the wave of dizziness that threatened him.

He should not have sat down to rest! Delay inevitably brought thoughts of how nice it would be never to go on at all; delay had caused him just now to sink down into the slow-dripping Wraithwaste day. He would not let that happen again! It would probably be necessary to die soon. But he would do it without a murmur. And he would do it on his feet!

And so would Rae and Orpaan—even if he had to hold them up!

He shouted, "Come here and bring him! Never mind the potatoes! We're going on right now!"

> *. . . the presence of the child evoked a feeling like that of a sailor who sees by the compass that the direction in which he is swiftly moving is far off the right course, but that he is incapable of stopping, that every minute is taking him farther and farther away from the right course, and that to acknowledge that he is off course would be just the same as acknowledging that he is undone.*
>
> —Leo Tolstoy, *Anna Karenina*

Nothing About Us

26 Avril 1893 A.D. The Raw: The Lovoshire Parallel:
Pilkinson's Shadowtown

Two days later, Crispin, Rae, and Orpaan entered the village of Pilkinson's Shadowtown, on the edge of the Raw, and certain things became far clearer to Crispin than they had in Ferupe, where people did not experience the approach of the war directly, as a blow which can be ducked or borne, but rather subtly, like the scent from an onrolling charnel cart, which is inescapable. In Shadowtown, by contrast, everything was as harsh and black and white as the sun at midday.

The century-long Kirekuni advance had caused the trickster women to batten their doors against outsiders and plant wards of oak around their gardens, but they, like the Wraiths, had existed before the war, and many of them hoped to survive it. Shadowtown had no such history or aspirations. In fact, as Crispin realized before he and Rae and the child were there long enough to get a square meal, it was no town at all. It was a toilet for soldiers' whims. Its demolition date had been fixed before it was even built. It was in no better a position than a sand castle in the way of the rising tide. (For at least twenty years, certain Kingsburg advisors to the Queen had annually predicted the ground Kirekune would gain that year, and they had consistently been proved right, for the figure did not change; though it was unlikely that the Queen heard anything of these estimates on her hill of silken pillows, with her Cypean cats in her lap, and her ears ringing with her courtiers' compliments.)

There were perhaps ten women to every man in Shadowtown. Dogs and cats—as opposed to daemons kept collared for food—were as rare as gold. People might be born in Shadowtown, live there, and die there, but the stammering fire that dropped out of the sky at night and burned holes in their houses worked on them from the minute they first took a breath. They thought no more about hope or fear than they did about love. Crispin, remembering his arrival much later, thought he must have realized this. The hopelessness of the place had settled immediately about his shoulders like a too-heavy coat. But he shrugged it off and led Rae and Orpaan down the rocky, dusty street—if it could be called a street—with the confidence of a prince.

Most of the houses were either half-built or half-burnt: it was difficult to tell which. Gray-painted tanks, trucks, and motorbikes were parked everywhere. Soldiers smoked cigarettes as they messed with the engines. They paid no attention to Crispin, Rae, and Orpaan. Shushing Rae's protests, Crispin pulled her and Orpaan straight through a group of them into a building that smelled like a tavern. There, he ordered them a slap-up dinner. He still had one pound of the money the Old Gentleman had given him, and though the bill was rubbed almost blank by months of unfolding and refolding with sweaty fingers, the Wraith barmaid took it without so much as a glance into his face.

They were halfway through their meal, Rae and Orpaan eating with a desperate speed which Crispin knew would make them sick later, he pacing himself with water, when soldiers with yellow epaulets on dark green uniforms surrounded their table and he knew his show of confidence had backfired.

He pushed back his chair and stood up. He saw a flicker of disconcertment in seven out of eight pairs of eyes, but not in those of the wiry, middle-aged man who faced him from behind Rae's stool. This man had double epaulets that stuck out six inches beyond his shoulders. He said conversationally, "Out of the Waste, are you?"

"And still weary from the journey," Crispin said with as much Millsy-style dignity as he could muster.

"Aye. Not many come that way."

"Last was before ye joined up, Snyder," one soldier said to another, a very old man, and sniggered.

"In fact, I'm sorry to admit I don't know exactly where we are." Crispin strove for a look of amiable puzzlement. "I left Valestock with my family more than a month ago. I don't even know if it's Marout or Avril."

"None but fools or them with the hangman behind them would go west. 'Spect them in Valestock would be interested to know of you. Aye, well, they won't be hearing for a good while yet," the two-epaulet man said drily. "You're in Pilkinson's Shadowtown, but all Shadowtowns are the same from Khyzlme down to Sudeland—isn't that so, boys?"

The men muttered a ragged yes. "But we got the best ho's for miles, right 'ere," one of them added boldly. The officer nodded and smiled, acknowledging his men's laughter. His gnarled hands rested on Rae's shoulders, massaging. Rae's carved-out face was white and dry; the food stains on her lips looked as garish as paint. The officer's index fingers wandered into the hollows of her throat, between the tendons that stood out in painful relief.

"Arrest them. Take him out to Chressamo. Do what you like with her; she seems used up. The child—" he shrugged. "Is he really yours?" he asked Crispin, giving a final cruel squeeze to Rae's shoulders and stepping back. "I think not. He's Shadow, and you are not."

Strong hands grabbed Crispin's wrists, ready to twist his arms behind his back. Even through the red haze that was clouding his mind, he knew that in his present state of weakness he wasn't going to be able to get free. Why wasn't Orpaan calling his daemons? Just when they could be really useful! The child's eyes darted wildly, but he did not move. One of his hands held a forkful of stew in midair, and it was trembling so violently that lumps of meat fell to the table. "He's my son!" Crispin shouted. "If you harm him, I'll kill you and every last one of your descendants!"

The officer laughed. He was at least forty, and his expression was pleasant. "Haven't any, my friend. You clearly know little about the war. It would be interesting to find out what you're doing here. Perhaps we'll talk again—I don't have much to do with Chressamo, but you never know. All right. Take him."

He turned away, and as if in slow motion Crispin saw his mouth open and the sound of words come out. He was hailing the bartender.

Orpaan knew when Crispin started fighting the soldiers that his new Dadda and his new Mama were going to die this time for real. Soldiers didn't stand for this kind of thing. Soldiers had sent ferrets with fire-fuses strapped to them down into the root houses of his village. Soldiers had slung him into a tree as if he was a dog that was worrying their legs. Soldiers were merciless. Jacithrew's words echoed in his head: *They hate us. They call us not Wraiths, but Shadows. They think we are less than human, created merely to serve and amuse, and if we fail to obey—and even when we do obey—they deem it their right to do what they will with us.* He had said that long, long ago, all the way back, when they stood watching the smoking ruins of the trees, a child and a harmless ancient, the only two survivors of their village, while the air ate away at the corpses of those who had been gunned down, and soldiers lit cigarettes off the embers. That was before they fled east, before Jacithrew went strange. Orpaan had still loved him after he went strange, but he no longer said things that made sense. The night Crispin came had been the first time in over a year that Jacithrew had mentioned the pale people, who had once been the subject of endless discourses. One of the reasons Orpaan had liked Crispin was because of this seemingly restabilizing effect he had on Jacithrew.

Which had turned out to be a bad thing, too, in the end!

He sat frozen at the table. Rae hugged him so tight it hurt. Crispin's struggles made everyone else flee the bar. Orpaan could not fend off the memory of Jacithrew lying in the ruins of his flying machine, nor could he fend off the far older memory of his parents' and neighbors' screams coming from beneath the ground, and the smoke . . . Usually he could make himself not think about those things, but now they met and mingled. He smelled burning daemons. He saw flames spilling out of the doors in the trees.

But it wasn't Crispin's fault!

Crispin! Oh, Crispin! He had knocked over a laden table, and his arm was bleeding freely. The barmaids had retreated to the far wall of the place, and they were passing a beer bottle among themselves, commenting on the fight. Orpaan's lungs had seized up as they did when he was too frightened even to call his daemons. *Amanse! Fremis! Sueras!*

Had Crispin not stumbled through the roof . . . But the jolt to his and Jacithrew's life had jolted Jacithrew's addled brains, too. The old mania had taken him, the mania which had made him an outcast within their village, humored but despised. *Jacithrew* meant The Old Man Who Wants To Be A Soldier. He was so named because it was his obsession to be able to fly. The night Crispin came, he had sat cackling by the fire until dawn, and the next morning, to Orpaan's horror, he had started work on the flying machine again.

The villagers had feared the soldiers, but not taken their threats seriously. At the water festival a man had dressed up as a soldier and people pelted him with pine cones.

Then the forest-clearing troops came, and nobody laughed any more.

With a scream Orpaan broke away from Rae and ran outside.

The sun was shining brilliantly. A group of children were shooting ball bearings for marbles in the dust. Orpaan dashed across the street and around a daemon tank with enormous, chain-ringed wheels. They shouted at him and scrambled to their feet. He knew he had knocked the game apart; he hoped they weren't angry. Across the street, a soldier came out of the tavern. "Kid! Where the fuck did 'e go?"

"Hide me," Orpaan begged the biggest boy, who was lanky and pinched-faced, dressed like the others in ragged shorts. His skin was so tanned—or so dirty—it was nearly black. Like the others, he smelled of sweat and filth. "They're killing my Dadda!" A mist of transparent bubbles rose and fell in front of his eyes. He felt as though he were going to faint.

The boy looked down at Orpaan. "You ain't got no Dadda," he said contemptuously. "No one ain't got no Dadda."

Scrupulously truthful, nearly in tears, Orpaan said, "Well, he isn't really my Dadda, but he tends after me. And they're hurting him. My Mama's there, but she can't do anything! Please, please—"

"T'ain't your Mama, is it?" a girl said with a giggle. She pointed at the door of the tavern where Rae stood with her hands over her mouth, trying to see between the soldiers in front of her. "She white as paper!"

"Pretty lady," said another girl.

"Well, she's Kirekuni." Orpaan fell over himself trying to explain. Why didn't they understand the emergency? He wanted to flee back into the tavern, try and pull the soldiers off Crispin by main force, but he had started this, and now he had to finish it. He sensed that the children would turn nasty faster than you might spin a knife in the air. "She's not really my Mama either but she—"

"Kirekuni!" two or three girls sang. Their hair fell to their knees in knotted masses. Even through his fright and dizziness Orpaan understood that they were singing softly so that the soldiers should not hear. "Long-tail rat-ass bone-face lady! Mouse-lady! Lizard-lady! Kire-cunt cunt cunt!"

Orpaan let out a sob, and tried to steady his voice. "I have daemons! Shut up 'bout my Mama, or you'll get it!"

"He has daemons."

"Sure he has daemons."

"You don't come out of the Waste, you come from Bennett's Shadowtown, you all fronting," said the littlest boy spitefully. "No guts."

"Show us them then, you baby prick," said the tallest boy. Orpaan felt a sting on the back of his neck, and knew someone had shied a ball bearing at him. He didn't turn around. "All right!" There was another sting, on his leg. "Amanse," he added softly, frowning as he drew the daemon toward him. The three had not followed at his heels, the way they usually did: they were hovering invisibly in the middle of the street, raising little puffs of dust as they snapped up the lizards that scuttled there. "Amanse. *Amanse.*"

Eight feet of green-furred muscle slid out of the air. "Special convoy!" she shouted shrilly. "Troop 170 Dragon to SP13! Eddie Brickett's gone south, haven't you heard?" The kids yelled in disbelief. Amanse interpreted this as a threat to Orpaan, and dug both hands into the tall boy's arm, twisting with her nails until she had ripped away a chunk of flesh. Meanwhile, she rubbed her bottom against Orpaan's middle in greeting. The tall boy screamed and backed away until he fell against the tank. His arm was gouting blood. Two of the girls rushed to him. Orpaan screamed, too, in horror. "Amanse! It's not my fault, it's not my—"

Someone growled in anger, and Orpaan was borne forward into the dirt. "Armaments 54 secure and present, sir!" Amanse shrieked, and Orpaan heard her teeth meeting with a crunch in human flesh, and the weight came off Orpaan's back for a minute, but then returned with a thud, winding him. Something crunched in his chest. His forehead banged rock.

The soldiers had handcuffed Crispin and they were frog-marching him out of the tavern, but the beast would not go quietly. It snarled at the sergeant and wrenched out of its captors' grip, out into the sunlight. Momentarily blinded, it shook its head and made a noise of fury. Even the sun was its enemy. Fight, fight, fight!

Orpaan lay unmoving on the other side of the street, blood on his skull and torso.

The beast rushed out of Crispin as quickly as a fire's heat when a door is opened.

A troop of soldiers leaned against a truck fifty yards away. Bright eyes watched from the windows of a half-charred house. Small brown hands gripped the windowsills. Crispin heard the children commenting on his stupidity.

The soldiers jostled up on either side of him, but he dashed away from them, across the street. "Orpie!" No response. Crispin dropped to his knees beside the small, inert body. His inability to free his hands frustrated him beyond words. Like a dog lapping water, he bent and laid his cheek on Orpaan's back. He tasted blood. It was bitter, and still warm.

The child was dead. The brilliance of the sun dissolved into diamonds. Crispin shouted. The caterpillars of the tank in front of him gleamed like a mosaic, an unreadable message encoded in the lost language of objects from whatever power had allowed a child to be killed this way. There was no explanation for the blood pooling sticky and black in the dust. No explanation for the blood on Crispin's fingers and lips. No explanation for the vast, metal-scored sapphire of the sky. No explanation for the handcuffs biting into his wrists or the soldiers yanking him to his feet.

He twisted against them with growing desperation. Must make

amends to Orpaan, must avenge him, but what could he do, what could he do? Half an hour ago there had been Rae, and with her beside him he could have done anything, but they had taken her away, Queen knew to where, Queen knew whether he would ever see her again! The small dark face, half-pressed into the dust, had no expression on it. Orpaan's life had been too short and too much scarred by violence to have been happy. But recently—recently, despite the direness of their circumstances—Crispin had often thought he glimpsed a look of peace on the child's face. If that were true, all the efforts Crispin had made on Orpaan's behalf, which Rae had some-times intimated to him were pointless, would have been worthwhile. But now he would never know.

From within the house came the sound of children's laughter, wild and merry, and something struck Crispin on the cheek. A ball bearing. It bounced into the middle of the road. Crispin roared and pulled free of the soldiers, who were so startled they actually let go, and plunged toward the house. Inside, feet thudded up creaking stairs. "You little bastards! I'll get you! Yeah, run, go on, you can't get away—"

The soldiers had him again, seven of them shoving all around him, and this time they made no attempt to avoid injuring him. It was all he could do not to shriek as they pulled his hands up behind his back and kicked his ankles with steel-tipped boots. Finally the epauleted officer intervened. "That'll be all," he said in his dry voice. "We want him able to walk. Intelligence has enough on their hands without sending an ambulance to Pilkinson's Shadowtown for an arrest of no consequence like this one."

"I'll give you no consequence," Crispin snarled. But the beast would not come back. The sergeant laughed and strode off. Crispin was pushed after him. Unutterably weary, he let his head drop between his shoulders and his eyes go out of focus, until a buffet of cold wind alerted him to the fact that they had come out from between the houses. He looked up.

It was the first real sight he had had of the Raw. The sky dwarfed everything on the ground. It was the hugest sky he'd ever seen, and the cleanest.

In the south, the sky was white-hot and creamy. In the north, a clear sunny day came maybe once every ten years. In the east, appro-priately enough considering the general temperament of the people there, the heavens were pure brass. Only in the heart of Ferupe (remember that glorious summer) had Crispin seen skies like this. A dome of pure lapis lazuli, unmarred by a single cumulus. Only the silver sky beetles in hot pursuit of each other, and burning streaks of red and yellow and blue and green arcing up from the horizon to catch them. They tracked their fiery dance across the inside of his head as he looked from the sky to the man-made badlands below. The landscape was cluttered with various buildings—abandoned settlements? military bases? and a pale brown road wound out into the hilly plain. There was no telling how far the desuetude spread. But the sharp gray shadows of mountains on the horizon looked no taller than the first joint of Crispin's index finger. The plain must be at least two hundred miles across.

Nothing moved out among the burnt-out buildings. There were dryland cypresses and baobabs. A few pines. Juniper and eyebright crawled at Crispin's feet, and creepers hazed the outlines of the rocks and ruins.

Could the fauna be as sparse as the greenery? If so, he had reached heaven.

Since he, Rae, and Orpaan came out of the last straggling bit of the woods into Pilkinson's Shadowtown, the throb of too many daemons had mercifully faded. Although the occult world was quiet, the mundane wasn't. The wind sighed and moaned over the bare desert with an insistency which spoke of never ever letting up.

The soldiers pulled Crispin toward a jeep which was idling on the road into the plain and pushed him under the tarp roof. Two of them got in after him and made him sit down with his back to the cab. The other five reached in to cuff him a few times for good luck, then moved off down the road toward Shadowtown.

"Bet you liked having me helpless, huh?" Crispin shouted after them, maddened by the punches. "Bet there's a shitload else you'd like to do to me—*cowards*!"

One private turned and spat, but none of the others paid any attention. The soldier on Crispin's left, a fat gingery fellow, slapped him on the side of the head. Through the dinning in his ears he heard the epauleted officer getting into the front of the jeep, speaking to the driver. Then the daemon whined in protest, and the jeep jolted into motion.

The naked land peeled away on either side of the road. Crispin felt sick: it was going backwards.

There was a crack between the tarp that covered the back of the jeep and the cabin. He tipped his head back. The metal lip dug into the back of his neck. High in the sky, a plane swung and dived. Another came after it, and there was the faint stammer of gunfire.

His heart pounded in his throat. The taste of spring embittered the wind.

Nothing about us except our neediness is, in this life, permanent.

—C. S. Lewis, *The Four Loves*

ℌ Picture of
ℌeartbreak

Crispin sat with his eyes closed on the edge of a cot which was so low that his knees came up to his ears. The cell was about seven feet by seven, with one barred window. It was high up in the tower named Chressamo. Crispin had spent hours watching jeeps and tanks rattle across the Raw, and craning his neck to watch the airplanes overhead. This morning, when he saw nine Kirekuni biplanes fire-strafe a Ferupian tower about two miles off, he realized why the holding cells for prisoners were in the top of the tower, which common sense would label the most prestigious bit; why the troops and staff of Chressamo lived underground. Even from two miles off, he could see the fire ripping through that other tower. But the Kirekunis had time for only one pass before they had to peel off into the sky to meet a group of avenging Ferupian monoplanes. The whole swarm wrangled off into the blueness, very small and not appearing at all deadly.

But Crispin had no stomach for watching the sky anymore. Last night he had had a dream—well, not a dream. A *hallucination*. And he knew now how he had come to let Prettie Valenta fall to her death in the center of the ring of Smithrebel's Fabulous Aerial and Animal Show, three months ago on a rainy Jevanary night. Right in the middle of an otherwise ordinary performance, he had been grabbed in the teeth of a vision and plomped down in another moment of his life. To be precise, the moment when humanity was coming to an end.

Not surprising, perhaps, as that was likely to be the single biggest event in Crispin's life—and everyone else's, too. Not surprising that supernatural phenomena should orbit around it.

Rae was right after all, he thought dully. Her and her tall tales.

No one knows exactly what shape the apocalypse will come in. All that has been revealed to us is that it will come.

But I know, Crispin thought. *Talk about revelations.*

Why me?

We are to die by fire.

The fires which devoured the anthill-city were the fires of the apocalypse. And Crispin had been there. He hadn't just dreamt it. He had *been there*, corporeal and solid—and in far better health than he was now, as if in the interval he had lived a relatively luxurious life. His hair had been cut so short the winter air chilled his scalp. His boots had skidded on the refuse in the street. His nostrils had stung with the smoke wafting on the wind. Terrified Kirekunis had shoved past, bumping heedlessly into him.

This time it had been much realer, a continuous experience uninterrupted by shifts in time and place. (Now he could remember the first vision just as well as the second. He marveled at the skill with which he'd blanked it out of his consciousness for three months.)

Last night he had been *searching* for the stranger he had so briefly met the first time around. That time, Crispin had failed to recognize the stranger; now he had to try to find him all over again. It was like looking for a gold coin in a mountain of sawdust, but he had no choice: he had to keep going. These were the fires, started by man or mystery, which would consume humanity, if not the entire world. And Crispin's only hope lay in finding the stranger whom he hunted in vain through the shouting crowds, behind overturned bazaar stalls, inside deserted houses, up narrow, twisting streets at the top of which the orange glow lurked. He knew he would recognize his quarry if and when he saw him, though he could not picture the man's face.

But the Kirekunis fleeing the city with their children and their useless valuables all looked the same. Many of them clutched amulets shaped like a woman's head, such as Rae had carried, as if they believed lumps of silver would ward off the flames; none of them paid Crispin any attention, except to glance at him in confusion when he pushed past them in the wrong direction, *toward* the fire.

He had come to a high street. It was empty. The air resounded with a rushing roar like a high wind. On both sides of the steep river of cobbles, narrow elaborate wedding cakes of buildings rose into the orange night. At the top of the hill the glow shone brightly, and he could actually feel the heat on his face. He was sweating, from the climb, from fear, from excitement. He was almost on his quarry.

What did he have to do to him when he found him? he wondered fleetingly. Was the stranger the personification of the apocalypse—was Crispin being given a chance to avert a future disaster by killing him? Or was he the one who must be saved at all costs, if there was to be any hope after the fires died down?

Crispin had not the least idea.

And the minute he thought to question his search, rainbow bubbles rose in front of his eyes and numbness rushed through his limbs, so that walking became as difficult as wading through water.

But before the rainbows completely obscured the street, Crispin glimpsed him against the light at the top of the hill.

He was a black silhouette. His clothes, unlike those of the Kirekunis, clung to his frame, making him look thinner than any human being should or could be. His shoulders were stooped. He had a tail.

And then the whole thing slipped away.

It dived like a fish, seeking to vanish without trace beneath the waters of memory. But he caught its slimy fin with his fingernails. As he lay breathing hard, with dawn's gray light growing in the room, it came swimming back to him. With it came the first vision. Both were so vivid, even in memory, that at times, as he relived them, the dawn in the window grew orange.

With a certainty greater than any he had ever felt, he knew they had not been dreams. Slowly he extracted the facts from the images. The former were few.

In a certain number of years—before he was very much older—he would find himself in a city in Kirekune, looking for someone who might or might not have some power to turn aside the fires of the end of the world.

If he ever met Rae again, how she would rub it in! How she would sneer—and then kiss him—

But he wouldn't mind, because he loved her—

But now his guess that he was unlikely ever to see her again was confirmed. She had not been anywhere in the vision.

He sat sweating, staring at the metal tray on the floor with its untouched plate of mush and mug of chicory coffee.

Why had the fires been *orange*? That was the color of ordinary fire. When spontaneous daemon combustion occurred, the flames were whitish blue, and all-devouring, though they gave off comparatively little heat. Crispin had once seen a truck careen off the road with incandescent flames bursting from the cabin windows, its driver flinging himself out, burnt so badly that he died within the hour. The hulk stood at rest in the field by the side of the Eastern Trunk Road, while every other trucker who happened by stopped to gawk. As its wooden frame was consumed, yellow flames adulterated the white.

Outside, "screamers" shrieked in the distance.

Pull yourself together!

But—

The end of the world. It was all going to happen as she had said. The death of the Queen. The destruction.

Unless this vision meant Crispin could *do* something about it.

But this was ridiculous. He was letting his nerves get the better of him. *Nobody* could see into the future, and even if that were possible, no one could *change* it! He remembered that on the occasion of both visions he had been strung out, wrought up. And there had been a third time, hadn't there, when he dozed in the truck he had stolen from Valestock—*that* hadn't been a fully fledged vision, but it had been clearer than any dream. On all of those occasions his nerves had been so tightly wound, his temper so high, that nobody would have found it strange if he started spouting gibberish. Seeing things was a relatively sane way of letting off steam.

Lifting his head to stare at the blank wall, he did not know what to believe.

The door opened. A man in the gray uniform ubiquitous in Chressamo entered the cell. A leather belt which looked as though it could deliver a nasty sting cinched his waist to a girl's narrow span.

He entered the room, followed by two guards, and the door closed behind them. Crispin did not get up.

A smile creased the man's seamed face. He was probably about fifty, but his face made him look a hundred. "You may salute."

"Actually, I'd rather not," Crispin said dully.

"You're not a soldier? You've never saluted your superiors? Let me tell you, it will make your life a good deal easier. Like this." The man demonstrated. Crispin sat back on his cot, knees apart. "You should be more frightened of me than of the Kirekunis."

"All you've done to me so far is lock me up." Crispin did not care what he said or what happened.

"Salute," the man said. "That's an order."

Reluctantly Crispin got to his feet and saluted.

"Much better. Much, *much* better." The man turned to the guards. "I'll have coffee. But I don't think this interview will be very protracted." He glanced at Crispin's untouched tray. "It doesn't look as though the young man wants anything."

"I wouldn't half mind a whiskey," Crispin said.

"Did you get that?" the man said, unbelievably. "A double shot of D'Aubier for the young man."

The door closed. "Thanks," Crispin said. "What should I call you—sir?" He owed him that now.

"Sostairs. Colonel. Can't you read?"

Crispin saw that one of the multicolored bars that decorated the man's chest was in fact lettering. He shrugged.

"Ahhh." Sostairs let out a long sigh. Crispin wondered if he had inadvertently saved his own life, or made a terrible mistake. Maybe the thing Sostairs hoped to pin on him—whatever it was—depended on his ability to read. In that case, Millsy had been right, after all!

But Sostairs was directing more questions at him. "Where were you born? What were you doing in Pilkinson's Shadowtown? I'm afraid it will be necessary for us to know more about you, Mr. Kateralbin."

Crispin didn't remember giving his captors his name. He shrugged again. "I was born in the heartlands in the back of a truck. I grew up in a circus. Smithrebel's Fabulous Aerial and Animal Show." He had nothing to lose by giving that information—were they to check up on him, they would find his record clean, at least as far as Smithrebel's went, for circus people's loyalty to their own, even after time passed, was stronger than their patriotism. Valestock was a different matter. So was the Wraithwaste. As he was wondering how to proceed, the guards saved him by coming back with two folding chairs and a laden table. Sostairs dismissed them and measured black coffee into his cup.

The unfolded furniture, fragile though it was, filled the little cell to overflowing. Crispin glanced out the window, where the noon sky glowed sapphire, imagining the heat, and the wind, and the stink of daemons blowing from the Wraithwaste. His throat closed; he raised his glass in a wordless valediction, and downed the amber liquid at a swallow. "Excellent spirits," he said when he could speak.

"Chressamo's cellars are among the best in the Raw, perhaps even in the whole country. We get shipments twice a year." The man looked up from his mug, and the corners of his eyes crinkled with amusement. "Once, our liquor-cellar supply plane—an old Blacheim—was shot down in the Wraithwaste by a KE-111 which had got hopelessly lost. I suppose the Shadow men got the bottles, those which didn't break. Imagine it: they must have been soused for months!" Sostairs laughed heartily, and Crispin joined in, though he didn't see the joke. "But I am not here to tell anecdotes." Sostairs became serious again. "Nobody just ends up in Shadowtown, Mr. Kateralbin. That is, unless he is a Shadow. Which you aren't." The bony fingers reached out and fingered the stubby braids Rae had made in Crispin's hair. "And you aren't Ferupian either. That is one of the reasons we're interested in you. This is a war between races, remember, and we are having trouble placing you on either side of the conflict."

"I'm as Ferupian as you are!" Crispin cried. "I'm half-Lamaroon by blood, but I'm just as ready to give my life for the Queen as the whitest man in the country!"

"A half-breed! I see." Sostairs's voice went as sharp as a rapier. "I'm going to be honest with you. You are not the real reason you are here. Understand? We want to know why you were bringing a Kirekuni girl into the war zone. There are Kirekunis resident in the domains. We are aware of this. And it is understandable that in a time of war and widespread prejudice, an alien might take drastic steps to disguise herself. As long as these easternized Kirekunis stay where they *are*, they are none of our concern. But circumstances like these give us reason . . ." He paused. "To intervene."

Crispin swallowed, his mind in turmoil. "She's my wife," he said. "We escaped into the Wraithwaste because of—of—we were being unfairly hounded by the authorities in Lovoshire. We were traveling with our adopted son. He was sick, we were trying to reach habitation, we'd gotten lost—"

Sostairs's voice cut like a knife across his babble. "She said she'd never seen you before the day you were arrested. Under coercion, she admitted that she had been traveling with you, but she swore up and down that you knew nothing of her purposes."

"She has no *purposes*!" Crispin gripped the edge of his chair with both hands. How could she have said that? Hadn't she realized that if either of them lied to the soldiers, their stories could not match? He wanted to fly at Sostairs's throat. Vividly, he remembered the despair which had come over Rae in the Wraithwaste. Her submissiveness had forced him to make all the decisions, to physically drag her onward when she said *I can't*. A few times she had turned her cheek so that he could slap her—her hand all the time clenched tight around that damned amulet—and he had had to work harder than he imagined possible not to slap her. The only explanation he could think of was that the time she had spent with the trickster women had damaged her more than she had known at the time. He wasn't sure she would ever recover. The thought of her in the soldiers' custody . . .

He bowed his head. Blood drummed in his ears. Anything that he said would either contradict her or condemn her.

Sostairs said, "Both of you have lied about your pasts. And you were traveling with a subhuman child who you say was your adopted son. Incidentally, she pretends to know no more of the child than of you. Frankly, Mr. Kateralbin, it reeks."

"What do you want?" Crispin asked without looking up.

"Another whiskey?" Sostairs said.

Crispin did not move. Cold drops slopped onto his knee; he heard liquid being poured. He felt blindly for the glass and drained it.

"It reeks of conspiracy," Sostairs said, his voice ringing implacably in the silence. "Perhaps between the Significant Empire and the Shadows. One would hardly suppose the Shadows capable of such complex planning, but no law, even that of stupidity, is hard and fast in times of war."

Crispin shook his head. "That's bloody ridiculous."

"Is it? She admitted to charges of counterintelligence work after an amulet of the Glorious Dynasty—I'm sure you know what that is, Mr. Kateralbin—was found on her person."

"After you *tortured* her?" Crispin poured himself more whiskey without thinking about it. "In the name of the Queen! I—well, in the first place, if she *was* a spy, and I was trying to get her back to the Kirekuni lines—"

"Is that what you were doing, Mr. Kateralbin?"

"—then walking straight into Shadowtown and ordering dinner would be a damned stupid way to go about it! You must see that! And I've *heard* of the Glorious Dynasty, and I know Rae had something to do with them once, but she hasn't spoken to any culties in years—"

"What has she been calling herself, again? I've forgotten." Sostairs smiled.

Crispin said sadly: "Ash. I believe that's her real name. But she might have used Clothwright. Or something else. Depending on how confident she was."

"She wasn't feeling confident." Sostairs shook his head. "Not at all."

"Damn you." Crispin ground his teeth, almost crying with frustration. "Damn you."

"She chopped off her tail. She wanted to disguise the fact that she is Kirekuni. It's a well-known trick of the lizard spies. Most of our soldiers learn to tell them by their skin, even if they have bleached their hair; but they pass themselves off on the common people of Ferupe with alarming ease. Had I to propose a scenario, I would say she was in Kingsburg, stealing secrets, and she is now returning to report to the Lizard Significant in Okimachi. She enlisted you as a guide, and you are probably telling the truth when you say you don't know anything of her purposes. It doesn't say much for you that you got her this badly lost; were you trying for the Salzeim War Route, perhaps? We have uncovered spies there, trying to lose themselves in the confusion. The safest, though lengthiest, way for you to take her would have been through the northern snows, which are frankly not worth the Queen's time to police, since they are so dangerous. But no one has ever praised Lamaroons for their intellect." He scrutinized Crispin as if he were trying to provoke him. "Mmm. Aesthetically the effect is not unpleasing, but in terms of temperament I cannot think of a worse crossbreed."

In any other circumstances, Sostairs's last words would have set Crispin afire; but he scarcely heard them. The colonel-in-chief's scenario was frighteningly plausible—*much* more plausible than Crispin's own wild tale. He couldn't tell Sostairs that he had stolen a truck and killed a man, and therefore he couldn't explain why he had entered the Wraithwaste. In any case, were he to try to explain the Wraithwaste, he could not leave out the deaths at Holstead House which had been his fault. Many times before he had experienced this angry, choking sensation of not being able to tell the truth because he knew it wouldn't be believed. Now it was worse than ever.

"I've never been near Kingsburg in my life," he said sullenly, aware that it was a lie—he had been to the outskirts three times with Smithrebel's. *Stop right there!* he thought furiously. *You're just getting yourself into deeper water! Sticking to the truth is the best way to lie!* That was not a Millsy saying but an Anuei one. "I'm not a spy!" he insisted. "Before I left the circus I was a catcher for a troupe of aerialists. Now I'm a professional daemon handler. I drive trucks." He opened his palms and put an innocuous expression on his face.

Sostairs raised one eyebrow pityingly, as if to say, *Really, you could do better.*

"It's the truth!" Crispin shouted.

Sostairs swallowed the last of his coffee and put down his cup. "I believe you."

"What?"

"*That* was off the record." Sostairs made a chopping motion with one hand. "I am not authorized to believe captives' stories. But I have had a great deal of experience in this field, and to me you look like a man whose story will not change even when you are in the torture chamber. Therefore, whether it is true or not is irrelevant, and I see no point in torturing you." Again, he smiled.

Quickly, so as not to lose this unexpected fair wind, Crispin said earnestly, "I've never done anything wrong. Ever."

"Oh, I believe you, I believe you," Sostairs said impatiently. Crispin rubbed his temples. He could not understand. No policeman would *ever* accept such a sketchy tale! Their interests lay in conviction. But perhaps the laws of the police were not the laws of the army.

That made a nasty kind of sense—after all, didn't Sostairs and his fellows all commit hanging crimes most days before lunch?

No law is hard and fast in times of war . . .

Now the workings of the colonel's clicking, humming, clockwork mind opened up to him. Sostairs had already decided on a version of the truth that was completely different from Crispin's, but sufficient for his purposes. And it made no difference whether he was right or wrong, or even whether Crispin confessed, because Sostairs had the power to make whatever he wanted true. Staring spellbound at the bright, cheerful, wrinkled face, Crispin guessed that the colonel anticipated complete satisfaction from Rae in the torture chamber. His real talent lay in separating his captives into those who would and would not crack.

But what did he do with those he thought too tough to bother torturing? Did he simply dispatch them? Innocent, criminal, or traitor to the Queen, it didn't matter once you were dead. . . .

Crispin took a deep breath.

Sostairs was leaning back in his chair. His gravelly voice measured out the sentences. "Mr. Kateralbin, you say you are wholly loyal to Ferupe. And I think you mean it. The fact that you were traveling with a Shadow child speaks in your favor, actually. We Ferupians are naturally more compassionate than the lizards, and if you thought to befriend a Shadow child, your Ferupian blood probably rules your Lamaroon blood, not the other way round. I believe you could be trustworthy."

Crispin nodded, trying to put a look of eagerness on his face. The colonel's condescension was offensive, but one's life was worth more than one's dignity.

The blue eyes glittered. "There are two options which we usually offer in cases like this. One is your freedom of the Raw."

I wouldn't last five minutes, Crispin thought. *They'd use me for target practice.* "And the other?" he said through numb lips.

Sostairs had been engaged in tilting the coffeepot to see whether there was any left. He glanced up. "Oh? Oh, yes. Of course we are always in need of recruits. You will be provided with employment. Nothing fancy. But if you are, as you say, a daemon handler, you'll get something a little better than a run-of-the-mill infantry position. I believe several of the QAF squadrons currently rotated to the front are in need of ground workers—riggers, fitters, daemon handlers, strippers, and so forth. Of course, if you were *lying*—"

He fixed Crispin with a glare which made Crispin very glad that he had told at least some of the truth. Sostairs was not the sort of man who forgave dishonesty—reticence being a different matter. Why, oh why, had Rae been stupid enough to lie to him? *Rae . . .*

"You will be sent for later today." Sostairs put down the coffeepot and stood up so fast Crispin thought a blow was coming. He nearly fell over backwards trying to avoid it. Awkwardly, almost knocking over the table in the confined space, he stood up and held out his hand. The look on Sostairs's face made him drop it fast and salute. "Sorry—sir."

"Not to worry." Sostairs favored him with an eagle smile. He looked almost human now, if supercilious. "I am glad. You have made a brave man's choice. You would be surprised how few do. Most of those who have got themselves on the wrong side of the law have an extraordinarily poor sense of their own well-being. All they want to do is run, and, given the chance, they run blindly."

"Not me, sir," Crispin said piously.

"As I said, I respect you for that, half-breed or no half-breed." Sostairs turned his head. "Freeman! Drown!" The guards entered the room and clacked their heels smartly.

"Sir," Crispin ventured. "These squadrons you mentioned—does QAF mean the air force? Not the infantry?"

"Yes. The air force. Depending on your aptitude, you may even be sent for flight training. However, there is a—mmm—" Sostairs looked Crispin up and down, frowning. "A *height* requirement," he said finally. "Not all of the squadron captains are as flexible as we here at Chressamo, where everyone is welcome. Eighty Squadron—where are they now? about thirty miles north of here, Pilkinson Air Base II—now, they have less rigorous standards. Flight Captain Vichuisse is laudably determined to foster unity among his men. Nonetheless, you may not fit in. I am merely warning you of the possibilities. I have nothing to do with the selection process."

Crispin's head danced at the thought of airplanes. The *air force.* Bigger daemons than any in trucks. Demogorgons the size of those used in factories. Monsters. Ogres of power.

Emboldened by Sostairs's apparent goodwill, Crispin reached out and stopped him as he opened the door. It was worth a try—"Sir, I don't know how promotions go around here. Is it possible to, is it possible—I know you have nothing to do with the process, but could you put in a good word for me? With the air force, I mean? So that I—so that I could be trained to fly?"

Sostairs turned in the doorway. He gave Crispin a withering look. "Your impudence is astounding, and astoundingly stupid. Be thankful I am not having you executed for crimes against the Queen! Technically you are a spy's accomplice, and that is high treachery! However, it is good for every squadron to have a traitor or two among its inferiors; they come in handy as scapegoats."

Both of the guards roared with laughter.

The door slammed.

Crispin was alone, his face burning.

They had not taken the folding furniture. There was no room to move as he desired. He lay carefully down on the cot.

In the barred blue square of the window, metal dragonflies danced. The screaming of the antiaircraft fire sounded disquietingly human.

He'd been lucky. Amazingly lucky. He shouldn't have pushed it! It would have been so easy for the kaleidoscope of regulations in Sostairs's brain to end up forming a different, equally random pattern, which condemned Crispin as Rae had been condemned. *I must have a charmed life, or something like that,* he thought dizzily.

Rae. Rae in Chressamo. Rae in Sostairs's torture chamber. Had she been his next appointment? What had he done to her already? Remember her not emaciated and weak, but smiling and voluptuous, her skin like cream, so opaque and smooth—

My wife. And son. He had invented the relationship between the three of them on the spur of the moment. But in memory the claim rippled back in time, back to Valestock, back to Jacithrew's house under the ground, gaining a repellently sentimental validity.

Crispin stared up at the window. The red beast turned around and around inside him, growling.

In the sky, two planes collided.

"Pilots must be lackwits," he whispered.

The little dark shapes did not, as he had expected, fuse together and spiral down like mating dragonflies; instead, one plane, which had been neatly severed in half, plummeted straight down, breaking into more and more pieces. The other fell far more slowly, its pilot obviously fighting a losing battle for control. White smoke streamed behind it. Crispin narrowed his eyes and saw that it was growing brighter and brighter as it fell. It was *burning*! The plane was no longer made of metal, but of white fire.

He had never before known metal to burn. Melt, yes, but not burn. The temperature at which that daemon was dying must be stupendous.

"Who would have thought. Who would ever have thought it?"

His head ached when he tried to contemplate his luck. He was very drunk. The womanish screaming seemed now to be coming from all around: faintly from outside the tower, and, muffled, from beneath his cell.

But he didn't care anymore who was dying. *He* was alive. He always survived—didn't he? Yes, and he would in the future, too. After all, he had to be in Kirekune in a few years. The world was going to end, and he had to be there! What a pity that she, who would have been so smug, was going to miss the grand spectacle!

Instinct told him the future was guaranteed; but common sense told him that *nothing* was guaranteed in the Raw. Not even survival. His blood pounded.

He was twenty-one, in prison, and starving hungry. Yet he was alive. He thought, *I wouldn't change places with the richest man in Kingsburg right now! Not the richest man—not—the—richest—*

He snuffled wetly. It appalled him to realize he was crying.

> *... in his mind was a picture of the heartbreaking years of squalid rooms in squalid towns, twice-nightly performances, and the awful ever-present fear of the bird. [He] had sung long for his supper; it was no wonder that the feast choked him.*
>
> —Josephine Tey, *The Man In The Queue*

BOOK FOUR

FLIGHT

Tumult in the Clouds

Novambar 1895 A.D. *The Lovoshire Parallel:*
The fringe of the Wraithwaste

About five miles into the Waste, hundreds of feet above the brown forest, Gorgonettees, Horogazis, and the Horogazis' escort of KE-122s dived, wrangled, and spat fire and daemons at each other. The Gorgonettees were small, light monoplanes made of wood and fabric. The Horogazis were deceitfully slippy three-man bombers, constructed almost entirely of metal, as were the KE-122s, which were the Lizards' devastatingly maneuverable improvements on the ubiquitous KE-111s. The 122s carried only one man, and their resulting speediness more than made up for their lack of a rear gunner. They had been appearing in greater and greater numbers for a year now, mostly doing the "dead man's duty" of guarding bombers on missions into enemy territory, but recently swooping in on Ferupian air bases in tightly controlled wedges of eighteen that were impossible to stop. When Crispin had heard what they did to the temp-base of 75 Squadron, ten miles to the south, his blood ran with ice and he longed vainly for a metal airplane. It was simply impossible for a Gorgonette to match a KE's speed and twistiness.

But thankfully, right now the Kirekuni fighters were so badly outnumbered that it was impossible for them to protect both themselves and the Horogazis. Rain darkened the winter afternoon. Flying conditions were terrible. The KEs' tracer fire spat thunderously as it arced orange through the wet. In response, the Gorgonettees loosed silent hails of screamers. Seven Kirekunis had already torn craters in the dense brown forest below. In the rain, instead of spreading, the crash fires had only burned blackened patches in the forest.

Crispin jinked *Princess Anuei* out of the path of an arc of tracer fire. Wind and rain whipped past the cockpit shell; his hands were numb with cold; the daemon engine roared as he let out the whipcord and pulled back the stick, gaining height and simultaneously circling, keeping *that* KE-122 in his sights. The pilot was already busy trying to avoid Eakin, one of Crispin's men. Crispin dived, opening up *Princess Anuei*'s screamer ports, and jewels streamed out in an arc.

The Kirekunis had been trying for the Pye Collins screamer factory. But it was not anywhere near here. For once, 80 Squadron had managed an intercept right. Screamer and munitions factories were all built underground, like old Wraith villages, and the roads that led to them were deliberately meandering and concealed under the trees, too narrow for trucks, barely navigable by jeeps; dead pines and spruces packed together so closely that they formed perfect cover. All the same, the Kirekunis succeeded entirely too often in strafing the factories. Nothing was worse by QAF standards than letting a screamer factory be fire-strafed; but it happened all the time. And the factories were not dispensable. Nor were their resident trickster women. These women came in two sorts: those who had once been independent, who were employed in producing screamers; and the "munitions women" recruited specifically by the military to do the mindless work of capturing mote-sized daemons for aircraft and mobile-unit fuel. All were the objects of much speculation and idealization on the part of the pilots whose job it was to defend them. The flowers of Ferupian womanhood, Festhre said, and composed an extempore poem in couplets. Crispin had laughed to himself—he was probably the only pilot ever to have met a trickster woman, although the encounter had lasted only a few minutes and finished with death. Then, he had not thought much of their morals. And Orpaan's daemon-handling skills had been far superior to theirs. But they were essential to the war effort. Their activities kept the QAF in business. Their very existence was a secret from everyone from whom it was practicable to keep it secret. A single destroyed screamer factory meant ten or fifteen air bases without ammo.

However, this time nothing except a few trees had been burned. Crispin grinned as he swooped at another 122, pouring screamers out of *Princess Anuei*'s ports. Just before he must have collided with her, he pulled back on the stick and shot straight through the center of the dogfight, out into empty air. Cruising, he had the satisfaction of watching his kill stall and plunge: the screamers which had found footholds on its wings and fuselage had clawed their way into the cockpit and eaten the Kirekuni's guts out. It was an ugly, but surprisingly unmessy, way of downing the enemy, And it left the wrecks intact. Right now, the Waste was a tangle of broken trees and broken airplanes. The metal from the wrecks would later be salvaged, but almost all of it would be shipped away to manufacture equipment for the infantry. The QAF was the vital element of the war effort the most often shortchanged on metal. But at times like this, Crispin thought they could keep going with only wooden planes forever.

Not a single Kirekuni was still airborne. Instead of a buzzing hornet swarm, a flock of painted birds circled serenely in the rain. They were three crews today: Crispin's, his friend Butch's, and that of Flight Captain Vichuisse. Crispin, flying patrol with his men, had spotted the Kirekuni strike force, so high that they were almost lost in the cloud cover. He had sent Eakin to fetch backup from Fostercy, and Butch and Vichuisse had arrived in time for all three crews to intercept the Kirekunis over the Wraithwaste before they reached Pye Collins. Victory lifted his heart like a balloon.

He waggled his wings, signaling his men. Far off through the gloom, Butch and Vichuisse were doing the same thing. With the precision of good ballroom dancers, the swarm of kites came apart into three separate wedges. Eighty Squadron was *not* the mess that popular opinion had it. At least not today; their problem was that they were erratic. But Vichuisse had not managed to cause any disasters this time. Crispin led his crew down to see the wreckage of the forest. It was difficult to make out through the rain, but nothing human seemed to be moving. The bright-colored screamer imps, oblivious to the shimmer of Waste daemons pressing close around them, were brawling over the flesh of the Kirekuni airmen.

Higher up, Vichuisse peeled his crew off toward home. Crispin quickly led his men up to follow. When Vichuisse pulled out, *you* pulled out—a necessity of the hierarchy which had contributed a good deal to 80 Squadron's reputation as a band of shirkers.

A show of independence would have been even more dangerous for Crispin, who owed Vichuisse his whole life, than for the others. The three crews strung out over the Waste, flying slowly to conserve their daemons' energy. The din of *Princess Anuei*'s engine slackened. Crispin flexed his stiff fingers and squinted through the rain-slicked windshield. He allowed himself a brief surge of pride as he saw that none of his five crewmen was too badly shot up. But Butch had lost one man. He thought it was Francke—a new, talented young pilot. Surprising that he had gone down. Vichuisse had lost two. But Vichuisse always lost men. A transfer to his crew was unofficially known as *the death sentence*.

If only Crispin did not owe so much to him! He was conscious of his indebtedness every waking moment, except perhaps during battle, when exhilaration blotted out the tangled web of obligations and friendships that he had to follow through if he was ever to find his way to any sort of future.

If only! He knew he could do a far better job of commanding this squadron than any arrogant northern squire! So could Butch. So could Keinze, or Redmanhey. So could even Festhre, probably.

Crispin smiled at the thought of his friends. The twilight roared around his Gorgonette. He signaled his crew that it was time to watch out for the flares that would go up to mark the runway when the ground crew at Fostercy heard the mission returning.

Triumphant. For once.

But no matter how many Kirekunis they, and the rest of the squadron, and the pilots of all the other squadrons in the Lovoshire Parallel and the Thrazen and the Galashire and the Weschess and the Salzeim and the Lynche and the Teilsche and the Sudeland Parallels, brought down, it was not enough. It was never enough. Are we winning? Are we losing? Nobody knew which to think. Patriotic phrases were on everyone's lips, and nobody dared to voice their secret guesses that with captains like Vichuisse all over the Raw, one could not possibly win any glory, let alone one's pension, let alone a war.

*   *   *

Fostercy Base lay in the arm of a low, scrub-covered hill about ten miles behind the front lines. When you went to the latrines at night you could see the screamers going up at the horizon: tiny, bright-colored shooting stars. But the distance silenced them. And during the daylight hours, the wind carried away the sound of gunfire. If a skirmish was in progress at the front, the clamor reached such a pitch that when the wind dropped for a second, a man standing in the open could hear a noise like a far-off earthquake. At such times motorbikes and jeeps could be seen in the distance, bouncing over the plain from the front lines to the command posts near Shadowtown. During skirmishes, almost all of 80 Squadron was in the air, providing assistance to the beleaguered infantry at the front. That was when being in a defensive unit was no longer a relatively cushy assignment. You landed, handed in your report to Vichuisse if you were a lieutenant, fell into your bunk, got shaken awake a few hours later, scrambled into your flight suit, and were in the air again before you'd rubbed the sand out of your eyes.

But clashes at the front occurred no more often than once a month. The rest of the time it was only when they were airborne that the pilots of Fostercy saw anything of the war. It was nearly always quiet on base: most of the pilots were constantly worn-out from the daemon handler's curse of weariness, and spent all their meager downtime either sleeping or eating. Right now, Festhre's, Redmanhey's, and Keinze's crews, the other half of the squadron, were either asleep or out on patrol. The men who had just returned pressed tightly around the fire that roared in the center of the mess, scooping up soup with the biscuits that constituted the greater part of their diet. Even indoors, it was too cold to take off their flight jackets, and the wet leather steamed, reeking. The firelight splashed up the rough plank walls. Carrie, the lurcher dog, moaned softly in her place by the embers. Crispin rolled his shoulders, wincing as pain stabbed through his muscles.

When he first arrived in 80 Squadron as a lowly rigger, he had thought the pilots' habitual silence, in contrast to the riggers' loquacity, weirdly primitive. Here were the hunters, huddling together about the campfire after returning from the kill. They meditated; and outside, the hunting beasts were rubbed down and fed by the tribe's inferior members. But that fancy was misleading. There was a hierarchy, of course—

but there was no initiative on anyone's part, not even Vichuisse's. Everything was done by the book and on orders. The system might have served to preclude resentment between pilots and ground crews, lieutenants and regulars. But living on his wits in Valestock and in the Wraithwaste had rendered Crispin unable to accept anything on face value: and very shortly after his arrival in 80 Squadron, keeping his eyes and ears open, he had realized that there *was* resentment—plenty of it. It was just kept under wraps, and confined, in its most corrosive manifestations, to the lieutenants—the only men, apart from Vichuisse's own crew, who had direct contact with the captain.

Crispin had not dreamed when he first arrived at Pilkinson's Air Base II that before long, he would become a lieutenant, and come to hate Vichuisse worse than any of them.

But everything was temporary. If two and a half years in the military had taught him a lesson, it was that nothing lasted.

The wind crept in through the cracks in the walls of the mess, and the men shrugged their collars up around their necks. Crispin glanced sideways at Butch, who was shoveling soup intently into his mouth. He had not spoken since they landed. His long, thin, serious face was pale orange in the firelight. Most people let the weakness apparent in that face blind them to the real Butch Keynes, who was a mercurial man capable of destructive anger and self-destructive misery, too good-hearted ever to be truly ambitious. It was Butch who had taught Crispin to read and write, after Vichuisse convinced him he ought to be literate. Education—and social class, which in the QAF almost always came hand in hand—were the hallmarks of a ranking officer. And Crispin was not going to be the odd one out. Millsy had been wrong, after all.

He nudged Butch. "Sorry you lost Francke. He had promise."

Butch stopped eating and turned burning eyes on Crispin. "He *did*. And do you want to know the worst thing? It wasn't his fault. He was slicing through 'em."

"What happened then?" Crispin shifted a bit closer on the bench so that the regulars wouldn't hear. "Tangled with his own screamers?"

"It was the Kirekuni." Butch spat the word out as if it tasted bad. Crispin knew instantly who he meant; not any of the Kirekunis whom they had shot down today, but the Kirekuni who served on Butch's own crew.

"What'd he do? Turn tail? Francke try to cover him?"

"No, he bloody well scored an own goal! It was right after we engaged them. Francke had his sights on this Horogazi. Showering him with screamers. Then the Kirekuni gets into the mix. He's about twenty feet off Francke's starboard wing, aiming to cross above him, cutting it *real* close, and he misjudges his margin. Fuckin' pathetic. And Francke sees they're gonna clash. So he has to lose height." Butch balanced his bowl on his knee and shoved an imaginary stick forward. "But things are crazy up there. And one of Vichuisse's boys is coming up right under the Horogazi, and Francke doesn't want to hit him. And first his propellers tap the Horogazi's undercarriage, and then he *tangles* with her."

Crispin grimaced. "What a way to go. At least he took the Horogazi down with him."

"She was screamer-infested already. And what makes it *sick* is that I saw it happen, and the Queen-damned Kirekuni got off scot-free. Made two kills after that. Totaling three for the afternoon," Butch said spitefully.

"Where is he anyway?" Crispin glanced around. The men were beginning to drift out of the mess. "Gone to earth?"

"Naw. See, he's got to learn—I dunno *what*!" Butch shook his head in frustration. "Stupid lizard always manages to save his own skin, even when he fucks the rest of us up! But after this long, we can't fairly suspect him of—of not being on our side. What's his kill tally? Ninety-something? Could be over a hundred. *Kirekunis*. How does he do it, Cris? He's been here as long as I have." Butch thumped his chest. Now that their men were gone he was speaking more loudly. "Three years. Same week I arrived from flight training, he arrived from Chressamo, and Vichuisse assigned him to my crew the same day. Worst piece of luck I've ever had!"

Crispin pulled a sympathetic face. He felt sorry for Butch, who, in addition to having to contend with a Kirekuni on his crew, had no feeling for what things looked like from the viewpoint of a regular: like most lieutenants, he had received his commission immediately on being posted to the front as a result of his background. He was the third son of a Dewisson Domain squire, one of that class for whom the army had been an honored profession even before there was a war. He had probably known he was going to be in the military before he was old enough to talk, Crispin thought, finishing his soup, and wondered, not for the first time, how it had been to grow up under that shadow, hoping and praying that the conflict would end before the time came for him to take part in it.

Then again, maybe Butch had hoped the *opposite*. He was that kind of man. It was the reason Crispin admired him.

"Not one of my boys from those days left except him! Queen damn it! He fucks up again and again, and what do you know? He turns up at the end of every battle like a bad penny. And it was always an accident, and no one can prove it wasn't. Much more of this, and *I'll* have to consider an own goal."

Crispin swallowed the last of his biscuit. "No, no, don't do that." He reached inside his flight jacket, pulled out a chocolate bar, and offered half to Butch, who stuffed it into his mouth as fiercely as if it had been a piece of the Kirekuni's flesh, barely bothering to pick off the colored wrapping. "He's just a coward, see. No backbone. You know how strictly disciplined the lizards are—well, I think discipline is all that holds them together. He doesn't understand that as one of us, he has a responsibility to *himself*, and to the *Queen*, to be brave. If one of our boys fucked up the way he does, he wouldn't be able to live with himself—but Ash doesn't get it, he doesn't hold himself responsible. You can't fault him for what he is. Just hope his luck turns on him, that's all."

"What gets me going," Butch said broodingly, "is that I have to let him off every time. Just because of what you said. If I were to start passing out punishments for plain old cowardice, I'd have to flog every man in my crew."

"*They'll* give him a razzing though, don't you worry. Francke was popular." Crispin turned to watch the last of the men leave. Their shoulders were slumped. Two had their arms around each other. Crispin's own crew had not come out of the battle as cleanly as he had thought; young Jack Harrowman was in the sick bay with a bullet wound to the shoulder. It was Harrowman's closest friend, Fergus Dupont, who was being supported by his comrade.

"If I know them, they will."

"They do often enough anyway. It's not like it has any effect. No." Butch turned to Crispin with a sudden, wicked grin. "I've taken some steps. Told him to report what *really* happened to Vichuisse. Not his version—*my* version. Made him repeat it after me until he knew it by heart."

"Good going," Crispin said, and forced himself to smile. Sometimes Butch's way of dealing with his men disgusted him. "It's about time Vee got an idea what really goes down around here."

"Especially what with all the strange noises we've been hearing lately. Promotion city, huh?" Butch shook his head. "If you ask *me*, he's getting a tad bit too big for his boots."

"They've been tight on him since day one, if you ask me," Crispin said with feeling.

Butch shifted in the warmth of the dying fire and rubbed Carrie's stomach with his foot. She whined in her sleep and rolled onto her back. Butch laughed, stretched, and peeled off his flight jacket. "Indeed! Any more choccy hidden about you, Cris?"

Silently, Crispin took out his second bar and broke it without removing the wrapper.

Half an hour later the fire went out. Crispin kissed Butch farewell outside the mess hall. This ritual had developed from the early days of their friendship into a superstitious touchstone, a charm for staying alive. Nights like this, when the moon hung wide and bright as a grin in the sky, were the lizards' favorite sort. Neither of them mentioned the possibility that they would later be wakened, or killed in their beds, by an attack. Watching Butch's back recede into the dark, Crispin felt a swell of affection for him. He put the last piece of chocolate into his mouth. Licking his fingers, he wandered around the corner of the mess, intending to stop by the regulars' barracks and see whether any of his men were awake.

The buildings lay low and dark in the moonlight. Not a sliver of light showed anywhere. Barracks and hangars alike were constructed out of knotty, poor-quality Wraithwaste-pine lumber, so there ought to have been thousands of chinks, but every building was painstakingly lightproofed inside with black canvas. The rain had stopped; the wind carried wetness on its back. Rounding the northeast corner of the mess hall, Crispin halted. Two figures were standing by the door next to the northwest corner of the building. The shorter pushed close against the taller, who was flattened against the wall. The thought that it was a lovers' tryst leapt into Crispin's mind. He was turning to retreat when he recognized Flight Captain Anthony Vichuisse's furious voice.

At this end of the mess hall, Vichuisse lived in lordly isolation: his quarters were not accessible from inside the mess, and his windows commanded a view of the empty Raw. Standing outside his front door, he was lambasting someone, not bothering to keep his voice down. A hissing, chinking sound punctuated his words: the cat-o'-nine-tails slapping against his thigh. Crispin sidled away. But he had been seen.

"Kateralbin!" He heard the unmistakable note of pleasure that entered Vichuisse's voice every time he spoke to Crispin. "Sneaking about at night? Still in an aggressive state of mind? Why don't you come and have a word with our friend here?"

Reluctantly Crispin went forward. Vichuisse stood back, hands on his hips. The moonlight cast his shadow in a bulky puddle around his feet. "Or are you here to join in the fun? Mmm?"

The Kirekuni stood with his back to the wall, his long, pale, ratlike tail lashing around his ankles.

"No—sir," Crispin said, his eyes on the Kirekuni. "I was just going to see if my men were still awake. Sir. I wanted to congratulate them on the job they did today. They handled the intercept marvelously. I thought."

"It's what they're trained for, Kateralbin."

"I was going to stop by sick bay, too, sir. Jack Harrowman is in with a shoulder."

"I know that," Vichuisse said. "I make it my business to stop by sick bay myself. So that my lieutenants don't have to." At the captain's voice, Crispin turned sharply to look at him. The moonlight blackened the sockets of the little, deep-set eyes. "Kateralbin, you tend to assume altogether too much responsibility for your own good," Vichuisse said gently.

"Any responsibility I have is your gift, sir."

"Tch, tch, tch! The past is the past!" Vichuisse clapped Crispin's shoulder, all fizzy good humor. "I suppose Lieutenant Keynes told you the story, mmm? The story of our little lizard friend's *cowardice* this afternoon?"

Crispin winced. The Kirekuni was anything but little. He was the tallest man in the squadron—taller even, by an inch, than Crispin. Somehow that made his silence in the face of the insult much worse.

"I know what chums you and Keynes are," Vichuisse said with vile innuendo.

"Yes, he told me about it, sir."

"I've been giving Ash a talking-to. But you'll agree that in a case like this—where a pilot's misjudgment caused the death of another pilot, a member of his own crew, no less—a talking-to is insufficient." Vichuisse swung the cat-o'-nine-tails against his palm. Only Vichuisse, Crispin thought with a surge of disproportionate anger, would indulge in a flogging by moonlight! Couldn't he have waited until tomorrow? And yet such bizarre acts were completely in character for the captain. There had been the time some money was stolen from his rooms, when Vichuisse made every man on the base turn out and stand on parade in the snow, in their underwear, while he personally searched their lockers.

The Kirekuni remained motionless.

"Yes, sir?" Crispin controlled his voice.

"Should you like to taste what responsibility *really* is, Kateralbin?" Vichuisse said, smirking.

Crispin and the Kirekuni stood face-to-face on the western side of the mess hall. Crispin had led him around the corner to ensure that Vichuisse would not be able to spy—there were no windows on that side, and what with the wind, unless the captain were actually to come outside, he would not be able to see or hear a thing. And to come outside would have been beneath Vichuisse's dignity—as well as proof that he did not trust Crispin to carry out his orders.

The thing is that he does trust me, Crispin thought. *If there's a single one of us lieutenants he trusts, it's me. That's why he made me a lieutenant.*

But hard on the heels of conscience's prickings came a thrill at the thought of depriving Vichuisse of one of his unfair victories over his men.

The Kirekuni was standing at ease, probably waiting to be ordered to unbutton his flight suit. In the moonlight his skin was as white as bone, his hair—slightly longer than the regulation buzz cut—sleek as the fur of a black cat.

Crispin jerked his chin in the direction of the regulars' barracks. "Dismissed, Ash." Then, when the Kirekuni did not move: "I said, you can go now."

"Ten of the best!" Ash's voice betrayed his astonishment. "Wasn't that what Vee said?"

"You don't get it, do you!" Crispin shifted the cat-o'-nine-tails to his left hand. "Go to bed! And if you don't have nightmares about what happened to Francke, I swear you're *not* human."

"You can't do this," Ash objected.

"You *want* a flogging?"

"I want one more than I want to be obliged to *you*."

"No payback involved." Crispin waved the cat-o'-nine-tails in the direction of the barracks. "Move."

Ash tilted his head and screwed up his face, as if he were trying to see right into Crispin. A thread of discomfort colored Crispin's determination. He did not know the Kirekuni; Ash was not in his crew, so there was no reason for them ever to speak. Besides, the last thing Crispin wanted was to be seen associating with the other outsider of the squadron. But it wasn't merely the racial stigma that made Crispin avoid him so assiduously. It was the way Ash *looked* at him. Whenever they were in the same room, Ash's gaze followed him, picking him out from the others. Of course, everyone had done that at first; even when he was just a rigger they had stared. But then they got used to him. New men soon learned that certain slurs which would have been perfectly acceptable anywhere else were not allowed in 80 Squadron: Crispin's crew saw to that. But the hungry way the Kirekuni looked at Crispin had not changed in two and a half years.

"Where did you get your last name, Ash?" Crispin said suddenly, without meaning to. "How would they say it in Okimachi?"

Ash shrugged. "My mother gave it to me."

Disappointment washed through Crispin.

"And her mother gave it to her, and her mother . . ." Ash took a step forward, as if trying to see into Crispin's face. "You're not jerking me around, are you? You're not."

"No."

"*Achino*. It's a very common name in Kirekune. Very old."

Crispin laughed. "And Mickey? That's not Kirekuni either!" *Ash had a given name when he came,* Butch had said once, *some funny-sounding lizard thing, but we took care of that quick enough . . . He took care of it himself, really . . . Declared one day that from now on he was going to be called Mickey, so we couldn't take the mickey out of him anymore. The boys laughed, of course—they thought it was rich . . .* "How would they say *that* in Okimachi?" He gave the word the lilt that had come in her voice whenever she said her name, or her mother's. *"Miki?"*

It took him completely by surprise when the Kirekuni flinched. Ash laughed, shook his head, and almost staggered against the wall. "Damn you, Lieutenant," he said, chuckling. "Mind if I smoke?"

"You're not on parade."

Ash extracted a cigarette case from a pocket of his jacket, then struck a lucifer dexterously with his tail, keeping both hands cupped around the cigarette. Crispin watched in unwilling fascination. It was a marvelous trick—made you wonder why all human beings had not been born with tails. When the Kirekuni got his cigarette burning, Crispin said without thinking, "Got another?"

"No problem," and Ash went through the whole routine again before Crispin could retract his words. But when the lit cigarette was in his fingers he felt a touch of panic. Now he would have to stay here until they had finished smoking. Their relations had been temporarily transformed from those of regular and lieutenant, to those of two pilots having a cigarette together after a harrowing evening. Ash must have felt the shift in the hierarchy, too. He leaned against the wall, the cigarette drooping from his fingers. "So Lieutenant, what do you think of this war?"

"Blessed Queen! What a *question*."

"Do you know what I think? It's a bloody farce."

"That's not a particularly original opinion."

"The freeze on negotiations is just *stupid*. If you'd had the opportunity to compare both sides, like I have, you'd know what I mean." Ash put his head back and looked at the sky. It was empty except for the bombers' moon. "We're going to be completely overwhelmed in ten years. Twenty at the most."

"Don't tell the captain that."

"Oh, I'd never *dare*!" Ash grinned and shuddered with exaggerated fear. It was unmistakably a fag gesture. "The only one I'd ever say it to is *you*!"

"Can't see why." Crispin exhaled smoke. "You don't know me."

"But I do know you, Lieutenant." Ash fixed him with that steady, dark gaze. "*You* just don't know *me*."

"You're taking liberties, Pilot. Watch it. And if I were you, I'd go to bed as soon as you've finished that. Your crew is on dawn patrol duty, if I remember right."

Ash gazed down at the cigarette in his hand. "I've never needed much sleep . . . Do you know why I give so much thought to the war?"

Crispin laughed. "Are you implying the rest of us daydream about Shadow girls while we're shooting down Kirekunis?"

"You'd be surprised how many do. No. It's because I'm not a fatalist. You lot are fatalists through and through. Say what you will, a century of defeats hasn't left the Ferupian spirit unharmed. I'd say every man in this squadron, apart from a few slackers, is prepared to lay down his life for the Queen. Assumes he *will* lay it down. I'm not like that. I think about how things are going to end."

"This isn't the infantry. One has to *want* to be a pilot. Maybe in Kirekune it's different."

"Just one of many things that's different. I never wanted to fly. Oh, sure, I got used to it. I even got to like it. But, Lieutenant, I'll admit it, I'm a coward at heart."

"No shit!" Crispin laughed. He took a drag of his cigarette and scrutinized the Kirekuni through the cloud of smoke.

Every trace of humor was gone from the pale face.

"You're the first man I've ever heard admit that," Crispin said slowly.

"I don't want to die! That's why I sometimes get spitting furious at the Queen and all her generals, whoever's responsible for making the negotiations break down, for keeping this war going on and on and on. I'm never going to get pensioned off; did you know that? I'm a traitor. They can't discharge me to wander freely around the Queen's country. And what's my chances of surviving another fifteen years at the rate I'm going? I hate it, but I'm going to lay my life down for Ferupe, too!"

"I've never thought much of the idea of dying either," Crispin said abruptly, surprising himself.

"But *you* aren't a coward, Lieutenant."

Crispin sucked the last drag from his cigarette and threw it to the mud. "You *wanted* me to give you ten of the best, didn't you?" he said with disgust.

The Kirekuni grimaced. Then, with motions so fast that Crispin flinched back, he took out and lit another cigarette. "Oh, yes, Lieutenant!" The self-mocking laughter was back in his voice. "I'd have just loved it! You still can if you want!"

"In the name of the Queen," Crispin said, and turned on his heel. He hesitated. Ash leaned against the wall, long limbs indolently askew, enjoying his cigarette with obviously exaggerated pleasure. "Tell me one more thing, Ash: *did* you mean to kill Francke?"

Ash's face twisted, and he spat on the ground. "Significant! I'd be more justified in suspecting *you* of offing Fischer in the heat of battle! You'd never have got to be a lieutenant if *your* lieutenant hadn't been shot down, would you?" He mimicked Crispin's tone. "Did *you* mean to kill *him*? I've been a pilot *three times* as long as you have! It happens to everyone."

"Not as often as it happens to you."

"You want to know the real reason I fuck up? It's the crap design of your damned Gorgonettees."

"What?" Crispin said.

"You're tall, too! You've got to have some idea of what it's like to crouch in that cockpit for hours at a time without being able to straighten your neck or your legs. Tends to make you antsy, doesn't it? Might even skew your judgment, having to look down through that thick windshield at an angle. That's one thing. And for another, I'm left-handed." Ash shook his left hand in the air. Stupidly, Crispin looked at it. "Nearly all Kirekunis are, the way nearly all Ferupians are right-handed. No, it never occurred to me, either, until I had to try and fly a plane with the controls reversed. I'm getting better at it. But still, the whipcord is so sensitive, and if you've been doing everything that requires delicacy with your good hand for twenty-one years, it's going to cause a few problems when you've suddenly got to exert microcontrol—and keep a two-ton daemon in check—with your worse hand. Just one tiny little unintentional spasm means a deviation of several degrees, or several dozen mph, when you're in the air. You're a pilot. You know what I'm talking about."

Crispin found his voice. "Why don't you get them to refurbish a KE for you? Or at least install the cockpit in a Gorgonette?"

"For me? I'm a *traitor*, Lieutenant. Come on. If I even *asked* I'd be daemonsmeat."

Crispin shook his head. "Wouldn't want your problems, Ash." He turned away. "Take my advice. Get some sleep."

"Yes, *sir*," Ash said mockingly behind him.

Crispin gritted his teeth and moved into the darkness.

Any thought of stopping in on his crew was long gone. As he opened the door to the officers' quarters, lifting it a little so that it didn't creak, he whispered: "Left-handed! Who would have thought it!"

It was a little warmer after he closed the door. A brazier of daemons burned at the far end of the room, between the bunks. The brazier was completely hooded, or else it would have lit the room bright as day; as it was, a thin line of white glowed on the floor around the hood. The room smelled of musk and unwashed bodies. As the most junior lieutenant, Crispin had the bunk closest to the ceiling. He laid Vichuisse's cat-o'-nine-tails on the lockers at the other end of the room. Standing by the brazier, he stripped and pulled on his pajamas, then climbed the ladder past Festhre's and Butch's sleeping forms. The sheetbag was icy. Forcing himself not to shiver, he thought:

Rae wasn't left-handed—

But she was brought up in Ferupe. Most likely when the culties taught her to write, she had to use her right hand. That would've taken care of it.

He hadn't thought of her in months. But she had been on his mind, consciously or unconsciously, most of the evening.

It's that damn lizard reminded me, he thought with sudden anger. *Got to avoid him in future. Got more important things to think about than the past. I was only a kid then. Must avoid—him in future— must remember to avoid . . .*

And sleep closed over him, the dreamless sleep of pure exhaustion to which all those who handle daemons succumb, and just as he was sinking he realized something that almost made him come awake again, something which talking to Mickey Ash had brought to the forefront of his mind.

He did not want to die.

Dying just didn't fit in with his plans to reap more honor and glory than any other pilot in 80 Squadron's history, and eventually be promoted to flight captain, from which position he would be pensioned off at the ripe age of thirty-five, when he would be able to lead a comfortable life in Kingsburg. Money and a military title would force society to accept him as it had not accepted the poor circus boy. He had vague plans to become part-owner of a *real* theater, a theater that staged classy dramas and operas for nobility in masks, to buy his way into a whole string of operations . . .

Yet death was a probability, not a possibility. How did he dare to plan for the future?

He *could* not die. He would not.

"Can't lose your nerve now, boy," he mumbled. "Gotta fly tomorrow."

He wrinkled his nose, turned over on his side, and slept. The crackling of flames which he had heard so clearly a moment ago stopped.

Nor law, nor duty bade me fight,
Nor public men, nor cheering crowds.
A lonely impulse of delight
Drove to this tumult in the clouds . . .

—W. B. Yeats

Not Everyone Dies
on the Battlefield

For almost three years, the disturbing hallucinations Crispin thought of as "visions" hadn't bothered him. When he first came to 80 Squadron as a rigger, their absence had been his only consolation. He had been desperately unhappy. He had not been able to make friends, and he yearned agonizingly to fly. His menial tasks bored and frustrated him to tears. It seemed cruelly unfair that the ranks of the regulars should be sealed to him. But then, unbelievably, Vichuisse had opened the doors wide, and the excitement of becoming a pilot, quickly followed by Fischer's death and Crispin's promotion to crew lieutenant, and the thousandfold complexities that entered his life that day, erased his nostalgia. Clearheaded in the absence of the visions, he understood that they, like his love for Rae, poor dead Rae, had merely been symptoms of the emotional weakness of his younger self. That self he now regarded with tolerance. Sometimes, secure in his rank and his plans for the future, he reminisced about Rae—revising the circumstances of their meeting to fit the version of his past his friends knew—and Butch would reciprocate with the story of *his* first love. This had been the daughter of a worker in Butch's father's copper mines. Butch had romanced her for four months before he departed for the QAF training camp in Lynche. The pair had corresponded— he with long, passionate letters he knew she would have to have read to her, she with gifts of chickens or cakes that inevitably arrived spoiled—until she announced she was marrying a laborer's son. Butch said his heart had never recovered from that blow. And indeed, for as long as Crispin had known him he had been celibate, unusually so for a pilot, rejecting the advances of both men and girls with sad smiles.

As a result of Crispin's repeated exposure to Butch's story, and his own dislike of the mawkish sentiment with which they toasted their "true loves," Rae, in Crispin's memory, had degenerated into a character similar to the village maiden: a shallow, naive music-hall girl whose only distinguishing characteristics were that she had happened to be a cultie and a Kirekuni. (And both those things he left out of the story he shared with Butch.) Perhaps it also had to do with Mickey Ash, the lizard traitor, happening to have the same very old, very common last name she had had. Occasionally Crispin found himself *forgetting* that the version of his life he told Butch was not true—and experiencing a sharp disappointment when he remembered.

In the story, he substituted Rae Clothwright for Prettie Valenta. He said he had simply grown tired of the circus life and decided to join up. To the lieutenants, who all came from privileged backgrounds, this was laudable. Crispin had taken a step up in the world.

It was lucky none of them knew that circus people looked down upon the military, officers and enlisted men alike, with the virulent contempt for those who follow orders that only entertainers can profess without hypocrisy.

Crispin slept: no longer an entertainer, but a participant in the real, deadly game. And both the vision of Okimachi and the real, the vibrant Rae poured back to him in a confused tumble of images.

It was Rae. But it was not Rae as he had known her.

Standing in a stone room, her arms folded, with a fierce, closed, proud expression on her face. Vanishing along a stone corridor in a flurry of women, their high heels clattering like gunfire: women dressed like Rae in black from head to toe. Rae standing in a sunny courtyard, shimmering in a haze of invisible daemons. Rae—and this was the worst image of all—smiling at a daemon, tall and purple and naked, that shambled beside her with its arm through hers—*talking* to her?

No!

Even in his dreams Crispin knew this was all wrong. She had sworn she would never have anything to do with daemons again, that they withered the souls as well as the bodies of those who tricked them. (Of course, that had been before she, Crispin, and Orpaan started to starve; hunger had made her turn around and unblushingly praise the kindness of the trickster women.)

Long black hair blowing across an orange sky. Rae standing above the pyre of Okimachi, as tall as a steeple and ethereal, like a cloud figure on the sunset.

No!

Four-fifths asleep, Crispin twisted onto his back and groaned, massaging his crotch. The image was powerfully erotic, but it was *wrong*. She had wanted more than anything to be homely. Her beauty and her race had combined to deny her the things in life she most wanted. And it made her miserable to be worshiped.

He could have sworn the sound of a voice woke him. He was lying in his bunk staring at the splintery ceiling three feet above. His body was clammy with sweat. The daemon brazier filled the room with a faint directionless glow. After a few seconds the glow got so strong that it could not possibly have been coming from the brazier. But this did not seem in the least strange to Crispin. He noted it only as one might note that the sun was rising after a long night. He sat up—ducking his head to avoid hitting the ceiling—and looked down.

She sat cross-legged on the strip of floor between the bunks. When she heard him moving, she looked up and smiled. The impact of her beauty hit him like a blow from a twenty-foot daemon. She held something in her lap. It was moving. "What the fuck is that?" Crispin said.

"This?" She lifted the bundle, holding it against her shoulder, bouncing it. With a shock Crispin saw it was a child. An octopus baby, with legs and arms as long in proportion to its small torso as an adult's should be. In the strange light its skin looked blue, unhealthy. "This is Jonathan," Rae said proudly. "My son."

"What?" Crispin sputtered. "All this time I've been yearning after you—" In the dream he did not flinch at saying things he would not even have let himself think in reality. "And you've been going off getting married and having *babies*? Queen damn it! It's just like what happened to Butch! I swear!"

"I haven't a clue who Butch is," she said with uncharacteristic asperity, patting the baby on its swaddled bottom, "but it would be a strange coincidence indeed if it was the same as what's happened to me. Which is a very long story indeed. I don't know if I should even begin—" Suddenly, the baby squalled. Its cry echoed through the officers' quarters. Rae's face fell. She looked around in fear. "Cris—"

There was an odd scent: it smelled like spicy food frying, something with chili peppers.

"Cris!" Rae almost wailed. "I'm not happy here! Please come and get me! I can't *believe* you've forgotten about me. Am I just a walk-on in your past? That's what I am here—a bit player. But I didn't think I was that to you. I thought I was more—more than I ever—"

Without thinking, Crispin started to jump down, to go to her. His head met the roof with a crack which certainly ought to have woken the others, even if the baby's crying and the strong smell had not. For a moment all he could see was blackness. Flecks of light spun in the void. He fell back onto his bunk.

And he was in Okimachi.

He was standing high up on the hill with the flames below him, in the very place from which missteps had taken him twice previously.

He glanced wildly about the broad, empty street. Several minutes must have passed. The fires lower down and higher up on the hill must be eating the goodness out of the air, for it was ridiculously difficult to breathe. His lungs worked like bellows. And the heat had grown so powerful that he could not understand how it was that no flames were in sight. The broken windows and open doors of the fantastic, pastrylike houses lining the street were black, empty.

Imperceptibly, he stopped being Lieutenant Kateralbin on the night of the fourth of Novambar with a patrol to lead tomorrow, and became Crispin-in-the-future. His hair was still buzzed in a Ferupian military-style cut, but he wore Kirekuni clothes. He was panting from the climb. He had no control over the urgency that drove him.

A minute ago he'd glimpsed him. The one he searched for. He'd taken one of the cross streets farther up the hill, heading uphill. Where did the dunghead think he was going?

Crispin would never find him. Not in an old city where all the houses were standing open, asking to be entered, holding out the promise of a thousand and one cubbyholes where a fevered mind might imagine it could escape the flames. Nonetheless, he had to try. It was his only hope. (*Their* only hope.)

He set off uphill again at a jog-trot, not hurrying anymore. There was no use in hurrying.

It was after he had passed the second, or third, west-twisting side street, that from up ahead, from the direction of the deadly orange glow that haloed the top of the mountain, he heard the sound of rushing water.

He came awake with a nauseating twitch. *Really* awake this time; the difference was self-awareness. The first thing he thought was that his dream had got one thing right. His sheetbag was soaked with sweat. Gradually, he became aware of a keening, groaning noise.

He forced himself to stop, and to open his eyes.

"Thank the Queen!" Festhre's mournful-clown face peered over the side of the bunk, gaunt in the first light of dawn. He must be standing on the edge of his own bunk, the bottommost one. As Crispin twisted to see what was clutching his shoulder and arm, Festhre rather shamefacedly eased his hands out from under Crispin's body. "You were shouting! I thought it was the bugle. But it's not time yet."

"Shit. Was I shouting?" Crispin found it hard to speak. He was still breathing hard.

"I can't imagine why none of the others woke up! We *did* have quite a wassail last night—before you and Butch got back—we invited a few crewmen in; perhaps Red and Keinze are sleeping the sleep of the remorseful."

"What did I say?"

"Unintelligible, my dear. Absolute gibberish."

"Not—no *names*?"

"Not that I heard." Festhre's tone grew just a little ugly. "Why, were you dreaming about poor Miss Clothwright? Your divinely beautiful long-lost love?"

Rae, and she's alive! Crispin wanted to shout. She's—do you hear—*alive!!!*

Then he remembered.

It had only been a dream.

"*Fuck* Miss Clothwright," he snarled. Festhre started back, only just managing to hold on to the bunk, his harlequinlike face falling. Crispin tore himself loose of his sheetbag and blankets. "I'm on today," he said between his teeth. "I might—as well—get up."

"Well, I'm not on today. And I'm going back to bed." Festhre dropped catlike to the floor with that grace peculiar to him, and so improbable, given his gawky body. "Sleep is at a premium in these parts, and I intend to get my full share. Good morning. Next time you have nightmares, I won't wake you."

If you hadn't wakened me, I might have found him, Crispin thought. *I wasn't making any mistakes this time!* Going for his locker at the other end of the room, he called over his shoulder, "Sorry, Brian. Thanks."

The only response he got from the bottom bunk was another sniff. But he knew Festhre wasn't insulted. It was impossible to insult him: he always bounced back like a billikin. Or else he was better at hiding his feelings than anyone Crispin had ever known. Out of all the men in the squadron, he would have done best in a circus. He had the face for it, anyway, Crispin thought. Wouldn't even need to wear paint.

He buttoned on his flight suit with vicious, jerky movements.

As he was tugging an extra sweater over his head, it happened.

A wall of flame burst roaring out of the floor, rising up all about him, surrounding him in seconds, arching over his head, frizzling his hair, parching his lungs, cracking his skin, blackening his hands in front of his face. The flesh was melting off the bones of his hands and there would be nothing left to protect his eyes. The heat. *The heat—*

In the windy wake of the flames' sudden absence he found himself bent over, trembling violently, the heel of his hand between his teeth and the taste of blood in his mouth. Dazed, he straightened up and looked around. There was no soot on the floor. In their bunks, Festhre and the other officers slept. The air was as chilly as one might expect on a winter's morning. Gray light fingered through the crack at the bottom of the door.

His faltering fingers encountered something on his scalp, clothed in the fuzz of hair the razor had left behind, but no less tender for that: a lump the size of a hard-boiled egg.

Probably not everyone dies on the battlefield. No! The determination not to die will guide us to a bright, mirror-like state of mind.

—Sonu Hwi

Supposed 2 Feel Nothing

Two and a half years earlier. 6 Maia 1893 A.D.
The Raw: Pilkinson's Air Base II

Two and a half years ago, 80 Squadron had had a better posting than Fostercy: Pilkinson's Air Base II, near Pilkinson's Shadowtown. Crispin arrived in spring, one of five recruits dropped off by a troop carrier on its way to Shadowtown. He'd only been free of Chressamo a week, and had spent most of that in trucks being shuttled here and there, north and south: a speck of dust on the game board of the Raw, wafted in the wind of much larger pieces being moved about. On the night of Maia 6 he was finally on his way to join 80 Squadron, trying not to fall asleep as the troop carrier jounced over the Raw. The other recruits destined for 80 Squadron—four boys several years younger than Crispin—were out cold, oblivious to the teeth-jarring jolting of the flatbed. They were fresh out of boot camp. Later Crispin discovered that they had had no idea what kind of posting they were getting; all they had been told was that they were joining a QAF squadron in a noncombat capacity. In this respect Crispin was better off. He had been given a rigger's job because he was actually a daemon handler, not because he had failed to pass the tests that would have sent him into combat.

He felt at once physically alert and mentally exhausted. His body was still sore from the sadistic attentions of the Chressamo guards, Freeman and Drown, with whom he had become exceedingly familiar. For twenty days he had been holding off sleep, keeping what he feared at bay; he slept only when he was too exhausted to keep it up any longer. He did not know he was wasting his energy—the visions had deserted him, and would leave him in peace until he was once again forced into confrontation with his own mortality two and a half years later.

He had had a good five hours of sleep in the canteen in Arvant's Shadowtown yesterday morning, so he sat up straight in the dark among the snoring boys, who were as yet so new to daemon handling, and so poorly trained, that they could not *feel* the daemon beneath them, feel it straining and shuddering every time it had to pull the troop carrier over a rise. It was old. Surprising that its driver hadn't detected how close it was to death. Or perhaps not so surprising. The few army handlers with whom Crispin had spoken had revealed in their conversation, whether voluntarily or unknowingly, the small extent of their expertise.

The wind blowing through the slatted sides smelled of dust. It licked over Crispin's newly shaved scalp like a big animal's breath. Spring had lasted perhaps four days. How different from everywhere else in Ferupe, where spring was a prolonged taste of paradise! But the Raw was not in Ferupe: its weather and the rhythm of its seasons were those of the plains of Kirekune. For four days the rain had been torrential and the sunlight slopped over one's hands like melted butter and the ground smelled wet. Even the carrion-crow voices of the women of Shadowtown had seemed to soften in response to the softening of the air. The hills had changed color, red earth and dark green scrub giving way to a blanket of pale green. But now, on the fifth day, although the blanket was still in place, it was starting to look dusty. The air was drying out and the winds were whispery and laden with shadows even at midday.

The nights were worse. The troop carrier labored loudly.

Leaving aside his personal fears, Crispin was irrationally afraid that if he stopped *listening* to the daemon, if he stopped encouraging its faltering will, it might lose heart altogether and strand them in the middle of the Raw. He resolved to stay awake all night.

But a resolution is merely a resolution when you're very tired. The next morning he woke with a jolt to see the other boys sitting up, their uniforms rumpled, questioning each other with their eyes. The truck had stopped. Apparently the old daemon had made it to its destination, after all. Outside, hoarse voices shouted over the roar of the wind.

"No use hanging about, here we are," said one of the four recruits, and they all slipped out from under the tarp that had been serving as a tailgate. Crispin followed more slowly. In the entrance of a vast barn, the officer who'd ridden in the truck cab was haranguing two tired-looking men in camouflage-patterned fatigues. Inside the open doors of the barn were two airplanes, the first Crispin had ever been close to. He took his place in the line of recruits. The machines were gigantic and weather-beaten. They looked as if every piece of them had been replaced at least once. One had a broken propeller: a fellow in black fatigues was standing on a ladder replacing a blade. The other was broken open below her nose, flaps hanging down as if she were laying an egg. A pair of human legs and feet showed beneath the flaps.

The scene was a far cry from the dance of the dragonflies a thousand feet up. But to Crispin it was even more thrilling. It was all he could do to yell his name without a trace of emotion. A short, dark man in a leather jacket strolled around the barn. As he went inside to talk to the riggers, he saw Crispin—*not* the line of recruits, as Crispin well knew by this time, but Crispin in the line—and he checked. His gaze sought Crispin's and held it. Then he went into the barn.

But Crispin had seen his face. Intelligence itself; and the hands, the confident, nonchalant walk.

Was he a pilot? Crispin wondered as the officer rounded on him and lambasted him for staring. Did they all look like that?

Later he was to realize that that had been Flight Captain Anthony Vichuisse himself. Although one can almost never remember the first time one sets eyes on a dear friend, or an enemy—there is usually only a haze of early impressions—with Vichuisse it was different. The moment when Crispin first locked gazes with the man who was to be his benefactor remained crystal-sharp in his memory until the day he died.

Avril—Okandar 1893 A.D.
The Raw: Pilkinson's Air Base II

Crispin's greatest fear had been that his coworkers would detect his lack of military experience. But he needn't have worried. No one asked where the new recruits had come from, let alone what sort of training they'd had. Just as soon as they could be issued fatigues and shown their lockers in the ground crew's barracks, they were thrust into the brutal routine of the ground crew. For a couple of weeks it was nothing but manual labor and carrying slops and falling into their bunks at night. At last Lieutenant Holmes, leader of the day shift, got around to testing their skills. He ordered each of the five to diagnose a daemon that was acting up. The other four had no idea how to begin, and were summarily assigned to older riggers who would show them the ropes. Crispin assessed the problem in a matter of minutes. The daemon was a thirty-foot beauty, and she was dying for the very simple reason that her cell had been made about a foot too narrow. After additional oak planks, dearly obtained, had been hammered onto the ends of the cell to enlarge it, and the daemon was made to clamber back in, her fury flowed out at Crispin like a proof of his ability.

He grinned at Holmes. His hands were sweating. He had been afraid—needlessly—that two weeks of toil had made him forget the trick of getting inside a daemon's head. But he had feared the same thing before, and been wrong. If anything, this time the empathy had come more easily.

Holmes squinted at him. "Civvy handler, were you?"

"Truck driver, sir," Crispin said radiantly.

"What on earth'd ya want to join up for?" Holmes asked testily, and made Crispin second-in-command of the night shift.

That was the first day of a horrible half-year.

The rest of the riggers understandably resented Crispin's having been placed in a position of authority without his having proved himself. After a month or so, he would have given anything to be demoted. But it was not to be. As Holmes had implied, none of the other riggers had had anything to do with daemons in civilian life; Crispin had a reputation to live up to. The other riggers' attitude toward the daemons was mistrustful and fearful at best, sadistic at worst. To them, Crispin's gentler approach proved that he was a sissy. In order to refute this assumption, he would have had to talk louder, boast bigger, walk with more of a swagger, and curse daemons more creatively than anyone else. For several months, during which he irretrievably damaged his reputation among the ground crews, he refused to walk the walk or talk the talk. Gibes, raspberries, and racial slurs followed him around. But he pretended, burning inside, that it didn't matter. He was still of the naive opinion that doing one's job was the important thing.

But the night shift was a closed community. There was no escape. One was either hated or liked; there was no such thing as keeping to oneself. Smithrebel's had been no preparation: the backdrop of the circus was a tapestry of new faces and new places. If you didn't want to get up close and personal with your fellows, you didn't have to. And Crispin's unique status—as a circus baby, a truck driver, and a performer—had enabled him to remain an outsider, a changeling without friends of his own age.

Here, he was constantly reminded he was an outsider, and derided for it. He thought he was slowly going crazy. For three months he hadn't seen daylight. The night shift got up late in the afternoon, when sunset was already blazing across the sky; they went to sleep at dawn. The advantage was that they didn't have to work in the blistering heat of the Raw summer. The disadvantage was that they had very little contact with the pilots or the rest of the ground crew. The airplanes in the hangars were their children. Gleaming glass and scrubbed floors were their pride. The work was not hard, once you got used to it, and they had the first, best helpings of the rations they prepared for everyone on base. On their rare days off, they knew no greater pleasure than consuming brandy until they were woozy enough to sleep for twenty-four hours straight. They were really just military janitors. Crispin would have gone crazy if not for the demogorgons in the Gorgonettees he tended. Their sugary hatred fortified him every night. It kept him on his toes.

He knew now that his hope of becoming a pilot had been a greenie's dream. The transition from groundsman to flyer was simply not possible. He might know the cockpit of a Gorgonette as well as Flight Captain Vichuisse himself, but in the night shift world, Gorgonettes existed only on the ground. Crispin's one remaining ambition was to do his job better than anyone else. In this, he surprised in himself a streak of perfectionism. Lieutenant Biggins, the boss of the night shift, said the shift had not been so efficient since he could remember. With Crispin and Greengage, the oldest man on the shift, sharing the duty of checking all the daemons on base, and the rest of the shift getting the maintenance work out of the way, all of them were generally finished with their duties by 3:00 A.M., and had the rest of the night to sit around smoking and waiting for the patrol to return. In the event that a victorious (or more often defeated) mission limped in late, the shift would spring into action and have the planes taxied into the hangars, the daemons fed, and repairs under way in less than an hour.

Crispin thought he gave his orders with the right touch of no-nonsense discipline. It stunned him when he found out that the shift considered him stuck-up and demanding.

"Shit," he said to Biggins. "What am I doing wrong? I don't fucking *like* ordering people about. But I've gotta do it. And nobody's gonna pull their weight if I stop yelling at them."

Biggins considered him from the other side of a tire they were changing. "Can't pretend you're comfortable doing it, then," he said. His eyes were kind. When Biggins was killed a year and a half later in a fire-strafing attack, Crispin, although they had long since lost touch, felt genuine grief. "They know you're not being real, Kateralbin. That's why they think you're stuck-up. I've been with this squadron since before you were born; I'm for the triple pension, me; but I've learned a thing or two. You gotta come down off your high horse, lad."

"Real," Crispin mused. "Mmm." The jack slipped, and he almost lost two fingers. "Damn it!"

He had to keep his past a secret if he was not to throw away the gift that Colonel Sostairs, back at Chressamo, had given him in return for Rae: anonymity. If the night shift knew he had come from *Chressamo*, life would be unbearable. So how was he to share the reminiscences about Home by means of which the riggers got to know each other?

Be real. It was impossible.

As it happened, his luck changed not by any doing of his own, but by his rotation to third-in-command of the day shift.

The day shift consisted of twenty men as opposed to eleven. The work varied more, and was more demanding. As a result the riggers had less time for petty rivalries. Soon Crispin realized that so far he had only seen the very worst that military life could bring out in men. The day shift, only dimly aware of his reputation as a civvy handler, treated him with indifference rather than distrust. For the first time he was able to become friendly with some of the other men.

And it was a relief to be on a normal schedule again. The mere sight of the sun—even though it was now the cruel orange autumn sun, under which men and trees withered alike—filled him with exuberance.

Not that he spent much time out in the sun. He commonly spent up to twelve hours a day in the crudely built hangars, working with the Gorgonette daemons on which the efficiency of the squadron depended. He could not have said what drove him to work until his fingers were numb. It was a compulsion far more demanding than love for the poor, hateful giants. Something to do not just with the power under his hands, but with the autumnal crackle that had come in the air, and with the whole, bitter, wind-flattened sweep of the Raw. Something he was catching from the day-shift men and from the pilots, who commonly had to be helped out of the cockpits, they were so drained. The awareness, *finally*, that he was in the middle of a war. Us versus them! For the first time in his life, he was part of an *us*. A tiny but essential part of Ferupe's defense machine.

Maybe his newfound enthusiasm for life was the thing that attracted Vichuisse to him. Crispin's first sight of the captain remained clear in his memory. But for the life of him he couldn't remember the first time the captain spoke to him. Had Vichuisse been pointing out the damage to his beautiful, metal Cerdres 500, stumbling with weariness as he circled the craft, Crispin two respectful paces behind? Had they encountered each other in some less orthodox setting? "Good work, Kateralbin." "Thank you, sir!" At first, Crispin had not hated the captain. "Keep it up." And Vichuisse might have touched his cap to the tall, shambling groundsman.

Crispin knew only that before he had been on the day shift a month, it seemed as if he and the captain had always been acquaintances. Whenever their paths crossed, Crispin was aware of Vichuisse's eyes on him. A couple of times he found humiliating little gifts on his bunk: chocolate or brand-name cigarettes. Such things could have come from no one else. It was this last which made him seek out old Biggins, on the night shift, and ask in a roundabout, embarrassed way whether it was possible Vichuisse was looking for a boy. Everyone knew that the captain's last favorite, a lieutenant named Savoy, had been transferred to another squadron by

Westanthraw himself, commandant of the Lovoshire Parallel: the liaison had become too public.

Biggins eyed Crispin in a way that made him flush. "It's not *that*." He reached out and rubbed Crispin's shaved head affectionately. "You numbskull."

"People are noticing," Crispin said, trying to defend himself. "Pretty soon everyone'll *think* it's that, even if it isn't—and as far as *I'm* concerned, it never will be!"

Biggins put his spatulate, broken-nailed thumbs to his lips. "If it was a matter of keeping your job, would you?"

"No! No . . . I don't know."

"Well, it isn't," Biggins said. "I may not see the captain that often, but I hear the stories, same as everyone else, and I've looked in on him from time to time, just to see his face. Could've stabbed him in his sleep as he lay slumped over his desk in that pretty-pretty office, me, a dozen times." Crispin stared in surprise. "And I can tell you he's not that easy a man, not so easy to make out. You're jumping to conclusions, Kateralbin. It's something else he wants from you."

"But what's that?" Crispin begged.

Biggins shrugged. "Damme if I know. Your tangle, not mine, m'lad. You're not on my shift anymore."

And with that Crispin was left with no other choice than to try to confront Vichuisse. The gossip was getting to be more malicious than joking. If the shift decided he was a favorite of the captain—the captain!—he would lose the few friends he had.

He chose a time toward the end of the shift, when most of the men had left the hangars. On days when Vichuisse was not flying, he often came into the hangar anyway, late in the afternoon, as if his kite was a mistress whom he could not neglect. Crispin contrived to save the Cerdres 500 for this hour. It was a couple of weeks before Vichuisse arrived on his own. But finally Crispin found himself face-to-face with him over the smooth bulge of the Cerdres's windshield.

Crispin was standing on a stepladder; Vichuisse was on the ground. Deliberately, Crispin climbed down the ladder. Something in his manner must have told the captain that things were not as usual. The captain remained still, with a mocking smile on his face, as Crispin walked around the nose of the Cerdres and saluted. "Evening, Captain!"

"Evening, Kateralbin. How's my love?"

Crispin blinked twice. Then he realized. "She's doing good, sir. Props running smoothly now. You shouldn't have any trouble."

"Was there something else, Kateralbin?" Vichuisse said, still smiling.

"There was." Crispin looked down at the captain from his greater height. For some reason Sostairs's tale about the QAF squadrons' *height requirement* flashed through his mind. He shoved his hands into his pockets. It was a gesture of extreme disrespect. Vichuisse stiffened. "Why did you have those things left on my bunk, Captain?"

Later he would wonder if his forwardness had in fact *pushed* the captain to decide what he wanted of Crispin. It must have been so. There was no other explanation for the way things had turned out.

"You're a smoker," Vichuisse said easily. "Nothing worse than going without a cigarette when you want one."

"True, sir. But that's not it at all," Crispin said stubbornly.

Vichuisse glanced around. Only his eyes moved; the smile remained fixed. There were eleven other planes in the hangar. Their props moved lazily in the wind that blew through the huge open doors. "Have you ever flown, Kateralbin?"

"Never had the chance."

"Would you like to?"

Would he? Suddenly he was choking on old, half-decayed dreams. But of course Vichuisse was only ragging him. "I haven't the training, sir."

"Why should you need training? You're so much brighter than the rest of the boys. Brighter than a good many of my pilots, even. Don't you think so?"

"That would be presumptuous of me, sir!"

"But you think so. Don't you? You think you're better than the rest of us."

The captain was already accusing Crispin, instead of Crispin accusing him. Such was the inertia of the hierarchy. With an effort Crispin recovered his self-possession. He met the captain's gaze. "I firmly believe I could fly a loop as well as *any* of them. 'Cept maybe yourself, of course." The minute the boast was out he wanted to take it back. But Vichuisse was smiling hugely now as if he had got what he was after.

"Could you? Could you, really? Well, why don't we find out?"

"But, sir—"

"No buts!" Vichuisse spun around. He was walking briskly toward the doors, and Crispin had to follow. His blood pumped with anxiety as he followed the little, trim figure out of the hangar—the doors ought to be closed, but obeying Vichuisse was more important—and across the muddy beginning of the runway, past the second and third hangars, to Hangar Four, the smallest, which stood right beside the barracks. Here the ground crew kept planes that needed complete rebuilding, or which were awaiting replacement daemons. Vichuisse gestured for Crispin to open the big doors. Trying not to grunt with effort, he heaved them wide and propped stones against their sills. Wings and beaks and bright eyes waited in the shadows inside.

Pilkinson's Air Base II was in the middle of a vacant stretch of plain. All that saved it from complete exposure to the enemy was the scattering of pine forest around the barracks. Many times Crispin had heard the pilots grousing about the short runway. It seemed that if your kite was a few pounds overweight, or you didn't lift off in time for some other reason, you got tangled in the trees before you could gain height. Indeed, the pines down at the far end of the runway were so badly damaged that it must have happened many times. They stood like splintered matchstick sculptures against the violet twilight.

"Your machine," Vichuisse said with mock gravity, indicating the interior of the hangar.

Crispin looked inside the hangar. Then at Vichuisse. Then back at the two airplanes that hulked inside. One was the ancient, broken-down Blacheim bomber which the squadron had had for donkey's years, it was said, since before they were phased out of bombing and became a purely defensive outfit. The other was a Gorgonette which had been shot to pieces shortly before Crispin joined the day shift. Its pilot had been dead five minutes after landing. The Gorgonette had still had its daemon, but its wings and fuselage were in tatters. Lieutenant Holmes had given it up as a bad job; Crispin thought differently. Working on his own time, using unwanted scrap lumber, he had repaired the sorry wreck. Did Vichuisse *know* about that? Was he being punished? The daemon was utterly ungrateful, of course—didn't know him from the Queen—and if it did, it hated him for putting its prison in working order again. He could feel it glowering at him from inside its cell, inside the bulky machine, in the shadows.

"Which one, sir?" he asked Vichuisse with a dry mouth.

The captain's laugh showed that he was not amused. "The Gorgonette, of course. Did you think I would send you up in the Blacheim? I'm not *completely* ignorant of the intricacies of the trans-formation engine—I *am* aware that without a daemon there's nothing doing. And the daemon of *that* heap of junk must have got thin enough five years ago to slip out the exhaust pipe. No, I should like you to test-fly the Gorgonette. I am aware that you have been working on it. If it fails you, it is no one's fault—and no one's loss—but your own."

Crispin started into the hangar. He stopped and looked at Vichuisse. "I never did anything to you, sir," he pleaded one last time.

"Never did anything," Vichuisse echoed. Then he turned on Crispin a smile so warm and radiant it made him take a step back. "I believe you're looking a gift horse in the mouth, Kateralbin! I thought you were brighter than that! No?" His tone made it obvious that for Crispin to contradict him would be inadvisable, if not fatal.

Crispin went to the Gorgonette and automatically began to check it over.

"None of that." Vichuisse's voice cut through his blue funk. "I haven't got all day."

"But we always check the kites before takeoffs," Crispin protested.

"Get a move on!" Vichuisse was still giving orders.

Scarcely aware of what he was doing, Crispin boosted himself up into the cockpit and strapped himself in. He had no helmet, or even goggles, no parachute; his rigger's overall was completely inappropri-ate, and his toolbelt got in the way. He unfastened it and dropped it over the side of the cockpit. It was difficult to swing the cockpit shell closed on his own. Suddenly it crashed down, nearly braining him, and through the glass he saw Vichuisse resting a long pole against the wall. The captain gestured impatiently.

Crispin sent a quick prayer to the Queen if she was listening, wrapped the whipcord around his fist, and jerked. The big daemon growled disconsolately as it stirred from sleep. In a remarkably short time it was purring and straining at the cord. It was powerful, hungry, and tired of inactivity. Its name was Toeleris. *How did he know that?*

Don't think about it. He maneuvered the Gorgonette out of the hangar. On the muddy downslope to the runway, it nearly ran away with him. That forced him to get the hang of the controls in a hurry. It was not *that* different from driving a truck—the Gorgonette felt about the same weight as a Dunlap ten-wheeler—although of course everything would change once he got up in the air. If he ever did get up in the air. The cockpit was a cell of unbearable noise. The self-starting props were whirring around at top speed. He was dimly aware of Vichuisse watching from outside the hangar as he turned the Gorgonette and geared the daemon for takeoff, doing everything by instinct, copycatting what he had seen the pilots do—he had no idea what half the dials were for, only the stick, landing gear, and whipcord. Thank the Queen it was a time of day when no one much was about—the afternoon patrol would not be returning for an hour or so. If anyone was watching, they must think him crazy. He thought *himself* crazy. The Gorgonette was a junk heap. His heart was beating so hard he was afraid he would pass out. Dizziness made his vision go jerky as the daemon, knowing its job better than he did, put on speed, and the Gorgonette's wheels tore up the ground and the pines loomed larger and larger, darker and darker.

And there was that horrible moment when he was convinced he was not going to make it—

And then the magical bounce that took him into the air, the engine coughing and the wind screaming around the cockpit, leaving his stomach and his worries and Vichuisse all on the ground.

The sky received the Gorgonette like a mother receiving a prodigal child.

Crispin never forgot that first flight, short and unadventurous though it was. The twilit sky grew huge around him and the land shrank and shrank until he saw how insignificant Pilkinson's Air Base II really was, just a clutch of shacks in a copse on the roiling desolation of the Raw; and there was the meandering gray line of the road to Shadowtown, and far off to the west, the antlike activity of the front. And away and above to the south, a formation of kites, Kirekunis from the look of them, flying serenely home.

Bank. Circle. *Mustn't get too high!*

A small figure on the runway beneath was jumping and waving its arms for him to come down.

* * *

Landing was far harder than taking off. He lost his nerve and circled twice more before he actually came in to the runway. By the time he taxied to a halt, he had realized there was a lot still wrong with the Gorgonette. The daemon might be willing, but something clanked ominously in the transformation engine, and one of the props was wobbling as it spun. He hadn't rebuilt the wings properly, either. The starboard ailerons were not working, so that it had been impossible for him to bank right when he was in the air. He came to a halt at the beginning of the runway, shut down the engine, and unwrapped the whipcord from his right hand, wincing.

Vichuisse was standing by the slowing port propeller. He helped Crispin to the ground.

In the air Crispin had been perfectly calm, but now he was shaking all over and wet with sweat. His fingers would not work when he tried to buckle the toolbelt Vichuisse handed him back on. Hopelessly, he let it fall to the ground and raised his gaze to meet the captain's.

Vichuisse smiled.

Crispin blinked.

The smile grew broader. Teeth showed. "Congratulations, Kateralbin." Vichuisse stepped forward and held out his hand.

Crispin shook it. It felt like the end of the world. There was no hint of displeasure in the blue eyes. For the first time that Crispin could remember, they looked kind. As Vichuisse gestured for him to kneel, he realized that this was the first time he had ever seen Vichuisse display the calm, oh-so-officerly poise he admired so much in the lieutenants, the demigods of the squadron. As a rule, Vichuisse was a sizzling, spitting enigma. A man to be feared. Not respected.

Crispin knelt in the mud, trying hard not to drop to his hands and knees. His thighs trembled.

Vichuisse tapped him gently on both shoulders with his boot knife. "By the power invested in me by our glorious Lithrea the Second, Queen Regnant, I authorize you to perform all the duties of a pilot of this squadron, the eightieth of the Lovoshire Parallel. I hereby relieve you of your duties as rigger-handler—though I by no means prohibit you from continuing to make your valuable expertise available to your erstwhile colleagues. Rise."

Crispin rose, stumbling. Vichuisse steadied him. A small wind had started to blow, bringing a scent of cooking from the mess hall. It had been beautiful weather for flying, but if the wind got any stronger, the afternoon patrol would have a hard time getting onto the ground. Crispin scrutinized Vichuisse for signs of his usual sneering cruelty. *Could* this all be an elaborate joke, a phase of what Crispin had believed, even before Vichuisse ordered him to test-fly the Gorgonette, to be the captain's vendetta against him? But Vichuisse had *dubbed him pilot*! Of course, no one had seen, no one could confirm the appointment—

"Pilot Kateralbin." The captain jerked his head toward the base. "If I were you, I'd put up your machine before those fellows get the whole squadron out of bed to watch."

Crispin turned and saw three riggers standing outside Hangar One. They were smoking and evidently regarding the scene with astonishment.

Crispin turned back toward the Gorgonette. He'd be lucky if he could get it into the hangar without it falling apart under him. Without *his* falling apart.

"Not Hangar Four," Vichuisse called as Crispin swung clumsily up into the cockpit. "Hangar Two. Park it with Lieutenant Fischer's other five. That way the riggers will know to give it a complete overhaul tomorrow—they'll do a much better job working in concert than you were able to in your spare time." The familiar, cruel note of laughter came into Vichuisse's voice. "And in the morning, I'll give you some personal landing lessons."

Okandar 1893 — Fessiery 1894 A.D.
The Raw: Pilkinson's Air Base II

Pilot Kateralbin.

It was what he had hoped for. It was far more than he had dared to hope for.

And he was grateful, of course. He was grateful every minute of every day, as he apprehended the complexities of flying solo and in formation with Lieutenant Fischer's crew. Yet he had to coach himself strictly in order to keep expressing that gratitude to Vichuisse. An unsilenceable voice inside him told him to steer clear of the captain, and when they did meet, to speak in the most formal terms—to widen the distance between them as much as possible. *He didn't really do you a favor,* the voice said. *Fischer's crew was short a man anyway. You didn't know that. Vichuisse simply chose the means of replacing that pilot which would be most amusing to himself, and cause everyone else the most bewilderment.*

But Crispin's sensible half kept him kowtowing to Vichuisse. And talking with him, when it could not be avoided, on a note of false conviviality. The captain seemed to think they were friends now. Sense told Crispin that this *ought* to be true. But he could not make himself like or trust the captain. Couldn't Vichuisse detect how despicably false his manner was?

Apparently not.

But they didn't encounter each other that much more frequently than before. And now Crispin had other things to think about. From the beginning, he was terrified that the other pilots in his crew looked down on him. Ground crew and pilots lived in two different worlds; he had not anticipated the difficulties of transferring from one to the other. His new world was smaller and narrower than any he had known before, though vast in terms of physical scope. Takeoff; flight; ENEMY; landing; food; sleep; and always, unceasingly, the kill tally sweepstakes, a game embittered by the competition between crews. Then there was the forced comradeship with one's own crew—a scant five other men. The tension stemming from who was "friends" with whom seemed at first to be overpowering. But after the first few weeks, Crispin realized the pilots' dependence on each other was largely emotional. In a defensive unit like 80 Squadron, the death toll wasn't as high as it was in the outfits assigned to cover the front lines, and so the mix of personalities, remaining more or less constant over periods of months, became inextricably blended—like different colors of paint mixing to make a single shade of brown.

Crispin's personal insecurity had made him standoffish and suspicious; but when he finally relaxed his guard, his crewmates accepted him without fanfare. It shocked him that they were willing to treat him no differently than they treated each other. They had not been shunning him; they had no time to spare for such pettiness. Crispin's flying improved markedly, and he let out his breath in relief. He had found his groove again. He coaxed his crewmate Martinson, who was good at painting, to do a buxom black woman on his kite, and although it looked nothing like his mother, he christened the Gorgonette *Princes Anuei*. He affected a slight Kingsburg drawl. He walked with a slouch to disguise the natural lightness of step which came from his Lamaroon resistance to gravity. To his astonishment, he found himself becoming popular.

The crews of 80 Squadron were identical organisms. This was the secret of their teamwork in the air. And yet the squadron was far from a harmonious unit. Eighty Squadron had a reputation for being something of a grab bag of pilots: a ragtag assemblage of human odds and ends. More, perhaps, than in other units, each of its men was an individual.

And each man wanted individual glory.

The kill.

It was on everyone's minds all the time.

The competition for glory.

And farther off, though not so far that they dared not think about it, *the pension*, the honorable (and lucrative) discharge. As old Biggins had said once, provoking derisive laughter among the riggers, none of whom would have dreamed of risking their lives in the air, no matter what the payoff: "They makes the kills, the Queen gets the bills."

But it was, of course, far more likely that the pilots would be killed first. It was almost impossible to survive a Kirekuni fire-tracer hit, much less an "own goal" of Ferupian screamers. In the short term they had only one dream: the kill. Perhaps because of his compulsion to prove himself, Crispin came to be more obsessed by it than any of the others. His crewmates teased him about it. There was an edge of bitterness in their voices. But on New Year's Eve, when the Queen's Greeting was read aloud and the tallies announced in the mess, Lieutenant Fischer commended Crispin. In two and a half months on the crew, he had shot down twenty-nine Kirekunis.

Crispin was ridiculously flattered. The truth was that the snob in him was utterly in awe of Fischer. Their lieutenant was a quiet, commanding man of thirty from the eastern domain of Ishane. He had the dark hair and fair skin of the heartlands. His ancestors, he told his crew, had in fact come from the heartlands, though for generations they had been squires to platinum-headed easterners. Fischer had a grain-trade fortune and a wife awaiting his discharge; he would not even need a pension. He had joined the QAF for the love of adventure.

But on a stormy morning in Fessiery of the new year, Fischer was smeared like marmalade across a hill in the Raw, shot down along with another man of their crew, two men of Keinze's, and four KE-111s. The wreckage was spectacularly complete. There was no piece of an aircraft larger than a man's hand: all eight were reduced to the same silvery jam. High above, fleeing for home, Crispin could hardly see for tears. All that anchored his concentration was the knowledge that it wouldn't do Fischer any good for Crispin to follow him down. When he climbed out of his Gorgonette back at Pilkinson's II, he saw that his three surviving crewmates, Potter, Harrowman, and Dupont, were crying, too, which only made it worse. The pines moaned in the wind. Ankle-deep mud lapped around the barracks. They tracked it across the floor when they went inside.

Later in the day they collected themselves for the eulogy, composed long before Fischer's death by Lieutenants Keinze and Festhre and read with a conspicuous lack of emotion by Vichuisse. Afterward they stood in the rain, sharing their outrage. Vichuisse had *deadpanned* the thing—made a *joke* of it! How dare he? Fischer had not been an easy man to know—but he had been their lieutenant! He had been *Fischer*! How dare Vichuisse?

And that night Crispin was wakened from a pitch-black, dreamless sleep by a night-shift groundsman bringing a summons from the captain himself. "Better not take too long about it either, Pilot," the boy said, dripping, watching Crispin struggle with his boots. "He's in a mighty mood. Cackling like a bloody jackdaw."

Crispin wondered vaguely how the boy dared speak to him like that. Then he remembered he had *known* him a lifetime ago when he worked the night shift. The weasel's name was Simmons, Smithson, Shitson . . . something like that. "Get lost, Shit . . . Simmons," he said. "Captain Vee's a skunk who should have been a policeman, not a pilot. You know it, I know it. Is there anything else? No. Get rid, then."

Gasping with delight, Simmons scuttled out. Crispin sat for a minute, his head in his hands. Then he slogged through the mud to the door at the far end of the mess hall. He knocked. If any response came, he could not hear it; the night was loud and wet. He went into the little entryway and removed his coat and boots. Another mackintosh was hanging beside Vichuisse's. Crispin's heart rose slightly.

But when he went in, he saw no sign of anyone else. Vichuisse sat in his big leather chair with his toes on the grate of a blazing fire. As Simmons had said, he was cackling. He stopped when he heard Crispin come into the office, and looked around the wing of his chair. "Ah! Kateralbin . . . Close the door, there's a good fellow, it's difficult enough as it is to keep the place warm. Sit down."

Another chair, less sumptuous, had been drawn up to the fire. Crispin eyed the bottle of brandy on the side table with longing, but when Vichuisse offered it to him, he shook his head.

"Cocoa then? . . . No? I suppose you're wondering why I got you out of your bunk." Vichuisse laughed. Crispin could not see the joke. The captain poured himself another tumblerful of brandy and took a long swig.

There were paintings on the walls and the paper-heaped desk was equipped with blotter, inkwell, and granite pen holder. A tiny stained-glass head of the Queen hung in front of the blackout shutter; it would catch the sun in the mornings. Probably the only metal in the room was the nib of the fountain pen. Vichuisse's illusion of luxury was just that. All the furnishings were tattered or repaired. Through the door on the other side of the room, Crispin could see the scarred bureau and the narrow bed. Someone's green pullover lay on the pillow. Was Vichuisse's guest concealed in there? Crispin could hear no sound. On the foot of the bed was a coverlet which looked as though it had been lovingly embroidered over a period of years. By whom? Vichuisse's mother? Did Vichuisse have a mother? Crispin had never heard of his having a wife. The motley decor gave off an indefinable impression of sadness. Crispin had heard that ever since he was appointed, the captain had carted every single bit of furniture in these two rooms around to every base where 80 Squadron was posted.

Vichuisse tapped Crispin on the knee. "Staring around! It's not as if you've never been here before! Eh? And it's only by your own choice that you're not less of a stranger to these humble quarters." By the time Crispin figured out the convoluted syntax of that remark, Vichuisse was leaning forward, his eyes gleaming brilliantly. "But I didn't get you here to make passes."

"Acknowledged, sir," Crispin said stiffly.

"Do you think I'm drunk?" Vichuisse said. "I'm not."

He smelled, indeed, of alcohol, but also of something else, something metallic. Crispin's skull prickled with fear. How absurd that he, the Lamaroon giant, should be so wary—no, call it what it was, *afraid*—of the good-looking but distinctly murine little captain. Afraid. Absurd, but true.

"I have two pieces of news for you, my dear fellow," Vichuisse said. "Curious? The first thing is that we're being moved to Fostercy Air Base."

Vichuisse picked something up off the floor that looked like a map of the entire Raw war front, all nine hundred miles of it, folded back to show the Lovoshire Parallel. *That brown streak is the Waste, so that must be Shadowtown,* Crispin thought—*and that,* there, *must be Pilkinson's II.* Maps were highly classified things: Crispin had only seen one since he was recruited. Yet illiterate, he couldn't decipher the lettering. Vichuisse's forefinger indicated a tiny blue star about four inches to the right of Pilkinson's II. "Fostercy Air Base. Isolated, true, but that's the point, I believe—I am not told much. You know that in cooperation with Seventy-eight Squadron at Pilkinson's I, we're supposed to protect Shadowtown. Well, we're not doing it well enough. Several ground-strafing forays have gotten through recently. So Commandant Smythe is switching us with Ninety-two Squadron."

What did this mean? The rain smacked the window hard. The fire crackled. Crispin's feet were drying out.

Vichuisse shook his head. "Fostercy is not a sought-after assignment, Kateralbin. Ninety-two Squadron was there for eleven years before this switch. We'll have to do awfully well if we ever want to get moved again. I'm counting on you to boost our tallies, my boy."

Crispin made a meaningless demurral. Had Vichuisse got him out of bed to tell him something the rest of the squadron would know in a few days?

The tips of Vichuisse's fingers were steepled together now, his elbows resting on the arms of his chair. The metallic smell grew stronger as he leaned back into the embrace of the leather. "I dislike having to bring this up so soon after poor Gerald's death. But there it is, a captain's duty. It is, as you know, customary to bring in new appointees from outside whenever a lieutenant is killed, but this time I do not believe it will be necessary. Your crew is already disarrayed, and with the additional trial of the move to Fostercy ahead, I see no need to burden you with an untried leader. So without further ado—get out of that chair, man! Kneel! One has to do these things properly—"

And Vichuisse made Crispin the new lieutenant of what had been Fischer's crew.

"I will simply have two new regulars sent to Fostercy. Does that sound acceptable, Lieutenant?"

"Yes, sir," Crispin breathed, still kneeling.

"I expect you are wondering why I choose you over the others," Vichuisse said with satisfaction as Crispin levered himself off his knees and sat down, queasily. "You should be aware that it is not just because I find you congenial. It is because you are . . . different."

That refrain will follow me all the days of my life! Crispin thought through the roaring in his ears.

For a moment Vichuisse seemed discomfited. Then he gave his cackling laugh. "To elaborate would be to violate one of the mysteries of authority."

"Of course I'm tremendously grateful . . . whatever your reasoning," Crispin managed. "I'll endeavor—to do—my best—to carry on Fischer's legacy."

He wanted to punch the wall, to kick the merry little fire into a rain of sparks. Even more he wanted to punch Vichuisse. His heart was pounding. His grief for Fischer had been superseded.

30,000 feet and still a-counting
The attack on my plane is steadily mounting
They killed my buddy, but I'm supposed 2 feel nothing
How can I live 4 love?

—The Artist Formerly Known as Prince

GLORY

16 Novambar, 1895 A.D. *The Raw: Fostercy Air Base*

The ecstasies and humiliations of the past had seldom been further from Crispin's mind as he stood outside Hangar Three with his crew. It was about two in the afternoon, but the cloud cover made the day as dark as if night were falling. The men's faces were as dark as the sky. An hour ago, along with Festhre's and Keinze's crews, they had participated in a total wipeout. Crispin's crew, fetched from fifteen miles away, had not arrived until the worst was over, and thus had not lost anyone; but Festhre's crew, though they had fought fearlessly, had lost three men. And Keinze's had lost four. Including Keinze himself. The oldest of the lieutenants, a year away from his pension, Keinze had been with 80 Squadron since before Vichuisse replaced Esethre as its captain. He, alone among the lieutenants, had been able to influence Vichuisse's decisions. Silent and cautious, he had kept to himself, holding no grudges against anyone. When he drank he was a different man: no one could tell funnier jokes or play better poker. He had commanded his crew with such efficiency, for so long, that it had been a running joke that he was immortal.

As always, they had been wrong.

Crispin looked around at his men. "We did well," he said heavily. "A kill for you, Eakin, a kill for you, Cochrane."

They did not react.

"We incurred minimal damage to matériel. We upheld our name.

We're the number one crew in this squadron, boys—you know that, and I know that. What happened wasn't *our* fault."

He couldn't allude any more closely to today's disaster. A lieutenant must never admit failure in front of his men. Crispin forced an upbeat tone.

"Keinze died honorably. He took three of them with him! It's official. Can you think of a better way to go?"

Reluctantly, they shook their heads.

"What's with all these long faces I see, then? As far as we were concerned, the engagement was a *success*. All right?" Crispin smacked his fist into his palm. "All right? We downed two lizards and lost no one! If that isn't a success, tell me what is!"

"Yes, sir," they mumbled.

Crispin suppressed a sigh as he looked around at them. Jack Harrowman, tall and lanky, surreptitiously rubbing his injured shoulder, which had healed well, but was still stiff. At his side, Fergus Dupont, a wiry young northerner with prematurely gray hair. Then Harry Potter, a Kingsburg man with a shady past and a face that showed every one of his thirty years. When Crispin was a regular, he had served with those three. When he was made lieutenant, they had accepted him without dissent, and continued to give him their best, as they had given it to Fischer. If they did not love him the way they had loved Fischer, that was understandable; after all, Crispin was still relatively new to his command. What mattered was that he and they trusted each other implicitly. He counted on them to boost the morale of the other two: Tim Cochrane, a southerner who looked far older than his nineteen years, and Sam Eakin, a talented newcomer to the squadron. But all five faces were slack with weariness and frustration. He knew intimately the mixture of euphoria—at having made it home alive, when so many had not—and guilt—over the same thing—that was running in their minds now.

"Go to the barracks," he finished, knowing he could do no more to stir them. "Debriefing is in one hour. Have your reports ready. You did a marvelous job. Keep your heads up."

They saluted and turned away. But Potter did not move. "Crispin?"

It was Potter's privilege, as it was Dupont's and Harrowman's, not to call him "Lieutenant."

"Yes?"

"When are they going to read Keinze's eulogy?"

"Oh, that's right, you knew him." Potter and Keinze, though not of equal rank, nor of the same crew, had been the two oldest men in the squadron; they had survived longer in combat than many new recruits dreamed possible. They had understood each other as few others could. "It might not be until tomorrow," Crispin said, remembering. "The captain has been closeted with his visitors. He may be too busy."

"Too busy for *Keinze*?" Potter said with quiet wrath. Crispin winced at the sight of his burning gaze, but he could not be openly disloyal to his captain. He could not admit that this time, he was not in Vichuisse's confidence: the visiting officers had arrived in a jeep two days ago, and Vichuisse had received them in his quarters. Nothing had been heard from any of them until yesterday, when the bizarre order for a full-squadron demonstration had come. Everyone asked Crispin what the occasion was; he gladly let them know he had no idea, either. It was ridiculous, but orders were orders: quietly cursing Vichuisse, all the able-bodied pilots on base turned out and flew formation over the base. The visitors and Vichuisse stood by the runway, watching. A good two-thirds of the squadron were still airborne, waiting their turn to land, when they went inside. That kind of rudeness came only from civilians, or *very* high-ranking officers. Crispin did not know what Potter guessed about the visitors' rank, and he wasn't about to venture any guesses himself. "The other lieutenants and I will put it to the captain later," he temporized. "If he says he's too busy, I'll put your name forward. Would you like to read the eulogy?"

"Isn't that irregular?"

It was, but Crispin felt he owed it to Potter to try and bend the rules for him. "Since he will have such a lot to deal with now, I daresay it'll be acceptable."

"Such a lot to deal with," Potter echoed.

"Yes."

They glanced around the hangars. Most of the activity following their return had died down: the injured men and damaged planes had been removed from the runway. But the stillness seemed to boil coldly—as if the air were full of frenetic, invisible activity.

"You wrote Keinze's eulogy—didn't you?" Potter said at length.

"Yes," Crispin said shortly. "With Lieutenant Redmanhey."

"How long ago—if I may ask?"

"Six months."

"I see," Potter said. "Downtime, then. See you in one hour." He saluted ironically and turned away. An injury sustained at the beginning of his career made him list sideways. Crispin watched him go. Then he started toward Hangar Two. He would have to see that the riggers were giving his crew's kites due attention. They were so lazy! Sometimes a catastrophe galvanized them, but more often, it worked the other way—not only would they protest that they were working as fast as they could, they would actually slow their pace, as if in defiance of their superiors. Donkeys!

Crispin stood outside the side door, clenching and opening his fists to try to get rid of the after-battle shakes.

"Lieutenant Kateralbin?"

Crispin's nerves were so taut that he actually yelped and spun around. *Fire*—

A slopboy. Such as Crispin himself had been at the very beginning.

"The c-c-captain." The boy was even more nervous than Crispin himself; he must think he had offended him. "The captain requires your p-p-presence in his quarters!"

"Oh, yes," Crispin said, collecting himself. "Of course." He nodded sagely. "Dismissed."

What the hell could Vichuisse want to call him from his affairs on a day like this? As he trudged toward the mess hall, he met Butch coming from the other direction. His eyes were bleary, and he was buttoning the neck of his sweater. He slid his arm around Crispin's shoulders and thumped him gently. "Heard. Sorry," he said with uncharacteristic succintness.

Crispin jerked his head. Butch dropped his arm. " 'S all right."

"Is it?"

"Didn't lose anyone. Didn't get there early enough to."

"Where?"

"Twenty-two miles southeast, by the front."

"What happened?"

"Keinze intercepted a whole flight of them on their way to ground-strafe an ordnance dump behind the front lines. He delayed them with three of his men while he sent the other two to find me and Festhre—"

"Four? Against sixteen?"

"Yeah. They were all winged by the time Festhre got there, and all down by the time I did. We couldn't get many of the bastards, but we delayed them long enough for one of Festhre's boys to go signal the ordnance dump what was coming. I don't know how many lizards finally got through. We had to run for home, or we would've been daemonsmeat."

"That's tough," Butch said. "It's all up to the ack-ack gunners in the end, isn't it?"

"Yup. Sometimes—" Crispin did not finish. He knew Butch knew what he meant. "Queen, I'd like to be in an offensive unit," he said vehemently.

Butch nodded, but said nothing, his long face set and thoughtful.

They had reached the door of Vichuisse's quarters. "Are you—he didn't send for you, too?" Crispin said.

Butch said only, "Yeah," but Crispin, glancing sideways, glimpsed a suppressed smile. They went in. The little, bare entryway smelled exactly as the entryway of Vichuisse's quarters in Pilkinson's Air Base II had—stale and somehow *older* than the rest of the base. Inside the office, the stale smell was worse. Vichuisse and his visitors lounged with their backs to the fire. Two of the officers occupied the only two chairs; Vichuisse himself sat on his clothes chest and the third officer on half an old barrel. The floor was tracked and dirty. Wine bottles lay everywhere like fallen ninepins. On the desk, maps were spread and pinned. The door to the bedroom was closed. Butch and Crispin remained standing. Crispin fought the urge to fidget. The three visitors were looking at them as if they were recalcitrant boys called in for a scolding. "Reporting, sir," Butch said, and Crispin joined in at the last possible moment.

"Lennox—Figueroa—Duncan." Vichuisse steepled his fingers. "These are my two best lieutenants, Daniel Keynes"—he pointed—"and Crispin Kateralbin."

"Honored, sirs," Butch said immediately, and again Crispin joined in when it was almost too late. What were these men here for? All three must be forty at least. He looked again at the one called Lennox, who was sitting in Vichuisse's own armchair. Crispin had heard

Vichuisse mention him before, with the elaborate casualness that accompanies name-dropping. Captain Lennox? *Commandant* Lennox?

Figueroa, an elderly man with sallow southern skin, lounging at ease on the half barrel, directed a withering stare at Butch. "Keynes? I thought it was *Keinze*."

"Perhaps I was not clear," Vichuisse replied. His laugh, always something of a cackle, sounded nervous. "This is not Keinze. Keinze was killed today, in that—um—unfortunate engagement of which we were recently notified."

"An alternate." Commandant Figueroa pursed his lips. "Keynes." He said it with distaste. "He had better be good, Tony. You understand that."

"I certainly do!" Vichuisse laughed nervously again. "Believe me, if he doesn't come up to par, he'll have me to reckon with!"

Butch looked paralyzed. *Small wonder*, Crispin thought. He dreaded the moment when they would turn their attention on him.

"They both seem awfully young," Lennox said. Though his face was lined and weary, his voice was as light as a boy's. "Haven't you others, Tony? Of course, I trust your judgment—and if they're not good enough, it'll be on your head, not mine—but . . ."

"But young blood is the hottest, isn't it?" Vichuisse said with another nervous cackle. Both Figueroa and Lennox winced visibly when he trotted out the old maxim. Duncan sat on the straight-backed office chair, his face wooden. Crispin guessed that he was not of equal rank with the others: an aide-de-camp, perhaps. He held a notebook in which he scribbled from time to time with a pencil. "And this"—Vichuisse reached over and patted Crispin's arm, as if he were a racehorse—"*this* is one of the best lieutenants I have been privileged to command in all my years leading this squadron. Before joining up, he was a professional daemon handler. He has a way with the regulars that is beyond belief."

Crispin felt a stab of panic.

"Where does he come from?" To Crispin's relief, Figueroa did not sound particularly enamored with Vichuisse's portrait of Crispin. "Cype? Why is his hair so curly?"

"His mother was a Pacific islander," Vichuisse explained. "But his temperament hasn't suffered by it. He's as Ferupian as they come."

Pride.

"Are you certain?" Duncan said suddenly.

"Oh, they'll do, they'll do, James," Lennox said. "We didn't see any flagrant muck-ups in the demonstration yesterday, did we? And this thing today—well . . ." Vichuisse seemed to shrink under Lennox's considering gaze. "I don't suppose it matters, after all, the paperwork is already complete . . ."

"It wasn't any of our faults." Crispin heard his own voice before he realized he was speaking. "Butch—Keynes, I mean—wasn't even *there*! We lost our very best lieutenant, that was Keinze, because we were spread too thin to get to him in time. It was four against sixteen of them, sirs. It was plain bad luck."

All four officers looked blank. With a shock of excitement Crispin realized he had surprised them. Then, simultaneously, Figueroa said:

"In war, Lieutenant, *nothing* can be blamed solely on bad luck."

And Duncan, speaking for almost the first time, said: "I like an independent spirit, Tony. Perhaps your judgment is not at fault. Theo, you're right. They'll do."

His voice was deep and confident. From the way the three others looked at him when he spoke, Crispin realized he had been wrong: not Lennox, but Duncan, was the highest-ranking of them. He scribbled something in his notes, then rose and shook Crispin's and Butch's hands. He was a lanky man, tall for a Ferupian: his eyes were on a level with Crispin's. "Pleased to make your acquaintance, Lieutenants. You would probably like to know what's just happened to your careers."

Crispin did not dare drop his gaze to Duncan's decorations, but out of the corner of his eye he saw Butch mouthing: *sublieutenant-marshal.*

A lieutenant-marshal was in charge of an entire parallel, giving orders to five to ten flight commandants, who each commanded a squadron themselves and had five more (like 80 Squadron) answering to them. The lieutenant-marshal's sub acted for him, exercising nearly identical powers. Westanthraw, lieutenant-marshal of Lovoshire Parallel, was practically a figure of myth, wielding the power of life and death over the careers of close to forty captains like Vichuisse.

"My name is James Duncan, acting for Lieutenant-Marshal Thraxsson of Salzeim Parallel. These are Commandants Lennox and Figueroa, both of Salzeim Parallel. Your Vichuisse is now a commandant, also of Salzeim Parallel." He did not give the bombshell time to sink in. "You two are now captains of Salzeim Parallel. You will be leading standard thirty-five-man squadrons in an offensive capacity, answering to Vichuisse, as before." The hint of a smile crossed Duncan's lean face. "We have had a good many vacancies open unexpectedly in the defensive units. We are reassigning several of these units to the offense, and we hope that with captains like yourselves in command, no more vacancies will open."

In the background, Vichuisse grimaced nervously.

Duncan said, "Congratulations, both of you."

A sweet taste filled Crispin's mouth. Flames were leaping in the corners of the room, sprouting like malignant fireworks from the necks of the empty bottles on the floor. When he heard Butch saying fervently, "I accept the assignment with all my heart, Sublieutenant-Marshal," he managed to prise his lips apart.

"Accept, sir."

"Then you are dismissed." Duncan turned his back on them. Crispin paid the rote obeisances to the officers and followed Butch out of the room, doing his best not to stumble. His skin stung from the biting heat, and he thought over the roaring of the flames, *It's a good thing I learned to read.*

"Vee has to have pulled strings," Carl Redmanhey said from his bunk. "There's no other way it could be possible."

It was past midnight, yet no one had suggested they get some much-needed sleep. The long, awful day of report-making and accounting for damages was over. Every minute of it, Crispin—and, he guessed, Butch, too—had vacillated between euphoria and acute nerviness. Vichuisse, unfathomably, had taken his crew out on the night patrol duty that should have been Festhre's. It was as if he *wanted* to give his remaining lieutenants some time alone to discuss the change in two of their fortunes. The visitors had not appeared in the mess at supper: Festhre and Redmanhey had taken this as a personal affront, and both of them were already in a bad mood when the lieutenants retired to their quarters after several hours of dissembling in front of their men.

"There's absolutely no other way," Redmanhey repeated irritatingly. "I don't mean to slander him, but he hasn't done anything to merit a commandancy! And commandancies are almost always given to captains from within the parallel, anyhow. A promotion to *Salzeim*? *Vichuisse*?" He blew a series of smoke rings. "I smell a rat. *Several* rats."

Butch was warming his hands at the brazier. "It's wildly improbable," he said wretchedly. "I thought that myself. Cris, *you* saw me!"

"You were a bloody wreck," Crispin agreed. In the presence of the commandants and the sublieutenant-marshal, Butch had been a model of reserve; but outside, in the wet, he had come as close as made no difference to breaking apart under the stresses of shame and honor and euphoria. And Crispin had been grateful, because the necessity of making Butch pull himself together had driven the flames away.

The flames.

They had come back, for the first time since that awful morning when they surrounded him and he thought he was going to die.

He added more kindly: "I was a wreck, too, if it comes to that."

"Oh, surely not *you*," Festhre said from his bunk. He, too, was smoking—not tobacco, but his "specials" that he kept for disasters and celebrations. "Surely you've always known you'd be the first one Vichuisse would choose, if something like this happened."

Crispin jumped to his feet. "I didn't fucking ask for it, if that's what you're implying!" Festhre looked up placidly at him. "The last thing I wanted was a Queen-damned promotion! He's plagued me because of I don't know what since day one, and now he's taking me to Salzeim so he can go on plaguing me! It's pure fucking sadism is what it is!"

"You know that isn't true," Festhre said.

"He hates me! Do you deny that?"

"I do, as it happens. I didn't think even *you* were paranoid enough to confuse favoritism with sadism."

"I'm not his favorite!" Crispin jabbed his thumb at Butch. "If he has a favorite, it's his man—the Kirekuni! Vichuisse favors him the same way he does me, only worse."

Crispin hadn't meant to mention the Kirekuni. But for the past twelve days Mickey Ash had been on his mind, in his peripheral vision, like the hallucinatory flames.

"But I meant the promotion," Festhre said as if Crispin had not interrupted. "You're more ambitious than any of us. You wanted it. If you deny *that*"—Festhre paused, as if trying to word his thoughts as delicately as possible—"I shall know you aren't half the man I have thought you."

Crispin could not deny it. The realization took the wind out of his sails, at the same moment as Butch said definitely, as if Festhre's jibes had been directed at him.

"I did want it. Who doesn't? But I wouldn't have wanted it at this cost."

"What cost?" Crispin shouted. "There was no fucking cost! It doesn't matter that we're an insignificant squadron in an insignificant parallel, it doesn't matter that we're on a ten-year losing streak, it doesn't matter that we got shifted to a dead-end base . . ." In the back of his mind he knew he was about to explode. His muscles were tight with frustration. "All that matters is that Vichuisse comes from a Kingsburg family with plenty of court connections, he's always known he wouldn't *have* to succeed to get promoted, and he's probably been pulling strings behind the scenes for years to set this up! It's absolutely literally a gift from the Queen! There *is* no cost!"

Redmanhey jumped down off his bunk and put an arm around Crispin's shoulders. "Calm down, boyo. You're all worked up and no wonder. Sit down." He guided Crispin by force to Keinze's bunk, its blankets neatly folded by the dead man that morning. Still gripping Crispin's shoulder, he fished in a pocket and lit another cigarette. Crispin took it thankfully.

Butch looked at him. "I meant Keinze."

"Oh, shit," Crispin mumbled. He took a deep drag, and coughed.

"Yeah." Redmanhey took his arm from around Crispin and braced his hands on his knees as if about to rise. But he did not move. "Poor old Keinze. He's going to get forgotten in all this excitement, if you ask me."

"I was supposed to ask Vichuisse if one of my men could read his eulogy," Crispin said.

"One of your men?" Redmanhey looked at him in surprise. "Whatever for? *I'm* gonna. And Vichuisse can stick me if he doesn't like it."

Crispin shook his head. They were all silent for a minute. Crispin guessed the others, too, were remembering Keinze. A loyal servant of the Queen for so many years, hardened by survival, a year away from the pension whose material value would not have meant much to him (for he had been the heir to a squiredom in Lynche) but the accolade of which would have made him a contented man, his services to Ferupe finally honored. All gone in a half minute of bad timing.

Bad timing gets every one of us in the end, Crispin thought.

The officers' quarters were chilly and oppressively neat, the half-hooded brazier gave off a light so cold that the temperature seemed ten degrees lower, the floor was tracked with muddy footprints, the lieutenants were gloomy; but the fact that Crispin was sitting here among them seemed suddenly the most precious gift he had ever been given. Far more precious than a promotion to Salzeim. *So far my luck's been good . . . extraordinarily good.* He shivered. *Look how far I've come. If it weren't for the Old Gentleman . . . if it weren't for Rae . . . if it weren't for Colonel Sostairs . . . If it weren't for the flames,* said the part of him that remembered Prettie Valenta lying crumpled on the red-and-white lino in the ring.

Festhre was smoking pensively. Butch was staring at the tiny daemons twisting in agony under the hood of the brazier.

Redmanhey got up. "I've had enough of this," he said. "I'm going to bed. You kids can stay up. I'm not particular."

"'Kids'? *Captains,* you mean," Festhre murmured.

"In the name of the Queen, lay off, Brian!" Crispin burst out.

Festhre looked up. "What, dearie? Does it really bother you?"

Butch let out a strangled snarl. "Yes!"

"Then, of course, your wish is my command . . . *sir.*"

"Fuck you, Festhre!"

"My pleasure." There might have been a twinkle in Festhre's eye. "Good night, dears. Don't forget to thank the Queen twice over." He kicked off his boots and wriggled under his blanket.

Some minutes later, when Festhre and Redmanhey were both snoring, Crispin sat down on the floor next to Butch and wrapped a blanket around his back as carefully as a mother. Butch shifted slightly, acknowledging his presence. "I can't stand that motherfucking fag sometimes," he mumbled. "Gonna be *glad* to get out of here. 'S truth."

"Yeah." Crispin confessed. "Me, too."

Butch was trembling. Crispin lit two cigarettes at once and gave him one. They used the brazier as an ashtray.

"Fucking shame we have to take Vichuisse with us though. All I was hoping for when he summoned me was that he was gonna tell me he'd got promoted or transferred or demoted. It wouldn't've made any difference as long as he was leaving and we were gonna have a new captain."

"I don't think there's much to choose between any of them," Crispin said.

"Not if those ponces we met today are a fair sample, no!"

"Scheming aristocratic fools," Crispin said vehemently, and then realized he had committed a faux pas. But the faint smile on Butch's face reassured him.

"*I'm* an aristocratic fool if it comes to that."

"Not a schemer, though. You'll make a better captain than any of them."

"Queen grant."

They could hear rain falling again. Crispin wished Vichuisse, out on patrol, joy of it.

Butch said suddenly, "But you know what *really* gets my goat? I have to take the fucking Kirekuni with me."

"Do you?"

"I can't exactly leave him and bring the others. And I'm not leaving Jansson, or Lance. They're my right-hand men."

"Yeah," Crispin said slowly. Then, "Listen, I'll take him off your hands."

"You'll *what*?"

He had said it. It was too late. "I'll give you Potter and take him. Do you a favor."

"Potter's your best man! You're crazy." Butch was breathing quickly, shallowly.

"Nope. This is what I figure." It hurt to say it, but he had to. "I figure him and me understand each other better than anyone else could. And Potter—Potter's getting just a bit too forward for his own good, lately. I don't trust him anymore."

"That thing with the eulogy," Butch said understandingly.

"Yeah. That was Potter. He shouldn't have asked." A minute later Crispin remembered that Potter had not asked, *he* had offered; but again, it was too late. The brazier sputtered blinding blue light as one of the daemons died.

Crispin wondered uncomfortably: *Did Butch look at me differently when I said that?* He had always tried to discourage even the ghost of the idea that he and the Kirekuni might be similar in any respect. He dreaded his friends' perceiving him as *other*—the thing that the Kirekuni indubitably was.

But Butch knew him better than that. They could say anything to each other.

The brazier was down to two-thirds power. "If you're sure, then," Butch said cautiously. "I'll tell him tomorrow."

"I'm certain." Crispin gave Butch's arm a squeeze. Butch looked at him in surprise, and then grinned.

"You're a peach, you know that?"

Crispin got up. "Give us the blanket . . ."

As he lay down in the top bunk, he saw the face of the Kirekuni like a ghost before him on the darkness. Mickey Ash was not wearing his usual closed, inscrutable expression but smiling superciliously. In an odd way the thought of him was comforting: as long as Ash was there, Crispin felt that he was in no danger from the flames, or the visions, which were really the daytime and nighttime aspects of a single horror, a horror that frightened him beyond reason, considering it was entirely in his head.

But he managed to forget both it and the Kirekuni without too much difficulty by dwelling on the uncomfortable prospect of telling Potter that he was coming to Salzeim, but not as a member of the crew with which he had served for eleven years.

22 Devambar, 1895 A.D. The Raw: Salzeim Parallel

Two, and only two, ground routes led through the Wraithwaste to the war front. Troops, supply convoys, messengers, and armaments trucks clogged them daily. One route started in Salzeim; the other in Thrazen Domain.

The Thrazen route had been opened in the 1850s, when it became apparent to the Queen's generals that the war had spread south, that it was not going to be won in the immediate future, and that a southern access was needed to prevent the Kirekunis from taking control of the South Waste. Thrazen had been chosen because in that domain, the daemonmongeries of the west existed side by side with the commercial culture of the south. Thrandon City was only two weeks by truck from Valestock and one week from Naftha, a southern port metropolis, the second biggest city in Ferupe. Before the war, Naftha had flourished hugely on profits from the metal-and-daemons trade with Kirekune; when war broke out, its economy started to collapse, only to be saved by the southern-spreading army's fortuitous need for supplies. Via the Thrazen War Route, Naftha drained the south of its young men and daemons, as Thrandon drained the west and the heartlands.

And Salzburg City, in Salzeim, drained the north and the east. The Salzeim War Route was older, broader, and shorter than the Thrazen. Its Ferupian terminus lay in rolling green farmland, whereas the Thrazen route led into the difficult western hills. It had been established in 1802, at the very beginning of the war, when Kirekuni forces first moved on the Wraithwaste. It was the first road anyone in living history had ever cut through the Waste. Ninety percent (so the soldiers' tale ran) of the troops ordered to hack that first path through the pines had died, some from overwork and accidents, most from stranger causes.

Even now that the Wraithwaste was being felled on a daily basis, its western fringe constantly eaten away by the Ferupian army's retreat, the soldiers still told horror stories about the deep forest. Not one of them, though they dreamed constantly about going to Shadowtown on leave, would have considered pursuing their dusky-skinned whores into the woods where the girls came from. They hated the Wraiths largely *because* the Shadow people weren't afraid of the forest—and the forest was not inimical to them! It was an outrage. Everyone knew that if a soldier marching on the war route strayed from his comrades, only his bones would be found in the morning! Wild daemons and humans *shouldn't* mix, and that was that. The Wraiths were simply unnatural. Unhuman.

A few objected that daemons didn't kill trickster women, either. And that traders invaded the forest regularly with impunity. Ah—but trickster women and traders never had to hack down Waste pines for cookfires with trembly-triggered sarges watching their backs—did they? The gorgons are *smart*! the soldiers averred. They know what's theirs, and they want to hold on to it!

In 1815, the daemon rifle was developed to defend troops against the dangers of the Waste, which was then taking a ridiculously high toll on recruits. "Kirekuni" guns with their metal bullets couldn't hurt a dematerialized demogorgon. Only another daemon, fired at high speed from a bazooka, had any effect at all. And even then, it could only slow a Waste daemon down, not kill it.

It was thus, through experimenting with a series of flawed prototypes, that the Ferupians discovered the "screamers'" effect on men. A few years later, the Kirekuni rampart gunners were being answered with hailstorms of screamers—a vast improvement over the sabers and flamethrowers with which the Ferupian soldiers had previously had to face the bullets.

Daemon engineering advanced by leaps and bounds, on both sides of the Raw. By 1830, hundreds of small aircraft—invented a half century earlier but never daemon-efficient enough for civil use—had been adapted for warfare. From these beginnings the QAF was born. The ever-resourceful Kirekunis quickly developed their own air force, which would soon be larger, better trained, and better equipped than the QAF; but during the few years when the Ferupian pilots owned the air, they were lauded as the instrument of Ferupe's salvation, and the lingering effects of this acclaim kept the QAF safe from criticism for several decades.

Only in the eighties did the eye of the court, constantly on the lookout for a scapegoat to blame for the Kirekunis' unstoppability, light on the air marshal general, by then a senile nonagenarian. He was replaced in quick succession by seventeen other air marshal generals—which instability hastened the decline into which the air force had already fallen. The facts were that the QAF budget had been surreptitiously tapped to provide for the ballooning infantry, and that most of the flight commandants and lieutenant-marshals were as incompetent as the notoriously pettifogging ranking officers of the army and of the minuscule navy that guarded the southern coast. Each QAF squadron was also having to cover a far vaster area than it had in the thirties and forties. Poor organization and a shortage of pilots meant inevitable defeats. And in the nineties, as the war seemed to be going worse and worse, blaming the air force became fashionable among the rank and file, too. *One* thing the QAF officers were doing a good job of was keeping their own men nearly as ignorant of the big picture as the general public at home in Ferupe. Of course, nothing could keep the pilots from tasting personal failure, but they had no idea how badly Ferupe was in fact losing—or how vitriolically the infantry blamed the air force for their own defeats. A QAF regular coming into first contact with an infantryman, whose experience of those defeats was far bloodier and more personal, would be in for a nasty shock.

And back in the twenties and thirties everything had been going so well for Ferupe! The distribution of screamer cannon had cut losses in half, and the near rout with which the war had begun had slowed to a manageable "strategic retreat." Some blamed the death of King Ethrew, and the succession of his infant daughter Lithrea to the throne, for Ferupe's inability to reverse that retreat. But it was widely guessed, if not admitted by anyone without decorations, that screamers were simply not as marvelous an innovation as they had seemed at first. They caused more devastation than bullets when they hit their targets. But they were just as apt to cause it among the men who had fired them in the first place. If a volley fell short in no-man's-land, it was quite possible the starved, ferocious tiddlers would get disoriented, turn around, and scramble back the way they had come. If you fumbled loading your screamer cannon it was nearly always fatal. And whereas a Kirekuni ammo dump strafed by Ferupian airplanes was no danger at all, a Ferupian ammo dump was literally a tinderbox. The only way to destroy a horde of escaped screamers was to set them on fire! Luckily, the Kirekuni flight commanders did not seem to realize this, for when they attacked Ferupian ammo dumps or screamer factories, they usually bombed them with fire-jennies—burning the screamers in their barrels, and causing far fewer deaths than they would have if they'd used bullets. Such delightful misapprehensions were what kept the Kirekunis from winning outright. The lizards might be military geniuses, but when it came to daemons they were remarkably stupid. And, of course, the Kirekuni war effort was hampered by their shortage of daemons, which almost, but not quite, negated the advantage of their access to most of Oceania's metal.

The Ferupian generals still held that daemon weapons were the technology of the coming century. When the right kind of magazines were developed, and screamer factories had been standardized like traditional houses of trickery, no force would be able to stand against Ferupians equipped with daemon rifles. The war would be over in a matter of months. But the regiments at the front still muttered longingly about bullets.

And not just bullets. Mechanisms, shielding, and metalware of every sort. By the 1890s, the Ferupian need for metal had become desperate.

Cookpots were made of pig copper. Privates' helmets were made of Cypean tin you could bend with two hands. Gun barrels were made of gold. Gold! Kirekuni iron and steel—*that* was what was needed! Forays into no-man's-land were just as often for the purpose of capturing Kirekuni matériel as for the ostensible purpose of recapturing lost ground. Often, a shot-down Kirekuni aircraft was requisitioned by a dozen different COs who all claimed it had crashed on their territory.

The Wraithwaste was a boundless reserve of lumber for everything that could possibly be manufactured of wood. But the fact remained: metal was necessary to a war effort. And the richest veins of ore in the world lay under the mountains of Kirekune. The biggest ironworks in the world were in Djicho; the only steelworks in Okinara. The Ferupian Snowlands—the domains of Thaulze, Cerelon, and Dewisson—had copper. The supplies were extremely limited, and of no better quality than the tin coming out of Ferupe's protectorate Cype. But it was all the authorities could offer the desperate quartermasters.

And the copper and tin all came, under heavy guard, along the Salzeim War Route into the Shadowtown which had grown up around the metal depots and smelteries.

Metal had made this Shadowtown into a city. A miniature city, and a filthy and unusual one, whose inhabitants were as used to seeing dogfights in the sky as they were to seeing clouds. Built in the middle of the Raw, it was populated by soldiers who passed to and fro, by Ferupians running the legitimate businesses which had sprung up, and by several thousand Wraiths, prohibited from most spheres of activity, who took care of the illegitimate side of things. (Although the word "illegitimate" was really inappropriate. So far from Ferupe, the city existed under the aegis of military law, which bore few resemblances to the laws enforced in civilized lands.)

Fittingly enough, the city was named after a long-dead general, a scion of *the* Cerelon family of Cerelon Domain, where most of Ferupe's copper was buried. Cerelon's Shadowtown.

Twenty-four QAF bases stood at varying distances from the city, scattered across the parallel. The pilots were seldom seen in the city, only above it. They got little free time, and so amplified were the standards to which they held themselves that they generally chose to spend it in the air, even if they were hallucinating from lack of sleep and were more likely to kill themselves than their enemies. The Salzeim Parallel saw heavier fighting than anywhere else on the front. The Kirekunis knew that Cerelon's Shadowtown lay a mere twenty miles behind the lines, and they knew its strategic importance to their enemies. But the concentration of Ferupian troops in the area had held them more or less at bay for twenty years. To the north and south, the front was creeping back, the war closing in around Cerelon's Shadowtown like the sea around a peninsula. But in Devambar of 1895, when Crispin transferred to Cerelon's Air Base XXI (or Sarehole, as it was known to its men), the Raw around the base was so quiet, so ghostridden, and the city of Cerelon so bustling by contrast, that for a time it seemed to him that he had come to a transposed bit of Ferupe. Only on his first free evening, a week later, did he discover how different Cerelon was. Nothing in the Lovoshire Parallel had prepared him for it.

On the day he arrived in Sarehole with Harrowman, Eakin, Ash, Dupont, and Cochrane, Crispin confronted his new men, having them dragged out of bed if necessary. They stood at attention, grouped in crews of five, on an open stretch of ground outside Hangar One. One-thirty Squadron had sustained heavy losses recently: there were numerous gaps in the ranks. Crispin, facing them with his predecessor's lieutenants at his back, felt as if he had met them all a hundred times before. Pilots living on their nerves, grappling daily with defeat, some of them spiritbroken (he would have the worst cases sent for a month's leave), but most as implacable as daemons. There was a proud tilt to their jaws, as if they were trying to stare him down. His heart swelled. The wind blew harder and colder in Sarehole than in the

Lovoshire Parallel. The pilots all wore layers of sweaters under their canvas macks. Their faces were chapped red.

Sarehole's ramshackle buildings crouched on a stretch of empty plain littered with stunted bristlecones. The base was right at the edge of the Cerelon's Shadowtown sector, and in fact right on the edge of the Salzeim Parallel. A few miles farther north and they would have been answering to a Lynche Parallel commandant. The chimneys of Cerelon puffed a black haze on the horizon.

"I am Captain Kateralbin." Crispin raised his voice to carry over the wind. "First of all, my condolences on your loss of Captain Jimenez. In taking command of this squadron I'll do my best to uphold his standards. I know how you must be grieving and I sympathize deeply."

None of them moved a muscle.

"Yes, well, it has been quite a week, hasn't it," Crispin said *sotto voce*. A few of them heard and laughed. He guessed that they were not so much amused by his sarcasm as by his tacit reference to the fact that Jimenez's death hadn't been much of a loss to anyone, let alone 130 Squadron. (Earlier, Vichuisse had cattily told Crispin that the man had been a moron and an incompetent.) If slandering Jimenez got them on his side, then well and good, but he'd better not carry it any further. "I've heard good things about you," he said instead, gauging their reaction to praise. "Your lieutenants speak highly of you."

A few smiles.

"I'm honored to have been offered the opportunity to command you. What leeway I have in the matter of offensives, I'll use to restore our victory ratio to what it *should* be, *can* be, and *will* be. This squadron has an illustrious record. I won't go into the reasons it's been slipping lately. Let's just blame it on the weather."

At that, a good many of them laughed. Crispin himself cracked a smile. But he had better change tack! Too much wink-wink-nudge-nudge and they wouldn't respect him as they must. He cleared his throat. "However, the lack of Captain Jimenez's influence is already showing."

Stony faces. They were waiting to see what he meant.

He gave it just long enough, and then said harshly, "A week without leadership has done nothing whatsoever for your standards. I've been snooping around. Several of your kite daemons are dangerously underfed. And do you realize the hangars are utter pigsties? It looks as if people have been camping out in there."

"People have," muttered Jones, one of Crispin's new lieutenants. "The riggers. It's warmer there than in their quarters."

"Thanks for *telling* me," Crispin said sarcastically out of the corner of his mouth.

"Didn't want to get my boys in trouble." But Jones did not sound resentful. When Crispin first met 130 Squadron's lieutenants this morning, they had openly expressed their philosophical view that no captain, however untried, however odd, could be worse than Jimenez had been. They were prepared to support Crispin. He just had to prove himself to them.

He rounded on the men again. "What if you had to scramble? You'd probably kill yourselves getting your kites out of the hangars, and if you didn't, you'd go nose down on the runway. There are potholes on the runway. *Potholes on the runway!"*

"Haven't been on any missions in a week," muttered an unshaven pilot in the first rank, defensively.

"Well, that's going to change soon enough," Crispin said. "The weather's been awful, I know, but I don't feel rain coming. And even if it was, it'd be no excuse."

All thirty of them knew what he meant now. No one dared to laugh. The unshaven pilot stared at Crispin, mouth hanging open as if he were paralyzed.

"And *you!*" Crispin said, pointing as if he'd only just noticed him. "Go scrape that hog-ugly gristle off your face! You—yes, you! Now!"

The fellow took one hesitant step out of line, and when Crispin snapped his fingers, he turned and shambled toward the barracks. Everyone watched him go. "Hold up your head, dammit, you're Ferupian!" Crispin shouted after him.

There were sniggers. Crispin faced the pilots again, praying he'd picked an unpopular man. It could make all the difference. The rest of the men's expressions ranged from relief that they hadn't been chosen to outright approval; Crispin breathed an inward sigh of thanks. "One-thirty Squadron's standards are higher than *that*," he told them. "One-thirty Squadron flies in rain, snow, and hail. One-thirty Squadron *slaughters Kirekunis* in rain, snow, and hail."

A few eyes slid toward Mickey Ash, standing among Crispin's own men at the back of the crowd, but most of the pilots seemed not to have realized their new squadmate's nationality yet. It was easy to miss when he was wearing a long coat.

"Most of you have come out here in half uniform! I'll let that slide this once, but from now on I don't want to see you—hear? I don't want to *see* you unless you look like *pilots*. You're not ground crew. You're not infantrymen. You're not, in the name of the Queen, *vagrants*! You are regulars in the Queen's Air Force! Are you aware of that? In the future, you will *look* like airmen, and you will *behave* like it. I've heard that many of you put in too much overtime. I admire your patriotism, but from now on that won't be necessary. Instead, we'll schedule *four* patrols a day, not three. Backup will come from the other five squadrons managed by Vichuisse, our new commandant. He, I, and Captains Keynes and Emthraze have agreed that shorter shifts will improve your health, your reflexes, and your kill tallies."

Vichuisse now commanded five captains. Out of those, Burns hadn't been there for the meeting, and Eastre had opposed Crispin's plan on the grounds that he liked to fly alone with his crews. But Eastre had been devoted to Commandant Elliott, Vichuisse's predecessor, and during the meeting he had made it obvious that he would oppose everything Vichuisse said as a matter of course. He had been overruled.

"Kill tallies. *That's* what we are here for, men. Make no mistake. We aren't here to fly *demonstrations*. We are here to shoot down so *many* of the enemy that the tide will turn back from the Salzeim Parallel!"

They were hanging on his words. Crispin's own crew, at the back, were chuckling among themselves. Crispin shot Harrowman a furious glance. They pulled straight faces.

"In cooperation with the other squadrons in and around Cerelon, we are going to mount a new offensive against the enemy. We are going to devastate him behind his lines, where it hurts him most, and recapture the Raw for Ferupe. Are you with me?"

Someone was breathing heavily: *ssss, ssss*. The wind swept coldly out of the Raw. Crispin squinted into it, his eyes watering. "Are you with me?"

"Yessir," roughly half of the pilots muttered.

"Are you with me?"

"Yessir!"

Ssss!

What *was* that? It came from the middle ranks. Crispin tried to locate it without letting them see he had heard.

Ss-ss-sss! Shshsss!

"Oh, Queen," Lieutenant Taft muttered behind Crispin, "*no*, I was afraid of this, ignore them, sir!"

That was when Crispin knew it wasn't his imagination. His stomach flopped sickeningly, for he recognized the hiss now. It was the noise soldiers in Shadowtown made at Wraiths.

Sssss! Shsh! Wraith! Wraith!

The cheek of them. The utter cheek of them!

He took a deep breath. What would Vichuisse do, what would any high-and-touchy aristo captain do in this situation? He would scream at them while pretending he had not heard. Therefore, Crispin would—

"Silence please," he said in a voice that was not loud, but pitched to carry to the last rank.

Ssss!

"It sounds as if a few of you disagree with something I've said. You can't be arguing with our need for a push to victory—and if you are, I suggest that you transfer to a noncombat capacity, because we don't want you *here*. Therefore, I can only assume you think I'm not qualified to ask these things of you."

On their faces, naked horror.

He had thrown them! He could not help grinning. "Perhaps you take me for a Wraith. Perhaps you're saying to yourselves, 'Our commandants must really be plucking at straws!' Frankly, I had thought you above such pettiness. But in light of *this* . . ."

Utter silence now. No more hissing.

Inwardly exulting, Crispin pointed at a boy whose face was browner than the rest, and whose bare head was fuzzed white-blond. "You look like an easterner. Are you?"

The boy's mouth opened and closed, fishlike, a couple of times. He had been one of the loudest hissers. "Yessir!"

"Name!"

"Teralbanin, sir!"

"Kateralbin," Crispin said, and tipped his cap with a smile, as if introducing himself. Teralbanin grinned sickly.

"My mother was Lamaroon," Crispin said. "My father was from Linhe Domain. I'm Ferupian, born and bred. But even if I weren't, it would be no reason for you to withhold your respect. I am astonished at your temerity. Among my crew is another non-Ferupian. Ash." He beckoned.

Mickey came up around the crowd, frowning. Crispin gestured for him to stand beside him.

"Ash was born Kirekuni." A few pilots gasped. "But he's not the enemy. He is one of us. It's *actions* that make the man, not origins, and Ash has shot down more lizards than half the pilots I know! You will tender him your courtesy as your squadmate, just as you will tender me your courtesy as your captain."

"Yessir," they said doubtfully.

Crispin held up one hand. "Your respect you may withhold until you have decided whether my command merits it. But your obedience I claim. And if you give it to me, I guarantee that we will earn more glory than any squadron in this sector."

"Yes, sir!"

They had come physically unfrozen. The crews came close to dissolving as pilots elbowed each other, raising eyebrows, smiling. "Good going, sir," Jones murmured behind Crispin. Another lieutenant seconded him. Crispin didn't think he'd won them over, he'd simply stunned them; but it didn't matter. "So, are we together?" he shouted at the regulars.

"Yes—"

"Yes *what*?"

"Yes, Captain!"

"Together?"

"Together!"

"What are we going to do?"

The responses came variously. "Kill 'em! Slaughter 'em! Shoot 'em down! Fuck the fuckers over! Make the pension! Give 'em woffor!"

Crispin had not known he was clenching his teeth until pain shot through his jaw. His fingers and toes were numb with cold. Beside him, Mickey lashed his tail in delight. Streaky dark clouds scudded across the gray sky, and in the distance, the lurid streaks of screamers marked an ongoing dogfight. The wind from Cerelon smelled of smoke. "I'm fucking proud of you," Crispin shouted at them when the voices died down. "Fucking *proud*, hear!"

"Captain!"

"Proud! I'll see Taft's crew in ten minutes for night patrol! I want Joffrey's crew in your bunks now; reveille's at 5:00 A.M. The rest of you—at ease!"

As they straggled away, they kept looking over their shoulders at him, grinning and shaking their heads. Crispin thought, *Still lucky. For now.* During the briefing meeting at QAF HQ in Cerelon, Captain Eastre's hostility had given him his first doubts as to whether he would have enough leeway to do his captaincy justice. His men, perhaps, he could handle, but they weren't the only factor. The sheets of drizzle sweeping over the runway bellied strangely, as if an invisible face were pressing itself against the wet gray curtains; the cackling of the crows on the bristlecones sounded human, like the voices of the night birds in the Wraithwaste nearly three years ago. Vichuisse's influence over Crispin's career had not been broken, only diffused.

Briefly we live. Briefly, then die. Wherefore, I say, he who hunts a glory, he who tracks some boundless, superhuman dream, may lose his harvest in the here and now and garner death.

— Euripides

CIVIL
VIRTUE

15 Jevanary 1896 A.D.
The Raw: Cerelon's Shadowtown

"So how's it going?" Butch said immediately, peering at Crispin as if he expected there to be something wrong with him.

"What do you mean, how's it going?"

They were in the Officers' Club in Cerelon. Crispin had arrived with Commandant Lennox, who had invited him for drinks at XII Base and then in town. Lennox said everyone who was anyone in the air force would be there: this was the monthly occasion when nearly all the captains and commandants got together and got drunk. The general briefing meeting the next day was known as the world's best cure for a hangover. Crispin had tried to get out of attending the night-before, but finally he had caved in to Lennox's insistence. When they arrived at the club, Lennox had been swooped up by a crowd of colleagues, and Crispin, not knowing anyone, had felt somewhat out of things until he spotted Butch on the other side of the room.

This was the first time he had seen Butch since leaving the Lovoshire Parallel. He hadn't been off base for a month—he could hardly believe it now, but the days went by so fast—knocking the squadron into shape. He had not let them know it, of course, but when he first took two crews of them on an offensive mission, their shoddy formation flight and poor aim had appalled him. They had lost two men, and only managed to strafe their target—a battalion of Kirekuni ground troops—once before they had to run for home.

"Everything's going great guns!" he told Butch.

Butch looked shifty and stirred his martini. "How're you getting on with the boys?"

"Marvelously! And you?"

"Takes some getting used to, but now I've promoted Lance and Potter and Jansson to lieutenant, it's not half-bad. Are you sure you—"

"What'd you do with the old lieutenants?"

"Demoted 'em of course," Butch said, puzzled.

Crispin bit back the caution that sprang to his lips. He would never have dreamed of demoting any of the lieutenants he had inherited from Jimenez. And none of the crewmen he'd brought from Lovoshire expected promotions, either. The barrier of class prevented them from even thinking about it. Potter was the only one who might have got difficult; that was why Crispin had not been sorry, in the end, to hand him over to Butch.

"Good, no, that's good, everything's going swimmingly," he repeated while he wondered what was going on in Butch's mind.

The Officers' Club consisted of several small rooms for gambling, snooker, and private conversation, a supper room, a roof terrace where receptions were held in better weather, and a large indoor clubroom with a bar in the corner. In the center of the room stood a curious sculpture: a cylindrical daemon glare taller than a man, its glass smoked to soften the light, around which a crystal bead curtain fell forever downward, sparkling, throwing prismatic light through the fog of tobacco smoke. Crispin hadn't been able to resist examining it up close. He had discovered that the "beads" were actually drops of water that slid down needle-thin rods to the base of the sculpture, and were recycled up to the top again. The ornament provided the only light in the room, although unlit daemon chandeliers hung from the ceiling. The walls were polished paneling. Potted trees stood here and there, between fat leather armchairs. Considering what city the club was in, considering the pasts and futures that enclosed every officer like a nacreous, impermeable shell, the atmosphere was astonishingly festive. Probably it was because they were all so drunk. Crispin had held off on the cognac, wanting to keep his head, but Lennox had been quite tipsy by the time they arrived, and from the fixed, insectile limpidity of Butch's gaze, Crispin guessed he was pretty far gone, too.

"Couldn't stop thinking about you," Butch said now, intensely. "After what I heard."

"What?"

"One-thirty! It's the worst squadron in the whole parallel. It's got an absolutely terrible reputation."

"Terrible reputations seem to be my lot in life, don't they?" Crispin knew this side of his friend. Butch was capable of fixating on an unfounded rumor or supposition and letting it consume him. "Finding out the truth behind them, I mean. I haven't heard the rumors, but there's nothing wrong with the men. They're willing and competent. Their last captain was a brainless idiot, but nothing's broken that I can't fix. According to the record our weekly tallies are already higher than they were under Jimenez. I had a spot of trouble the first day, but that's water under the bridge now."

"What sort of trouble?"

"What do you think?" Crispin gave Butch a wry look.

"I knew it!"

"Well, what else? Be reasonable."

"Cris, I was *worried*," Butch said all in a rush. He was very drunk, Crispin saw now. "I heard about your squadron. The worst possible assignment you could've been given. One-thirty's last captain, he was a southeasterner, right, and they said he had Lamaroon blood, too, he was curly-headed, browner than a Cypean! And you know the way regulars' minds work! It was completely unnecessary to send you there!"

"They must've thought they were fucking cursed," Crispin said, keeping his voice light. "It's a good thing I didn't know that, or I'd never've had the guts to deal with them the way I did."

"You got screwed!" Butch said. "Someone—"

"Did it deliberately. Yeah. . . ."

The room was a sea of noise and smoke, the talk of the officers and Wraith girls so heavily punctuated with laughter that Crispin had a momentary flashback to the evening he'd spent in the pit of the Old Linny Music Hall in Valestock, Lovoshire. The atmosphere was the same here, except for the cultivated accents and the violence of their educated repartee, each word a bludgeon designed to bruise and wound. Even when QAF officers were off duty, they were still at war.

A party of officers was bearing down on Crispin and Butch where they stood by the wall.

"Someone wanted me to fuck up," Crispin said finally. "Whoa."

Butch rolled his eyes. "If you're going to start on Vee again—"

"You bloody well told me yourself that One-thirty was the last place any reasonable commandant would've posted me! He's trying to see how much I can take. He's trying to break me."

"Mistakes happen," Butch said. His eyes were wide and strange. He gulped the last of his martini. "Shouldn't have mentioned it. Just had to find out how you were getting along, that's all. Forget it—" He swung toward the approaching officers, holding out both hands. "Collins! Allendez! Guterman! Let me introduce you to—"

The way the captains brushed him off was expert, Crispin thought. Their tones held just the right mixture of heartiness and indifference. Before he knew what was happening, he and Butch had been separated, and Crispin had been introduced all around and was caught up in a party of men by the bar arguing raucously over aerial strategy, and Butch was still standing by the wall, half-hidden behind a potted miniature elm, an unreadable expression on his face. He looked as if he had just bitten into a sour olive.

Before long Crispin found himself a center of attention. It was as if now that his colleagues had decided to include him, they were going the whole hog. Vichuisse was there; Crispin felt a thread of pleasure when it became apparent that the Salzeim officers weren't paying half as much attention to the commandant as they were to *him*, a lowly captain. In fact the other commandants seemed to make no secret of the fact that they found Vichuisse tiresome. If Crispin had been them, he would have felt the same, and might not have managed to conceal it as well: he had never seen Vichuisse so ingratiating, or heard his laugh so whinnying. To Crispin, the commandants' talk of strategy was fascinating and informative. But Vichuisse kept silent when the rest were discussing the war, breaking in only when the topic shifted to who had made what faux pas or been seen with what young pilot. The captains kept their faces expressionless at such times; Lennox, Figueroa, and Hawthorne maintained a semblance of weary interest.

For the second time in his life, Crispin came close to feeling sorry for Vichuisse. The commandant was not stupid. He could not fail to be aware that he was being disrespected.

And why were they hanging on his, Crispin's, words, and plying him with drink? Probably it was just because he was a new face in a crowd of old ones. And maybe they hoped he could replace Captain Eastre, who had been killed earlier in the month after being a favorite of his colleagues for six years, and who had to all accounts been a fabulous wit.

Crispin had a natural wariness of getting drunk, and he'd already had too much, really. He lit another cigarette and leaned toward Salemantle, a captain of Lennox's who seemed more intelligent than most of them. "You were surrounded over no-man's-land? Have to hear how you got out of that one. Never know when it might happen to me. Knock wood."

"Knock. See, I have these signals for my wingmen. I carry noise flares, and I set them off when things are getting bad. One for 'every man for himself,' two for 'by me,' and so on."

"Useful trick!"

"Try it! It works! So I signal them to clear off up out of it. They told me later they thought I'd gone mad, but they did it. That left me alone in the middle of the lizards—"

There was a disturbance by the door, and Crispin and Salemantle turned with the rest. A tall, thin man came in, taking off his overcoat, passing it to a servant. His hair and trouser bottoms were wet with rain. Though Crispin had never seen him smile so widely before, he recognized that face: it was Sublieutenant-Marshal James Duncan, arriving late.

"Duncan!" Vichuisse got up and hurried toward him. "My dear man! We thought you weren't coming!"

Duncan cut him dead. He walked straight past him and shook the hands of the less obtrusive commandants Figueroa, Lennox, and Hawthorne.

"Kateralbin!" Now Duncan was facing him, beaming. Crispin stood and automatically shook the sublieutenant-marshal's hand. "I wasn't going to come tonight, but I wanted to see you. Congratulations on your successes!"

"Thank you, sir—it's only been a month," Crispin stammered.

"Nonetheless! We all thought One-thirty Squadron was beyond redemption. And your four-shift plan is working out rather well."

Crispin glanced involuntarily at Vichuisse.

"Tony told me the idea originated with you," Duncan said.

"Upright of him, eh? Lieutenant-Marshal Thraxsson plans to extend the system to the rest of the sector, and possibly the entire parallel, depending on whether tallies continue to improve. It's a viable alternative to increasing squadron size, a measure we have been debating for some time. We have only lost one ranking officer under this system, and that was Captain Eastre; but that was nothing to do with you. In fact, if we were to blame *anyone* for Eastre's death, it would have to be the officer who was flying command with him."

That had been Vichuisse.

"Eastre was a man of great competence. It is regrettable. But all in all, losses are down and kills up."

"Thank you again, sir!" Crispin's mind was whirling.

Duncan turned to Vichuisse, bold-faced. "And my congratulations to you, Tony, for your shrewd choice of captains! I have heard good reports of Kateralbin, obviously, but also of Keynes. Is he here? I should like to speak with him, too."

Everyone watched while Duncan found Butch and congratulated him with the same effusion he had used toward Crispin. Then the sublieutenant-marshal moved on to the next man. It became apparent that he was making a point of speaking individually with every officer in the room. The knot in Crispin's stomach loosened. He even felt a touch of pride. Duncan had approached him first! That had to be a mark of honor.

It took the best part of an hour for the sublieutenant-marshal to make the rounds of everyone in the club, including the bargirls. By the time Duncan and Vichuisse could be seen retiring to a corner, Crispin was enjoying his third whiskey and soda, and paying less attention to the political undercurrents of the party than before. But all the same, he cringed when he saw Vichuisse practically bobbing up and down before the sublieutenant-marshal. It was obvious that Duncan was criticizing Vichuisse for his role in Eastre's death. But still. *He has no sense of self-respect!* Crispin thought in disgust, not for the first time.

He slumped back in his armchair and took a long swig of liquor. No one seemed to hold Vichuisse against *him*, or against Butch, Emthraze, or Burns; but he could not escape the feeling that in shaming himself, Vichuisse shamed his captains, too.

The officers occupying the circle of armchairs they had drawn up were arguing, hotly and illogically, over the merits of screamers from different local factories. Captain Emthraze, who had been hovering near Crispin most of the evening, leaned toward him and said in an undertone, "That was quite a dressing-down Duncan gave him!"

"I couldn't hear. How do you know?"

"Oh, I know Duncan! He doesn't mince his words. But on the other hand, I *don't* know Vichuisse. He was your captain; you're far more familiar with his ways than Burns or Salemantle or I. What do you think?"

"Of *Vichuisse*?"

"Mmm."

Crispin narrowed his eyes at Emthraze. The intelligent dark face puckered with earnestness. Emthraze didn't look as if he were trying to trap Crispin. But if he wasn't, what did he want? A southerner (so it was said) from an ancient, molding aristocratic house, Emthraze had so far joined in the carousal with less gusto than the rest. In flight, he was a solid team player, lacking the competitiveness which had been Eastre's downfall. If anyone around here knew about keeping his mouth shut, it would be Emthraze.

And yet—

Crispin's loyalty to Vichuisse was stronger than he had known. It swayed him.

"Why don't you ask Keynes? He's over there." Crispin jerked a thumb at the corner where Butch sat nursing a drink in silence.

"We've already asked him. He seems perfectly reliable." *And weak-spirited*, said the rueful smile on Emthraze's face. "It's you who hasn't committed one way or the other."

One way or the other? "What's that supposed to mean?"

Emthraze just smiled.

"What did Keynes say then?" Crispin tried.

"We are all in agreement."

Crispin was silent. Matters political had to be communicated through manner and deference (or lack of it), not words. Anything else would have been suicide. That, of course, was why Emthraze was being so vague. But it all came down to politics in the end. The rest of the captains were banging their fists good-humoredly on their armchairs as they argued. The Wraith girls behind the bar looked exhausted. The air was sour with smoke. Emthraze regarded him with serious brown eyes.

In his drunken state Crispin knew it would be very easy to commit himself to words he would regret later. He took a sip of his drink. "Let *me* ask *you*—what did you think of our last commandant? Elliott?"

"Oh, Elliott . . ." Emthraze shook his head. "No one could compare to him. His loss—a tragedy." He seemed to mean it. "We were all certain Burns would get the appointment, but then . . ." He let the sentence hang.

"Burns seems capable enough," Crispin said. "I haven't really spoken to him. Not man to man."

And what can they do about Vichuisse now he's got the commandancy? Crispin thought. *Nothing. Why don't they concentrate on scheming against the lizards, not each other? Honestly, sometimes I wish I was in the* Kirekuni *army—at least, according to Mickey, they respect their superiors!* He drained his glass.

"He's appropriately named," Emthraze said. "Burns, that is. D'you know why?"

Flames . . .

"If he's that teed off by not getting a promotion, I daresay he didn't deserve one in the first place," Crispin said. "Now if you'll excuse me—"

"We wouldn't have cared *which* of us got the promotion," Emthraze called softly after him. "But when it's a question of our men's lives, and influence, not competence, determines the hierarchy, one has to wonder if—" Emthraze broke off, as if he realized that he was getting dangerously close to treason and that people could hear. "Kateralbin, just talk to Burns! I strongly suggest it."

"Tomorrow, all right?" Crispin called over his shoulder. Without giving Emthraze a chance to reply, he circled the water-dripping sculpture to the corner where Butch sat alone.

Butch looked up. Even in the half-light, Crispin could see his eyes were bloodshot.

"Come on."

Butch didn't move. Crispin took his arms and pulled him to his feet.

"I've had enough of this fancy-ass backbiting. Enough. I don't know how you stand it."

"Nor do I," Butch said wonderingly.
"Let's get shot of this dump."

They made their good nights and left the Club; by common consent, they wandered out of headquarters. Cerelon after curfew was a miserable sight. The night was cold even for Jevanary, and drizzly. A fetid mist clouded the moonlight. Lacking any normalizing agency such as a comptroller's office, Cerelon knew nothing of plumbing, running water, gas, or street cleaning. Unpaved and badly littered, the streets were really just twisting routes between the habitations which, over time, had encrusted the land between the Army HQ, the QAF HQ, the depots, and the metalworks. Few of them were wide enough to take a jeep. When they were on duty, soldiers stuck to the main thoroughfare. Off duty, they stole to the civil sectors like ferrets to a rabbit warren. The houses here were shabby, dark, and uninhabited-looking. A flash of light as a door was opened, or a burst of laughter from behind blackout shutters, betrayed the fact that Cerelon was packed as full of people as a Kingsburg slum. When Crispin drove through the city in daylight with Lennox, he had been struck by the grim tension in the air. It had taken him a few minutes to understand that there were no children in Cerelon. No one loitered, no one played in the gutters. Men and women scurried warily about their business, dead-eyed as Wraiths in Shadowtown. But even in Shadowtowns there were children. Cerelon had its Wraiths, of course, thousands of them; but except for a few madams, they did not live in the Ferupian sector. They had their own shantytowns on the outskirts. Like the Ferupians, their business was to bleed the soldiers of their temp pay. One had to wonder, Crispin thought as he and Butch passed a young Wraith woman and a private, arm in arm, where all the pay the soldiers frittered away *went*.

Butch looked after the pair as they passed into the dark. Crispin looked at Butch. "You know this place better than I do. Where're we going?"

"To hell in a handbasket," Butch said. "Fringetown's crawling with half-breed kids. Lots of them are already grown-up, and they can pass. David Burns is one . . ." He looked at Crispin, not too drunk for instant contrition. "You know what I mean."

"I meant where are we *going*," Crispin said.

Butch stopped walking and stared up at the moon. "My driver's gonna collect me at dawn. I wasn't thinking . . . Jeep's parked back at HQ, but I don't know where Waller's at." He tore his gaze from the white half shell in the sky and looked around the shadowed lane. "Around here somewhere, if I know him . . ."

Crispin had no inclination to turn back to HQ. He started walking again. Butch followed, stumbling. Crispin steadied him and found that Butch needed the support; if Crispin let go, he would fall over. Butch's heart was beating wildly. His breath seemed not so much labored as absentminded—as if at any moment he might forget to inhale. Crispin wrapped his arm around his back. The other's body was as hot as the outside of a daemon cell after a five-hour flight. "We'd better sit down for a bit." Crispin pulled him toward an outside staircase that zigzagged up the front of a two-story building.

"What, here, are you crazy? They'd have us in five minutes!"

"They?"

"It's after curfew, nobrain. You think just because there's soldiers, there aren't cat burglars and pickpockets and knife boys and suchlike scum, too?" Butch spat.

Crispin *hadn't* thought. The exclusive society of pilots had deconditioned him to towns; but Cerelon was just as much a town as it was an army base—more the former, if anything. He adjusted their course so that they were walking in the shadows of the eaves. After a couple of minutes, warily surveying the side streets, he said, "Butch. What do you think of Emthraze?"

They turned a corner, passing a windowless building from within which came the notes of an accordion.

"He's all right."

"That it?"

Butch turned his face toward Crispin. His breath reeked. "Course not! A man's a man, isn't he? Course Sade's got his thing, just like everyone else! But, Cris, I dunno—"

"Dunno—"

"Him and Burns and Salemantle . . . and I dunno who else. Lennox maybe. Though I can't credit it. I can't understand it. I don't know why they won't just leave me out of it." Butch shook his head in anger. "I joined up to *fly*, by the Queen, not to play at conspiracies like some damned courtier!" He paused. "I was presented at court once, did I ever tell you that, Cris? Dad presented me. I didn't hardly dare to look at her. It was June—"

"What year?"

"Queen, who can remember? I was eleven. No, ten, it was the year Cassie was born. My fifth sister. Squires' wives have so many babies, Cris, more than commoners ever do. I've always thought that's weird. Maybe it's so there'll be enough officers if they keep on enlarging the army the way they're doing . . . I'm twenty-five. That means it was '81."

"I was there, too," Crispin said, laughing.

"At *court*?"

"No, in the suburbs with the circus. Smithrebel's Fabulous Aerial and Animal Show. Running around half-dressed—do you remember how hot the summer was in Kingsburg that year?—riding an elephant in a little Eo Ioriel getup in spec!" Crispin shook his head.

In the moonlight, Butch smiled. "I *hated* court! It was supposed to be a special treat that Dad was taking me along . . . he had to go and pay the copper taxes every year, but he usually took Edward, my oldest brother. The shit I had to wear was so stiff with rhinestones and embroidery I could hardly move. Had to kneel to everyone we saw. My knees hurt for weeks. Black-and-blue!"

"I don't suppose your dad ever took you to the circus."

"Queen, no! He'd sooner have taken me to an opium den. Or the music hall."

My girl worked in the music hall, Crispin almost said, and then remembered he had to lie to Butch. A wave of sadness passed over him. As if sensing it, Butch squeezed his arm with his elbow and said frankly, "Nostalgia's a bitch, huh?"

A crowd of people surged out of a doorway ahead of them, laughing and talking, and crossed the road to vanish as quickly as they had appeared. A sweet breath of incense hung for a moment on the rank air.

Butch squinted up at the sign, its colors muted in moonlight. "Look out for the Dancing Pig . . . that's Waller's spiritual home, that is!" As he spoke, he squeezed Crispin's arm again, affectionately.

Crispin thought, *Butch, I—*

Butch, you're drunk, drunk!

He shook his head, trying to clear it.

"Was the circus an amazing place?" Butch asked.

"What do you mean, amazing?"

"Sometimes I wish I'd been you. Where have I ever gone? One nasty, cold corner of Dewisson. Kingsburg. Training camp. And the fucking Raw. Growing up in the circus . . . that must've been something else."

"Wasn't all that. We went hungry. And we lived in the backs of trucks. And we worked like dogs. I was trained for the ring, and then as soon as I got bigger the ringmaster started me on heavy labor, and thank the Queen if I'd never had the chance to learn daemon handling I'd still be doing that. Killing myself to show people a good time."

"But you've been *everywhere*. The south, the heartlands, the east, the west, the north, the cities! I never even *thought* about seeing other places before I met you." He paused. "Too late now. Been thinking a lot lately about what I've missed . . . but it's too late now."

The night swirled like liquid around them. In the distance, over the grumble of the city, they could hear screamers shrilling. The flames had never been farther away; Crispin was completely rooted in the instant; and yet the awareness of death hanging over his head filled him with dread of the next instant, and the next. Adrenaline pounded through his body. His heart beat in a lumbering rhythm he could almost hear. "Daniel. I appreciate your confidence in me."

"Friends to the end," Butch said, and put his other arm around Crispin. It would have been an embrace except that they were both facing the empty street. For a fraction of a second everything mutated, eddying, and the street was the pathway of Crispin's vision, lined with strange people in foreign clothes. The air coruscated. And who was that grinning as he vanished into an alley? But almost immediately Crispin was back in Cerelon. A woman started hoarsely to sing in a second-story room. Crispin sought Butch's hand and gripped it clumsily.

"I thought you'd changed," he said.

"*You're* the one that's changed," Butch said seriously.

"Bullshit," Crispin said, laughing, and pulled away. The sign over the nearest door bore rude script: *the dancing bore*. He couldn't stop laughing. When Butch saw the sign he joined in, too. "Betcha this is your Waller's hideaway!"

"It better be; I'm far too drunk to drive a daemon," Butch said grimly, and they entered a bar misty with smoke, lit by daemon glares shaded with red cloth, packed with tables over which brown and white faces hung close together, smiling and sweating; but Waller was not among them; and as the patrons noticed Crispin and Butch's captains' bars (for everyone in Cerelon could read decorations, even if they couldn't read books) and fell silent, they left, and found their way with some difficulty and a great many accusations of stupidity back to the QAF HQ, where they located Butch's jeep and requisitioned a disapproving sentry to drive them to Air Base XV, five miles outside Cerelon. This he did with an appalling lack of control over the daemon, several times nearly overturning the jeep in potholes. When they reached XV it was 4:20 A.M. by Crispin's pocket watch. The night patrol had returned and the dawn patrol taken off an hour ago. Apart from the noise of the wind over the Raw, all was silent. They kept their voices down as they slunk toward Butch's quarters. Crispin did not want to be seen by any night-shift groundsmen: the plan had been for him to stay in town with Lennox. They entered the captain's office. The blackout shutters had been pulled and everything was dark.

When they lay down to sleep after a substantial nightcap, Crispin realized just how drunk he was. Too drunk. Butch's quarters were pitch-black. Crispin felt weightless, disoriented, as though he were lying on the top of the carousel Smithrebel's had had when he was a child and it was spinning; he could hear the chiming national anthem it played, and yet his limbs were so heavy he couldn't move. A leg lying across him, an arm under his neck. He was fully clothed except for his boots, and yet he felt cold. He wriggled closer against the warm body beside him. The person sighed and wrapped arms around him. Some impulse made Crispin turn his head to see the face on the pillow. Pale skin over jutting bones . . . thin-lipped mouth . . . it was Butch, of course. His friend. He had never had such a friend.

For an instant his head cleared, but the dizziness reclaimed him and he shifted closer to Butch, seeking warmth, the embrace, the safety of two-ness. Butch sighed again—asleep or not?—and hugged him so close that their faces touched and their legs entwined.

Friendship. This was all new.

Crispin had grown to manhood in the society of older men and women. There had been no boys his age in Smithrebel's. And except for that one summer when he was fifteen, he had never known any local kids. Never had a friend before. Never. He wanted to tell Butch that, what he hadn't been able to say earlier, when they were in Cerelon, but his mind was not working well enough, so he kissed him instead. He meant it as a cheek kiss but somehow it ended up a mouth kiss. And then came something he hadn't felt in months: but it wasn't urgent, it was only pleasurable . . . and Butch was kissing him back.

Crispin's eyes fluttered closed.

Lips. Tongues. Warm and brandy-flavored. The strange familiarity of the male mouth.

Hands. Hands and mouths on skin that had never before seemed desirable.

Try as he might, afterward, torturing himself with the effort, he could not remember at what point he drifted asleep.

The next day, the captains, commandants, mistresses of the screamer factories, Sublieutenant-Marshal Duncan, and Lieutenant-Marshal Thraxsson of the Salzeim Parallel sat in the briefing room in QAF HQ. A dogfight was going on overhead. The city lay quiet, cowering. It would have been bad form to so much as glance out a window; the officers and trickster women kept their faces stony as they strained to hear Thraxsson's voice over the noise. All the men were nursing hangovers. The women seemed more alert, but they did not speak. Two had a truculent, militant demeanor; the other looked browbeaten and rested her head on her hand. She wore the trickster woman's traditional brown wool, where her companions wore feminine versions of QAF uniform.

The briefing was merely a formality; the offensive and the defensive would continue along the same lines as before. Except in terms of success or failure, which were not the concerns of this meeting, it made no difference that three of the officers at the table were new. Next month one or two more would have changed.

Crispin scribbled a few details of Thraxsson's strategy on the fly-leaf of a pamphlet containing exhortations to glory by the Queen, which he was supposed to read to his men. (Most of them were illiterate, as he had been.) He would receive a more comprehensive transcript from the shorthand clerk later. Butch, sitting on the other side of the table, would not meet his eyes. It was the first sign Crispin had received from him that the events of the night before could not simply be a forgotten indiscretion. Of course neither of them had said a word that morning. Treating the whole thing as a drunk dream, Crispin had more or less succeeded in putting it out of his mind. But the part of him that remembered was furious with Butch for acting so oddly. Did he want everyone to *know*?

But after the briefing, when the officers lit cigarettes and mingled around the table, Butch behaved quite normally, though he still would not look directly at Crispin. He even went so far as to introduce Crispin to Captain Burns.

"Delighted," Burns said, his dark eyes level. Now that Crispin knew he was a Wraith half-breed, it was impossible to miss, although one could have taken him for a southerner, or a dark-haired easterner who had not been long out of the sun. He was in his late twenties. "I'm looking forward to flying with you, Captain. I like the four-shift plan. It means each of us will get a chance to see how the others operate."

"You and I are flying patrol together next week," Crispin said. "Unless there's an emergency in the meantime."

"Knock wood." Burns's voice was deep and carrying. He actually turned and rapped the briefing table with his knuckles, as if calling a meeting to attention. The conversation quieted.

To ease the awkward moment, Crispin said, "How long have you been in the parallel, Burns?"

"David, call me David. Long as I've been flying. Eleven years—twelve this summer."

Crispin whistled. Burns's face crinkled in a grin. "Pure luck."

"I need some of the good kind! Come out to XXI when you're free and we'll discuss it over a beer or two," Crispin invited him.

"Mmm, XXI!" Burns said in his loud voice. "I was stuck in that shithole for a year and a half! It was my first assignment." He chuckled. "I'll visit, but I won't stay. I wish you the best of luck, Captain, because you're gonna need the Queen's intervention if you ever want to get out of there alive!"

Vichuisse was standing not five feet away, arms folded, watching them with an unreadable expression. Crispin made a horrified face at Burns.

"Yeah!" Burns went on, seemingly oblivious. "Sarehole! That base is right in the line of flight from one of the biggest Kirekuni air bases on the front to Cerelon. They used to fire-strafe us just for fun. We'd always be scrambling!"

"That hasn't happened to me yet, but—"

"Must be because we've got a bunch of ace captains in our sector this year. You, me, Sade, Butch, and Alan Eastre was the very best of us, Queen keep his soul—we're holding 'em off." Burns winked. Crispin nearly choked. The older man knew exactly what he was doing. "Because it's certainly not due to the quality of our command, think you? I haven't received a communiqué that made sense in weeks. And I know who Alan was flying with when he went down. The hierarchy these days . . . appalling! When a war drags on and on and on, the bureaucracy can get away with slack. They know they can drag their feet, the real men will carry them."

Vichuisse walked away, his steps measured, clicking.

"No offense, Lieutenant-Marshal, I'm sure," Burns added wickedly, pulling a face in the direction of Thraxsson, who was chatting with Lennox, Figueroa, Hawthorne, and the trickster women on the far side of the briefing room.

"Captain, I hope your luck is *good*." Crispin shook his head. "You're pushing it."

And the smile vanished from Burns's face, and Crispin remembered what Emthraze had said last night, that Burns was on fire. He could believe that now. He decided to trust the Wraith-blooded captain.

"I hate him," he murmured, jerking his head in the direction Vichuisse had gone. "I owe him everything—I came up from the ranks, did you know that? From *rigger*. He boosted me. And I hate him. You'll probably think I'm an ungrateful sod—but, Queen's body, I don't *need* him anymore!" He shook his head, unable to put his distaste for

Vichuisse into words. Right now he wanted to be flying. He wanted wind roaring past his ears and a KE-122 in his sights. He couldn't bear another minute of this sticky crisscrossing web of plot and counterplot.

"None of us need him," Burns said. "I came up from the ranks, too, and every promotion I've gained, I've had to fight men like him for it. I'll take you up on that offer of hospitality. In a week or two, when I have space to breathe. They're coming at us like gnats out at XVII right now." He made warding-off gestures as if he were evading the Kirekunis where he stood. "And I'm gonna have to oversee Alan's squadron, too, until they decide which of his lieutenants to promote . . . None of us need a millstone around our necks."

And then the smile was back, for Commandant Figueroa had moved up to them with two captains from his sector.

Early that afternoon, Crispin flew solo back to Sarehole. Among other things, he considered Burns. He was dubious about the captain's revolutionary talk—surely Vichuisse could not be that much worse a commandant than Elliott had been, or than Lennox, Figueroa, or Hawthorne? But all the same, Crispin liked Burns. He was clearly all there. Which was more than could be said for a lot of the fellows Crispin had met last night. Crispin had not trusted Emthraze or Duncan—or for that matter, Butch, the first time they met—the way he had instinctively trusted Burns. And since Butch was acting so strangely now . . .

The Raw scrolled past beneath *Princess Anuei*'s wings, moving as fast as a bolt of camouflage fabric unrolled down a hill. The daemon responded with gratifying sensitivity to the whipcord. It was a young, strong beast, and before coming to Sarehole Crispin had fed it personally, handpicking the healthiest splinterons from the seething barrels in the storerooms. Now he no longer had time for that, but he'd put the fear of the Queen into the riggers, and they seemed to be doing a good job. He ought to trade *Princess Anuei* for a Cerdres or a Killer Bee, a machine that suited his dignity, but he was putting it off—this kite was *his*. He'd rebuilt her in the scrap hangar of Pilkinson's Air Base II. Of course she'd been refurbished countless times since then, but she was still *Princess Anuei*. One Anuei had brought him into the world; it would be fitting for another *Anuei* to accompany him out of it.

But not yet, Queen, not yet!

He flew close to the ground, jinking through lulls and blasts as the wind rushed over the hills, keeping an eye on the reflectors. The sky was as good as empty—a Ferupian patrol several miles to the north, nothing to worry about. From time to time, flames leapt up, orange and flickering, from hollows on the ground or from around the boles of trees. He was used to them—they came whenever he found himself alone—and he concentrated on ignoring them. The smell of open air braced him. Blowing from the battle lines, the wind was so cold it was spicy.

The noon patrol hadn't yet returned, and the runway was clear when he landed at Sarehole in the middle of the afternoon. No damage seemed to have been done to the base while he was gone. Had it only been one day? Seemed like forever. A few pilots were up and about. They greeted him with delighted salutations.

He had gained his men's liking as Vichuisse had never been able to. That in itself was a victory, he thought as he listened to his lieutenants' reports later, sipping a brandy, keeping his counsel. Jones, Taft, Carnation, Kimble, and Hammersmith were all first-rate officers, and they trusted him.

But he had half-consciously come to accept what Burns had said: that his squadron, like Butch's and Emthraze's, like the late Eastre's, could never live up to potential under their current command. Burns's prognosis seemed truer yet when Crispin learned that Lieutenant Taft had lost two of his men, and sustained damage to his own Gorgonette, in an offensive mission he'd flown in conjunction with a crew of Vichuisse's yesterday.

From rude darkness the hero rose; amid songs of praise, destiny chose him; in wind and dust, his three-foot sword, armor donned for the altars of the land; wings to his father, pure in civil virtue . . .

—Tu Fu

The Shadow
of the Waxwing

23 Marout 1896 A.D.
The Raw: the Kirekuni front lines: 1,500 feet

Orange fire arched through the air, crossing and recrossing the lurid rainbows of screamers. The gusty Marout wind pulled the arcs out of shape, warping them ragged. Among them, KE's and Gorgonettees lumbered and lifted like heavy sea beasts chasing each other through a grove of thread-fine seaweed. Death enacted its ribbon show on its own, a thousand feet above the Kirekuni Raw; the aircraft merely happened to have stumbled into the midst of it.

Or that, at least, was how it looked to Crispin from 1,500 feet. He had made his second kill of the day and he was circling above the dogfight, out of range of the ground fire, catching his breath, trying to see who was down, who missing. The two flights of KE-111s and 122s that had intercepted Vichuisse's strike force—though reduced from eighteen craft to twelve—darted about so fast that they seemed twice as many. But the odds were on their side. And the sky was clear. Kirekuni backups weren't pouring out of every corner of the compass, as they usually did when the enemy encroached even a half mile into their airspace. The simultaneous attacks north and south of here must have them on the hop.

The bunkers behind the Kirekuni lines were cracked open, burning. Antlike figures rushed to and fro on the ground. Screamers that had fallen from the air chased them like ravenous fireflies.

Crispin took *Princess Anuei* down into the action, yelling, his voice lost in the wind. Triumph—all too rare a feeling—surged through him.

It was the role of QAF officers to make their men believe every mission was the one which would decide the war. Morale was a function of hype. But work as Crispin and the rest might, the regulars had got wind of the fact that this was an unusually important strike. Last week, the infantry had lost a whole mile of ground in a defeat of unprecedented dimensions. Something had to be done to keep the rout from snowballing. The specter of losing Cerelon's Shadowtown—everyone's nightmare for fifty years—loomed large and solid. If Ferupe lost Cerelon, it lost the metalworks, which would probably mean the loss of the northern Raw . . . And that, in turn, could mean the loss of the war.

Night-long closet sessions between QAF and Army high-ups had resulted, among other things, in this mission: two crews each of Vichuisse's, Crispin's, Eastre's replacement Matheson's, and Burns's squadrons joining forces to stage an all-out attack on the section of the Kirekuni battle lines which the Queen's infantry hoped to overwhelm that night. To the north and south, Lennox and Hawthorne's men were mirroring their attack.

Crispin circled into the fiery gap where he'd last seen Jones. Screamer ports open, he roared straight at a KE-111 and pulled up at the last moment. In his rear sights the lizard stalled and plunged.

Easy as scalding babies.

He was *Princess Anuei*. He was her daemon. He was screaming. He was consciousness divided in twelve—single-mindedly pursuing his own prey, and at the same time keeping an eye on every man of his and Jones's crews. Thank the Queen, none of them had been lost. Yet. He was flying. He could not have said how many minutes it was until he caught a glimpse of a signal in the corner of his eye. He twisted. It was Vichuisse's lieutenant, Morton, performing the left-right-home. *What?*

Others had noticed, too. The flowing moment eddied into confusion. To port, a man of Burns's crew, caught off guard, was entangled in orange fire.

High and to the east, Vichuisse's Cerdres 500 looped the loop determinedly.

Obey orders!

It was so deeply ingrained that they had to do it even though the orders made no sense. The battle was by no means over. Kirekunis remained alive in the air and on the ground. The strike force had the odds in their favor—but their commandant wanted them to run for home, now.

Crispin's blood burned. *Bastard deserves everything Burns has planned for him!* he thought furiously.

Obey orders! But he had to make a token show of defiance—fool-hardy though it might be. He signaled his crew and Jones's and took them down for a last pass over the lines. Burns picked up the cue and followed with his ten remaining kites. One after another, moving too fast to be caught in the feeble ground fire, they emptied their screamer magazines into the disarrayed Kirekuni infantry. Finally they followed the rest of the strike force into the east.

The Cerdres 500 was a silver glint in the distance. Behind it, the wedges of Gorgonettees and Killer B-99s straggled out for miles. A good many of them, Crispin saw, had been damaged to the point where they were scarcely aloft. Burns's Bee was wobbling badly, its rudder broken half-off. Matheson, Eastre's successor, was gone. If a captain survived his initial dunking in the deep waters of combat, then he learned how to swim. Matheson, apparently, hadn't even been able to tread water. Perhaps Vichuisse had been right, after all, to pull out. *But still—*

In Crispin's reflectors, the surviving Kirekunis fled into the massed clouds on the western horizon. Seven KEs. Seven enemies who should have died today. They were strung far apart, probably suspecting a pincer maneuver, unable to believe they had been allowed to escape, seven tiny monoplanes like insects against the gigantic violet cumulonimbus that had threatened storm all day.

A dozen pilots of other squadrons who judged their planes too badly damaged to make it home, Burns among them, set down at Sarehole. After four months, Crispin was accustomed to this use of his base. He rattled off orders for accommodations to be made in the hangars without even thinking about it. Yet as he inspected the bullet holes in the wings of his men's kites, and soothed the trembling daemons with calm, a disconnected part of his mind wondered if Burns had exaggerated the damage to his plane in order to land at Sarehole and have another go at convincing Crispin to "commit."

If so, he had chosen his moment well! Crispin had never been angrier with Vichuisse. Only his knowledge of Burns's essential sneakiness made him cautious. When Crispin first met the Wraithblooded captain, he'd thought him as honest as the day was long. Now that he knew him better—and was party to his and Emthraze's deadly serious scheme against their commandant—he understood that although Burns *did* embody the virtues cherished by the QAF, honesty, bravery, patriotism, and a fighting spirit, there was not an ounce of traditional morality in his makeup.

The tension in the mess that evening was as electric as the storm-heavy air. Vichuisse's baseless decision to pull out had cheated the pilots of the catharsis of victory or defeat that usually followed an engagement. Aggression uglified their voices. Sitting at the captain's table, Crispin reached up to rub his neck. His body was rigid with tension. Usually when he landed after a battle he was shaking so badly he couldn't light a cigarette; tonight he was in perfect control of his limbs, but he felt as if he were about to explode. When he opened his mouth he was not sure at any point what was going to come out—harmless small talk or a vicious indictment of the commandant. It wasn't the first time in his two and a half years of flying with Vichuisse that such bizarre things had happened. And near catastrophes had become far more common since they moved to Salzeim.

The night was high and windy and dark when Crispin and Burns finally left the mess. Not a sliver of moon or one star showed through the clouds. "Something's got to be done," Burns said furiously, aloud. "We've got to *act*! Talk can't avert farces like this! Talk can't avenge Matheson! Something's got to be done!"

"Vichuisse didn't kill Matheson," Crispin said, though he had no particular desire to defend their commandant. "Man just wasn't good enough to cut it."

Burns snorted. "Think you? *He* deliberately assigned him first place in the attack. That's as good as telling a green captain to commit suicide."

"All the evidence in the world isn't going to get him indicted. Don't bother."

"Fuck that! How can you *not* be angry?" Lines of weariness showed on the Wraith half-breed's face as he lit a Belize cigarette. The wind blew several lucifers out and he cursed explosively before succeeding on the fourth try.

"Let's go for a walk," Crispin said.

"Let's go to your quarters and get drunk!"

"You want to talk treason with my men listening through the walls?"

Burns started to retort angrily, but then he shook his head. Side by side, they walked away from the mess hall, between the hangars where chinks of light around the big doors told them that 130 Squadron's riggers were working overtime on the damaged kites, into the grassy open. Behind them, the base lay invisible in the night, blacked out. The ground was wet, treacherous. Clods gave way to muddy sinkholes.

"Been talking to Sade," Burns said now in a confiding undertone. "Been talking to Lennox. I got an audience with Duncan last time I was in Cerelon. He gave us the go-ahead. Not in so many words of course. But what it comes down to is, even if they *know* what happened, even if someone, though I can't imagine who, kicks up a fuss—Thraxsson won't beef. Duncan promised me that."

"You trust him?"

Burns was silent for a moment. "He's a bit too good to be true, isn't he?" he said at last. "But we don't have much choice."

We. Us. The unspoken assumption of a shared purpose irked Crispin, although it should not have. "Why do you keep saying *we*?"

"I thought you were with us! Shit!"

"Look, of *course* I'm with you! I trusted you before you trusted me, remember?"

"The fuck is your problem then?"

"My question is, exactly who is *we*? Now that Matheson's gone, and Figueroa, is it just you, me, Keynes, and Emthraze? And who are we to take the law into our own hands?" Crispin had to force out the rational objection: the red beast wanted Vichuisse's blood, wanted him to burn. Three lieutenants had died since Crispin took over 130 Squadron—all of them flying with Vichuisse when they went down.

Taft. Kimble. Hammersmith. Crispin missed them sorely, but that wasn't the real reason he wished Vichuisse erased from the world. Three years of compelled gratitude and swallowed indignity could not find expression in words.

"Look," Burns said. "What good is the law if it gives us a commandant like him? The law is corrupt! The law is made in Kingsburg! This is *war*—and in war the insulted strike back! That's what it's all about! Would you rather have the *law* or your *life*? Because that's what it's going to come to sooner or later." He paused, then said more softly: "And besides, what has any Ferupian law ever done for you, Lamaroon?"

So that was the shape of it! Crispin had suspected it, but knowing nothing of Burns's past, had never asked. "If it comes to that," he said, "what has the law ever done for you, Wraith?"

"Ohhh," Burns said, his voice soft and terrifying the way Jacithrew Humdroner's had been when he called his daemons. "I'm not going to forget that." He made a hissing noise that could have been laughter, or not. "You'd better believe I won't forget that."

Crispin shrugged. It was what he had suspected. But what he wondered now was whether Burns had inherited that daemon-calling gift from one of his parents; Crispin had assumed he had it, and that that was why he'd survived so long in combat, but now he doubted it was true. Ferupian law would in one way or another have prevented a man with that gift, (Orpaan's gift, Jacithrew's gift, the trickster woman's gift a hundred times distilled) from getting anywhere near a QAF captaincy. If they had known about Crispin's resistance to gravity—which gave him a tiny but appreciable edge in combat, in that he could make up the weight with screamers—he probably would not have got his captaincy, either. He probably wouldn't even have got his wings. *Princess Anuei.*

They came to one of the small, sluggish streams that trickled across the expanses of the Raw. The water gurgled between grassy banks, as black as the sky, gleaming only slightly. Burns lit another cigarette. The wind blew the smoke into Crispin's face. *"Queen,* I wish we hadn't lost Matheson," Burns exploded. "He'd agreed to do it. Did you know that? I persuaded him. Sure, the giggling little fool would have agreed to anything in order to get connections—if *Vichuisse* had asked him to assassinate *me,* he would've agreed just as fast, I bet—

stupid snot just wanted to be *in* with someone so he'd make commandant—but no matter! He'd agreed! And then he has to go and fucking *die* on me!"

"Your persuasive powers are admirable," Crispin said drily. The sarcasm was lost on Burns, who was in full flow.

"I'd do it myself, I could even have done it today, and believe me I was burning to, but too many of those regulars didn't have a clue, they would've reported me faster than you can say toady. And it's not as if I'll have another chance. Vichuisse *never* assigns me to fly with him. I wouldn't even have been on the strike force today if he had drawn up the lists, but Thraxsson did it at HQ because of this situation we're in. Vichuisse must have been shitting his pants! He isn't stupid, he knows something's afoot, and he guesses it has to do with me, because I don't pretend to like him—I've never been any good at that kind of fakery—"

"Too fucking true!"

"Now you—he likes you—"

Crispin closed his eyes. He dug his nails into his palms.

"I've never understood that." Burns took a deep drag on his cigarette and cocked his head inquiringly. "Were you? At one point?"

"No! Queen, no!" Crispin spat into the stream, nauseated by the very idea.

"No need to jump down my throat. I've never seen you with a girl."

"That's because there was only ever one for me, and she's dead."

Cris, I'm not happy here! Please come and get me! I can't believe you've forgotten about me . . . For a moment the howling night rang with her voice. In the west, thunder growled like rocks moving.

"I'm sorry," Burns said.

"It was a long time ago."

"And you haven't since?" Burns laughed. "Queen."

For some reason, though it had nothing to do with the question, Crispin thought of the night he had spent at Air Base XV, the night he and Butch had sworn eternal friendship. Try as he might to forget it in the intervening months, it kept popping back into memory at the oddest moments. That night had been the beginning of the end of their friendship. He regretted Butch right now more than ever.

"Damn! You've got harder balls than I do!" Burns laughed so hard he coughed. He must have noticed Crispin's silence then, for he stopped and said in a completely different tone, "So? Are you willing?"

"What?"

"Oh, tch, tch, your gutter mind!" Burns laughed again, but it was gentle. "You youngsters! If only I weren't so fucking transparent to him, I'd do it myself. I've always hated that about myself: that I can't hide my thoughts. Sade Emthraze is the same, or he would do it, too. But he suspects us both. It's got to be you or Keynes. You were his men, he won't see it coming until he's being eaten alive by your screamers. And though I hate to admit it, both of you are more popular with your squadrons than Sade and me are with ours. You'll have a better chance of swearing them to silence."

"Have you asked Butch?" Crispin stared at the stream. How could water so black be so visibly in motion? Lightning flashed far to the west. The wind skirled a few drops of rain into their faces.

Burns made an "ugh" noise and pulled his muffler up round his ears. "Yes. But he's . . . I'm sorry, Crispin. But he's a liver lily. His teeth chattered—I swear to the Queen he nearly jumped out of his skin when I asked. Even if we *did* manage to pressure him into it, he'd probably fuck up or back down at the last minute and create a shambles we'd never hear the last of. It's got to be you. I truly am sorry."

"I . . . I can't." Embarrassment at his own weakness heated Crispin's face. He looked full at Burns. "It's my luck. I'm afraid—David—if it turns—"

Even in the darkness, he could see the harsh lines appearing on Burns's face. "I never took *you* for a coward!"

Shame and pride filled Crispin. He knew exactly what Burns was doing, and yet he could not resist. Burns embodied the pragmatic, diplomatically skilled, and yet hot-blooded ideal of a QAF officer, where Vichuisse embodied the reality: the death of the soul, paranoia, the foolish aristocrat's pride, the incompetence and stubbornness that had kept this war dragging out and dragging and dragging well beyond its allotted life span. Crispin wanted to kill Vichuisse, wanted to see him spiral down out of control into no-man's-land. And Burns knew that.

Burns's frown grew deeper. "I always thought you were one of the bravest men I know." He shook his head. "I'm not usually so wrong about people!"

Sincerity and manipulativeness were the flip sides of Burns's character, and sometimes, as now, they coexisted: Crispin *knew* he was being manipulated, and yet he could not stand for Burns, his one remaining real friend, to think him a coward. "I'm no liver lily," he heard himself say. "I'll do it."

"—Crispin?"

"I said I'll do it! Just give me the word!"

Burns grinned disbelievingly and held out his hand. Not for him the embrace, which smacked of the patronizing squire! Numbly Crispin shook his hand. "Queen! I *knew* you'd come through!"

In the west lightning flared again, silhouetting Burns against the horizon, and it seemed to Crispin that the brightness did not die down: rather, the bolts of lightning multiplied and changed color, going from blue to yellow, and now they no longer came from the clouds but the ground, leaping up from the miserable ramparts of the far-off battle lines which themselves looked strangely different, black and heaped, towering; and huge tongues of orange shot into the sky, reddening half the heavens as if an all-consuming dawn were coming from the wrong side of the world.

And Crispin could not answer Burns's questions about date and place and strategy, because it was dark, insufferably dark, and he had just seen Okimachi for the third time.

Avril 1896 A.D.
The Raw: Salzeim Parallel: Cerelon's Air Base XXI

In the middle of Avril, spring came. These tender yellow days were scandalously few. But while they lasted, the sunlight dripped with honey and the ephemeral scent of primroses and dog violets blowing on the breeze sweetened the moods of men. Victories were few, but no one seemed to care much. In summer, when the dust winds blew, skirling up the soil of the denuded Raw, aggravating hot-weather chills and fevers, the moment would catch hold of them again. It always did. But for these few days the QAF captains were hard put to knock a sense of urgency into their men—even though the army–air force initiative to prevent the Kirekunis from pushing forward to Cerelon had largely failed. The infantry retreat continued at an undignified pace. The troops were falling back so fast that the workforces scarcely had time to construct new ramparts before the soldiers were among them.

Among the supplies lost to the enemy were several hundred barrels of screamers. This security breach caused a flurry of panic at Army HQ. But even after sixty years of falling victim to screamers, the Kirekunis had no clear idea of how to use them, and in a series of fatal barrel-openings, they killed more of their own weapons experts than the Ferupians had all year. The real disaster was that they finally put two and two together in the matter of fire and daemons. Soon the SAF was no longer strafing Ferupian ammo dumps with fire-jennies, but bullets. Now it was up to the Ferupian soldiers to try to contain the destruction with flamethrowers—and to ferret through the ashes afterward in search of the precious nuggets of metal from the KEs' guns.

The retreat continued apace, and, by the end of Avril, as summer drew its first burning breath, one could see the new ramparts from the rise behind Sarehole.

The QAF was affected only indirectly by the streak of setbacks that had transformed Army HQ into a forcing bed for nervous breakdowns. The nature of the pilots' job did not change; succeeding merely became more important. And though the officers knew the missions they flew now *could* determine the war, it was difficult to make the regulars, whom experience had convinced that the fighting would never end, feel the same urgency. The only reason their hype continued to have any effect at all was because the death rate was so high, and climbing, that at any given moment, less than half the regulars in any squadron had served for more than a year, and so were unused to emergency as a way of life.

And this dreadful spring seemed to have induced fatalism in even the youngest hotbloods. Crispin fretted his days and nights away, wondering if 130 Squadron's relapse into the Jimenez pattern of loss after loss was due not to the yellow season, but to him: namely, to his distraction. The anti-Vichuisse conspiracy consumed most of his physical and mental energy. Even when he, Burns, and Emthraze were not meeting in secret to discuss their plans, he was pondering the deed he had agreed to do, and wondering how on earth he was going to slip it past his crew. He would have to enlist one of them, at least, to back him up. But who? Or could he go it alone? The moment he had imagined countless times already (sight-lock, screamers, tailspin, pieces of Cerdres 500 all over the Raw) had got into his bones. He could no longer place it in context.

The date they had set was the thirtieth of Avril. On that day, he, Vichuisse, and Butch were scheduled to fly a mission into no-man's-land.

On the twenty-seventh of Avril, a jeep drove up to Sarehole as Crispin was getting ready to take off on patrol. A groundsman came to Hangar One with the news that Flight Commandant Vichuisse had arrived to see the captain.

Crispin's heart thudded sickeningly. *He knows,* he thought. *He knows.*

His own voice sounded strange in his ears as he told the groundsman to ask the commandant to wait in his office. He looked around the hangar, seeing it with different eyes. The riggers were making the final check over the crew's kites, rushing here and there with silver nails, canvas glue, and last-minute tidbits for the daemons. In accordance with the bizarre superstitions of their trade (which Crispin did not condemn, having been immersed in them himself, and knowing they did the daemons no harm), they would not feed the daemons splinterons before a flight, instead pushing morsels of chocolate through the mesh hatches. The daemons loved chocolate, although they wouldn't touch any other human food. The side door opened, and the rest of Crispin's crew came in, suited up, carrying their helmets. Among them was Mickey, tail flicking. "Captain!" he shouted. "Do you know who's here?"

"Change of plans, don't worry!" Crispin called back. He grabbed a rigger. "Go fetch Lieutenant Jones! On the double! Give him my apologies and say due to unforeseen circumstances he'll have to take my patrol this afternoon!"

Unforeseen circumstances—the men were sure to assume the worst. Few reasons existed for a commandant to pay a surprise call to one of his squadrons, even given the rate at which briefs were being chopped and changed in Cerelon. After Vichuisse left, Crispin would have to dissemble better than ever before.

Always assuming he was still there to do it!

He gritted his teeth. On the way to his office he stopped in the lieutenants' quarters to make sure Jones had got the message and to change out of his flight suit into dress trousers and a jacket borrowed from Carnation, the tallest of the lieutenants. Carnation woke from a deathlike sleep to mumble, "Yeah, course, Captain, what's mine's yours, anytime . . ." and then rolled over on his face again. Crispin dragged somebody's comb over his scalp and tried on a welcoming smile in the tarnished mirror over the washpail. *Damned if I'll let him see he's caught me off guard!*

The day had started off sweet and fresh after a night rain, but it had rapidly turned blowzy. The sun was invisible behind a cloud haze, and the sky glowed as bright as an unshaded daemon glare. Horseflies buzzed around the slops outside the mess. Inside Crispin's office, the blackout curtains were three-quarters drawn, though he was sure he'd opened them that morning. Woodsmoke thickened the dimness. Vichuisse had opened two bottles of Crispin's Beaudonne lager and set out glasses on the overturned crate that served as a table; he was squatting by the hearth, trying inexpertly to start a fire. The day was so warm that it was unnecessary, but Crispin controlled his irritation. "Let me, sir." He nudged Vichuisse respectfully aside, arranged the kindling into a pyramid, and lit it with the speed of twenty years on the road. Then he opened the window to let the smoke out and sat down on a half barrel across from Vichuisse.

All his mental and sartorial preparation had been in vain. Vichuisse was clearly not in any state to notice what Crispin was wearing, let alone the nuances of his manner. As they exchanged pleasantries, Crispin wondered what state Vichuisse *was* in. The commandant had not shaved. Wrinkles marred his uniform. He smelled as if he had been drinking. A less definable scent—that metallic, nose-wrinkling whiff Crispin had associated with him since the earliest days of their acquaintance, which he had not since been able to identify with any brand of cologne—also hung about him. He tapped his foot with the incessant jerkiness of a drug addict. Yet his speech was as precise as ever. "It has been a long time since we talked, hasn't it, Kateralbin? I do miss those chats we used to have."

"Both of our posts are demanding, Commandant."

"Demanding, yes, yes, indeed. It is a strain." Vichuisse laced and unlaced his fingers. His mouth twitched.

Crispin eyed him dubiously. "Commandant—have you thought about taking some leave? You haven't had any in years, to my knowledge."

"You're implying that I need a rest!" Vichuisse smiled. "But why should I fritter away what time I have left?"

He does know! Crispin thought, nauseated with horror. Somehow he managed to control his voice. "Why do you say that, sir? Are you ill?"

"Only as we all are."

"Sir?"

"Is it unlucky to admit that one is going to die?" Vichuisse smiled pityingly. "I am going to die; you are going to die; so are all your fine young men, and their Shadow women. Every last one of us is sick with glory. This war is almost over, Kateralbin. We are making a heroic last stand, but had you heard what I have at HQ, you would know it is useless. The Kirekunis will be on us by the time the year is out, and they are without mercy."

"It isn't their intention to crush us, according to Mickey," Crispin said before he could stop himself.

"Mickey . . . ? Oh, Ash, Eighty Squadron, our pet lizard, yes." Vichuisse nodded. "He and I were once so close . . . I should like to see him. He's on base, isn't he?"

"I can have him sent when he gets back from patrol," Crispin said, and whistled to summon the sentry he had placed outside the window. "Yes. Pilot Ash. The commandant wishes to see him . . . I *know* he's out. Have someone tell him to come as soon as Lieutenant Jones debriefs the crew on their return."

"Thank you, sir." The door closed. As Crispin turned back to Vichuisse, he felt the irrational dislike and fear that the commandant always engendered in him. But now it was diluted with pity. What was Vichuisse, after all, but a withered little drunkard with food stains on the breast of his uniform? His eyes swam like red-dyed Queen's Birthday eggs in their sunken sockets. He looked older than his thirty-odd years. Had he *deteriorated* in recent months? Or had he ever been more than this? Had his superiority and seeming omniscience merely been illusions produced by the hierarchy? He relaxed on the half barrel as easily as if it were his own leather armchair, leaning against the wall, knees apart, one hand beating a careless tattoo on his thigh. But his face wore a pinched, tense expression, like the face of a neophyte walking a high wire for the first time, and Crispin realized what had changed. Every time he and Vichuisse had met before, they had been in the commandant's territory, or on neutral ground. This time they were in *Crispin's* territory. Crispin's very own office, in fact, the seat of the captain's power, which, lacking possessions, he'd furnished with jerry-built furniture and a few selections from Jimenez's leavings. He cherished it because it was the only space of his own he'd ever had; but it was the accidental simplicity of the decor he ended up defending to visitors who had grown up, one and all, in mansions full of chockablock rooms. Eventually he had decided he wouldn't change a thing even if he could. Now, for the first time, he understood why he felt so much at home here. The office could not have been less like Vichuisse's bourgeois sanctuary. Against the spartan backdrop, the commandant with his stylish neck scarf and shined shoes looked not just out of place, but flamboyant, superfluous.

Watching him drain his wineglass, Crispin said, "Sir, I'm busy. Was there a reason you wanted to speak with me? Something urgent?"

"No." Vichuisse smiled. "I simply wanted company. The time hangs heavy on one's hands, you know."

Crispin did not know.

"When one has no one to talk to . . . You and Ash. You were the only two men I ever commanded whom I could be honest with. When the Queen sent me first him, and then you, in the space of less than a year, I thought I was being rewarded for my perseverance in the face of dislike and subverted mutiny. I used to wonder what I'd done to deserve my men's disrespect! Now I know it was just that I was too passionate. Too passionate, at least, for these mercenary regulars and honor-obsessed lieutenants with whom we must contend."

Crispin winced. "Commandant, haven't you at least considered taking a couple of weeks off to fly home, see your family, take it easy—don't you think it would do you good?"

"And leave six squadrons in Burns's hands?" Vichuisse smiled. "No, the truth is, Kateralbin, that I could not abide to return to Ferupe without going home. And I cannot go home. Should you like to know why?"

Crispin shrugged.

"I was my parents' second child." Vichuisse paused, as if expecting Crispin to object at his starting from the beginning. After a moment he went on. "Shortly after I joined up, my older brother died of a fever—in no way akin to the fever that is consuming me now—but undoubtedly designed by the same evil. It was his unrequited love for a shepherdess on our estate. The physician called it pneumonia, but I knew better. I was the only one he confided in. After his death I had the option of being demobilized, but I stayed on the front."

"Why?"

It seemed to Crispin that as he spoke that one word, the faint bad smell in the room got stronger. Vichuisse wrinkled his nose as if he, too, scented it.

"I could not face taking responsibility for our unfertile lands—this is northern Lynche of which I speak, on the edge of the snowlands—our ungrateful villagers, and our cumbersome flocks of sheep. All my life I had longed to escape, and I was not about to let my brother's weakness cheat me out of my freedom. Besides, I was already in love with the air force." He smiled as if remembering. "The affair has lasted ten years now, and *my* passion has not cooled—although I have seen evidence lately which tells me *hers* has. Love's tragedy is that it must be unequal. Yet someone said that 'if there must be a lover and a beloved, let me then be the one who loves too much,' and I have lived by those words."

He cracked a smile. Crispin took a gulp of ale. The Beaudonne flamed in his insides.

"So I left the estate in the hands of my aging mother. About five years ago, she was taken in by cult charlatans who offered to buy our mansion and lands for a magnificent sum of money. She accepted, but no contract was signed; and in the absence of a written agreement, and since possession is nine-tenths of the law, she cannot do anything to get the land back, despite the fact that she is a daughter of one of the oldest families in Ferupe, and the supposed buyers are nothing but gutter scum, half of them lizards to boot. I suspect the nobility ignored her appeal because she disgraced herself long ago by marrying my father and forcing her family, the Amithres of Lynche, to accept him.

They have long memories, the Amithres, like all northern families. And they have great influence in Kingsburg."

Was that how you got your promotion to Salzeim? Crispin wondered, pitying him. *Your Amithres must have guessed, given your record, that any promotion would be a two-edged sword, as likely to destroy you as make you. They must have seen their chance to be rid of the blot on their name. Did you know that?*

Vichuisse sighed. "Mother writes to me, from the house in southern Lynche of her even more aged sister and my repulsive cousins, that she has been back to see the estate and that it has fallen into an appalling state of decay. The lizards have let all the servants go and let all the house daemons out of their cells; they have let the lawn go wild and carved ciphers into the teak furniture. The roof repairmen were turned away last winter. In short, Kateralbin"—the self-deprecating smile flashed again—"I'd rather die than go back to see it. I left once; and as an indirect result, the house—where I was born, and where, since I was not aware of the stratification in my family, I spent a happy childhood—as a result, that house has been destroyed. I cannot go back. Even though now that I sense my last days approaching, I have woken from dreams of the stone kitchen below stairs, and the taste of a new potato eaten out of one's hand with butter dripping between one's fingers—there is *nothing* like a new potato boiled straight out of the ground—and skating along the stream under the naked branches of the willows in winter, and the trout under the weir."

The colors of Vichuisse's uniform and decorations seemed to have faded as he told his little story. He seemed no more than a shade of his former self, a ghost lingering for a few moments before it fled to Lynche.

"I'm sorry," Crispin said at last.

"I didn't come here for your *sympathy*, Kateralbin, although it is touching in the extreme!" The commandant laughed, swung around, and lit a cigarette with a brand from the fire. "I merely came—one might say—to settle my affairs."

"Sir?"

"In the past I have not conducted myself toward you as a commanding officer should. I have come to make my apologies."

Crispin actually yelped in surprise.

"Yes!" Vichuisse's eyes glinted. "I condescended toward you when

I knew in my heart you would surpass me. Not wishing to see you ostracized, I concealed from my men the fact that you had spent time in Chressamo, when I should have let you account for your past yourself."

Crispin hadn't thought *Vichuisse* knew about Chressamo. If he had, he would never have gone anywhere near the captain. But of *course* Vichuisse had known! And as large as Crispin's debt to him had been, now it was infinitely larger.

"I treated you like the worst sort of recruit scum at the same time as I made you my protégé and gave you every advantage! I want to apologize both for picking you out of the mud and for throwing it in your face! Do you forgive me?"

Yes, Crispin wanted to say, *yes! You are my commandant!*

"Well, honest forgiveness can never be got just for the asking. I am glad you did not lie." Vichuisse shook his head and exhaled slowly.

"Why—sir—*why* did you favor me? Was it for the same reason you favored Ash?"

Vichuisse laughed, and evaded the question. "I always had a yearning for the exotic. You and Ash were as close as I was ever able to come to it. What I should really have liked to do was to travel to Cype, Lamaroon, Eo Ioria, the Americas . . . if there had not been a war . . . Oh, make no mistake, I am dedicated to this air force as I believe few are. But . . . well, it is too late now."

And Crispin remembered Butch standing in a moonlit alley in Cerelon, smiling and saying in the same self-deprecating, vaguely amused tone, *Too late now. Been thinking a lot lately about what I've missed . . . but it's too late now.*

Too late now. That night had put an untimely end to Crispin and Butch's friendship. Too late—

Jacithrew Humdroner, the mad Wraith, standing tippy-toe at the top of a dead pine, flapping his wooden wings and shouting delightedly, *I will fly and fly and fly away from this dead place to a land where all is life, I will fly south to Izte Kchebuk'ara where the sun shines all day and there are beautiful red-skinned women, where there is wine to be drunk beside a sparkling sea—*

Too late!

A dreadful flickering dimmed the room.

There had to be some way to escape the parade of skulls, the ribbon show—

But it's too late now! Flames in the hollows, and either I'm mad or the world is going to end in Okimachi, and I will be there, and I've visioned nothing beyond that night—

Vichuisse was staring at him with amusement. "Was that a goose walking over your grave? You look positively pale."

Crispin forced his fists to unclench. "Have you ever loved anyone, sir? A girl, I mean? I mean, *loved*?"

"Not as such . . . what does that matter?"

"I did," Crispin said, hearing his voice shake. "I did."

The familiar mocking smile leapt onto Vichuisse's face. "And never once said a word! You are a dark horse and no mistake, Kateralbin! To think that all this time I believed you and Keynes . . . And that was the only reason I offered him a post in Salzeim!"

Crispin shrugged. He was trying too hard not to see the pale flames coming out from under the skirting to take offense. "I had a girl, Rae her name was," he said thickly. "They killed her in Chressamo."

The amusement vanished from Vichuisse's face. "I am sorry!" He sounded as if he meant it. So had Burns, although neither of them knew Rae from the Queen. Everyone meant it, the first time; then the thrill of vicarious misery paled and they left you alone with your grief. Only this time the trouble was that Crispin could not locate his *own* grief. Despite having spoken the charm of her name, he still felt keyed up to the point of screaming, imprisoned in the coils of the plot into which he had thrown himself so recklessly, with no release in sight. Over the course of the last three years, the stirring of the red beast had continuously prompted him to seek refuge, consciously or unconsciously, in the old grief, which was immutable, certain, and above all, understandable both to himself and to others. But this time the ploy had failed. Rae had no power to free him from the enigma of Vichuisse. He tried to conjure an image of her face and saw Gorgonettees and KE-122s reeling in a blank sky. Words replaced coherent thoughts. "Black hair—Rae. I miss her. I don't know why I'm talking like this! I—"

"You mustn't brood. It will take the edge off your brain," Vichuisse reproved. "I want you to be more than I ever was. And I want you to succeed by the brilliance of your prowess alone, as I could not. You have the potential, you can be a commandant, maybe even lieutenant-marshal in time! If you let your career slip away over some girl, I will kill you!"

It was said in jest, but in Crispin's wretched state, every word resonated. "But I don't miss her anymore!" he protested. "I don't!"

"Good, then! Good! The QAF must be your first love, as she has been mine, if you are to succeed. And right now, her only hope is for those few who truly love her to give her their all—"

There was a knock outside. "Come in!" Vichuisse called—just as if it were his office, Crispin thought in a flash of renewed dislike—and Mickey entered, grinning, his cheeks flushed with altitude. When he saw Vichuisse his grin snapped off like a light. Watching the commandant as if he thought the unkempt little man would spring, he sidled inside and took a seat on the third half barrel. As if by magic, the flames died down. The air thinned and became breathable again as the tension surged, redirecting itself into new channels. Crispin's pulse slackened. "Have some Beaudonne, Mick!" he said expansively. "It's warm, but it's perfect!"

"What I need." Mickey knocked down half a glass straight.

Vichuisse's eyes sparkled. "I came especially to see you, Ash!" He made a dramatic gesture, placing one hand on his heart. "How long it's been!"

"Commandant . . ." Mickey had clearly noticed Vichuisse's bedraggled drunkard's appearance. He shook his head mutely.

"I am ill," Vichuisse said lightly. "You on the other hand, you're looking well!"

"The northern climate suits me. But I hate summer."

"Better alive in summer than dead in winter," Crispin said with a wink. "How was patrol? Sightings? Encounters?"

And in a few minutes he had managed to downshift the conversation smoothly into flight talk such as any three pilots, anywhere, might have shared. The topic held little interest for Vichuisse; it was obvious that he wanted to say certain things to Mickey which Crispin should not hear. As soon as Crispin saw the shape of things he made an excuse to leave, but Mickey kicked him in the ankle so hard that he stayed put. Vichuisse grinned knowingly, and proceeded to reminisce without a trace of embarrassment, as if he and Mickey were alone, although he did not fail to include Crispin in his repulsive innuendos. The Kirekuni deflected the stabs at his pride with astonishing grace. The only sign that the unraveling of his private life affected him at all was the rate at which his glass emptied. As Vichuisse chuckled on and on, Crispin was struck again by the strange impression that the commandant was *fading*: it was as if despite the lascivious anecdotes issuing from his lips, he possessed no more substance than a shadow in the corner twittering of the time when it had a body, and steadily dissolving as it poured out the memories that had given it an existence in this world.

But Mickey, especially now that he was drunk, was there enough to make up for Vichuisse and five more besides. Tail switching, scalp bristling black, smoke puffing from his mouth, he was more corporeal than a materialized daemon. Watching him, Crispin thought it was a wonder how he pulled off his blending-in act all day, every day. Was this special corporeality the reason he and the flames could not exist in the same place? Or was it because he was Kirekuni? Crispin did not know: it was enough to have gained a reprieve. In the absence of his personal horror, liberated from grief, nothing could faze him, not even Vichuisse's distressing indiscretions. Vichuisse was going to die two days from now anyway, so what did it matter? What did anything matter?

Vichuisse finally took his leave as twilight was falling. The fire in the hearth had died to embers, and the smoke haze in the room glowed orange as the sunset slanted in between the blackout curtains. Crispin and Mickey saw the commandant off in his jeep. They exchanged a sigh of relief as they reentered the office. "Hind leg off a donkey," Crispin said, and rolled his eyes.

Mickey laughed. "I'll leave you in peace, too, Captain." He turned to go.

Crispin stopped Mickey before the Kirekuni reached the door. "No. Stay. I have something I want to talk over with you."

Mickey's smile vanished. He looked suspicious and tired.

"I'll have supper sent in. You are hungry, aren't you?"

"Ravenous," Mickey said without a smile. He was rigid with tension. It showed in his shoulders, his stance. He must hate Vichuisse more than any other man in 130 Squadron. He would do.

"That simply wasn't on, was it?" Crispin said, sounding him out. "I would have left, but you—"

Mickey whirled around twice and threw up his hands in one of his operatic foreign gestures. "I thought he wouldn't bring it up with you there! The last thing I wanted was to be alone with him! And what the fuck was he thinking, anyway? What the fuck was he thinking?"

His vehemence startled Crispin as much as if a songbird had cawed like a crow.

"What does whatever happened in the Lovoshire Parallel between him and me have to do with the fact that I have a *patrol* to fly at dawn and I haven't slept for *days* and he's a bloody commandant and he should have more *sense*? Nothing! That's what! He's an insane inbred aristocrat worse than any of the rest of them! I always knew it, and now I've *seen* it! Mad! Mad! Mad! He's mad!"

"He's just a drunkard, but it comes to the same thing," Crispin said.

"No fucking joke! He—"

"He thinks he's dying."

"Ho, *does* he? Hypochondriac! Dying my ass! He's gonna live to be a hundred after he's killed us all with his fucking incompetence or *bored* us all to death with his slimy anecdotes!"

A breath of wind crept in through the open door. The slit between the curtains glowed red. The windows faced west, toward the sunset. Toward Kirekune. Crispin had never once asked Mickey about his native country. Although their acquaintance was as close as the gap of rank permitted, they had never spoken of anything personal. Not, at any rate, since the night at Fostercy when Mickey revealed that he was left-handed. For him, *that* was personal.

I'm a fool to confide in him, Crispin thought, and then said, "But you know, Vichuisse may be right. I should be extremely surprised if he survives the mission two days from now."

It took Mickey an astonishing two seconds to get the idea. His eyes lit up and his body spasmed as if he were about to hug Crispin. Then he flung himself across the room, pacing. "Who? Who? Who's in on it? What can I do?"

Crispin chuckled. "Not so fast! Captain Burns. Captain Emthraze. Captain Keynes."

"Everyone!"

"Not the fellow who took Matheson's place; Lang's a brown-nosing weasel. But Commandant Lennox. And Sublieutenant-Marshal Duncan."

"That means Thraxsson," Mickey said, and then something quick. Crispin asked him to translate. "Sorry! I said: 'Tell it to the Significant!' It means sort of, 'This is too good to be true!'"

Crispin smiled.

"What's the plan? A pincer maneuver? Who's going to—"

"It shouldn't be difficult. We'll be engaged by the enemy. It'll be reported as an accident—that is, if anyone even *notices* he was taken down by his own side."

Mickey frowned. "But they will. Have you ever seen Vichuisse put himself in danger in an engagement? He keeps to the edges and plays umpire. That's how he's lasted so damned long. It'll just have to look like a blunder—like somebody got disoriented. Do you want me—"

"No," Crispin said more sharply than he had meant to. "I want you to back me up. To edge him into my sights. And second me if I have to explain. That's all."

Mickey squinted. "You want him bad, don't you?"

Crispin half nodded, half shrugged.

Mickey sank down on a barrel-chair and performed his cigarette-lighting trick with his tail. "I love it! It's so Queen-damned Ferupian! I love it!"

"Don't *your* people bear grudges, then?"

"*Your people* . . . I haven't heard that for months! Nobody gives me shit around here like they used to. I think you terrified it out of them."

"I didn't mean that."

"If you had, you would've said *you lizards*. But no, we don't, we don't even *think* in terms of grudges. We don't ask questions. Orders are orders. If you're commanded to commit kamikaze, you're supposed to thank the Significant on bended knee for singling you out. I could never have done that, and I knew it—that's why I made such a terrible Disciple. That's why I ended up here."

"But what do you mean it's so *Ferupian*? Seems to me it's un-any-thing."

"Oh, no, no, no!" Mickey shook his head. "It's been too long since you were a regular, Captain! The rumors . . . In this parallel, they fly like birds. This death . . . *that* death . . . well, it wasn't an *accident*, you know, *he* wanted a promotion . . . well, *he* had a grudge against him for stealing his girl . . . and so forth and so on . . . sometimes I can't help laughing because it's just so parochial. War on the other side of the Raw, it's this gigantic finely tuned operation, the army and the air force and the Chadou, that's the civilians they moved in from the other side of the mountains, all following the same set of orders, all synchronizing like the different bits of a transformation engine. Our command is totally centralized and all our communications go by air. And it works because we're *winning*, Captain. There's an energy which reproduces every time the SAPpers gain ground. But over here . . . well, there's nothing organized about it! It's really just sanctioned murder of whoever you happen not to like, and all too often that isn't the enemy, but the fellow you see every day! The Ferupian military is eating itself."

"That's rather harsh."

"But it's true! The only explanation I've been able to think of, short of a difference in the national temperament, is that one hundred fucking years of defeat has—how can I put it—killed the daemon in the Ferupian war machine. And it's fallen apart into this gigantic mess of aggression which is so poorly directed that a hell of a lot of the time, people take it out on their own officers. And some of those officers, like Vichuisse, are trying to hold the system together, but it's absolutely fucking useless, because they're incompetent to practice what they preach, because of the ridiculous system you have for selecting officers, which is based on *social class*, of all qualifications, and which in my opinion is the *real* reason Ferupe started losing the war in the first place . . . And meanwhile, you all have this ridiculous faith in the Queen, as if she can't lose the war even though she really has nothing to do with it, as if she's some unstoppable force of *nature*!" He stopped, abashed, as if finally realizing he was treading on forbidden ground. "At least, that's what I think . . ."

"Do you despise us, then?" Crispin asked eventually. Mickey's words had stung him to the quick, and yet he had expressed more or less the same opinions accepted by all the officers Crispin knew, merely having arrived at them from a different, clearer perspective.

"Despise you? Significant, no!" Suddenly Mickey was serious. "How could I? This is my adopted country, isn't it? I *belong* here. In Ferupe. In the middle of this defeat. And no, I'm not having you on!

There's a family history of Ferupian tendencies—my aunt joined a Ferupian cult, and so did my uncle, ten years later. My mother's dream is to get Ferupian girls in her brothel: she knows what sells. I joined the Disciples, but now look at me, here I am, just like them! It's funny the way it comes out."

"And yet for a Ferupian, you have some very odd ideas," Crispin said.

"I do, don't I! Maybe I'm just trying to justify my own cowardice by deciding everyone else over here is a coward, too . . . But . . . but . . ." He closed his eyes and touched his lips with the tip of his tail. Then he opened his eyes again. Liquid black pools, almost perfectly round.

Crispin took pity on him. "Not that odd, actually. All the commanding officers think more or less the same thing, if you can get them to admit it. Congratulate yourself on your perspicacity, rather."

"Don't flatter me."

"I wasn't."

Mickey bit his lip. It was an oddly endearing gesture. "You aren't going to change your mind, are you? You're still going to . . . involve me?"

"There isn't anyone else in this squadron," Crispin said. "There's Butch. Captain Keynes of One-forty-five Squadron, I mean. But I—I can't depend on him."

"I hate Keynes's guts. He hates mine. He blames me for everything that ever went wrong when I was in his crew. I'd kill *him* if I thought I could get away with it . . . Does *that* change your mind?"

"Bit late now," Crispin said dryly. "You could rat on all of us. I've *got* to involve you!"

And for a second the flames appeared again, dancing high between him and the Kirekuni, blotting out his vision; but they had no heat, no power, and they vanished as quickly as they came. The air was dim and sharp. The smoke from the cigarette Mickey was holding in a twist of his tail smelled like campfires, like toasting bread, and Crispin suddenly realized how hungry he was. Outside, the first night patrol was taking off. The grumble of daemon engines came almost too low to be heard. Voices yelled over the wind, which blew chilly through the open window—summer was not *quite* here yet.

"I've always thought you were different from the rest of them,

Captain," Mickey said. He had been observing Crispin with his head on one side.

"So has everyone else."

"I mean as an airman. The rest of them just say they love glory, they *say* they live for the kill . . . but you, you really do. You may be bloodthirsty, but that's so refreshing. And you value your squadron's efficiency over your personal advancement. Or at least, that's how I've perceived it."

Four years in Ferupe had given Mickey an irritating habit of qualifying everything he said, which detracted not a whit from the inflammatory nature of his opinions. "Don't suck up to me, Pilot," Crispin said. He was wondering how he could seal the other's complicity and dismiss him. Mickey was simply too perspicacious and opinionated. He made Crispin uncomfortable.

"I wasn't sucking up! I just wanted to tell you that I admire you! Is that a breach of propriety?"

"Call me Crispin. As if propriety hasn't been breached just about as thoroughly as it can be, this afternoon."

"Yes! But that's what I mean! You're so *different* from *him* . . . Even in a matter like this you're straightforward. When I first came here, I thought all Ferupians were such bastions of honor! I thought they did from their hearts what we do because we're ordered to. Then I realized the truth. And I thought, there has to be someone who really *is* like that, who embodies grace and selflessness and bravery and all the rest of it, what they praise in the anthems. But I never met him until you joined Eighty Squadron. Do you remember when you wouldn't flog me because you knew it wasn't fair? I thought, this man is the real thing. I couldn't believe my luck when you traded me with Captain Keynes."

He's a boy, Crispin thought, gazing at the pale, excited face. He was twenty-three, the same age as Crispin, but right now he did not look it. *A boy, hero-worshiping someone who once did him a good turn.* That night outside Vichuisse's quarters . . . Crispin had forgotten all about the flogging until this moment. "Don't be ridiculous, Pilot," he said coldly. "You don't know the half of it."

"What's the other half, then?"

"Nothing that would improve your pretty picture of me."

"But I don't really know *anything* about you, Captain," Mickey said. "I'm just going on what I've seen. See . . . I think you're going to crash and burn. If you want to know the honest truth, I don't like the sound of this thing we've got ourselves into. Burns . . . Emthraze . . . Keynes . . . Lennox . . . Duncan . . . and all their men . . . why must *you* be the one who actually *does* it?"

"Think about it."

"Well, I'm all for exing Vichuisse, but *you're* the one in the pilot's seat! And I think you're going to hit turbulence, but I can't say whether it'll be good or bad . . . I don't want to speculate, either. I just wanted to tell you that I'll be at your back when it happens."

Crispin had never had a worse hex laid on him. Paralyzed, he felt his luck oozing away from him, beading out of his skin like sweat, dripping to the ground. He rubbed his eyes with the heels of his hands, rubbing away the premonition, and when he looked at Mickey before the other had time to rearrange his features, he saw that revealed on the Kirekuni's face which he had hoped not to see.

Mickey *would* have Crispin's back two days from now, then, even if something went horribly wrong, which pray the Queen . . .

Such a depressing explanation for his enthusiasm. But was there ever any other explanation? Crispin wondered in a fit of gloom. Or did all human interactions reduce eventually to that one viscous back-and-forth tide?

A cough and a shuffle outside the door alerted him to the silence inside the room. He and Mickey had been closeted in here far too long. And after Vichuisse's visit, the men probably already suspected something was afoot! "At ease, Mick," he said, and clearing his throat, called to the groundsman outside the door: "Come in, damn your eyes, don't stand outside eavesdropping like a bloody Shadow! Come in!"

"Captain Burns to see you, sir," the night-shift man said as he opened the door.

Crispin saw the unspoken *Again* in the man's face. He blew out his breath and spared Mickey a quick smile. "Tell him I'm waiting to receive him . . . and have our suppers sent from the mess, with three plates. Oh, what the hell, tell them to whip up something a bit better than usual. Have them go through stores. This is going to be an all-nighter."

*   *   *

Twenty-four hours later, he was in the Officers' Club at the once-a-month get-together. He had no more liking for these civilized orgies of booze and hypocrisy than he had had before he ever attended one. The gatherings were meant to reinforce amity among the captains and commandants, but everyone deplored them as a waste of time, even though they attended religiously. Crispin usually just flew in to Cerelon the next morning for the briefing meetings. But tonight, in light of the secret drama which was to unfold the day after tomorrow, he had to be at the club.

No one except the conspirators themselves was supposed to know about the plot. Crispin had come to see whether, in fact, they *did.*

But all seemed as usual. Smoke and talk filled the clubroom. Cocktails were consumed faster than beer at a public flogging in Kingsburg. Burns was at his suavest; Emthraze sat in a corner, exchanging secret smiles with his vodka; Vichuisse was giving his all to anyone with an iota of compassion; Butch was doing the rounds to a warm reception. Crispin wondered if he was imagining that since Butch and he had stopped being friends, both of them had become more popular with the rest of the officers. The first time they had both attended one of these gatherings—on what Crispin thought of as *that terrible night*—Butch's efforts to ingratiate himself with their colleagues had been largely spurned. Now he was the life of the party. Had he been networking behind Crispin's back? One thing was certain, he was uproariously drunk. When he performed a Dewisson song-and-dance number on top of a coffee table, heels clacking like out-of-sync castanets, Crispin wanted to sink into the floor.

But this was not possible, even metaphorically. Despite his efforts to keep a low profile, one officer after another claimed his attention, pressing drinks on him, smiling toothily, regaling him with meaningless good wishes. Crispin watched their eyes. Were those flashes of complicity—or merely the wet gleam of drunkenness?

"Good job on One-thirty, Kateralbin! Keep it up!"

"Glad to see you in town at last. We thought you'd kicked the bucket!"

"Where's your sidekick, Captain? The Kirekuni, I mean! Ha!"

Their hearty, double-edged jocularity convinced Crispin that a good many of them knew more than they ought. He shot a vengeful glance at Burns, who was holding court in another corner, as if he already possessed the commandancy that would surely be his within the week. Burns looked up. Their gazes met across the crowded room. Crispin frowned at him. *What the hell?*

Burns mouthed something that looked like *Don't worry*—and then the crowd surged between them, blocking Crispin's view.

Furiously, Crispin plunked his drink down on the arm of someone's chair. How *dare* Burns? The occupant of the armchair shifted and knocked the drink onto the carpet. Neither he nor Crispin bothered with apologies. The Shadow maids would clean up a hundred such accidents before dawn. *How dare he?* Crispin stared in the Wraith-blooded captain's direction as if by the sheer magnetism of his gaze he could force Burns to look at him again. But the water-dripping obelisk stood in the way. It glowed like a column of light, like the answer to all questions, casting those answers in little bright undecipherable fragments on men's faces and on the backs of their jackets.

Crispin had not had any sleep the night before. He, Burns, and Mickey had talked until dawn, when Crispin and Mickey were scheduled to fly, and Burns departed in a mist of good humor. The fatigue was getting to him. He'd leave soon, go to the room he'd commandeered in HQ, and sleep, blessedly alone—

"Cris!" It was Butch, flanked by a bevy of captains. "How *are* you? Haven't seen you in *years*!"

He held a cocktail with a little wooden monkey perching on the rim of the glass. His face was flushed from the exertions of his dance routine, his lips wet, his jacket buttoned askew. A horrible chord twanged in Crispin's gut. He wanted to pretend nothing had ever happened to drive them apart; but Butch had blundered so badly at first, in ignoring Crispin, that now, no matter how friendly he acted, it would be impossible to revise the past. "You're not a particularly appealing sight when you're drunk, my friend," Crispin said wryly.

"I'm stone raving sober! And I'm about to get even soberer!"

The rest laughed appreciatively.

"We're gonna make an *excursion*, Cris. Discover 'the dark beauty inherent in the night'!" More laughter. "Ask you if you wanted to come!"

"Underage Shadow girls may be your cup of tea, they aren't

mine," Crispin said. His own rudeness astonished him. "And your *actions* led me to believe they weren't yours, either."

Everybody grinned. There were too many jokes made daily on that topic for them not to know what was meant. Butch's eyes clouded briefly as the jab hit home, and then opened wide. He was going to choose not to get it. "Ah, yes, my poor, beloved Katerina! But, Cris, she's five hundred miles away and happily married, too; I daresay *she* won't be offended! Nor will your Miss Duckworth! Or was it *Cloth*worth? Duckwright? Do come."

"Clothwright," Crispin said. He felt his patience about to snap. "As if it mattered."

"He's had a drop," one of Butch's followers said. "Let's go, Keynes. Leave him."

"Hot-shot ace, my ass."

"Shut up." Butch turned to them. "And fuck off, why don't you?"

They laughed. Apparently even when Butch cursed at them he could do no wrong. "I'll catch up with you outside. Be just a minute. Grab my coat, will you?"

And they moved off and Crispin and Butch were momentarily isolated among the loud eddies of the gathering. In that instant the mask of joviality melted off Butch's face, revealing distress. "Cris! When it goes off—I wanted to talk to you, tell you—"

"Tell me *what*?" Crispin said bad-temperedly. The realization that he had misjudged Butch's degree of inebriation made him feel even worse than before, and therefore crankier. He despised Butch. He missed him.

"Not here! Can't tell you here!"

"And I'm Queen-damned well not coming with you to some sleazy Shadow brothel!"

Butch cast a desperate look around, as if expecting inspiration to spring from the air. "You, me, and Vee on the thirtieth, two crews each, right?"

"Right."

"Word is they're gonna revise the composition tomorrow. Burns got Duncan to throw his weight about a bit. He—Burns—is in and I'm out."

"Frankly, I'd rather have Burns than you at my back, anyway," Crispin said. "And I'm gonna find this all out tomorrow, right? So—"

Butch moaned. His gaze darted over the crowd, the air, the ceiling, everywhere except Crispin's face. "All right, all right! It was me who badgered Duncan! Burns was pissed as all hell."

Whatever Butch was trying to communicate was getting less comprehensible by the minute. Crispin sighed. "Go away! You've said your piece."

"You—I—oh, all right. I just wanted to say good-bye, that's all!" Butch rooted in one pocket after another. "Shit!" With an air of desperation, he pulled the monkey decoration off the rim of his glass and thrust it into Crispin's hand. "Here. I want you to keep this. It's a bit of nothing, I know, but it comes from me, I want you to remember that. Please. All right?"

"All right!" Crispin said bemusedly, pocketing the monkey, thinking that Butch must have meant to bring some good-luck charm for Crispin to take on the fateful mission. It was quite sweet of him. Or else—

"Hey, screw her brains out for me. Okay? I'd come if I weren't so tired."

"You would bloody well not, and I wouldn't either," Butch said, giving Crispin a look of disgust. "You think I do this shit because I enjoy it? It's public relations, boyo, pure PR." And then he was gone, swaggering with perfectly faked tipsiness through the crowd to his cronies, who were hailing him loudly from the door, waving his greatcoat at him like a flag.

Left alone, Crispin took the monkey out again and looked at it. It was carved of some dark brown hardwood and it had long legs, realistically crafted so that it could cling to the rim of a glass as if that were a tree branch. It had a skinny curled tail. Its face wore an almost human expression. Funny, he'd seen these little trinkets a hundred times but never noticed the workmanship that went into them. What craftsman in what far-off domain—or faraway country—had carved this little "bit of nothing" all unaware that it would end up on the war front in someone's martini?

What I should really have liked to do was to travel to Cype, Lamaroon, Eo Ioria . . . If there had not been a war . . .

Crispin did not move from his corner, but he found himself exchanging identical phrases of small talk with an unending parade of faces. Everyone of any importance, all the way up to the lieutenant-marshal himself, was seeking him out. What on earth did they all want from him? The only possibility he could come up with was that those in the know—which seemed to be just about everyone except Vichuisse himself, who was still bumping and buzzing against the walls on the other side of the room, getting no more attention than a half-dead bluebottle—those in the know had chosen him to be the next commandant, not Burns, and that they were subtly congratulating him on it. But that was not possible.

On the other hand, Burns was angry about something. When Crispin exchanged the rote pleasantries with him, the Wraith-blooded captain's evil expression belied his tone. He mentioned Butch several times, needlessly. Crispin gathered the two conspirators had had a falling out.

Faces. Pink, flushed faces. White, sweating faces. White scalps showing through close-shaved fair hair. One slightly darker face, belonging to Burns, who actually looked good in the military buzz cut, since his head was shaped as beautifully as if it had been turned on a lathe. One luxuriant shock of pepper and salt, neatly parted on the side—that belonged to Thraxsson, whose rank permitted him to forgo the buzz cut. What was Thraxsson doing here, anyway? He almost never attended these gatherings. Maybe that was why the crowd was so lively.

In the midst of the noise Crispin felt horribly alone. He hadn't intended to get drunk, but somehow, by taking polite sips of each of the drinks people handed him, he had become so inebriated that his mind had stopped working properly. Finally he gave himself up to the flow of the night. An endless string of affirmatives.

Faces—

I was the shadow of the waxwing slain
By the false azure in the windowpane;
I was the smudge of ashen fluff—and I
Lived on, flew on, in the reflected sky.

—Vladimir Nabokov

Here's the Real Truth, Kid

30 Avril 1896 A.D. *The Raw: Cerelon's Air Base XXI*

The morning of the thirtieth dawned bright and clear. When Crispin stepped outside he realized it was the first real day of summer. The air was absolutely still; the sun had already bleached the sky. The only sound was the sharp tan-tara of the bugle floating from somewhere near the barracks, where the talented pilot who regularly performed the reveille was ornamenting it with trills and minor notes. It was a perfect day for flying.

An unsuitable day for murder. Everything would be visible for miles.

Don't hex yourself, Crispin thought, and he rapped his knuckles against the wall of the mess. A splinter caught in his skin, drawing a bead of blood.

At 9:35 he gave a pep talk to his crew and to Jones's. At 9:45 everyone scrambled for their kites with perfectly choreographed haste. Crispin admired the way they followed each other onto the runway at precise intervals, taking off far enough apart for safety, yet close enough that not a fraction of a minute was wasted. How much they'd improved! Jimenez would not have known them.

Crispin himself took off at the very end of the queue. The wind whipped past the cockpit as *Princess Anuei* gained speed. The bellowing of the daemon sounded like music in his ears—full of energy, sharp like trumpets, deep as a double bass. Then the kite lifted, and Toeleris's roar died to a purr. Helmeted and goggled, Crispin took a brief look down. It never failed to amaze him how unassuming Sarehole appeared from the air. Just a handful of wooden dice without spots thrown down on the vast flatness of the Raw. No trees to shade the base; only the threadlike stream from which the ground crews drew water, some two hundred feet away. No one would ever guess that fifty men lived and worked here day in and day out. The buildings looked deserted. Perhaps *that* was why the base had thus far, in Crispin's tenure, escaped the ground-strafing of which Burns had warned him—the lizards thought it *was* deserted now.

Or maybe they simply had better things to attend to.

Crispin gave the signal for his crews to form one large wedge, with himself at its leading tip. They headed south. The warm gale exhilarated him. His hands were perfectly steady on stick and whip-cord. Several miles to the east, they sighted the wedge of aircraft spearheaded by the silver Cerdres 500, and farther off, the identically sized wedge which could only be Burns and his men. The plan was for them all to converge over the Ferupian front, ten miles to the south. Then they would make for their target—the Kirekuni infantry which scouts said had been massing for days opposite the spot where the strafing of an ammo dump had weakened the Queen's lines. It was in the middle of the battle which was sure to ensue, as soon as a Kirekuni patrol got wind of them, that Crispin planned to act.

10:36 A.M.
The child that the wind and the earth had when they danced

But eleven years earlier, when he watched his mother die (although he had not known that was what was happening), he had *not* acted. He had knelt frozen behind the curtain among Anuei's prohibited props, caught between the instinct which told him to scream and the fear of betraying his presence in the black top, where his mother had forbidden him ever to set foot on pain of "the worst beating you ever had from the biggest roughneck in this circus and break my heart, too."

* * *

Joie 1885 A.D.
Ferupe: Linhe Domain: Gilye City

Breaking Anuei's heart was the only childhood nightmare that still
frightened Crispin, now he was training on the flying trapezes and
growing an inch a week. Anuei's regular threats had not lost their
power, but gained it, if anything, now that he felt himself maturing
beyond the *ability* to obey her. She hated the fact that he was training
with the Valentas, but he couldn't give it up just for her. And here in
the hot dry east, the smell of Millsy's uncollared daemons pervaded
the circus lot like dust, and he could not help scanning the crowds
who trickled past the ticket booth, looking for his father's relatives.

And Anuei was saying, "No! No!" and she was struggling,
"Don't!" in the middle of the act in which she had engaged with her
customer. Crispin knew what they were doing, but he had never seen
it done like this, and he wanted to be sick. And Anuei was crying
weakly, "Stop, it hurts!" and then something in Lamaroon, and then
she was still. And after an obscenely long time the little tanned easterner pulled away from her and scrambled around the tent like a huge,
desperate spider, picking up this, putting down that, checking her
pulse, whimpering, and finally seizing on what he must have seen as
the only possible solution—but Crispin didn't understand that, nor
would he *ever* understand, for in later years he would not allow himself even to remember those moments when he crouched, a terrified
pair of eyes and ears, hearing (uncomprehending) the first crackle of
flame, seeing the bright flower in Anuei's long hair, and not being able
to move.

She had always taken a metal fire-bowl into the tent with her, for
burning incense. It was one of the many ironies of her career that
incense was not a Lamaroon tradition. It had first been introduced to
Ferupe by eleventh-century explorers who traveled to the far-off
Asias. Seven centuries later, it was popular in many parts of the continent, and the cheapest and best sorts all came from Cype; but it had
never caught on in Lamaroon, perhaps because people there were too
poor for frivolities, and uninterested in mysticism, or perhaps
because the natural smells of that island country were so powerful

and delightful that no artificially produced scent could compete. But then again, almost none of the accessories Anuei used to set the mood in her tent were authentically Lamaroon. In the nineteenth century, Lamaroon—Anuei had philosophically told her son—was just too much like a hotter Ferupe. At least the Lamaroon that people *knew* was. Authenticity would have bored them. Most of the props were Cypean trash-deco, with the odd trinket from Izte Kchebuk'ara.

And here the circus was on the Cypean border again, and Anuei had told her son she'd asked Saul Smithrebel, as a special favor which everyone had known he would grant her, because he always did, to show the outskirts of Gilye for three days straight while she made a shopping expedition into the Cypean sector to replenish her supplies of incense, glass beads, tattoo inks, and suchlike. The border between Ferupe and Cype, as it had most recently been redesigned, cut straight through the city. Anuei had told Crispin that this time he was old enough to accompany her. He anticipated the trip with avid curiosity. The roustabouts had tried to scare him with horror stories about Cypean ghosts and vampires and religiosos—he half expected that as soon as he and Anuei crossed that invisible line down the middle of Border Street, these oddities would start popping out of the walls; he wanted to be able to report to his older friends that they *hadn't*. All his friends were grown men, but he did not consider them any different from himself. At twelve, he stood on the borderline; his childish curiosity was beginning to be tinged with the darker, more dangerous curiosity of the adolescent. He had just been initiated into the firing of daemon rifles, and promoted to the roster of sentries who stood duty every night outside the circled trucks.

It was a combination of these things that made him, for the first time in his life, risk breaking his mother's heart. He wanted to witness her exotic dancing and her inking of tattoos on stunned men's biceps and backs. Surely, even if she discovered him, she was pleased enough with him at the moment, as evidenced by the offer of the shopping trip, that her heart wouldn't break?

And she *couldn't* discover him!

What he did not know as he wormed under the edge of the black top, having coaxed a reluctant Millsy to stand guard while he worked out one of the tent pegs, was that Anuei's heart was going to break— or rather to *pop*, as a result of her obesity and a particularly unnatural sexual position—that very afternoon. The inside of the tent was black after the dazzling eastern sun. Wriggling under the canvas, laying it flat behind him so that not a crack of light should enter, he found himself in a narrow curtained-off space full of boxes. He eased them aside to make room to kneel. His fingers itched to lift the lids of the boxes—anticipating wetness, smoothness, lumpiness, he did not know what—but he sought the overlap between the curtains. He could already hear the sounds. Such sounds, inadequately disguised by the chirping of Anuei's rare birds!

The curtains were heavy and dark red. Cheeks burning with shame, Crispin eased them apart just far enough to see.

Gilye, everyone agreed, was a strange city. None of the performers or roustabouts liked it. They hailed from northern and central Ferupe, and they did not like the east in general. During the middle hours of the day, Gilye was deserted; at night, it came alive with gaslight and crowds and weird, tuneless tinkly-tonk music. But the Gilyanese, like most easterners, thought entertainment was as important as food and sleep—that was because they were all half-Cypean, the Old Gentleman maintained—and so they flocked to the circus, not knowing or caring that Smithrebel's was just a mud show. They had never seen Murk & Nail's, or Gazelle's, or the Stix Brothers'. To them, Smithrebel's Fabulous Aerial and Animal Show was as exotic as their honky-tonk music was to the Ferupian circus band. "And that's why we keep coming back here!" the Old Gentleman railed when his people grumbled. "Where d'you think your salaries come from when we're stuck in some western dirthole? Eh? They come from *these* sons of bitches and their triple-Queen-damned Cypean trade route! *Now* who says I don't know about saving for a rainy day?"

It was on the eastern swing before last, Anuei told her son with an artful mist in her eyes, that she had met Joe Kateralbin, Crispin's father.

"He told me he loved me," she said.

He had come to see her act. Then he had come again. And again. And again, paying twice what she charged each time.

"First I didn't believe him when he said he couldn't live without me. Then he signed on as a roustabout—one of our men did run off with a Cype girl. And after that he didn't talk to me no more, just sat staring at me with those big sad eyes across the fires at night. Couple of months down the road, I had to believe him."

She sighed nostalgically. Crispin, as a child, had pressed her to continue. The middle of the story varied—Anuei enjoyed inventing romantic vignettes too much to keep repeating the same thing over and over—but it always ended the same way. "Joe couldn't stand this cold northern climate. He got feverous. He needed the sun, that man, like you and me need air. I nursed him for weeks—you being just a new baby I wasn't performing anyhow—but he died no matter what. Aah!" She pulled a horrible face. "Saul cried crocodile tears at Joe's graveside, him. He was joyous!"

And the postscript of the story, which Crispin recited in silence, grinding his teeth, was that after Joe Kateralbin's death Saul had got .Anuei back.

Crispin did not know, of course, that Saul had had her to himself all along; that the stories of Joe were an elaborate fiction created by Anuei because she hated Saul and was ashamed of having let him father her child; that she had chosen his surname because there had been a roustabout named Kateralbin who died of fever around the time of Crispin's birth. Crispin had no ties to the east except the ones of which he convinced himself. In the fullness of time he would find out the truth. By then, he would feel so strongly about the east that that particular element of Anuei's fiction would have passed into reality. But now he was only twelve, and it was the middle of the day in that hot city where he believed Anuei had met Joe, and the customers drifting along Smithrebel's tiny midway were probably the only people awake in the entire city, for most of the circus people, too, had succumbed to the heat and were resting in the trucks before the evening performance. And inside the incense-gloom of the black top, Crispin watched in terror as flames sizzled in Anuei's hair and leapt up the painted hangings. The rare birds beat against their cages. Anuei did not move even when the fire caught her wooden beads (she wore nothing else) and spread to her pubic hair. The john was long gone—he had gibbered, setting the fire, and slipped out as silently as a thief—and Crispin knelt paralyzed behind the curtain, tears pouring down his cheeks.

Only when the smoke got thick enough to throw him into a spasm of coughing did he move. He struggled out from under the side of the tent, choking, his eyes running. Millsy had been waiting anxiously outside; he wondered why Crispin had not yet reemerged, but he hadn't seen the threads of smoke escaping through the seams of the tent. He tried to catch Crispin, but the boy eluded him. Sobbing, Crispin dashed toward Sunflower 1, shouting for Saul. "Old Gentleman! Old Gentleman! Anuei—fire—the fucking *bastard*—help—fire—"

In his terror, Crispin had used his private name for Saul, and so neither Smithrebel nor anyone else knew who he was calling. But his distress alerted a good number of locals and midway vendors. When they saw the flames bursting from the roof of Anuei's tent, the crowd dissolved briefly into chaos, but inside a minute everybody was organizing one of those spontaneous efforts to combat disaster which some say are a measure of our humanity. A local man, a complete stranger, took it on himself to crawl into the black top and try to rescue Anuei. It was far too late, of course. By the time Saul arrived on the scene four minutes later, the flames had been put out, and Crispin, hysterical for the second and last time in his life, was being held back from the steaming wet ruin.

Some of Anuei's props were salvaged—although Crispin never found out what happened to them after that (he suspected Saul of confiscating them). But the Balloon Lady herself was unsalvageable. The exotic dancer, the skilled prostitute, the tattoo artist, the mother of one and lover of one who wept all night for her (Crispin in the multiple arms of the Flying Valentas, Saul alone), the woman who had had the distinction of being the only full-blooded Lamaroon performing in a Ferupian circus at that time—Anuei Eixeiizeli was three-quarters cremated already.

Saul canceled both the performances that night. No one objected. Anuei had been better loved than she had been appreciated. They cremated the rest of her on the spot. The Gilyanese came in crowds to see the circus, and when they found that it was off, they stayed to watch the funeral pyre. Some of them helped the festival atmosphere along by setting off fireworks and tossing strings of red crackers into the fire. Others started a tuneless, catchy Cypean chant. Crispin was staring miserably into the fire when he found himself caught up in an impromptu conga line snaking around him. A toothless, grinning Cypean woman gripped one of his hands; a boy a few years older than himself took the other. His feet were drawn into the stamping, shuffling dance step. The other boy bent forward and shouted, "Sing up!" Timidly, Crispin added his voice to the chorus. Soon he was singing so loudly and being tugged about so fast that the tears were dry on his cheeks. He could not cry. He could not even think.

Saul and Millsy both found the Gilyanese people's disrespect horrendous. Joining forces for what was probably the first time in their lives, they encouraged the Ferupian roustabouts to break up the party. The locals departed, cursing quietly. Saul shot their dirty looks back at them; he was thinking, wildly, that Gilye no longer seemed so hospitable, and that with Anuei gone there was no reason to stay, they'd move on this very night, yes, move on, and with an armed man riding on the roof of every truck—

Detached from his companions, his back to the dying bonfire, Crispin scuffed his feet in the dust. The night wind blew cold. The stars shone faintly overhead, misted by the lights of the circus lot.

Saul's hand closed on his shoulder.

10:37 A.M.
Kherouge: Center City: the Enclave of the Most Patriotic
Consecrated Sisters
Sun-time

"My blood is Royal!" chanted Rain with the others. "My body is Royal!"

The pianola's slow, majestic chords rolled out from the back of the chapel like waves of sound, breaking over the veiled heads of the Consecrated, whence the foam of voices rose. Rain knelt in the back row, where the pianola was loudest. Sister Fairday clasped her right hand, Sister Breeze her left. The chapel was full of summer dust— right outside the windows lay the courtyard in the middle of the Enclave—and the musky incense the Consecrated used to combat the dust added to the weight of the air: but by moving her head infinitesimally to one side or the other, she could smell Fairday and

Breeze's good, familiar soap-and-onions perfume. The women prayed slowly, in a manner that tested both vocal pitch and lung capacity, prolonging each word on note after downsliding note, so that what might originally have been conceived as a hymn became a mantra. Repeat after repeat, Rain's lips and lungs formed the words on their own, and her mind wandered where it had been wandering far too often lately: out of the Enclave, out of the familiar streets of Kherouge, into the vast, terrifying, scintillating world where she had been Rae, and from which she had fled. The memories of that flight still gave her nightmares. She was all of twenty-one now, and a mother, and she had been safe in the Enclave for two years. But she still cried in her sleep. And Breeze had to slide into bed with her and hold her to keep her from scratching herself as she clutched for the silver amulet that no longer hung around her neck. She'd had to discard the amulet when she entered the Enclave, along with the gowns Master Player Authrond had given her, and his necklaces and earrings. Silver made the Royals' skin break out; and a Sister wore only black.

But amulet or no amulet, even with nothing to remind her of the past, her mind still wandered. The letter she had received from Okimachi worried her. She could remember her mother mentioning a sister in Kirekune, but she had not imagined the woman was still *alive*, far less up to locating a long-lost niece, and she had never heard of any of the other family members Saia Ash mentioned. She did not know whether to reply, or what to say. She did not know how Saia Ash had found her. That was worrying, too. And her mind slid farther back into the past: to the toothlike tower, and Colonel Sostairs, the author of the worst pain she had ever felt; to Master Player Authrond. Had he grieved when she ran away? Had he found another floozy yet?

Finally, inevitably, her thoughts went to *him*. She always ended up thinking of him. It saddened her that she had forgotten his face. She remembered only striking details: his massive, callused hands, the thin white marks on his huge pectorals, the way he had felt inside her when they made love, she biting her lips not to cry out because the orphaned boy was sleeping right there beside them. Where might *he* be now? And where was Crispin?

They were both dead, they had to be dead, and she hoped they were, prayed they were, for she wished them well. She wished them the bliss of the Royal embrace, not the dreariness and pain of sun-time.

She wished Crispin dead. She wished him *here*.

No!

"My heart is Royal!"

Sunlight slanted through the window slits. They had already been kneeling for over two hours on the stone-flagged floor of the chapel. Rain's knees were throbbing, and her back ached. She welcomed the pain as a distraction from her thoughts of him. But her discomfort brought a different, equally familiar worry. Why was it that she could no longer lose herself in prayer as she had been able to in her first year with the Consecrated?

"My offspring is Royal!"

It wasn't that her thoughts were *wrong*—no thoughts were wrong, for there *was* no wrong, only a single Right—but thinking distracted her from praying.

As always, the first order of the day after their morning chores had been communion with the Resident Royals. Communion drained her of any lingering sleepiness, leaving her with a marvelous sense of lightness and emptiness that was the closest thing to bliss anyone could achieve in sun-time. After communion, she generally sailed through the subsequent three hours of hymns and cued prayer on wings of pure spirituality. The blooming heat of a Kherouge summer could do nothing to wilt *that* energy. Each word from whichever Sister was leading the prayer sparked chain reactions of understanding in the bright emptiness of her mind.

But lately she had been coming out of the confessional more tired than euphoric. And her mind had been drifting unconscionably.

The sun would be high in the sky before they ate anything. But she could already feel her stomach growling.

It was probably just the fatigue of Jonathan's birth, lingering on longer than normal because she was not yet accustomed to the life.

"Consecrated—my laughter! Consecrated—my tears! Consecrated—my breath! *My sun-time is Royal!*"

Her Sisters would care for her if she became sick. Her Sisters would not let her fail.

"My body is Royal!"

Jonathan was only six months old. He was still suckling. She nearly lost her place in the chant as she imagined the piercing cries that would greet her when she hurried to the nursery to give him a feed before noon. Only six months old, and he could scream like a vulture.

"My blood is Royal!"

Six months old and still so *ugly*—

(His little hands and feet were as well developed as those of an infant three times his age, and he was already beginning to sit up—it was unnatural—)

So *ugly*!

Jonathan. My son.

Where is the one who should have been his father?

"My heart is Royal!"

An expression of pure joy shone on the face of Cloud, Speaking Sister. She clawed the air above her head, reaching for the ceiling. Cloud was a stout woman—she had borne seven offspring—but right now she looked as though she might fly weightless through the roof, her black robes flapping like birds' wings. The pianola chords swelled. The women raised their voices in the final cadenza of the hymn, and the very dust that danced in the walls of sunlight seemed to vibrate. The barking of a courtyard dog outside was almost inaudible. "My offspring is Royal!"

Oh, dear Queen, my Queen, do something

But at that moment in the depths of the palace-fortress in Kingsburg, the Queen was not doing anything at all. Lithrea the Second floated on a sea of cushions in the sixth parlor of the Royal suite nine stories below the ground, her face a dark, wrinkled little raisin in the magnificent candy of her morning gown, whose ruff stood up behind her head like the frill of a lizard. Her bib of jewels encircled her neck as tightly as a collar. The total weight of the gown was about forty pounds. She could not have moved so much as an arm without help.

*   *   *

10:38 A.M. Ferupe: Kingsburg: the underground fortress

The Queen listened with what, for her, approximated pleasure as her Royal Cousin Farthred played his harmonium. The tune was called "A Sweet Rain in the Heartlands," and it was composed through with no choruses. Farthred played loudly and accurately, though mechanically: this was one of his best days, Lithrea thought, and even on his bad days he was good enough to command the attention of the gathered ladies and courtiers and even the Royals, who unlike their inferiors would not have pretended interest if they hadn't felt it. Even if they had been bored, however, the Cousins and Aunts and Uncles would still have had to listen, for Lithrea had asked Farthred to play, and the Queen's request was law. Farthred would have had to play even if he had ten broken fingers!

But of course in that case, Lithrea thought vaguely, she would not have made the request! For she was the kindest monarch in centuries, wasn't she, a kind Queen and a gentle one, everyone called her Lithrea the Compassionate, at least everyone around her did, and as for the outsiders she didn't know, it was only rarely she remembered that there *were* outsiders. Remembered on her own, that is. Her other self remembered them all the time like needles in its nonflesh, and hated them, my goodness how it hated them! But all the same Lithrea was kind to them, and if she was kind to the *commoners*, well, of course, she was the very spirit of beneficence where her own relatives were concerned.

And she had a special soft place in her heart for Farthred, or at least she had had when she still had a place in her heart for anyone. She liked Far even though he had not been able to give her a child, any more than her other male Cousins (of whom there were fewer and fewer as the oldest ones died off) had been able to. None of them had sired a child on any of the other Royal women either. It had been a proper old game of musical beds when she was young! But the hurdy-gurdy had played, and then stopped, and it was all of no avail. There were no Royals young enough to have children anymore, and the sycophants went about with terror and greed in their eyes.

Despite the fires in the many hearths, it was freezing cold in the parlor. It always got cold whenever two or more Royals gathered together. The courtiers' lips were blue, and they chafed their hands as they smiled and tapped their toes to the music. They understood nothing about Lithrea and her relatives; they were too stupid to understand, her father had told her, even were the Royals to try to explain. Lithrea knew this, and so she had never tried. She simply took it for granted that no one except herself and her Cousins—and perhaps the Significants, but she could only feel them as a hostile shimmer in the white distance, she had heard nothing from them in twenty years, ever since that imbecile ambassador flubbed his mission and communications froze—that no one except these few knew the true, terrible immensity of the situation. If they did, perhaps they would give Lithrea a little more credit. Perhaps. They thought she was as crazy as a crab in boiling water, and as close to dying. She had glimpsed looks of dread on the faces of even her most trusted advisers when she missed what they said because a daemon had been jabbering in her ear, or when she stopped in the middle of a sentence because for a second she had been no longer *Lithrea* but a daemon in the far-off Wraithwaste, where Lithrea had never been, the whipcord choking her as she fled from the pain at thirty miles an hour.

But still and still, Farthred was good on his harmonium. And music was the only thing that could distract her from the immaterial for so much as an instant, these days. Only music could banish her Cousins' relentless non sequiturs.

She adjusted her face into an expression of bliss, intending to doze for a few moments, cocooned in the music. And the variously beringed courtiers must have been so relieved that she was not twitching, or calling out fragments of street barkers' pitches she had never heard, that they did not see her hand slip off the head of her idiot lapdog. They did not see her eyelids flutter closed. No one—especially not her Cousins, who like her were enclosed in the world of their heritage, hemmed off from the courtiers and from each other by the frantic jabbering of the other cousins who twined invisibly about them—saw the slow rise and fall of her bodice stop.

Lithrea's seventy-two-year-old face relaxed. Miles of fine wrinkles smoothed out of her skin. A thread of drool crept out of the corner of her red-painted mouth.

Inside her head she was running, galloping, flying, worming, crawling (for she had all forms and none) across a dark landscape shot across with lightning. She was daemon. She was Wraith. She was Royal. She was in every last corner of the world at once. She was darkness hemmed in by the light that roiled at all her horizons, hearing the distant screams of pain from those cousins who had already been embraced by the light, *feeling* their agony. Their/her necks were collared with cruel silver, they/her were burned alive in hardwood saucers, they/her were choked by silver-braided whipcords, they/her were fired half-dead out of blunderbusses, they/her were crammed into tiny cells whose oak walls irritated them beyond pain to madness. They/her in the distance were all mad. Nothing remained in any of their/her minds except pain and fury and fear: *kill, flee, kill, escape, flee!*

And the light was closing in. The last bastion of darkness where she ran, galloped, flew, wormed, crawled, slept, ate, sang, talked, and groomed herself was shrinking faster than she would have believed possible. The western horizon was loud with gunfire, red with blood.

Lithrea moaned. She wasn't her father, able to calm the darkness with a silent command. Her old heart pounded. The darkness was a lake and the lake was dammed up, and the shores were closing in. Where were the fish to go? Where? She had to escape before the dam burst—

In the sixth parlor, Royal Cousin Alithry's head jerked up and she let out a raw, bubbling cry. Then she slumped sideways in her chair. Her wig fell off and dangled. None of the other Royal Cousins paid any attention; they went on smiling vaguely, listening to Cousin Farthred, who kept on playing, like a windup music box that cannot be stopped until it has finished its tune. But the courtiers leapt out of their chairs, pressing around Alithry, and the Queen's parrot on its golden perch sensed their panic and screeched, "Kingsburg's burning! Kingsburg's burning! Fire fire! Fire fire! Pour on water. Pour on water—" a jingle it had heard from the mouth of the Queen, which she had got from her invisible cousins, who had got it from a gang of street children in the Razia district. "Kingsburg's burning! Kingsburg's burning—"

"Royal Alithry! Open your eyes!"

"Alithry!"

"Fire fire! Pour on water!"

"If somebody doesn't shut that damned parrot *up*—"

"She was just *sitting* here, and then—"

"We all saw what happened. It's the same thing happened to Royal Melithra. Go get Physician Exupery, quick!"

"Don't be a fool! If you have him down here for nothing, he'll—"

"It's not nothing." A youth with blond hair was pressing Alithry's shriveled, sallow wrist. "Her heart's not beating."

"*Queen*, no—"

"It's not, I tell you."

And as children looking to the oldest of their crew when disaster strikes, all of their faces turned like sunflowers to the Queen, who had not moved, nor paid any attention to the minidrama going on below her dais. She lay still on her cushions, under her midnight blue canopy with its dripping swags of topazes. Her idiot lapdog was licking her face. Her bosom was not moving, and her eyes were half-open, slits of yellow whites showing in her face like bones through crescent-shaped gashes.

The panic that had previously been contained within the parameters of a *familiar* disaster lit the room on fire. Faster than any fire, it moved out into the rest of the suite, upstairs, through the rest of the palace. Soon the courtiers—none of whom had dared to come closer to the Queen than five feet—were crowded out of the parlor by sentries, ministers, policy makers, generals, advisers, clerks, and a host of physicians. These packed in around the Queen like voyeurs at the scene of a violent crime. Exupery himself was hustled through the crowd. The top brass willingly gave ground to him. Fussily, he extracted his stethoscope and placed it on the least jewel-encrusted part of the Queen's bodice.

"There are vital signs," he said at last. The ministers, generals, and advisers controlled a collective urge to strangle him. They had already ascertained that Lithrea wasn't *dead*—not like poor Royal Cousin Alithry! "But what's *wrong* with her?" someone shouted. "Is she sleeping? In a swoon? In a coma? Or is it—"

"We are all aware that the patient is prone to fits," Exupery said calmly. "However, this time her withdrawal appears more pronounced. She does not respond to external stimuli. I shall have to examine her at length." He put down his stethoscope and started to fiddle with the Queen's bodice, possibly in the hope of finding the fastenings. His chances were poor: every man in the room knew it took six ladies to dress the Queen—three to hold her gown while the others lifted her into it. The air took on a sudden metallic bite. The ministers and advisers closest to the Queen sneezed.

Lithrea started violently up off her cushions. Her skull met Exupery's nose and he fell backwards with a screech. "Freesias!" Lithrea screamed. *"Fresh-picked freesias from country gardens! Melon ice, ma'am? Strawberries cherries blue raspberries, who'll buy me raspberries, only two shillin's the quarter, I gotta sell 'em cheap, me little daughter cried when I was going to drown 'em, only a shilling for the black an' two for the calico, their mum's the best mouser in Razia, shine ya shoes, sir? Kingsburg's burning! I kin tell yer lonely—it's a dark evenin'—Kingsburg's burning—"*

A rasping noise came from her throat and she fell back. Everyone gathered was momentarily stunned. Exupery recovered first, and stumbled to his feet, trying vainly to staunch his bleeding nose. "Hot tea!" he shouted, windmilling his free hand, spraying drops of blood over the ministers and military men. "Hot tea, and five drops of my tonic number seven, and have her ladies take her to her *boudoir*! *Now!* On the *double*! Are you all *half-wits*?"

Lithrea opened her eyes.

What are all these people doing here? she thought vaguely. *They will excite the cousins and we will have no peace for days.*

Her whole body ached. If only they wouldn't all come running every time she . . .

"Why has Farthred stopped playing?" she said suddenly. "Have I been asleep?" She attempted a joke. "That's really no cause for alarm, you know. Even *I* have to sleep occasionally. Although I admit, it was rude of me to drop off while my dear cousin was performing."

"I—I believe he has finished now, Queen," stammered one of the overhanging faces.

"Then tell him to give us another tune. He is so clever with that harmonium of his."

The fire flickers and dies.

* * *

10:39 A.M.
The Raw: Salzeim Parallel: the Kirekuni lines, 3,000 feet

The Kirekunis took much longer than Crispin had expected to mount a counterattack. The Gorgonettees, led by Vichuisse's Cerdres, were making their fourth dive at the scattering ground troops. Their screamer holds were nearly empty, their mission of destruction close to complete. When Crispin heard bullets directly above him, he thanked the Queen silently. He had been afraid the Kirekunis weren't going to put in an appearance after all. He dragged *Princess Anuei* sideways to avoid an orange fountain of ground fire and pulled her up out of her dive. Behind him, a Gorgonette spun sideways and burst into flame. Not all the troops on the ground were too demoralized to strike back at their killers, and at the lowest point of the attack dive, when the Gorgonettees opened their screamer ports, the little monoplanes were particularly vulnerable to ack-ack. This was neither the first loss of the day nor, from the look of the sky, would it be the last. As *Princess Anuei* gained altitude, Crispin cursed silently. There were far more of them than he had hoped for. Although to hope for any at all had been unpatriotic, really, hadn't it? KE-111s, 122s, old-style Shuilies, and even some Horogazi firebombers. They were fairly pouring out of the east, five or six dozen of them, raining fire on the Gorgonettees caught down at rooftop height.

Several Ferupian planes in succession nose-dived into the ground. The rhythm of the attack dive faltered and broke apart. Two Gorgonettees collided and instantly self-destructed. The shrapnel from that collision would kill more Kirekunis than the two planes ever could have by firing on them—that was the idea behind kamikaze, of course—yet what an ignoble way to die. Crispin winced to see it. The battle was boiling up toward him. Coolly, he assessed the odds. The Kirekunis' style of attack was not far off air kamikaze today. They were flinging their aircraft about with nerveless abandon. They had the advantages of surprise, altitude, and numbers. The Ferupian pilots were all out of formation and firing wildly—apparently forgetting that they were as good as out of ammunition.

Crispin banked so fast that *Princess Anuei* nearly stalled, and plunged down into the fray, signaling his crews to rally to him. Escape obviously had to be their first priority. Vichuisse would just have to wait—that's all—have to wait—

As a squadron captain, he had trained himself to resist the killing frenzy which even the tamest engagements had once provoked in him. But his men, even stoic Jones, had not. Battle was an addictive sort of candy, no matter how bitter the odds. One taste, and you could not stop. You *wanted* that lizard, *that* one, and your daemon howled and thundered, egging you on, and you didn't care if you died trying, you *wanted* him—

Crispin couldn't catch his men's attention, far less make them rally to him. Not even Mickey responded to his signals. Through the clatter and the fire, he could see Burns desperately trying to marshal his own men, with as little success. Didn't the fools understand that if they didn't turn tail and run *now*, they wouldn't get out of there alive? There were just too many KEs, and they were attacking too wildly!

Princess Anuei juddered as bullets ripped across her port wing. *Kill or be killed.*

Crispin did not know how much later it was when he depressed his firing button and—

—nothing happened.

A thin stream of tinies sputtered from his ports. The KE-122 he'd been targeting dodged them easily.

If he had even one burst of screamers left, it would be a weak one.

His thoughts resolved themselves into a single word, a word like a drop of freezing water hitting his brain softly, coldly, relentlessly.

Vichuisse.

It was the water torture to which he had been subject for months, which distracted him from everything else, amplified all of a sudden to an immediacy that could not conceivably be denied. Forcing himself not to touch the screamer button, he maneuvered *Princess Anuei* out of the deadly center of the action.

Vichuisse.

Tremors came over him, shaking his body like a leaf in the wind. In the past he had never started to shake until *after* a battle, but this time his teeth were chattering, and he could scarcely maintain his hold over *Princess Anuei*'s speed-maddened daemon. Vichuisse was not hard to spot. There he was in Crispin's reflectors, circling, high up and far out of the action, "playing umpire," as Mickey had said, his Cerdres 500 glinting like a noon star on the whitewashed sky. Crispin did not waste a second as he took *Princess Anuei* into a climb.

Queen, oh Queen. He felt his lips forming the words, felt them buzz in his throat, though he could not hear a thing. *I don't have a second but help me. Send Mickey. I'm nearly out of ammo, and if I try for Vee and can't do for him, then I'm done for, I might as well commit kamikaze! Queen, send Mickey, and let him have some screamers left in his hold. Let him have been frugal—Queen—*

He swore aloud, disbelievingly, as a winged fleck climbing ahead of him out of the west, toward the same 4,000-foot pinnacle where Vichuisse circled, proved to be not Mickey, but *Burns.* The fuselage of the Wraith-blooded captain's Killer B-99 was painted with a lewd arrangement of red petals that was impossible to mistake even from a distance. "Shit!" Crispin said as relief washed through him, making his hands shake so badly he could scarcely grip the stick. "From now on I say my prayers every day! *Queen!*"

Burns had professed inability to take part in the actual murder because Vichuisse already suspected him of treacherous inclinations. But Burns hadn't known he even would have the *chance* to take part until two days ago. This mission was to have been Butch's. And Burns hated Vichuisse even more than Crispin did. It would have been sheer humiliation for him to watch Crispin make the kill he wanted so badly. He, too, must have succumbed to the water torture.

With difficulty, Crispin stalled his climb and looped the loop. It was the simple signal he and Mickey had decided upon in Burns's hearing. It meant: *Go for it.*

Vichuisse must have seen the two Gorgonettees ascending toward him. He thought nothing of it, of course. Or perhaps, Crispin thought, he believed his two captains had taken his own sensible approach to the massacre below: get the hell out and wait and see who wins.

Whatever was passing through his mind, he did not make any attempt to escape.

The sky shone leaden white. Visibility had been one hundred percent this morning; now the distance was hazy. A heavy blue mist hovered at the horizons. The sun was nearly at its zenith. Neither side could use the solar advantage unless they were diving straight down on their enemies, and by this time, such measures were no longer necessary anyway. The KEs had all but wiped out the Gorgonettees. The QAF was being paid back in spades for the havoc it had wreaked among the Kirekuni troops. Nothing moved in the dust of no-man's-land except screamers: jewel-colored points of light zipping to and fro until they happened on a corpse, of which there were literally hundreds. There would be no SAPper attack on the Ferupian lines tomorrow—but QAF Squadrons 125, 130, and 139 would never be the same again. Crispin and Burns had a few moments, if that, before the KEs turned their sights upward.

They reached Vichuisse's altitude and kept climbing—4,500 feet; 5,000 feet. Crispin's ears popped. He and Burns were forcing their kites toward the apex of a gigantic triangle with one foot in no-man's-land and one in the Kirekuni Raw. Finally, at 5,300 feet, they met and circled. Vichuisse was directly below them. Right about now he must be starting to wonder what was going on.

The windshields of Burns's Killer B-99 were frosted with a multitude of cracks. Crispin found it slightly unnerving not to be able to see Burns inside as they passed within forty feet of each other, coasting, letting their daemons catch their breath. Then Burns waggled his rudder: the Bee did a little waltz step in the air. Crispin took his hand off the stick for an instant to give Burns the thumbs-up.

They dived.

Gravity pressed Crispin back into his seat. His vision strobed black. *Princess Anuei*'s daemon bellowed in pain. He was vaguely aware of Burns diving beside him, wingtip to wingtip, as if they were flying an exhibition. For whom were they parading their skills? Vichuisse? The orange-streaked mess of the battle spun upward, with the single star of the Cerdres 500 superimposed on it, metal wings reflecting the sunlight into Crispin's eyes. Somehow, he managed to fix Vichuisse in his sights. How was Burns able to target through the opaque ruin of his windshield? He was edging dangerously close aport. Crispin sheered off a little.

The Cerdres filled his sights. He opened fire and *felt* a fair-sized burst of screamers leave the ports: the dive must have forced every last one of them back into the gun chambers. Emeralds and rubies and sapphires streamed out ahead. He actually *saw* Vichuisse's pale face in the shadow of the cockpit as the little daemons glommed onto the

Cerdres's fuselage, which after all contained no real silver, nothing to repel them. Then he yanked the stick hard sideways, forcing the Gorgonette into a port-side spin which was necessary so that he should not dive into his own fire, and as he fought to bring *Princess Anuei* under control, he blacked out. A split second later he was jerked back to consciousness by an unbearable pain in his leg.

A screamer.

He must have flown into his own fire after all.

This is how pilots die! Quick, quick!—side revolver, safety catch, aim, bring her out of the spin damn it, what if I shoot my foot off—pain—

The crack of the shot deafened him. Gunpowder filled the cockpit. The screamer that had attacked him, and the screamer from his revolver, fell wrangling into the space under his feet. But there were more of them. On the windshield, skinny arms splayed. They were trying to gnaw through the glass. On the wings. Bits of screamer caught in the props. The cockpit wasn't a sealed chamber; they would have no trouble getting in.

His revolver only held six rounds.

Crispin dispatched the three that found their way into the cockpit, and *Princess Anuei*'s vertiginous spin shook the rest off. But the trouble was that in order to shoot at them, he had had to take his left hand off the stick—there was no letting go of the whipcord—which meant the spin worsened. And he was losing altitude without regaining control—3,500 feet; 3,000 feet.

Just as he was on the brink of leveling her out, a double fountain of garnet arched across his wings.

The shock made him lose control again. Quite accidentally, *Princess Anuei* tumbled out of the way of the jeweled rain. Crispin cursed as he struggled once more to level her out. A *Ferupian* enemy on his tail! Had the attack somehow failed to finish Vichuisse off—was he now chasing Crispin to exact his vengeance? That couldn't be right! Vichuisse wouldn't try to kill Crispin! Knowing him, he'd probably promote him instead!

In Crispin's reflectors.

Burns.

And it all fell into place.

Every smile, every handshake, every conspiratorial nudge, every last fucking minute of their hypocrisy. "Damn it," Crispin said. "Damn them all, and me, to hell and back."

How stupid had he *been*? How trusting, how gullible, how *wrong*?

He did not lose control again, even though his hands were shaking worse than before, and his left arm ached from the kick of the revolver. He *could* not lose control again. The determination to get out of this made his blood run cold and slow. The Bee was a black silhouette against the whiteness that filled his reflectors. The dead eye of its shot-up windshield seemed to glow: opaque, merciless. The sun shone brilliantly above. The sky had taken on an overbaked sheen. Crispin could not shake Burns off. Burns fired again: he must have been conserving his ammunition specially for this. This time Crispin did not lose control, and a few of the screamers caught *Princess Anuei*'s wings. Two of them found their way into the cockpit. He dispatched them. Now his revolver was empty.

Out of ammo, *completely* out! He couldn't keep this up! If Burns fired successfully on him again, he would be done for. And in the game of cat and mouse, Burns was chasing him downward toward the buzzing swarm of KEs. The Kirekunis had surrounded the few remaining Gorgonettees and were picking them off with deliberate cruelty. Crispin wondered in a moment of black humor what they thought of the spectacle above—one Ferupian hell-bent on shooting down another.

We're doing their job for them, aren't we, and have been all along!

Burns fired yet again, and Crispin stalled *Princess Anuei* dead. It was an old trick. The screamers fell ahead of the Gorgonette's nose, dropping into the void. For a minute Crispin thought Burns would overshoot him, cheated by his own velocity—but not for nothing had the Wraith half-breed worked his way up through the ranks, any more than Crispin had; and they had both learned their craft in the same school. There Burns was again, firing a long burst, maddened now by the determination to destroy his prey. Crispin knew that feeling well, too. This time the screamers fell just short of *Princess Anuei*'s tail.

And then came salvation in the form of a Gorgonette out of the sun. Mickey had not got out of the battle, no one could have escaped *that*: he had evidently fought free earlier, and been circling high, high up, watching and waiting for his moment. Burns, concentrating on targeting Crispin, was taken completely by surprise. Mickey's screamers poured over the Killer B-99 like a waterfall. Burns shook the craft like a wet cat, but the screamers clung to it like leeches. One stuck right in the middle of the frosted windshield, giving the opaque eye a red pupil. Now it was Burns's turn to defend himself with his revolver. Crispin's disbelief turned to jubilation as he watched the Bee's windshield shatter wide open to a shot from inside the cockpit. "Finish him off, Mick!" he shouted, forcing *Princess Anuei* around out of danger. "Finish him *off*!"

But Mickey wasn't firing again, just waggling his wings frantically, and almost immediately he turned his Gorgonette and fled east. Of course, Crispin realized, he, too, was out of ammo. That must have been his last burst. Thank the Queen he'd had it! Thank the Queen he'd been frugal!

His leg felt as if it were on fire. He didn't need to touch the wound to know it was still bleeding. With difficulty, he turned *Princess Anuei*'s nose eastward and jerked the whipcord cruelly, forcing the exhausted, disoriented daemon to put on speed. Ahead of him, the sky was completely empty. Mickey's Gorgonette was the only fleck on the lavender-colored haze hanging above the Wraithwaste. Behind him, the KEs were finishing off the last of his crewmates. Quite possibly, he and Mickey were the only survivors of the engagement. No one else could have escaped, not unless they had fled earlier—in which case they were cowards.

And Mickey calls himself a coward . . . ! Crispin thought. *I've never seen such . . . !*

And far to the south, a third little wooden monoplane fled east. From the drunken way it was dipping and rolling, Crispin could tell it was Burns, navigating blind. With his windshield shot out, he must be in agony, scarcely able to breathe. But Crispin felt sure he would make it back to base—if not *his* base, then somewhere he could put down in safety. *Damn!* Crispin should have guessed he, too, would escape: he was too good a shot for one burst of screamers to finish him off, and too good a pilot not to make a successful getaway.

Vichuisse: bits of aluminium across no-man's-land: a death: a daemon burned alive in its collar, in its cell.

But at what a *cost*! What a massacre!

If Burns and I hadn't been so fixated, *each on our own secret ambition,* Crispin thought, *maybe we could've got our men out of there—maybe we could've saved—Jones, Harrowman, Dupont, Eakin, Cochrane—*

It did not bear thinking about.

He was soaked with sweat. His nose and eyes stung from the residue of gunpowder in the air of the cockpit. His ears rang. He had never in his life felt so battered, wounded, and despondent. Vichuisse was dead. There was that. *But maybe he would have died anyway, in a disaster like that! Maybe we should have fought our real enemies and let the war take its toll! Because it does, even on cowards, as we have just witnessed, ladiesangentlemen! What a nightmare—what a Queen-awful show—*

But at least I found out—

Mickey: *I think you're going to crash and burn. If you want to know the honest truth, I don't like the sound of this business.*

He had guessed at Burns's scheme. But Crispin had not. How could he have been so gullible?

In his heart, he knew why. His own weakness, after the fact, was painfully apparent to him. He could not permit himself to name it—he could only vow never to make the same mistake again. But even as he promised himself *never, never, never,* he felt an ocean of loss in that resolve, and through the spume he glimpsed the colder shores of cynicism, distant and blue.

Grief braided itself into a rope, binding him in regret, sealing the knots with truth. He wanted to kick himself for his own stupidity. In retrospect, each detail of the plot was crystal clear, each motive outstanding, each dropped hint so obvious that he wondered uselessly how he could have failed to smell a rat. The future whirled before him, a white void. The names of the conspirators sounded in his head: Burns, Emthraze, Thraxsson—oh, that you could stoop so low, Lieutenant-Marshal!—Lennox, Duncan, Butch.

Butch.

Knife in the heart, twist, flourish, keep this, it's a bit of nothing, I know, but it comes from me, I want you to remember that. Crispin was actually *wearing* that little wooden monkey today; he'd tied a string on it and hung it around his neck, under his flight suit.

Some good-luck charm!

Butch!

Below, the Raw of the Cerelon sector lay peaceful and still in the sunlight. The day was so calm and clear under the blazing white sky that the land looked like an artificial construct: hills of papier-mâché under a daemon glare. Drawing strength from the spirit of Millsy, the spirit of Anuei, the spirit of the circus, Crispin thought, *There is nothing to be gained from stopping here. The show must go on! My leg hurts like the devil, is all, my leg hurts—*

—and he wanted a cigarette and a drink, he *needed* a cigarette and a drink, Queen, his hands were shaking, and no matter how soon Burns carried his tale of treachery to HQ, no matter how soon they came for him, he would not meet them before he had a cigarette, a drink, a wash, and a change of clothes, even condemned men were allowed such things! Even traitors had their rights—

Sarehole came into view below, weathered pine buildings gleaming softly in the sun. It was the most welcome sight Crispin could imagine. His remaining squaddies did not know their captain was a wanted man. They would succor him.

His pocket watch said it was 1:30. As he came in to land, the riggers were putting Mickey's plane away. Mickey himself stood at the end of the runway. Even from this height, Crispin could see his tail switching. When Crispin climbed stiffly down out of *Princess Anuei*'s cockpit—the shakes already making a comeback—Mickey hurried up to him and hissed, grabbing his arm with clawed fingers: "You've got to get out of here."

"One hairbreadth escape a day is enough for me. I hope you've broken the bad news to the rest. I'm not up to it. I need a drink."

"Don't you *understand*? He was shooting at *y*—"

"A triple whiskey."

"You've got to *escape*."

My man is my man only some of the time
Cause some of the time he's like hard to find —
Living kind of hard for a lot of his days
Cause see, in our days he had the phrase that pays —
And now I never see him while he do a bid
While he do a bid
Here's the real truth, kid:

—Terminator X

Base

Treacherous World

It was 4:15 P.M. and the remaining lieutenants of 130 Squadron—Smith, Dixon, Carnation, and Kimbrough—had just left Crispin's office. After he described the multiple disasters of the day, there had been a long interval during which no one said anything much. Perhaps their stunned silence had been due in part to Mickey's presence. Crispin had kept trying to catch his eye and indicate that it was inappropriate for him to be at an officers' meeting; but he had hovered, mixing drinks, like a self-appointed waiter.

Crispin went into the bedroom and sank down on the edge of his bed. Mickey stood before him, tail flicking. Over one shoulder he had slung a carpetbag, a Jimenez relic, into which he had packed what he must have assumed were Crispin's most treasured possessions. In fact, Crispin owned nothing that he treasured—nothing that had not once been somebody else's. Soon, shorn of his rank and his Gorgonette, he would be as free of material ties as a newborn baby. The few things he'd taken from Smithrebel's that had survived his flight through the Wraithwaste had been lost forever in Chressamo. He had emerged from the toothlike tower with a shaved head, a cast-off uniform, a kit bag, and a resolve to do right for the first time in his life—not by the law of the land, which had given him up before it gave him a chance, but by the law of the armed forces, which was firmer, cleaner, and based on survival of the fittest, not the petty concerns of respectable people.

But he had not known that at a certain level of the hierarchy, military law, too, stopped applying—or at least, became fuzzy. The tensions of power, ambition, and greed warped pure survivalism into neoaristocratic immorality. Murdering one's personal enemies and expecting to get away with it was not a practice of soldiers, nor of the right-living masses. It was a practice of the gutter, and also of the Ferupian nobility—who, Crispin thought now, must surely be the most desolate people on earth.

All was quiet outside. The base had sunk into a torpor, stunned by the loss of a third of its men. It would not be much longer before the jeeps rolled up. Even taking into account the fact that Sarehole was a forty-five-minute drive from Cerelon, Burns would not need more than five hours, if he was hurrying. And Crispin guessed he would hurry. The possibility that Crispin might not try to escape wouldn't even cross that sneaky half-Wraith mind.

It had been three and a half hours.

"You've got to get away," Mickey said, breaking the silence.

"No, no. No."

"If you don't get out of here, they're going to court-martial you! You'll be in front of a firing squad before you can say it wasn't me!"

"Leave off, Mick. I *did* it. I'll have to pay for it."

Insidiously, perhaps while he flew over the Raw, perhaps while he drank whiskey with the stoic lieutenants, shouldering their silent blame—guilt had infiltrated Crispin's heart. The idea of fleeing his fate had become unacceptable. He had fired on Vichuisse a split second before Burns did. It had almost certainly been one of *Princess Anuei*'s screamers that had eaten Vichuisse's vital organs. And how could a traitor get off by complaining that he had been betrayed?

"There's such a thing as being too scrupulous," Mickey said urgently.

"I'll take that as a compliment."

"Since I've known you, Captain, you haven't been prone to stupid heroics! What's *happened*?"

"You yourself said that I was the very embodiment of grace and selflessness and bravery. And all the rest of it."

"Yes, but it's gone beyond that now! That stuff is fine, but none of it applies anymore! It was all very well to risk your life and your reputation for the good of six squadrons—"

And a personal vendetta, Crispin corrected him silently.

"But now it's gone beyond that. It's got personal."

It always was personal! Why, oh why does he think so highly of me?

"Burns isn't an abstract cause, he's an ambitious, treacherous, double-crossing bastard. They're all double-crossing bastards! Are you going to die for *them*?"

"Someone's got to carry the can!"

"They *could* say Vichuisse was shot down by the enemy. If they wanted. But you're a danger to them now, Captain. They want to take you out. Of course *you* know that, too, now. But I saw it even back then, the way Burns looked at you. You have to desert! Take *Princess Anuei* and fly back across the Wraithwaste! Put her down in an empty field in western Ferupe—"

"You're out of your mind."

"It's the only possible—

Crispin looked up. "I haven't told anyone this in three years. But I don't suppose it makes any difference now. I got into trouble with the police in Lovoshire. I stole a truck. And I was fingered for arson. That's a serious crime—a *hanging* crime, if anyone was killed, which I don't know. What I do know is that the white-coats had it in for me. If they found out about the man I did kill, after I got away from them the first time round, in all likelihood they circulated my description to the cities. It's been three years—they probably wouldn't come down on me right away—but I can't even *contemplate* spending the rest of my days on the mud-show circuit with military and civil charges hanging over my head. I wouldn't be able to perform; I might get to drive trucks if I could find an owner who'd overlook my sketchy history; but I'd probably end up as a laborer. I'd rather die."

Even to him, it sounded melodramatic. But then he remembered Vichuisse saying *I'd rather die than go home . . . even though I sense my last days approaching . . .*

At the time, he had thought the commandant a fool, but now he understood, because he stood in the very same trap that had been closing on Vichuisse three days ago. Anyone for whom heroism—or even the *belief* in heroism—had been a way of life was inevitably ambushed at the end, even after he had discarded his pretensions to glory, by his own pride. His own need for a heroic end. Vichuisse's talk of being ill had been his way of saying that he was going to go out in a blaze of glory—a final, visible commitment to the ideals he had lived for. During his career, he had failed to be a hero. But a noble death was within the grasp of even the chronically cowardly. It required nothing except determination.

But Vichuisse had been prevented from whatever apotheosis he had planned for himself. He had died in the least noble way possible. By Crispin's hand.

Did Crispin himself, therefore, deserve the end he had denied the commandant? Was heroism his lot in life—as he had assumed, as he had hoped it was? Or had he already, back in Jevanary when things first "got personal," slipped without knowing it out of the plane in which heroes moved?

He massaged his eyes hard, his head spinning with unwelcome yet unexpectedly appealing logic.

Desertion. Yes . . . it would have to be. But where, when, and how?

Possibilities opened up before him, very quickly shedding their disguise of self-abnegation.

He shook himself and ran his hands over his scalp and down his neck, locating an incredible number of bruises and sore muscles.

Mickey still looked stunned by Crispin's revelation. *Never broke a law in his life,* Crispin thought contemptuously.

Then he remembered that Mickey had been a deserter and a traitor to his own long before Crispin so much as set foot in the Raw.

"Well?" he snapped. "Anything to say to that?"

Mickey swallowed and said, "There's another possibility. You could go to Kirekune."

Crispin said nothing. Mickey rushed on.

"If you make it across the Raw, you can make it to Okimachi. The first bit will be the hardest, not to get shot down. Then you can hop, skip, and jump. Load up on splinterons; there are no daemons to be had in the plains, they've all been requisitioned. I'll give you my family's address in Okimachi, they'll help you out if you say you're a friend of mine—I mean, I know you might not want to say you're a friend of mine, but I promise they'll help you out, if you'll try." He paused again, obviously taking Crispin's silence as rejection of his suggestion. "Look, you've *got* to—if you ever *I*—if you ever took me seriously—*please*—"

Crispin reached out and took his sleeve, pulling him closer. "You knew about Burns, didn't you?" he said softly, looking up into the worried face. "Isn't that what you said?"

Something had shifted inside him: something, he did not know what, was changing. Vichuisse's death had not been the solution, but the catalyst. He felt as if he were about to explode, or fall to pieces. And no one was near to help, or to bear the brunt, except Mickey. "You knew!"

Slowly, Mickey said, "I guessed."

"When?"

"When you told me what was going on. After we talked to him that night, I was practically sure of it."

"*How* could you have been sure?"

Mickey tossed his head. "I dunno . . . the way he looked at you."

The way he looked at me! "Then why the *hell* didn't you *say* anything?"

Mickey closed his eyes. "You wouldn't have believed me. You wanted to think they were . . ."

"Stop right there!" Crispin's voice cracked out like a whip. "Not another word! Not another fucking word, all right?"

"Then I'm sorry," Mickey whispered. "Significant."

The sunlight coming in the window slanted onto the bare wooden floor and the carpetbag. Dust danced in the rays. An air patrol churned noisily by, flying low. Crispin closed his eyes.

I can't *go on*, he thought in a moment of absolute clarity.

When he opened his eyes again the world looked different: sharper-edged, multidimensional, unknowable. The air patrol passed overhead and was gone. The only sounds were Mickey's breath and the wind outside rustling over the grassy rise. Freed from the manacles of false humility, Crispin's thoughts hurtled ahead, out of control. Minutes, hours, days. The Blacheim, and its daemon of dubious health. The explanations he would concoct to put the riggers and lieutenants off the scent. Provisions. Weights. Splinterons. Maps. Money. The Kirekuni Raw. Okimachi, the city of fire. There were so many unknowns it made his head hurt even to think about it. And underneath, of course, the blank gray horror that Mickey's suggestion of flying to Kirekune had seeded, which had bloomed when Crispin realized there was no real reason not to go. There is nothing quite as unnerving as seeing a component of a hallucination tumbling out of the world of dreams, into possibility, crossing a gulf which nothing should be able to survive undamaged.

Crispin braced himself and forced a grin. "I apologize!"

He rose and clapped Mickey on the shoulder.

"It's no business of mine grilling you about something that's in the past! Especially when you're my ticket out of here! Queen, I should be thanking you on my knees!"

"That won't be necessary," Mickey said stiffly, obviously suspecting another outbreak of sarcasm.

Crispin grabbed him by the arm and swung him around. "Listen, don't be a fucking prima donna!" He kept the false grin plastered on his face. "Time's passing! And we have to think of some pretext for getting the Blacheim out and having her checked over!"

"The *Blacheim*?"

"She's the only two-man kite on base. She's old, but as far as I know, her daemon is still alive—I've been having them feed it, no point letting it die." He swooped the carpetbag up off the floor and took a look inside. Mickey seemed to have an eye for anything which might possibly be of monetary value—that, at least, was the only explanation for his egregious taste in souvenirs. Crispin went to Jimenez's wardrobe and stuffed a dress suit and a smoking suit into the bag. Jimenez had not been a big man; Crispin had had his clothes altered to fit. They would crumple, but it didn't matter. Such garments were ubiquitous the world over, and so were hot irons.

Mickey stood unmoving in the rhomboid of sunlight on the floor. "Captain?"

"Call me by my name! We're partners now!"

"You're *not* suggesting . . ."

"Suggesting?" Crispin caroled.

"That I . . ."

"That you come with me? I wasn't aware there was any question of your *not* coming!"

"Someone's got to cover for you," Mickey said desperately.

Crispin turned on him. He felt disgustingly incapable of matching Mickey's capacity for self-sacrifice. "What do you think I *am*? A snake like Burns? A daemon in human form? Has it slipped your mind that *you* fired on Burns, not me—as far as he's concerned, you're a worse traitor than I am! Talk about treachery! Talk about firing squads! You wouldn't even get the travesty of a trial. You're coming, no question about it."

"But . . . but! I *can't*! Not to *Kirekune*!" Mickey looked as if he were about to break down.

Oh, Queen, Crispin thought. "Look, we're in this together. I pulled you in. That means I've got to pull you out."

The sun highlighted the meaningless tattoo patterns on Mickey's lashing tail. "You're *not* responsible for me! I can take care of myself!"

"Don't be childish. If it weren't for you, I might already have flown into Cerelon and given myself up. I owe you that much, at least."

"You don't understand . . ."

His voice was halfhearted. Crispin pressed his advantage. "I *need* you. There's no guarantee I'll even make it over the Kirekuni Raw. And if I get shot down on my own, I'm dead."

"You'll have more of a chance on your own than you would with me," Mickey whispered.

Crispin ignored him. "And supposing I make Kirekune; it might as well be the dark side of the moon for all I know about it! Just how far d'you think I'd get in Okimachi without someone who speaks the language?" Galvanized by the thought of danger, both distant and impending, he chivvied Mickey across the room and through the office. "The Blacheim's in Hangar Four. You deal with the riggers— tell them it's my say-so, we have to make a trip to Cerelon, tell them the commandants are recalling all the antiquated bombers, tell them what you like. I'm going to say good-bye to the lieutenants. There are a few things . . . I have a few apologies to make. Then I'll come back here and pick up some maps. Make sure to get as many barrels of extra splinterons into her as she'll hold. Use the bomb holds. Food isn't that important. But water is. If we're flying for long stretches at a time, the radiator will blow if we don't cool down the engine. Got it?"

"Got it, sir," Mickey said sadly.

He saluted. It should have been an ironic, even humorous gesture; but when Crispin glanced at his face, he saw a look of—fear? longing? craven terror? A look such as he had never seen before.

Why had Mickey overreacted so violently to a plan that was, after all, his own? Was there something Crispin did not know?

There was a great deal, Crispin thought, that he did not know.

No time to ponder. Five hours, and four of those were gone. They went out into the summer evening.

Delight is to him whose strong arms yet support him, when the ship of this base treacherous world has gone down beneath him.

— Herman Melville, *Moby Dick*

Crispin and Mickey's adventures continue in

The Daemon in the Machine.

Fleeing the trap laid for them by the treacherous David Burns, they strike out for Okimachi, where Mickey is reunited with the family he abandoned to join the Disciples. Crispin struggles to reconcile his apocryphal visions with the political realities of Okimachi. Meanwhile, on the far side of the continent, Rae faces the appalling truth about the cult to which she has attached herself. Kirekune is winning the war, but a Significant victory will have terrible consequences for humans and daemons alike.